on paper

a novel

SARAH MADELIN

spindlefern
PRESS

Copyright © 2022 Sarah Madelin
All rights reserved.
ISBN: 978-1-955853-03-3

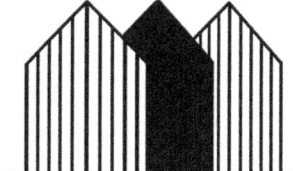

AMAZON REVIEWERS ARE DELIGHTED BY *LOVE ON PAPER*

"A sweet, smart romance novel that leaves people thankful for the stories that make up our lives. *Love on Paper* isn't just about romance...there's also forgiveness, family, grief, friendship, and humor on these pages, thanks to characters who have to navigate the ups and downs and swirls of life."

"*Love on Paper* is charming from the get go, and truthfully, hard to put down! A novel that captures human emotions that we have all felt. Definitely check out this for a feel-good love story that will stay with you a long time after reading!"

"I loved this book and found myself thinking about the characters long after I finished it. Beautifully written, with some unexpected twists, I was sad when I turned the last page!"

"Warning! This book will make you forget to cook dinner!"

"Sarah Madelin's women's fiction debut was such an enjoyable read. Charming and heartfelt with lovable characters, a beautiful setting and real, relatable problems, *Love on Paper* will suck you in and keep you invested until the very end."

For Mike
who always delivers on his vow to support my dreams

For Mom
who reads every word I write and somehow loves them all

For Dad
who encouraged my writing from the very beginning

For My Kiddos
who make each day better, who make each day matter

And For Allyson
because it simply would not exist without her

CHAPTER ONE

This first part? It's kind of a prologue. An introduction. A less risqué summary of what happened first. But I might as well call it what it really was:

The end of the life I had planned.

"Do it," Julie said, pulling me in front of her patio fire pit. "You'll feel better."

"You spent hours printing each one by hand on that ancient letterpress," I told her. "I can't burn them right in front of you."

The box of elegant cards trembled in my hand. My closest friend grabbed a handful. She tore them in half and dropped them onto the flames.

"Do it," she said again. "It will make *me* feel better."

Julie's husband Garrett poked my favorite rose-print

bedsheets deeper into the fire. "Roast them, Marin. You know you want to."

I know I should want to, I thought, wincing as a custom orchid illustration vanished in the flames. My eyes began to sting.

If they ask, I'll say it's because of the smoke, I told myself, swallowing hard. But I knew they wouldn't ask.

"Don't judge," I said as I tucked one card into my purse.

I just wanted one. And only to keep until I didn't want it anymore.

"I'm sorry you wasted all that time," I told Julie, pitching the box into the fire.

One hundred wedding invitations spilled out onto the flames, flaring up fast. Like they wanted to burn.

Julie linked her arm through mine.

"I'm sorry you did, too," she whispered, and I knew she wasn't talking about invitations anymore.

Sparks snapped upward and disappeared into the heavy July night. Before I turned away, I saw the corner of one invitation curl in. I made myself look, but I was too late. Our names were already gone.

In the third week of my breakup—and subsequent breakdown—my mother staged an intervention. Not being an overly subtle woman, she didn't lead me into a room filled with scented candles and my dearest friends. There was no mediator or moderator or whoever conducts those things. It was just my mom and my stepsister cornering me in the all-night diner beside my condo building to ask how long I planned to avoid my home.

"Not sure," I said with a glibness that only my mother can inspire. "When I stop craving chili-cheese fries?"

My mother drew upon years of practice to expertly ignore this. "I noticed you're still sleeping in your guest room."

"You were at my place?" I directed this question at Nandila, my sister, and the only person left in my life who still had a key.

"We're saving you from yourself. Get over it," Nandi said, sticking her tongue out at me even as she abandoned the other side of the booth to slide in with me. But that was Nandi, thriving in her proprietary blend of loyalty and sass. We were sisters, despite our lack of shared blood and decade-plus age difference. The stepsister thing did not apply.

To be fair, the stepdaughter thing had never mattered, either. I saw my mom's eyes get misty as this spirited younger daughter locked her lithe brown fingers into the elder's wan, weary hand. But then her mission to rehabilitate the elder—to rehabilitate me—sharpened her focus.

"Well," Mom said after clearing that rare sentimentality from her throat. "Are you going to spend the rest of your life hiding out in diners and catching three hours a night on the sofa bed? Or can we help you move back into your bedroom?"

"Sofa bed," I told her. "My regular mattress is too soft anyway."

"Don't listen to her, she's minimizing," Nandi said.

"And masking her emotions with sarcasm. Two classic Marin Beckett moves."

"Did you switch your major from art to psychology?"

"Deflecting attention from yourself to someone else," she replied with the smugness unique to bossy teenagers. "Another signature move."

"The important thing, Marin, is to acknowledge your feelings," my mom and her years as a professional therapist said. "If avoiding your condo will help you adjust, we'll respect that. But you need to get some rest."

I decided she was right, so in Week Four I swapped places with my sister. I left Alfred purring in my condo's window seat; a dorm is no place for a cat.

"If you're planning to work on your book, try Sunday and Friday. Most people on my floor will be hung over, so it won't be as loud," Nandi said. "Don't take the back stairs, some dudes keep grilling on the landing. Hopefully you don't mind the hot dog smells."

I did my best, but after a week of frat boys puking in the halls and headboards knocking against the walls, I felt every one of my thirty-three years. Plus, my sister's dorm was in the middle of campus. I could too easily bump into David, my ex-fiancé, who teaches literature at the university. Or into the co-ed I'd caught him bumping in our bed.

Five days later, at the start of Week Five, I smuggled Alfred into our new room at the Heart 'O Chicago Motel. I chose the Heart 'O Chicago for its vintage neon sign and reasonable weekly rate. The neon blinked in through the window all night, but I was up. It was good company.

Week Six. I was back on the sofa bed. Alfred was back in the window seat. And my parents, God bless them, took unprecedented steps to push me out of my self-pity, out of the country, and into a new frame of mind.

"Hello, Mariana," my dad said over the phone later that week—he's the only person outside the publishing world who always uses my full name. It was almost midnight, but I'm nocturnal even when not avoiding sleep, so he never hesitates to call me late.

For the sake of my digestive system, I had moved from the diner to the bar next door. While I guzzled coffee to keep myself awake, my brilliant-author father told me he was juxtaposing two obscure literary forms for the one essay he manages to publish each year, this one commissioned by *The New Yorker*. I did not mention that I was trying not to gag while thinking up euphemisms for various intimate acts. I'd been asked to write an article on sex and metaphor for the American Association of Romance Authors.

We spent a few minutes discussing his struggle to put words on paper—a struggle I had sadly come to know well in the weeks since becoming a cuckquean. If you're wondering, that's the female equivalent of a cuckold. And if you're wondering how I know this, it's from spending six years dating the literature expert who would eventually turn me into one.

"Can you visit tomorrow?" my dad finally said.

"Of course." That he has health problems is an understatement, so I was instantly filled with concern. "Are you all right?"

"This is not about me. Your mother and I want to meet with you."

I paused, certain I had misheard him. My mom had divorced my dad twenty years earlier. They hadn't seen each other even one time since. "You and mom want to meet with me together?"

"That's the idea, yes."

So many emotions rushed through me—joy, shock, maybe even dread—that I choked. My coffee cup was empty, so to soothe my throat, I had to chug the cold espresso I'd started carrying in one of the silver flasks David had bought for his groomsmen. This one was engraved with a Matthew Arnold quote, something about true friends beating down foes. Because a professor of Victorian poetry can't just say *thanks, man* in plain English.

"Mariana?"

The apprehensive tremble in his voice triggered my own bout of nerves. I forced some cheer into my voice for his sake and told him I would love to come.

"Your mother said she'll pick you up. Be here by six, please. And you could bring me some Black Forest cake from Cafe Selmarie."

"Do you need anything else?"

"Some more of my pens, if it's not too much trouble."

Sure, sure, I thought, because remember how I said he has health problems? Of course I would get him the pens. And while I was out, I'd get myself a t-shirt with the word *Enabler* on the front.

My mother's nose had already wrinkled at what she considered excessive middle-class privilege when I slid into her car the next afternoon.

"Does everyone in the plaza have a Starbucks addiction?" she said, watching four women clutching Ventis push strollers toward the fountain in my neighborhood of Lincoln Square. She sighed at their careful distribution of organic, DHA-supplemented milk. "Do they realize some kids don't have milk at all?"

I expect my mother's judgy brand of activism, so I didn't respond. What I did not expect, however, was how her fingers knocked against the steering wheel throughout the drive from Chicago to my dad's place in southern Wisconsin.

"Are you nervous about seeing Dad?" I finally asked at the outskirts of Wind Point.

Her hands fell flat.

"I was married to your father for seventeen years. I can spend an evening with him." The words hadn't left her mouth before the tapping resumed.

I lay my hand on my own anxious stomach. The butterflies I'd had all day were suddenly more like birds.

We pulled down my dad's long drive to find him sitting on the patio with his back to us, watching the indigo swash of Lake Michigan bump against his yard. My mother gasped, maybe at the view but more likely at how the former love of her life had aged.

My attention snagged on his shabby little house. David had been planning to replace the cracked cedar shakes and repaint the porch before his fall semester began. Now I could either make the repairs myself or endure requesting the help of Ulrich Thompson, my dad's landlord, who once told me while ogling my breasts that he not only reads my dirty novels but enjoys picturing me as the leading lady.

Dad's thick white hair had blown over his forehead. Although it was mid-August, it was windy, and he was wearing one of his trademark cardigans. A brown fedora was perched on his knee. In his own way, he was bringing it, which did nothing to ease my nerves.

"Hi, Dad," I said, draping my arm around his shoulders. I caught an atypical whiff of cologne when I kissed his cheek and the birds in my stomach beat their wings.

He patted my hand. "Hello, Petite."

I should mention, I'm not that petite. I'm five-eight. But some nicknames refuse to die.

My dad was trying to be casual, but I felt him stiffen when Mom approached. She lingered behind the two of us, shifting her weight uncertainly from foot to foot.

I grabbed her hand.

"Well, here we are. Mom, you remember Dad," I said, trying to lighten the mood as I prodded her toward the chair opposite his. "Dad, this is Mom."

My parents stared at each other without speaking. Dad sat motionless but Mom teetered on the edge of her chair, her hands jittering awkwardly. I sighed when she began absently twisting her wedding ring.

I rested my hand on my dad's shoulder again. "I brought your cake."

He didn't look at it.

"And a big bunch of pens," I sang, waving around a Costco-sized box of Bics. That's right, the simple black ballpoint is the writing utensil favored by renowned author John Robert Beckett. Reporters love this bit of trivia. One wrote an entire article comparing my dad's literary style with this stark, no-frills pen. I've always wondered what that reporter might have written if I'd opened up the closets to reveal thousands of these literary metaphors hoarded within.

I left my parents staring at each other and went inside to cut the cake. While our coffee brewed, I poked around the house as I always did to make sure his panic disorder was still in check. Mantras? Displayed on every wall. Floors? Meticulously swept. Windows? Polished to perfection, bringing the calming waters of Lake Michigan as close to inside as they could get.

So, that's some mischief managed, I said to myself, mustering a half-hearted laugh as I gathered up our cake.

My parents had moved from staring to chatting when I made it back outside. There were a few minutes of forks scraping against plates; these people are, after all, the ones who sired me and I'm not one to neglect a cake. But at last my dad cleared his throat.

"Mariana, we're concerned for you." His voice was strong and direct, and for some reason this made me slump into my chair.

"Really? I thought you guys wanted to get together after all these years to play cards. Maybe Old Maid?"

The look my parents exchanged was an exact replica of one I'd seen as a kid—the She-Inherited-That-Smart-Mouth-From-You smirk.

"It's been more than a month and your mother tells me you can barely set foot in your own home. Did you really spend all of last week in a place called the Heart 'O Chicago Motel?"

I have to confess, I absolutely loved hearing my father, the literary legend, use the word *'O* in something other than a reading of Keats.

"Mariana? Is this true?"

"Yes, I stayed there," I finally said. "It was nice."

Have you ever seen a Raul Fletcher International Book Prize winner roll their eyes? It's awesome.

"Obviously our concern is not whether it was nice but why you felt the need to avoid your own home."

"I'll be honest. Walking in on an English major straddling my fiancé turned me off the place."

"Marin…" My mom sighed, and my habit of firing back at her disappointment in me triggered what tumbled out next.

"Did I mention they were on top of Grandma's quilt? The one she made me for my eleventh birthday, which makes the twenty-two-year-old quilt the exact same age as the girl David was with. It really killed the cozy vibe of home."

I turned back to the lake so I wouldn't see them trade She's-Clearly-Overwrought nods. Also, I was a little embarrassed about the images I'd just unloaded on them, even though I knew that was silly. Twice a year, my mom and stepfather visit his native Zambia and sow condoms like seeds to fight HIV. I learned about the birds and the bees at age nine—at my dad's own public reading of his memoir.

When I risked a look at them, their eyes were locked like they were deep in conversation. Seriously, twenty years without one bit of contact and these two people could still read each other's thoughts? No wonder my dad has problems.

"We don't blame you for avoiding the place," Dad said. And then, as if they'd telepathically choreographed it, he and Mom leaned toward me and uttered the same words at once:

"We want to help you get away."

"You do?"

"We do," Mom said, her voice softer than I'd heard it in years.

Dad picked up his fedora and twirled it around his finger. I actually smiled; he's so Frank Sinatra-cute sometimes. Then he said, "I'm selling the Seasalter house," with a matter-of-fact look like this wasn't the end of the world as we knew it.

I glanced from his face to my mom's. They were both sober. I mean to say that they were both serious, but it's also worth noting that they were not drunk. Because selling the Seasalter house was an idea they'd have to be drunk to consider.

It wasn't just that it was the setting of *Salt in the Sea*, his bestselling memoir about his slide into mental illness—about how he'd clung to my mom and to me. It was that it was his childhood home, and mine. We hadn't lived there since I was six years old, I could barely remember it, but I had been reading about it my entire life.

The house in Seasalter, the small coastal town in southeast England—a town with a name you could taste, could smell—that house was all that was left of my parents and me. It was us as a family, before the divorce, before panicked delusions and desperate tears that eventually forced us apart. It was the three of us sloshing through pebbled beaches, shrieking at lapping waves. My dad, so tall and tan, his hair white-blond in the sun. My mom freckling despite her huge straw hat, her own hair hanging down her back like a copper rope. It was what he had written about me, their Bell Petite, and the alchemy that had melded platinum and copper into a little girl with golden curls. These images, pieced together from my own memories and the pen of my father, were all I remembered of our life when it was only the three of us.

And the Seasalter house was proof it had been real.

"The London Literary Archive contacted me in May," Dad said. "They're planning a permanent exhibit on *Salt in the Sea* and want memorabilia. Papers and personal effects, things that belonged to us while we lived in Seasalter. It started me thinking I might unload the lot of it."

"Dad, you've been planning this since May? Why didn't you say anything?"

"You've been busy for the past few months, love," he said gently.

Right. I had been busy. I had been trying on dresses and picking out flowers and enjoying all the cake tastings I could justify.

I winced at the idea, then winced again as I whispered my next words.

"What will you do without the income from the rent?" I hated to mention it in front of my mom, even if it was public knowledge. During their stormy divorce, his frazzled mental state had led him to donate all his money—including all future royalties from *Salt in the Sea*—to psychiatric research. He hadn't published more than a handful of essays since my mother left. He barely got by.

"I'll just visit the restroom," Mom said tactfully. My dad's eyes clung to her all the way through the front door before he turned back to me.

"Okay, Dad, what's going on? Do you need money? Is there a problem I don't know about?"

"Ulrich is selling this house." My stomach flipped completely upside down, but before I could panic, he said, "If I can raise the money, he'll sell it to me. It means I'll never have to move."

There was no way to argue with that. My dad's tiny cottage on the shore of Lake Michigan was his only haven, the refuge in which he had sequestered himself to manage his complex OCD. I don't know how renting affected my dad's anxiety, but the idea that he might have to uproot himself from the one place he felt relatively safe was a constant source of stress for me.

"Values have climbed so in that part of England, you won't believe the price the realtor quoted me for the cottage. The Seasalter property will bring more than enough for me to purchase this house, with money left over for necessities." My dad looked at the ground. "What kind of fool throws away all his money? Without even bothering to buy a home first? I should have realized the burden would fall to you."

"Dad, I don't mind helping you," I mumbled. "I love helping you."

My father touched my cheek. "Then help me buy this place so I can stay."

Behind us, the screen door banged shut. I turned to see my mother bent over the tangled hydrangeas blooming by the porch. Her long linen skirt caught on their branches. She pulled it free, laughing as a flurry of petals swirled to her feet. When I looked at my dad, the ache he was usually able to hide had bled across his face.

"Isobel," he whispered as she disappeared around the side of the house. He squinted like the weak sun hurt his eyes, then he focused on me and his cheeks sagged.

"Mariana. My little bell. Help me let the Seasalter house go."

And let go of the love for my mother that the house represented. I could read the words as clearly as if they were etched into the lines on his face. His eyes, blue like the water he needs to be near—blue like mine—were wet.

I took his hand in both my own. We sat in silence until my mom returned. And somehow he summoned the strength to his voice.

"The last regular tenants moved out in April. The Seasalter house has been a weekly rental all summer. I spoke with the property manager last week. The house is furnished and it's been well-tended, but we need to clear out the attic. We moved out in such a hurry, I don't remember what we left behind, but you know the book as well as anyone, Mariana. You can pull out some items worth giving to the Archive. See what, if anything, you want to keep."

"You can get away for a few months," my mother said. "And you can write as easily in Seasalter as you can here."

I almost groaned. If that were the case, I wouldn't churn out a word. When my own relationship fell apart, romance seemed to have been driven out of me.

"When is your next book due to your publisher?"

"March. It was supposed to be September, but they extended it. I earned some good grace when my *Jane Eyre* spin-off was optioned."

"Rightly so. Not every novel gets made into a TV movie." My dad is thrilled that I'm a writer. He doesn't mind that my forte is torrid love.

My mom, however, is less enthused. "Which name do you use for the historical books again?"

"Mariana Rose. The contemporary novels are Beckett Bell." Don't worry, I almost told her. *None of them can be traced back to you.*

"It's filming in England, right?" She pushed some enthusiasm into her voice. "Weren't you invited to visit the set? Now you can go."

"The set visit was scheduled for the week I called off the wedding. I was not in the mood for a meet-and-greet. I'm still not in the mood."

"You can't shut yourself away forever, Marin."

"I'm not!"

"Skipping the set visit? That sounds like avoidance to me."

"Back to our Seasalter idea." My dad's sharp tone silenced us both. "Ulrich is retiring next spring and wants to sell this house before then. But he's agreed to give me time to get the money together. You can leave anytime. And you would have a few months in England to figure things out."

"To figure things out or to sort through the house?"

"However you choose to see it."

I picked up his hand again, focusing on the freckles scattered over his pale skin. "Dad. I don't want to leave you alone."

When he squeezed my fingers, his grip was firm, like he was trying to prove he wasn't as frail as I feared.

"I have everything I need right here. What I want most is for you to be happy."

"You can have your own adventure, Marin," my mom said. "Anything could happen."

I stared out at the lake once more. A late-summer firefly flickered near the shore.

"And I could see the Seasalter house," I said, more to myself than anyone else.

When I looked back at my parents, they were gazing at each other with the same satisfied smile, like they already knew I had decided to go.

CHAPTER TWO

I THOUGHT IT WOULD BE BIGGER.

In my mottled little-girl memories, the Seasalter house was colossal—a grim stone manor shadowed by a heaving sea. When it turned out to be two narrow stories of clapboard painted a friendly baby blue, I won't deny some surprise. Apparently in my youth I'd consumed too many gothic novels alongside *Salt in the Sea*.

"You probably thought I would be smaller," I told the little house with a shrug. "Twenty-seven years. We were both bound to change."

I hauled my suitcase out of my rental car, still in disbelief that I had managed to drive on the opposite side of the road even the seven miles from the Canterbury train station to the house. "I'm a city girl. Next time, the bus," I promised myself. But who was I kidding? I had no plans to go out.

Our realtor had anchored a For Sale sign into the yard. I slipped a flier from the brochure holder attached to the base.

"'Own a bit of bookish history. Enjoy uninterrupted sea views in the charming two-bed home from famed *Salt in the Sea*,'" I read aloud. "'Let literature's finest love story inspire your own great romance in this inviting coastal cottage.'"

Brilliant, I snorted, unless potential buyers know that literature's finest love story ended in reality's ugliest split.

I tiptoed across the tiny yard, crushing the thyme curled around a sunken stone path. The crisp scent mingled with the September breeze. It was bittersweet and familiar, but with an untamed edge. Autumn with a briny, seaside tang.

At the threshold of the pretty cobalt blue door, I froze. Three handprints, a tangible reminder of my Seasalter childhood, were pressed into the concrete step. Two adult palms, six inches apart, tilted together until the fingertips touched. Sheltered below them was the imprint of my own four-year-old hand. I pressed my palm against the rough shapes, against the proof of a truth so easy to forget: that despite how fractured my family was now, once upon a time, we had been a team.

The magic of this idea clung to me as I unlocked the heavy front door. A tiny foyer welcomed me in. The narrow staircase to my right jogged recollections of two small bedrooms and a bath overhead. A snug living room unfolded on my left, full of overstuffed linen furniture and quaint built-ins lining the creamy painted walls. It was everything a little beach house should be, only bare and impersonal. But as I passed through the few small rooms, memories bloomed before me: crewelwork tapestries and hanging plants and copious books crammed onto shelves. My drawings taped to the wood-paneled walls, my sea glass collection lining the windowsills. The jumbled comforts of a life well lived.

I gave the bare kitchen walls a friendly tap.

"I'll find some things to liven you up. You I'm keeping for vintage flair," I told a curly-corded phone and ancient answering machine.

Through the French doors in the dining nook, the fading sun flickered on the gleaming North Sea. Even the waves were genteel compared to the brute force I'd always remembered. A champagne sunset spilled into the house—polished the wood floors, made the pale walls glow. I raised the windows and listened as the water washed over the shore. When the salt wind teased at my hair, I did my best to lose myself in the romance. A cozy English cottage by the sea. An actual fantasy come to life.

"Maybe it's jet lag," I told myself when my heart didn't skip.

But maybe it was just the new me.

If you've read *Salt in the Sea*, you know about the boat trip that signaled the end of our time in England. You know that one afternoon, despite his fear of boats—the result of a childhood accident off the Seasalter coast that had drowned his family and nearly drowned him—my dad had rented a sailboat and snuck me out to sea. Already mentally faltering, he was convinced that if he and I relived his family's failed sailing trip, he could cure the panic disorder bearing down on him. When a storm blew in, he had a critical mental break—an episode so severe he'd been paralyzed with fear. To keep me safe, he shut me in the cabin below the deck, so close and cramped that, at six years old, I could barely stand upright.

You know that we were rescued the next morning. What you don't know is that, throughout the day, I watched him through the cabin's small porthole as he huddled above-deck in the rain. When night fell and I could no longer see him, I frantically tried to claw my way out. By the time we were found, my nails had splintered off, my fingertips were raw, and I was battered all over from throwing myself at the door. I came away with some bruises, some bandages, and a blood phobia so severe that a hangnail can drop me. I was lucky. My dad left the boat with a lifelong panic disorder that locks him in his house and a guilt that, no matter what I say, he still hasn't managed to shake.

For the most part, my blood phobia doesn't hold me back. I'm an expert at blindly tending to my cuts, my scrapes, and—because *everyone* asks—yes, even my time of the month. The catch is unfamiliar environments. I have to be especially careful until I master the layout. Which is why I passed out during a call with my sister that first night in the Seasalter house.

"Marin! Mare!" Nandila was yelping from the phone at my side when I finally came to. I lifted it to my ear and groggily reassured her that I was alive.

"Sorry. The bedside lamp is this steel bird sculpture. I cut my knuckle on his beak turning on the light and didn't notice until I was more awake. You know it's one a.m. here, right?"

"Oh, please. You're always up. So can I borrow it?"

"I've been unconscious, Nandi. Remind me of what you want."

"The matte-sequined top. From your engagement—" She paused, but my little sister does not do awkward. "—from your 'I almost married a pig' party."

I managed a laugh. "Keep it. But housesitting does not include closet privileges."

"I'm young and lit, Marc. My interest in your wardrobe is a compliment," she said. "So? Aside from the killer lamp, how's the new place?"

"Charming. Surreal. How's my old place? How's Alfred?" This new bed felt huge without my fluff-ball cat pushing me to the edge.

"Alfred keeps barfing up dead orchids," she said pointedly. "I thought you were throwing them out."

"I enjoyed watching them die first," I said just to sound cool. In truth, it had been too hard. A few months before, those orchids had been living jewels that David had given me each year on the anniversary of our first date. For six years, I had faithfully nurtured each one. In July, I'd watched them wither away.

"I wish—" I stopped myself, but Nandi listens closely to what goes unsaid.

"I hate David," she growled. "Did he have to ruin your home along with everything else? Why didn't they just go to her place?"

"You tell me, she lives in the dorms, too. Would people notice the Homecoming Queen sneaking her English professor past the front desk?"

She faked a puking sound. "Moving on. Where are you going first?"

"First? To bed."

"You know what I mean. You're in England! Go explore."

I tried to think back to the days when Nandila had been content to be my sister and not my mother. Then I remembered: there weren't any. My mom had begun seeing

Charles when Nandi was only five, but the minute this kid had burst into my world, she'd begun bossing me around and fighting my battles. And I'd been nineteen years old at the time, so you can imagine how she runs my life now that we're both adults.

"I know you, Marin. When you're upset, you pull away. You'll turn into a hermit if I don't hound you to get out. I'm not letting this go. I expect regular slideshows of your adventures."

"Okay."

"I mean it."

"I said okay." Yeesh, this kid.

"I'm calling you in three days. Pictures, Marin. Get on it," she said, so I did.

For the rest of September, I filled Nandi's inbox with unbearably sweet shots of my quaint cottage and its idyllic view; of the vibrant beach huts lining the shore; of that long, quiet stretch of sea—its tossing waves my clearest memory of my Seasalter childhood.

I wrote her emails detailing my daily walks on the beach, how I'd learned the schedule of the tides and where to find the most sea glass. I told her to visit, that I would take her for the best fish and chips in town and show her the cute boutiques lining nearby Whitstable's seaside streets. I did not tell her I'd never browsed the boutiques. That I still hadn't tasted the fish or the chips.

I told her some truths: that each afternoon, I sat down to write at the dining table overlooking the back garden. That I opened the French doors wide to let in the fresh sea air, layering sweaters as the days grew cold. That I made myself stay every day until six, even if all I did was count the flash of the cursor. I didn't tell her that every line I managed to write felt like lying. Like selling an idea I knew wasn't true.

I didn't mention that, late each night, I flung myself on the bed and hoped for a dreamless sleep. I did not mention David, or how I always woke at three a.m. with cold sweat dripping in lines down my back as some scene from our life together faded away. I didn't tell her when the nightmares and the sweating stopped, when I dried out like the orchids I'd allowed to die. When I stopped being unsettled by all the absence—of myself and my life and what had once defined it. That I liked it just fine, being holed up alone, watching the dusk fall over the beach.

CHAPTER THREE

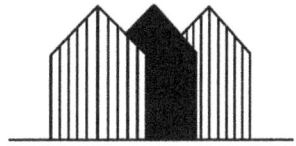

Richard Glenister and I got off to a rough start.

To begin with, my dad forgot to mention the meeting he'd scheduled for me with Mr. Glenister, director of the London Literary Archive. Which meant, of course, he hadn't mentioned that the meeting was at my house. So it wasn't with a warm smile and a hot cup of tea that I welcomed the poor man; rather, it was with an apology for the bras drip-drying on the line I'd strung between the open French doors.

"Such a charming garden," Mr. Glenister said around a C-cup or two of blush-pink silk and a couple more of sensible white cotton. I snatched them down so he could step into the backyard, where he folded his hands and sighed. "Roses overlooking the shore, just as your father described in his book. How lovely they must be in summer."

"I'm sure they are," I said, stuffing my underwear behind a shrub.

We both heard the click, but I was used to it, so only Mr. Glenister looked up.

"Did that couple just photograph your house?"

"Probably. Our realtor referenced *Salt in the Sea* in the property listing. It's encouraged more gawkers than buyers, unfortunately."

"Few books attain that level of devotion with the public as well as critics. Such gestures prove your father's collection belongs in the Archive," he said. "Your father mentioned you're also a writer, Ms. Beckett—er, Mariana. I know your father always refers to you as Bell Petite in public, but he let slip your given name. May I call you Mariana?"

"Sure. Or Marin. I usually go by Marin."

"Of course, Mariana to Marin. Because Bell Petite couldn't pronounce her own name. Would you mind—how did you—"

"Marinana."

His prim lips twitched into a grin. "Forgive me. I'm such an admirer of your father's book that learning your name is akin to solving a riddle. And you're also a writer! Might I have seen your work?"

Something told me that a Mariana Rose classic like *Doyenne of Desire* had never rested on Richard Glenister's nightstand. I offered him the safer answer.

"I wrote a prequel to *Jane Eyre*, my favorite novel. *The Young Edward Rochester* didn't gain much traction as a book, but it was made into a film for public television this summer."

"How very interesting. I'll be sure to read it." I smiled and tried not to envision him comparing my work to *Salt in the Sea*.

"I heard tell that the poem your dad painted on the

bedroom ceiling is still visible. Might I see it? Of course, I don't wish to intrude upon your privacy," he said as I led him upstairs.

You've already seen my bras, I contemplated saying. Might as well glimpse last night's pajamas in the hamper, too.

"Wonderful!" Mr. Glenister clasped his hands beneath his chin. The lavender words above my bed had faded like a fresco, but the tribute my dad had written for my mom was still legible.

> *We live in the shadow of our dream,*
> *But you're kind, you're quiet,*
> *You're calm, you're bright;*
> *You shine for me in the dark and the deep.*

"Incredible," he whispered. "That this symbol of your parents' love remains is simply enthralling."

Over tea, Mr. Glenister explained the plan for my dad's papers. Everything would be thoroughly catalogued, then select pieces would make a circuit across the UK. Finally, the complete collection would be permanently installed at the British Library.

"Alongside those of so many other great minds, from Virginia Woolf to Shakespeare himself. We couldn't be happier to welcome John Robert Beckett into the fold."

I paused to wonder what donations Shakespeare's daughter might have pulled from his stockpile. Probably not the six cartons of ancient ballpoint pens I'd found in a closet the week before.

"What items would the Archive like to receive?"

Richard Glenister looked at me pleasantly over his cup as he took an elegant sip.

"Anything you choose to part with, Ms. Beckett. We plan to make your father's collection highly personal to correspond with the intimate nature of the book."

Of course, I thought. What kind of collection would it be without shining a light on what remains of the Beckett family's privacy?

"We'll entertain any item. Why, Dorothy Walker-Ward offered us custody of her cockatiel. We declined, of course, for sanitary reasons. She's a wonderful woman. A bit eccentric, you know…" He flushed and was suddenly fascinated by the inside of his teacup.

Don't worry about it, I wanted to tell him. Eccentric writers are a penny a peck, as my dad likes to say. In the words of John Robert Beckett himself: "It's too hackneyed to be tragic. A reclusive writer who authored one acclaimed work and then shut himself away? It's laughable. Who knew I would become a living cliché?"

Mr. Glenister recovered enough to say, "Your father is well, I hope. Such a shock it was to his readership when we learned your mother had left him."

"Yes, well, it was a shock to him, too," I said, trying to be glib.

"Just imagine, John and Isobel Beckett. If they could divorce, do any of us stand a chance?"

"I have no idea," I told him, more honestly than he knew.

On his way out, Mr. Glenister smiled timidly. "I must say, it was remarkable to meet you. To think I just enjoyed a cup of tea with one of the most captivating children in modern letters."

In the twenty-five years since my dad had published *Salt in the Sea,* I've received many comments like this. I should be prepared, but somehow they always catch me off guard. I usually stammer a red-faced *I enjoyed meeting you, too.*

Therefore: "Thank you, Mr. Glenister. I enjoyed meeting you, too."

"I don't suppose you keep a pet oyster these days." He looked at me sentimentally. "Bell Petite, all grown up."

I leaned against the door when it clicked shut behind him. To my right, the staircase loomed like a warden, ready to march me up to the attic. Richard Glenister's enthusiasm for the treasures within hadn't rubbed off on me. I've been curling up with *Salt in the Sea* since I was eleven years old, and I enjoy letting myself believe in my parents' love story when I do. Pulling apart the remnants for a public exhibit was not a tempting way to spend a day.

On the other hand...

To my left, the blank document on my laptop glared at me. The cursor grew more insolent with every flash.

So those were my choices—inventing a passionate fake romance or deconstructing a failed real one. I glanced again at the computer and made for the stairs.

The attic space was tucked beneath the eaves, stretching between my childhood bedroom and my parents' old room and accessible at each end by short doors in the walls. I started toward my parents' side, which I had claimed for myself when I'd arrived, but a gold-tipped memory stopped me. I stepped into my childhood room and, after dislodging a heavy padlock, popped open the little attic door.

A swatch of cornflower-blue stars still twinkled on the back.

"We'll sprinkle your walls with sparkling stars," my dad

had said so many years ago, pasting a long sheet of the same paper from the ceiling to the floor.

"Stars," I heard myself echo. The British tones in my four-year-old voice rocked through my memory, just like his American accent had dawned on me then. "Daddy, you don't sound like me."

"Not anymore. When I was small, I sounded like you."

"Were you big when you moved to America?"

"Bigger than you, but I was still small." I'd been pasting the lopsided square onto the back of the attic door. My dad smoothed it down.

"Mrs. Wickens said now that you watch me all day instead of her, I'll start waffling on in a dreadful American voice." He laughed while wiping my sticky fingers clean, until I added, "Daddy, why don't you work anymore?"

He had frozen with his hand still clasped around mine. The crusty rag bit into my skin. I pulled away. He blinked.

"We couldn't make your room this pretty if I was working. When I was your age, I shared this room with my brother. We had boats on our walls."

"I like boats," I remember saying. And I remember the ragged fear in his voice when he whispered, "I don't."

His hand, level with my little-girl face, had gripped the brush until his knuckles turned white.

"Daddy?"

The brush had clattered to the floor.

"No boats for you, Petite. You get stars. Stars to watch over my bell while she sleeps."

"Stars," I whispered, running my fingers over the faded wallpaper again. I knelt and peered into the attic space. At five, I'd built a secret club in the corner, so maybe it was muscle memory; my hand shot through the darkness straight to the switch.

Dust lay like a quilt over boxes and trunks and sheet-covered lumps filling the narrow space. Twenty feet long, four feet deep, five feet high at its tallest point. It would take me roughly nine years to plow through it all.

"Live and let live, okay?" I called to any creatures residing within. "If I don't know you're here, I won't hire an exterminator to break up your happy home."

I hunkered down and began to pick my way through our belongings. Something bright in the corner caught my eye.

My little yellow rocking chair, handmade for me by my Granddad Cal and shipped all the way from South Carolina. He'd painted a ribbon of roses along the top. I traced the curve of one red petal and let the needle-fine strokes of my grandfather's brush pull me into the past, to my bare toes pushing off the wooden floor, to the slats smacking my shoulder blades as I rocked back. To my dad pouring secrets of love and sickness into the keys of his green Olivetti as his fitful words snapped onto the page.

I started a keep pile by shoving the little chair near the door, then hurried toward a box inscribed with *Mariana* in my dad's lean, sharp print. I popped off the top and gasped. We had left the house in such a hurry that I had few mementos from my Seasalter years, but here were Golden Books and my four-color pen and erasers shaped like oranges and grapes. I lifted out a stack of drawings. My fingers slid across a sad family—a yellow-haired girl crying projectile tears, flanked by an absurdly tall stick-figure dad and a mom whose cherry-red ponytail pointed to the sky.

And floating in the heavens, surrounded by hearts, a dearly departed oyster-grey lump.

My dad's six-page tribute to this incident in his memoir had turned Pearl the Oyster, my little short-lived pet, into a cultural punchline, even to me. But when I caught sight of the lace handkerchief beneath the drawing, she turned back into the solid, slimy treasure I had wrapped in my jacket and smuggled upstairs, a living creature I had nurtured all day. The soft lace cloth in my hand had been an ideal coverlet for her Kleenex-box bed, until a desperate thought had woken me. What if oysters were like fish and couldn't breathe air? It had been life or death. What else could I do at two a.m. but slip her into the toilet until I came up with a plan? And what could be done the next morning but grieve when my mom had unknowingly flushed her away?

I piled the drawing and handkerchief onto my little rocking chair. But the nostalgic warmth in my chest froze over when I dug into the box again. My fingers trembled as I lifted out a faded clothbound book identical to one that, until July, had rested on my dresser at home.

Tennyson. *Poems, Chiefly Lyrical*, with its pessimistic heroine, Mariana, smothering herself slowly in her moated grange.

The attic seemed to close in around me, even as the image of my condo in Chicago crowded it out. My bedroom, the coziest room in my home, with a putrid new sickness boiling off the walls. A shocked, shaking girl in the corner, sobbing as she threw on her twisted sundress. Framed love poems on my French flea-market dresser, and the hand that had written them clutching my favorite quilt around his waist to hide his shame. The desperate words he flung at me: *love, doubt, sorry.* Especially *sorry.*

And then he had whispered, "Mariana."

I gripped the book in my hands the way I'd gripped David's copy then, but this time I didn't hurl it across the room. I flipped straight to the poem that, after six years together, was permanently lodged in my brain. Poor lovelorn Mariana, so fulfilled by despair that she refuses to hope. Six years of jokes from Doctor David Lauer, Tennyson expert: that I dream up romance but lock it in books and anchor real life with caution. Jokes that had gradually lost their lightness, that he had laced with reproach as time wore on. Poor skeptical Marin, who watched her parents' love die and couldn't or wouldn't trust her own to survive. I had always ignored his teasing jabs—I loved him, I was marrying him, I was happy to be doing so—but what if he'd seen something I couldn't?

I looked around at the remnants of my family's life in Seasalter—a life that had been shelved, in the truest sense of the word. Too much chaos roiled through the pages of *Salt in the Sea* for me to have idealized it fully, but for years I'd been cocooning into my dad's account of our Seasalter life. What if David was right? What if, without meaning to, I let fictional love run wild but kept real love caged to protect myself? And what if I sifted through the fragments of the most beautiful part of my parents' romance—of all that remained of my family when we were whole—and realized that, even then, we were destined to fail?

I was so lost in thought that it took a minute for the banging on the front door to register. By the time I got downstairs, the delivery driver was gone, but a package from my editor was waiting. Inside was a book. My book. *The Young Edward Rochester*.

"It's the second edition we printed to tie in with the TV movie," Gretchen said when I called. "What do you think?"

"It doesn't look like my other books, does it?" I ran my fingers over the thick matte cover with its spot-gloss details —and noticeably without a shirtless man on the front. The man on this book was fully clothed, a dim figure silhouetted against a misty English landscape.

"The cover is a still of Simon Quinn from the film. That's a first look at your real-life Edward Rochester."

This was almost too much to handle. His face was cloaked in shadow, but he looked sexy. In a literary way, of course.

"He looks right for the part, don't you think?" Gretchen said.

"I can't make out what he looks like, but they captured the Rochester spirit. He seems just melancholy enough."

"You'll have to tell me after the wrap party if he's as dark and romantic in person."

"What wrap party?"

"Look in the envelope."

Among the papers I'd tossed aside was an invitation to celebrate the end of filming for the brand-new TV movie. And lucky me. The party was in London. In only three days.

"SaladBar," I read. "Seems like a lame place for a party."

"Are you serious? SaladBar pioneered fusion destinations. Raw-cuisine lunch spot by day, organic cocktails and the hottest emerging bands at night. *The Vegan Voice* gave it four beets."

"Oh, in that case…" I said, mimicking the sanctity in Gretchen's voice. "Anyway, I'm sure they don't expect me to go."

"Flip it over."

A boldly scrawled note filled the back of the invitation.

Ms. Howard,

How fabulous to hear that Mariana Rose is in England! Everyone involved in our production has scoured her book to bring it to life. We were disappointed when she canceled her set visit during filming, but her company at the wrap party would be ideal. Please forward this invitation to Ms. Rose, along with my sincerest wish that she join us.

~ Jordan Palomo

Jordan Palomo. The film's director. Her personal note to Gretchen did not bode well for me. I tried anyway.

"I'm uncomfortable at networking events. You know, the introverted writer thing."

"Look, I was supportive when you skipped the set visit in July. Flying to England the day after you walked in on your fiancé and his—well, no one expected you to go after that. But the breakup was months ago, and now you're an hour away."

"I think it might be an hour and a half."

"Do what you want," she said, feigning indifference. "But Yvonne knows you're invited to the wrap party. She said it's a great way to build relations between the network and Velicity. And you know she still hasn't formally signed off on your renegotiated publishing deal."

Yvonne Lee was head of the Lee family publishing dynasty—the book industry's answer to the Corleones. She was also Velicity's hands-on new owner. I was doomed. Given the smug silence on her end, Gretchen could tell that I knew it, too.

"Look at it this way," she said. "You get to spend an evening with Edward Rochester."

CHAPTER FOUR

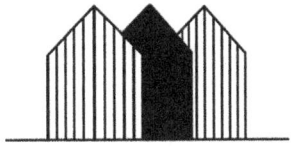

As the double-decker bus rolled south from St. Pancras railway station toward the cramped London neighborhood where the wrap party was being held, the vibrant downtown colors washing over the streets turned orphan's-undershirt grey. The bus dumped me out on a dreary corner, made more Dickensian by the icy rain. Ten seconds after it pulled away, I realized I'd left my jacket on the seat. Cursing myself for not even thinking to wear tights with my skirt, I froze as I wandered the sidewalks in search of my haute vegan destination. The handful of businesses I passed were closed. The crowd of guys gathered outside the bar that was open crowed loudly as they leered at me. When I started to shiver, I felt I had earned the comfort of some easy directions and a friendly voice.

"The wrap party is tonight?" Nandi said. "How do I not know this? I could have ditched school to go with you. I've always wanted to date an actor."

"Then start hanging out in the theater department. I'm not staying long. In and out. Thirty minutes."

"Don't you dare leave! You're supposed to be adventurous."

I ignored her. "Can you look up the address for this salad club thing? I'm dying a slow death out here in this rain."

"I told you public Wi-Fi would be crap. You should have gotten the international data plan."

"You were right. It's insanely expensive, but I'll add it tonight."

"Oh, Marc. Say it again, slowly: *I was right.*" Her laughter ended in a giddy squeak. "Phil's at the door! It's our first real date. Let me answer it, then I'll look up the address. Call you right back."

She hung up. I glanced around and spotted a boiler repair shop that seemed to be open; maybe I could ask for directions. But as I started to cross the street, the wind ripped my umbrella from my hand and hurled it against the building behind me. I thought the spokes were only tangled in the iron grille covering a low window, but when I jerked the handle, I heard a metallic rip. Seconds later, a light flipped on inside.

And then my phone rang. I fumbled to answer it without looking, too busy gaping at the gash I had torn in the screen.

"I was starting to think you forgot about me," I said, confident Nandi was on the line. Instead, an unwelcome voice knocked the breath out of me.

"I could never forget you. I love you."

David.

My heart punched into my throat as image after image hit me in the face. It had been three months since I'd walked in on him with his student—three months of reliving that anger and shame.

"Can we talk?" His deep voice, laced with desperation, sliced into my ear. I pictured his green eyes, wide and desperate, when he'd seen me in the bedroom doorway. "Please, will you talk to me?"

The cool English rain smacked into my hot face, which burned even more when he whispered my name.

"I'm sorry," he said, just as he had when he'd chased after me that horrible day. "Marin, believe me, I'm so sorry."

My shaking fingers managed to end the call.

Why? Why now? I had scraped together just enough courage to go to this wrap party alone, the very last thing I'd have chosen to do. David, so composed and well-spoken, always chatted me through my dreaded networking events. Why, of all moments, had he called now?

I pulled in a few steadying breaths but then the phone rang again, startling me so much I dropped it into a puddle. When I bent to retrieve it, I was shaking so much that I lost my balance and pitched forward. My knee slammed full force into one of the sharp iron spikes on the window grille.

"Do you need help?"

A hand clasped my arm and gently pulled me to my feet. I looked up into eyes so dark and warm that, for a moment, I forgot the graphic images seared into my brain, forgot the pain tearing through my knee and the rain smacking my face. For a moment, I felt calm, in an oddly breathless way.

Until that wretched phone rang again. This time I practically threw it into the puddle. The warm eyes blurred as mine filled with tears.

Don't! I barked over the echo of David's voice in my head. Don't. He's not worth it.

I clamped my teeth over my trembling bottom lip and tried to distract myself with my stinging knee. But I was careless. Too flustered to focus, I swiped at the scrape and saw a red smear across my palm. Fog flooded my head. I felt myself sway. Desperate, I grabbed for the man in front of me as the world around me went dark.

CHAPTER FIVE

DESPITE FAINTING LIKE THIS SINCE CHILDHOOD, I'VE NEVER woken up in a completely foreign place. But the next time I opened my eyes, I was on a rough tweed couch in a dim basement apartment. It took a minute of frantically glancing around to recognize my yellow umbrella, still flapping at the window above my head.

"It's chucking it down out there, so I carried her inside, but now what?" an unfamiliar male voice said from behind me. "Should I ring for an ambulance?"

This last bit kept me from panicking about being in an underground room with an unknown man hovering out of sight.

"Because you're a doctor." After a long pause, the voice snapped, "Of course not. Look, will you help her or shall I ring 999?"

Another dizzy spell hit me. When I opened my eyes, I saw the guy from earlier lifting my feet above my heart. I spent two seconds hoping he wouldn't look up my skirt before I glimpsed my bloody leg and it was lights out again. This happened twice before I had the wherewithal upon waking to keep my eyes shut.

"…pulse seems fine. No, her lips aren't blue."

I lifted my hand before speaking so I wouldn't scare him with my sudden resurrection. "I'm okay. It's vasovagal syncope."

"Dad, she's awake. She says it's, er, vaso…"

"Vasovagal syncope. It's nothing. I just faint when I see my own blood."

"Oh, is that all?" I kept my eyes shut, but he sounded amused. "What, Dad? Apply pressure, use antiseptic. Right. Thank you." I was careful not to look for fear of passing out, but it sounded like he'd tossed his phone aside. "Sorry about that. My dad is a decent physician but it took a moment to get this situation through to him. Fortunately, he walked me through how to try and stop the bleeding."

"That's too much trouble. I'm used to this. If you give me a wet paper towel, I'll be all set."

"Shouldn't I do it? A river of blood is pouring into your boot." Unfortunately, I was still lightheaded. At this vivid description, I passed out again.

When I came to, he'd pressed a warm, wet cloth against my knee and was sponging my nose with another. "Sorry, that was a stupid thing to say. I'll have to work on my bedside manner."

"Your bedside manner is great, I'm just a pitiful patient. Did I hit my face?" I asked as he dabbed at my cheek.

"No, it's just silt from your fall." He rubbed at a spot. "Whoops. Those specks are freckles. I'll leave them be."

The warmth in his voice helped cut the tension, but I was still mortified.

"I'm so sorry. I bash in your window, pass out at your feet, bleed on your couch, and now you're cleaning me up. This is the worst first impression I've ever made."

"I'm just glad I was here. Does this happen often?"

"Not anymore, thankfully. But I was a pretty uncoordinated middle-school runner. Fun times—when I was awake." Restless and embarrassed, I tapped my fingers on my stomach in time with the Neil Young he had playing in the background. But my rhythm was thrown off when a snarling guitar split through the room. I recognized the weirdly wonderful version of "Long May You Run" by a punk-rock Neil Young cover band. "Hey. This is Third-Wheel Neil."

"You know them?"

"I've seen them. They're from Milwaukee. They're not a big-name band. I didn't expect to hear them in England."

"My friend started me listening to them a while ago. Do you know a lot about punk bands?"

"Not really, I just like live music." I blindly picked at a clump of wet muck ground into my shirt. "I live to rock, can't you tell?"

"You do make quite an entrance," he said. "I'm a Neil Young fanatic. Tell me about the Third-Wheel Neil show."

As he worked on my knee, we spent the next few minutes discussing how, despite their differences, punk rock and Neil Young are a perfect fit. Laughing with him about the stress of screaming all eight minutes of "Ambulance Blues" took some of the sting out of the past half-hour.

"The bleeding has slowed, which I believe means no stitches," he said finally. "But I need to take off this boot to clean up the—er, to clean up your leg. Do you mind?"

His hand brushed my calf as he unzipped the boot, leaving behind a line that tingled until he scrubbed it away.

"All done. It should be safe to look, if you avoid your knee while I bandage it."

My eyes blinked open and locked onto his, which were as warm as I remembered, the deep amber of sunlight filtering through strong tea. They crinkled at the corners when he smiled at me.

Our gaze held a moment too long. I glanced away, embarrassed. But he seemed so relaxed about patching me up that, before long, I felt more relaxed, too. He was easy to watch. Tall and broad-shouldered, with golden skin and thick lashes and—he glanced up and grinned—mmm, a perfect smile. The rain had made his dark hair curl.

I studied the casual way he moved and his laid-back style—worn-out jeans and a faded shirt, slightly ripped at the neck. The stubble on his face wasn't stylishly trimmed, just plain old couldn't be bothered to shave. He seemed like he didn't give much thought to his looks, which was impressive, considering he looked as good as he did.

He drew a soft square of cotton over my knee. The sting of the cut seemed to melt away. His lips curved into a tempting—

Mariana Beckett! I yelped in my head. Quit romanticizing this!

Although, to be honest, I didn't want to stop. After three months without a hint of inspiration, I was thrilled that I had so easily slipped into idealizing the moment. It was a lifelong habit that, since my disaster with David, I'd feared might be lost for good.

Still, I reminded myself, have some dignity. You're not

plotting a book, you're bleeding in a stranger's basement. Get it together.

"Don't watch," he said, pulling me back into reality as he removed the cotton from my knee and sponged the cut one last time. I kept my eyes on his ceiling while he smoothed on a row of plastic bandages. "They're small, but they'll work if we line them up."

I started to thank him but paused when the unusual Band-Aid design caught my eye—they were solid black, adorned with white skulls.

"My sister was a pirate at a fancy-dress party," he said at my inquisitive look. "I bought her these plasters so she would look tough."

"They're working. I feel tougher already." Then I ruined the effect by shivering.

"Your top is soaked. I'm sure I can find something that will do." He left the room, returning with a hand towel as well as a red V-neck sweater. It looked my size, which made me nervous that some gorgeous underwear-model girlfriend was going to burst in and catch me ogling her man while wearing her clothes.

"Are you sure?" I said when he offered me the sweater. "I don't want to get into a whole 'Who's been eating my porridge?' thing with your girlfriend."

Was it the genuine way he laughed at that or how his eyes seemed to gleam when he looked at me? Whatever it was, I suddenly felt warmer than I had in weeks, and I hadn't even slipped on the sweater yet.

"Don't worry, the jumper is mine. I didn't know it would shrink in the tumble dryer." He steadied me as I got to my feet and led me down the hall. "You can change in the loo."

In his tiny bathroom, I stripped off my sopping shirt and threw on his cozy sweater. After a horrifying glance in the mirror, I swiped away the mascara streaking down my cheeks and smoothed my dripping hair.

"Definitely better on you than me," he said when I reappeared. As I tried not to feel too flattered, my phone squeaked out a rusty ring. Nandi's picture appeared on the flickering screen.

"Oh, great," I muttered, stupidly realizing that the calls after David's had likely been her. "My sister is probably planning my funeral."

I snatched up my phone. It flickered again and died for good.

"Here. Use mine."

"It's an international call," I said, shaking my head, but he pressed it into my hand.

Nandi's hello was anxious, but when I said, "Hey, it's me," she sighed explosively.

"Dude, I've been freaking out. Do you know how often Americans die in England while crossing the street? When this strange number popped up, I thought someone was notifying your next of kin."

"I'm fine. Did you find the address for the restaurant?" Nandi's call had jolted me back to reality. My romance-writer's block had already hurt my career, and I was twenty minutes late for a pre-party cocktail with director Jordan Palomo.

"I've been calling for ages. Why didn't you answer?"

I knew better than to mention David's call to Nandi. "My phone is messed up. Yell at me later, okay? I'm late."

She growled the address at me, then said, "Seriously,

Marin, pick a personality. First you don't even want to go, now you're—"

"Look, make a list. You can tell me off when I call you back. Loveyoubye," I added guiltily before hanging up.

I repeated the address aloud as I sponged the mud off my leather boots.

"You're going to SaladBar? It's upstairs. The front door is just round the corner."

"Oh, perfect," I said, slipping on my boots.

When I looked up, he was holding out an adorable dotted umbrella. "I think yours is buggered, but you can take this. I trust you'll wield it responsibly."

"I promise. Can you write down your address for me? I'll have the sweater cleaned and mail everything back to you."

"No need. The jumper fits you better than it ever fit me, and that umbrella has been here forever. I've no idea whose it is."

I'll bet you don't, I smiled to myself. Some poor girl probably left it behind hoping you would call.

"I'll pay for the window," I told him. "And the phone call. And I should have your couch cleaned, too."

"That's not necessary." When I hesitated, he said, "Don't waste time worrying over it. What would your sister say if you were late after cutting her off?"

It was nice, laughing with someone about home.

"I'd let her think she slowed me down. All right, you win. And really, thank you. For everything."

In the open doorway, I looked up at him. I suddenly felt ridiculous. After all that time, I hadn't asked his name.

Well. Better ridiculous than rude. I held out my hand.

"I'm Marin. Sorry it took me so long to say so."

"Sam," he said, folding my fingers in his. "Pleased to meet you, Marin."

"Nice to meet you, Sam."

He smiled again and I felt irritated that I had to go. And then I felt irritated for feeling that way, so I waved and ducked out into the rain, clutching my new umbrella tight.

CHAPTER SIX

JORDAN PALOMO KNEW JUST HOW THINGS SHOULD BE DONE. Over one glass of wine, she'd informed me that I had taken the wrong bus to the bar, that Whitstable's world-famous oysters were "nothing to tweet about," and that her hometown of Los Angeles outranked Chicago in every way.

When she left to lecture her frazzled assistant, who was struggling to hang some kind of photo display, I entertained myself with ideas on how to best model a book character on Jordan. In a classic work of literature, she'd be the ruthlessly beautiful adversary. In an original work by Yours Truly, she would be the belligerent boss bent on stealing your man.

"House red for the lady." Prisms danced on the bartender's hand as he slid me a new glass. I thought I detected a Scottish trill in his voice when he added, "Sulfite-free, of course."

"Of course," I said, and he grinned from behind his red-gold beard. But he fled when Jordan slumped onto her barstool again. She had romance novel looks to match the personality—long dark hair and smoky green eyes. Skin sun-bronzed but bent on remaining unlined. She looked familiar. Like the Homecoming Queen might look when she grows up.

Maybe that's why I feel sort of hostile toward her, I thought. Then she opened her mouth again and I realized that the resemblance wasn't the only problem.

"Will!" she snapped at the bartender, smacking her palm on the bar. He sent a martini whizzing into her hand.

"Do you come here often?" I asked as she bit into three olives at once.

"Often enough. This is where I met Simon. When he isn't striding around the moors in wool breeches, he works here."

Simon as in Simon Quinn, the young Edward Rochester himself. A few minutes earlier, Jordan had told me she'd personally discovered the film's lead actor at his band's live show. Apparently, he was "a dedicated performer, a brilliant musician, and an absolutely unquestionable talent." I doubted that anyone dared to question her, which must've worked out for them both.

I knew almost nothing about Simon Quinn, but even I could attest to his musical talent. The day my relationship had imploded, I'd been meeting with my publisher, who sent me a track from the film that he'd written and performed. I loved that song immediately, so much that I binged it for hours on my way home from New York to Chicago. Of course, I had promptly forgotten it after walking in on David that night. But remembering the song made me more interested in meeting the man who'd written it.

"Wait until you see him," Jordan told me again, leaning

conspiratorially over her glass. "He's the epitome of the classic romantic hero. Tall, dark, brooding. He's the most beautiful guy I've ever seen. Although there's something rugged about him that makes him…ahem. All man."

This was an idea that I didn't love. "Edward Rochester isn't described as handsome. Quite the opposite, in fact."

"Well, this isn't a blockbuster film. We need a face that grabs attention and doesn't let go." She smiled slyly. "Of course, his body's just as captivating. Trust me."

Okay, I get it. You've tamed that beast. Congratulations, I wanted to say.

Jordan seemed disappointed that I didn't press for details of her conquest. She had probably decided that she couldn't bond over cocktails with someone who preferred literary accuracy to a gorgeous man.

And you know what? I was okay with that.

But you're here on business, I reminded myself, and forced a pleasant expression onto my face.

"You're very pretty when you smile," Jordan said. "Have you ever done any acting?"

I did my best not to laugh in her face. "No. I'm the behind-the-scenes type." Then I'm sorry to say I did that stupid thing people sometimes do and interpreted a compliment as a slight. You know the trick: How do I look when I'm *not* smiling? Right.

Jordan's eyes jerked behind me. "Simon. Finally!"

Across the dimly lit restaurant, I saw someone new helping Jordan's assistant tack the display to the wall. Even from a distance, he looked too tall to be Edward Rochester, who was, according to Jane Eyre herself, of medium height. This guy was at least six feet tall. But he had the broad shoulders Jane had described, I'd give him that.

"What is he doing?" Jordan growled. "I'll bring him over. You have to meet him." Her stilettos pecked at the wood floor as she stalked away.

The bearded bartender faked a shudder. "That woman is mental. Do not turn your back on her. But I'll admit, she's right about one thing. You are very pretty when you smile."

I promise I tried not to grin excessively at him. "Come on. You say that to all your customers."

"No!" He threw up his hands innocently, then winked at me. "Only the blondes."

I heard the approaching click of Jordan's heels and feigned a look of fright. The bartender mouthed the words "watch your back" before I turned to face Jordan and the man she held by the arm.

I'm still not sure what I expected. Not the character I'd envisioned while writing the book, thanks to Jordan. Her oversexed description had tampered with my own image of a younger, yet-to-be-thwarted version of my favorite romantic hero.

I can tell you, however, what I didn't expect. I didn't expect it to be that guy from downstairs. Sam.

My eyes widened in surprise. His crinkled into a confused smile.

Jordan's fingers brushed his sleeve possessively. "Simon Quinn, meet Mariana Rose. I don't need to tell you who she is. You've been devouring her book for months."

"You're Simon Quinn?"

"Mariana?" he asked pointedly. "Is that a pen name?"

I smiled. "No, it's just a mouthful. Professionally, I use Mariana. In my real life, everyone calls me Marin. Except my dad. And a few people who no longer speak to me. They call me something else altogether."

The wine was kicking in. I heard my bartender friend laugh into his sleeve.

"Is Simon your…" The wine again. I couldn't remember the word. "…actor name?"

He smiled. "My dad's given name is Simon as well. I've always been called Sam."

"I see. So you're Simon Junior."

"Surprisingly, that is not the image I'm cultivating, professionally or personally."

We both smiled this time. But Jordan pinched her lips into a sour line.

"You know each other? What an absolutely unbelievable coincidence."

Whatever she was implying, I didn't like it—or the way she was glaring at Sam.

"We met this evening," I snapped. Sam's eyes sparkled with silent laughter, but Jordan's scowl reminded me again that I was representing my publisher, who had a whole backlist of books she'd like optioned for film. I lightened up.

"Sam—uh, Simon—was my stylist earlier. If he had any idea how to care for cashmere, I'd be really underdressed tonight."

He explained our earlier meeting, politely sidestepping the more embarrassing moments. Like me fainting dead at his feet.

"I should have known you'd be a film hero, too," I said.

"And I should've known you possess a talent for drama," he replied.

I took a second to admire his dark eyes again. "I have to

work at the fictional drama, but it does come naturally in real life."

It felt like we had formed our own little club, complete with code names. If we talked much more, I was pretty sure we'd come up with a secret handshake. While I was surprised at how much that idea appealed to me, I was not surprised when Jordan intervened.

"Great," she said, taking my arm. "Now let's introduce you to the rest of the cast." She shot Sam another sullen look before pulling me across the room, as far away from him as we could get. When I glanced back a few minutes later, he was leaning against the bar, laughing with the group that had gathered around him. But before I turned away, he looked straight at me. His smile this time was roguish. Like he knew as well as I that we were on the same team.

NANDI WOULD BE PROUD. I STUCK IT OUT THROUGH TWO whole hours of polite conversation before slipping outside for a break. The rain had finally stopped, but heavy drops still fell from the trees that marked the restaurant's entrance. Strands of tiny white lights, strung through the branches, sparkled on the wet leaves when the breeze stole through.

The moon shone bright and steady as the clouds streaked past. The clean night air that swept through my hair made me long for Seasalter, for the whispering waves and my sweet blue house, the firelight flickering on the diamond windowpanes. It was comforting to realize that it felt like home.

Time to go, I decided, but someone scuffed the pavement behind me.

"I'm attempting to be noisy so I don't startle you. Is it working?" It was Sam. Simon? He looked around. "What are you doing out here?"

"Catching my breath. I'm not much for big parties."

"Really? As a writer, don't you often go to events like these?"

I almost snorted. Believe it or not, the author of such classics as *Pounding Hearts* and *Once More, With Feeling* has yet to be invited to a National Book Awards bash.

"I'm not really that kind of writer."

"What do you mean?" he said, God bless him. Too many people needed no clarification—they explained it to me all the time.

I groped for a mild way to describe the narrative sex shop that is Velicity Books.

"I write romance novels," I finally said, trusting the stereotypes would fill in the blanks. "But my publisher is adding some mainstream lines to expand its market. *The Young Edward Rochester* is quite a bit different from my other books."

Meaning I had reduced the sex to suggestion. How could I not? It was Edward Rochester. He might be passionate, but writing about someone bedding down with him was scandalous. Like a kid seeing their teacher during summer vacation. In a swimsuit. Just wrong.

"Anyway, film sets and wrap parties are foreign to me," I told him.

"To me as well. I knew nothing of making films before this. But it was a break from waiting tables and hustling for gigs. It's fortunate I rented the flat downstairs last year.

Through it, I found a job serving overpriced, undercooked vegetables, and met Will, the bartender, with whom I formed my band, which led to meeting Jordan, which led to the film." Our eyes met, and he added, "I owe quite a debt to that flat, actually." I pretended that the little smile teasing his lips had something to do with me. But before I could indulge the fantasy, he added, "How is your knee?"

"Honestly? You did a wonderful job patching me up, but it hurts. I think I twisted it when I fell."

"Shall I take a look? At least check your bandages? We don't need you passing out again."

When he knelt in front of me, I transformed it into a scene for a book: his long fingers caressing my knee, the moonlight glinting off his dark hair. Was he a hero who'd brush his lips across the cut to make it better? Or one who would sweep up the heroine to keep her safe?

He smoothed my pirate bandages to ensure they were holding tight.

No, I decided. He's the kind who cleans things up while making the heroine laugh. He's real.

Sam looked up. "It's not bleeding. Beyond that, I have no idea what I'm doing."

Yep. Definitely my kind of hero.

"You should sit down." And before I could tell him I was leaving, he'd led me to a nearby café table.

Okay, maybe a few more minutes, I told myself as he sat opposite me. He is the star of the film. Gretchen would want me to make a special effort with him.

That's right. I said Gretchen would want it.

"So. You live in Chicago."

"I do." I paused. "How do you know that?"

"'About the Author.' Jordan's right, I've carried your

book with me for months. I have your biography memorized. 'Mariana Rose grew up in South Carolina dreaming of Edward Rochester. She lives in Chicago with her fiancé and an overindulged grey cat.'"

A new reminder of my canceled engagement, this one immortalized in print.

"You must have a good memory," I said, sounding steadier than I felt.

"A compulsion, more like. It was my first acting job. I clung to your book so I wouldn't be a disaster."

"I'm sure you were great." I relayed Jordan's opinion that he was partly human, mostly divine. He grimaced like he had heard this too often.

What had Jordan been saying to him? And had she really been saying it to him in bed?

Jordan and I had different definitions of brooding; the guy in front of me was decidedly relaxed. He'd exchanged his torn t-shirt for a thin grey sweater, but the jeans were still worn and the stubble was still obvious. Not too fussy, just like I'd thought.

He ran a hand through his short, rumpled curls.

Not fussy, but undeniably gorgeous—too gorgeous to portray Edward Rochester, for sure. The man's true love called him ugly to his face, I grumbled inwardly. Then he glanced at me and I no longer cared. Plus, Brontë's description of Mr. Rochester's *dark and very fine eyes* had echoed through my brain. It was hardly Sam's fault that his dark eyes came with chiseled cheekbones and that strong jawline.

His very fine eyes crinkled into a smile. I realized it had been a while since my own less-fine eyes had left his face. Okay. Moving on.

"So, what now?" I said. "Will you keep acting?"

"Honestly, I wasn't even pursuing acting when I fell into the Rochester film, so I've nothing else lined up. For now, I'll keep serving at SaladBar and hopefully playing gigs with the band. Jordan mentioned working together on another film. And then there's my father, who wants me to finish university and go to work for him."

I heard some crestfallen little part of me say, His *dad* wants him to go to *college*? How young is this person? but I shut her down and said, "What were you studying?"

"Psychology."

"That's a big jump, psychology student to movie star."

"I'm not a movie star. I'm barely an actor." He shrugged. "I'm more focused on playing music and writing songs. It's cathartic."

"It is, right? I always feel more sane when I write."

Except for lately, I could have added. But he was nodding at me.

"Exactly. I quite enjoyed your book. It was clever. Very original."

"For a story full of borrowed characters and settings."

He tipped his head thoughtfully. "Are you always like this? So hard on yourself?"

Since I could feel the truth rushing into my cheeks, I didn't bother to deny it. "Yes. I am." It felt abnormally good to admit.

"You shouldn't be. The book was good. Thank you for emphasizing the musical side of Edward's character. It's why I got the part."

"You were in the back of my mind all along." I was joking, but I realized it felt true.

And that was my cue to leave.

"It's getting late. I should catch the bus to St. Pancras so I don't miss my train," I said as I stood, keeping my weight on my good knee. "Thank you again for earlier. I don't know what I'd have done without your help."

"It was my pleasure."

That nagging irritation about telling him goodbye returned. And even while I stood there asking myself if I'd completely lost my mind, my heart skipped when he stepped toward me and stretched out his hand.

I gave it a business-like shake, wishing I could shake off the flutter in my pulse as well.

"Nice meeting you, Simon Quinn. Sam."

"It was nice meeting you, Marin. Mariana Rose."

"Oh. It's Beckett." For some reason, I wanted him to know the real me.

"Pardon?"

"I lied when you asked if I use a pen name. Mariana is my real name. Rose is my pen name. Well, it's my middle name. My last name is Beckett."

"Are you letting me in on a trade secret?"

"After what I put you through earlier, you deserve to know who you were dealing with." The left corner of his grin lifted just above the right. I commanded myself to leave. But I'd only taken a few steps and he was beside me again.

"You know, I should walk you to your bus. This area can be a bit dodgy at night."

I opened my mouth to tell him that I was fine, that I often trek across Chicago alone at night. But upon consideration, I snapped it shut. A few minutes more with him sounded just fine.

"Where are you staying while you're here?" he said, falling into step with me.

"In Seasalter. Near Canterbury."

"You're staying in Kent? That's where I grew up. What do you think of it?"

"It's perfect," I said, surprising myself by how much I meant it.

"How long are you staying?"

"Until I finish my new book. It's due in March and I may need every minute. Typically, I'm a fast writer, but… it's not going well."

"What's the trouble?"

I kept my eyes on the sidewalk. "I'm not really in the mood for romance. I can't come up with anything worthwhile."

"Oh."

"Sorry. I should think up a diplomatic response. Bad breakup," I murmured as those awful images flooded my head again.

He paused. "I'll update your author bio on my copy of the book. Do you still have the cat or shall I scratch him out as well?" His reassuring smile eased the tightness in my chest. "Anyway, you'll be around for a while."

"Well, I'll be in Seasalter." I pictured Nandi trying to kill me. "I mean, yeah. I'll be around."

"If you're *around* next Friday, my band is playing at Three Wastrels in Canterbury. Have you been?"

"No. I've been here a month and can barely drive my rental car. That whole opposite-side-of-the-road, backward-car thing is daunting."

"If you feel like giving it a try, I'd love you to come."

Nandi's face loomed before me as I considered turning

him down. But as I looked at him, I realized—I didn't want to say no.

"If you're busy, of course, I understand," he added, shoving his hands in his jacket pockets.

"I'm never busy," I said without thinking, then immediately looked away. "I just mean I haven't gone out much yet."

"I know what you mean." He said this casually, but I had that same unsettling feeling he'd seen through me again.

The bus was barreling toward us. "Next Friday?"

"Eight o'clock. Three Wastrels Pub on Dover Street."

Maybe it's time to be brave, I told myself. Besides, it would be nice to know someone here in England.

This was not a lie, but it wasn't the whole truth. I was already thinking it would be nice to know Sam.

The bus's headlights cut a bright path down the wet street. I didn't let myself reconsider.

"I'll see you then."

CHAPTER SEVEN

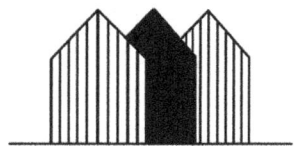

I'D BEEN TAPPING MY FINGERS AGAINST THE DESK FOR fifteen minutes. Prior to that, I had rearranged the sun porch that was once my dad's office, cleaned out every scrap of paper in every desk drawer, and stared out the window at the waves for an hour. I had written exactly zero words.

Maybe chanting? Meditation? I'll try anything to get something down, I thought.

Since it had worked so well with *The Young Edward Rochester*, I planned to write another literary spin-off. One more success in that genre would vault me permanently from the metal rack of romance novels to the smooth wooden shelf of historical fiction—and get my disappointed mother off my back. But I was getting nowhere.

I put my forehead on the desktop, resisting the urge to bang it. The pile of pens I'd sorted through rolled against my head. I seized the opportunity to waste more time by lining them up in the top drawer, first by color, then by height. Some Foreman Property Management notepads went in next. Then scissors. Tape. Paper clips.

If I ever come up with a decent idea, this desk is good to go, I told myself, centering my laptop just so. I glanced around the little white room, not more than eight feet across. It used to seem so big. As a little girl, I would spread out on the floor with a stack of my dad's typing paper. While he filled his pages with literary greatness, I filled mine with elaborate strings of fake cursive writing. I'd discovered a packet of letters in his desk and had been desperate to mimic the fancy words.

Hmm.

I pulled open the lower left drawer and ran my finger around the base. Thirty years earlier, while scavenging for Sharpies and other forbidden treasures, I'd found something even more exciting—my dad's secret hiding place.

My fingertip snagged on a silky loop. The drawer's false bottom lifted out.

"Busted," I told him from three decades and four thousand miles away as I pulled out half a pack of Pall Malls. Isobel Beckett would not have approved.

For an interesting guy, my dad's secret stash was surprisingly lame. Aside from the cigarettes and at least sixty treasured ballpoint pens, that bundle of letters was all that remained. I tossed them onto the desk and wished for one madcap moment that cigarettes don't make me puke. But they do, and even if they didn't, thirty-year-old nicotine had probably lost its edge.

Think, Marin. Think about literature. Think about well-loved characters and how to use them for profit.

I lowered my head to the tabletop and this time I did bang it. Well, it was more of a tap, but you know what I mean.

Okay, process of elimination, I told myself. Mr. Darcy is not a candidate. Darcy spin-offs have been done to death. Heathcliff? I can't idealize a brute. Maybe Mr. Knightley? I like him.

But Mr. Knightley was no Edward Rochester. It had been easy to spend months writing about him. I'd spent my whole life loving him.

And speaking of Mr. Rochester...

My mind drifted to the night before. For some reason, I couldn't stop thinking about Sam. Or the fact that he was an absolute smokeshow.

"Marin!" I snapped aloud—I'd upped my occasional asides to full-fledged conversations, since I had no one else to talk to. "Quit objectifying him!"

Sam was more than a gorgeous heartthrob. He'd been so considerate of me. So thoughtful and kind and tall and strong, with his rumpled hair and those rich brown eyes. His sincere smile. That sexy mouth—

"Mariana Beckett! There's a word for what you're doing right now."

There is. It's *lusting*.

My conscience took a moment to remind me that, whether he looked it or not, he was too young for me. Quit acting like a cougar, it said.

I shoved my conscience away. "I hate the term *cougar*," I told it, picturing his broad shoulders. I spent a few blissful minutes with Sam in my head. And while my chin rested on the heel of my hand, I had an idea.

Maybe I needed a break from the pressure to Create

Real Literature. Maybe, to help my words start flowing, I should play around with the only inspiration I'd had in months.

Maybe I should write about Sam.

There was definitely material to work with. The whole scenario of the girl in distress and the guy rushing to her aid is the set-up of half my novels—the other half featuring guys rescued by my dauntless heroines, of course. That he was the leading man in a film based on a book I had written was undeniably unique. Even the hidden-identity aspect of the way we'd met had a certain road-tested appeal.

I could fictionalize what had happened with Sam. A writing exercise. A fun way to get myself back on track.

There's also the bonus of reliving my time with that delicious man while I do, I thought with a devious smile. Because maybe, if it fit, I might work in a love scene or two. Sure, I was supposed to be moving away from romance toward more literary fiction, but I'd worked hard to master the spicy stuff. I pictured his sexy mouth again. Yes. I had a responsibility to maintain that skill.

It was worth a try. I couldn't spend another day forcing a tired idea into something unworthy of a three-hundred-page book. If writing about Sam helped me break through my block, it would be time well spent.

I turned back to my laptop and cleared the screen. For a moment, I closed my eyes and pictured Sam's face. When I looked up again, I was ready.

"Umbrellas always let Marin—"

Nope, that was weird. I'd have to rename myself.

"Umbrellas always let Madison down. So when the wind ripped hers from her hand and whirled it into the window of the building beside her, she had no idea that, this time, the umbrella would be fixing her up…"

CHAPTER EIGHT

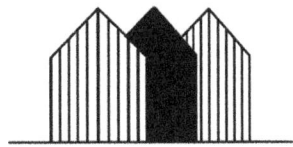

"How's the writing coming?" my friend Julie wanted to know when she called a few days later. I paused, unsure if I should mention my new project.

"I've been playing with some writer's block exercises. It's been fun."

Fun, indeed. In the week since the wrap party, I'd written forty-eight pages about meeting Sam—or Sean, as I had decided to call him. Inspiration was flowing, and it felt so good.

I caved when Julie asked for details. I told her about Sam and his starring roles in both *The Young Edward Rochester* and the new stuff I'd written.

"That's great! I love that you're turning real life into fantasy. That's how it should be."

"Shouldn't people use fantasy to inspire real life? In this case, reality stays the same. I'm just plumping it up for a story."

"Then let fantasy inspire reality and make a move on him at his show tonight."

"I'm not making a move on him. He's eighteen years old."

"He doesn't sound eighteen to me."

"He doesn't look eighteen either," I said.

"He's old enough to drop out of college. He can't be that young. Anyway, who cares if he's younger? Men do it all the time."

"Yeah, a thirty-six-year-old snake sent me that memo in July."

"So get back at him. Land yourself a gorgeous young guy—"

"Not happening."

"I read about this in one of Garrett's magazines. Older women and younger men are hot these days. Guys of his generation were raised by sensitive dads and strong working moms. They like the role reversal. He's probably waiting by the phone for your call."

I burst out laughing. "I'm sure he's writing about me in his diary right now. *If only that neurotic American would ring me!*"

"Yup, and dotting every 'i' with a little heart."

"With a hot pink Gelly Roll pen! Oh, Jules, I miss you. I'm so bored here all alone."

"So call up the teenager. Or should we call him the Prom King?"

"What would I do with a younger man dripping sex appeal? I'm used to prematurely graying hair and a little paunch."

The paunch part was a lie; David's racquetball habit kept him in shape. I allowed myself a total of five seconds to miss the silver flecks in his stubble when he didn't shave. It's weird, the stuff you miss about someone. It's weird that you keep missing it even when you know they suck.

"—to it."

What? In the five seconds I had been gone, I'd missed something Julie had said, but my ears perked up at what came next.

"Have a fling. It will do you good."

Despite the appeal of this idea, that night I suffered a small neurovascular hemorrhage over the prospect of going to Sam's show. Suddenly all those pages of reality-based romance seemed like a horrible idea. And the things I had written! That knee-bandaging scene, for example, was R-rated in the fictional version. How could I look him in the face?

Nevertheless, I summoned my courage and drove to the pub. A bell over the door jangled when I stepped inside. Part parlor, part woodshed, part hipster dive, its rough-hewn tables and overstuffed chairs created a cozy, hodgepodge warmth. I pushed away the ache-inducing image of David and me tucked into a corner of our favorite cafe and focused on the small stage strung with globe lights. My heart fluttered when I saw a guitar case with a Sam-I-Am sticker on the side.

Get a grip, I told myself as I approached the hostess, a grandmotherly woman in geek-chic glasses.

"I'm sorry, dear, we're at capacity unless your name is on the band's list."

Maybe. But what name should I give her?

"It's Mariana Rose," I said, figuring the one on the book Sam had studied was the safest bet. She shook her head.

"Mariana Beckett?"

"I'm sorry," she said kindly.

"Marin Beckett?"

She looked at me like I had a personality disorder. Then she glanced at the list again and said, "Oi! There you are. Marin Beckett."

Marin Beckett.

A smile spread across my face. It's amazing how someone knowing you even a little bit can boost morale when you've been on your own.

"You should've told me you're a friend of Sam," the hostess said in a vaguely reproachful way. "Exceptions can be made, where appropriate."

Her face looked flushed. Was it possible that this grandma was in love with him, too? I pictured him in my mind and felt my own face flush. But the woman was talking again.

"You're down as his guest, so there's no fee. Go right in."

The crowd waiting for the show to start was as varied in style as the pub: old and casually hip, young and deliberately square. I even glimpsed a couple of kids as I edged toward a seat in back.

"Marin!" I heard Sam call, and then he was cutting through the crowd toward me, looking as tall, dark, and handsome as I'd envisioned him all week. He touched my elbow. "I'm glad you came."

He's glad I came, I mooned to myself. And then I snapped, Oh shut up, Marin! and tried to act sane.

"Jordan shared the theme song you wrote for the film with my publisher. We all loved it. I'm excited to hear you play," I said casually. You know, like I hadn't spent the afternoon writing about undressing him.

"I hope you won't be disappointed, knowing this is the voice of your character."

I didn't bother to tell him what he already knew—that Mr. Rochester was Charlotte Brontë's character. I also left out the drivel David would've been compelled to preach—that such a beloved character belonged to The World.

Sam looked back at the stage.

"I'll let you finish setting up," I told him. "Good luck."

"Wait. My sisters are here. They'd love you to sit with them." He waved to a table near the stage, where a beautiful girl about Sam's age sat with the two little kids I'd spotted earlier. The smallest girl grinned. She was missing a tooth.

"Those little girls are your sisters?"

"My parents enjoyed another honeymoon period a few years ago. My other sisters and I tried to block out this knowledge, but the babies that kept coming were hard to ignore."

"Other sisters? How many do you have?"

"Five. All younger."

"Five sisters! Wow. Which one's the pirate?"

"Pardon?"

"When you gave me the skull Band-Aids, you said they were for your sister's pirate costume." The youngest girl's curls bounced as she wriggled. "My money's on the little one. She's got the look of a swashbuckler."

"So true. Lily is six and could command a pirate ship."

"Yeah, I have a sister like that, too."

The little blonde patted the empty seat beside her.

"That's Ella. She's eight and is already determined to be a writer. She may ask for career advice. And this is Amy." He grinned at the dark-haired older girl as we approached the table. "Technically an adult, but so immature."

Sam ducked when Amy tossed her car keys at his head. "Point proven," he said, laughing as he left to set up.

Lily had my scarf looped around her neck seconds after I sat down. Of the three girls, she looked the most like Sam, with the same dark curls and laughing brown eyes. Despite her energy, she was concentrating hard on a vibrant drawing. Among the hearts and flowers she'd drawn, the words *Slap and Tickle* stood out on the page.

"Slap and Tickle?" I asked.

Amy glanced at the drawing. "Lily! That's impolite!" she said, but she was laughing. "Our grandmother liked to joke that Sam's last girlfriend was clearly always after a bit of slap and tickle. Unfortunately, Lily fancies the phrase."

"I do. Ella writes lovelier than me so she did the words. But it's my drawing, not hers."

"My drawing is better anyway," Ella said. "I'm sure Sam will love it and keep it on his fridge."

Amy sighed. "Please excuse them, Marin. They constantly compete for Sam's attention, and he couldn't spoil them more. They should both be in bed but our dad is working tonight, so Sam convinced me to bring them out for his show."

Ella began describing a skit she was writing for their school's autumn festival. "I work on it every night. Sometimes it's all I can think of," she sighed.

"That's how you know you're a real writer. When it's something you have to do and nothing can stop you." Ella smiled at my answer and even I took heart, because it was true. I've always been a writer. Eventually my words would come back.

Just then, Sam stepped onstage alongside a guy with an electric bass, a girl who sat behind the drums, and the bartender from SaladBar, who had traded his cocktail shaker for a battered violin. I smiled when he gave me another exaggerated wink.

The fiddler was cute, but within minutes I gave up my pretense of paying attention to the band as a whole. I couldn't pull my eyes off Sam—the expert way his fingers slid down the neck of his guitar, how easily they skipped over the strings. Sometimes he closed his eyes as he sang; in his low voice, the words shimmered like a prayer. When the quiet songs gave way to a harder sound, they pulsed in my core until my nerves shuddered together. A slow refrain at the end of the set rocked all that heat to a simmer.

The house lights remained dim after the show as people lingered over drinks. Midway through the set, Ella had leaned on my shoulder with a drowsy smile. Sam smiled when he found her sleeping soundly against me.

"You've made a friend. Shall I take her?"

"I can wait until they're ready to go."

He bumped the table when he sat. This woke Lily, who leapt up like she had never been asleep and climbed onto his lap, slinging her small arm around his shoulders.

"Your music was lovely," she told him, planting a kiss on his cheek before shoving her picture at him. "See my drawing? It's for you."

Sam blinked at the risqué message on top.

"Wow," he said slowly. "Won't Granny be pleased by how closely you've listened to her." He glanced at the drawing and then at me. "Er, that's an old family joke. Not worth explaining, really."

I grinned wickedly. "Slap and tickle. Randy ex-girlfriend. I've been debriefed."

Even in the low light of the pub, I saw his cheeks fill with color. Amy laughed loudly, then gave Sam her keys.

"Can you put Ella into the car? Miss Lily and I will visit the loo before we leave."

"She is so cute," I said as Lily pranced away.

"Yeah, she's a right gem." He tried to grimace, then gave up and laughed before sliding his arm beneath mine to pull Ella toward him. She groaned and leaned into me. "Come on, El. Time to go."

She pressed her nose into my side.

"No. I want to stay with Mummy."

I started to smile, but Sam flinched.

"Ella," he said. And then, although he tried to speak, his words seemed lodged in his throat.

Ella opened her eyes. She looked up at Sam, then back at me. Her contented smile faded to confusion, then despair.

"You smell like my mummy," she said, and her little face crumpled. She pushed it into my shirt with a sob.

I pressed her close as her shoulders shook. She felt so small and fragile against me. Sam bent close and whispered into her ear, so gently I couldn't hear his words. In a few minutes, she was calm. But she clung to me a moment longer before climbing into her brother's arms.

I opened the door as he carried her outside, took the keys from him to unlock Amy's car. Ella slumped into the backseat. Sam slipped his jacket beneath her head and reached in to fasten her seatbelt. I watched him smooth the hair from her face. Ella looked up at me.

"Goodbye, Marin."

"Goodbye," I whispered, as something inside me cracked.

Sam closed the door and leaned against the car. When he turned toward me, he almost looked old.

"Our mother passed away in June. Cancer. It's still quite difficult."

Before I could speak, Lily's lively voice echoed through the night. I watched Sam shrug the slump from his shoulders and match his little sister, laugh for laugh, while he buckled her in.

"Do they have far to go?" I asked, watching his forced smile die as Amy's car pulled away.

"West Malling, outside Maidstone." At my blank look, he added, "About thirty miles west." He ran his hand over his face and looked toward the pub. "I should go pack up our gear. Goodnight."

"Goodnight," I said, but he didn't look back.

A cold wind swept through the street as I walked to my car, toward my silent, empty house—my silent, empty, upended life. I imagined Sam and his sisters and the space where their mother had been. Empty.

I didn't make it to Seasalter before I had to pull over. Driving in England was hard enough when I was calm; with tears in my eyes, it was impossible. I shut off the car and let myself cry, for Sam and his sisters and their lost mother, for myself and the lost parts of my own life. I cried in gulps, in shudders, until my ribs ached and the driest, stiffest parts of me fell limp.

On the wrong side of the road, in a backward car, I sobbed, until the pieces of me that had toppled three months before began to pull themselves upright.

CHAPTER NINE

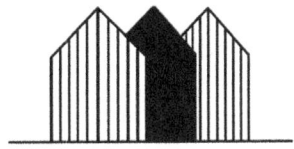

THE NEXT MORNING, I WOKE WITH A MISSION: TO BEFRIEND more of my home away from home. While tiny Seasalter and I had become good pals, I'd done nothing but dash through nearby Whitstable for necessities. I snuggled into my favorite sweater and let the crisp October breeze propel me up the shore.

I slipped bits of sea glass into my pockets as I walked. On the stretch of beach below Preston Parade, I watched a little girl and her father run at the shallow waves, dashing back before they lapped their feet. It was like watching a remade film of my dad and me; brighter color, better sound —but the same laughter ringing through the air.

When the little girl shrieked, it struck me. I was in Seasalter. Despite limited memories of my childhood in England, the idea of Seasalter was wound into my identity, inextricable as my left-handedness or the blue of my eyes. Almost mythical to me, it was the setting for bedtime stories my parents had told me and stories about my family complete strangers could tell.

I had avoided visiting it for the same reasons I avoid articles about my family and scholarly dissections of my dad's book—I didn't want to tarnish what has always seemed so ideal. But as I stared out at the sea, the memories that rolled over me were nothing to fear: tangles of rope washing up on the shore, fog blanching the bright beach huts to pastel. Footprints—four large, two small—entwining together through the sand.

Whitstable and I got along swimmingly. After a cream-smeared scone and steaming tea, I wandered with no plan at all. British pounds flowed from my purse, became shell-handled letter openers for my dad and Charles, locally crafted earrings for my mom and Nandi. Oyster shucking at the fish market was my afternoon show, but the gritty scrape proved too harsh for a girl who had once whispered secrets to a ruffled shell named Pearl.

At last, I walked down the high street and arrived at the only shop I'd deliberately sought, a narrow storefront with books lining the walls. An orange cat snoozed on the sunny front sill, but when the door stuck as I tried to open it, the cat scowled up at me.

"Put your hip into it," a grainy voice called from within. Maybe I shoved too heartily; it popped open with a bang.

"Now that was impressive," said the tall, sturdy woman behind the counter. "I would never have supposed such skinny hips could muster that much force."

My hips are fairly regular, I think, but who among us wouldn't like to hear those words? I took a second to let my delight settle before asking if she carried journals.

She pointed out a black leather-bound book, but the sunshiny cover beside it caught my eye. Ella deserved some cheer.

"I'll take the yellow one. And the orange sketchbook, too," I added, remembering Lily's slap-and-tickle drawing with a smile.

"At first, I thought Canadian," the shopkeeper said as she collected the books. "But no. You're American."

"What tipped you off?"

"You're masking a Confederate A and have a slight lower-back vowel merger. You were undoubtedly raised in the south, but I wager you've lived in the Midwest for at least five years."

I blinked. "I grew up in South Carolina, but I've lived in Chicago since I was twelve. That's amazing."

"No, just practiced. I was a dialect coach in New York for years. This was before I married a photographer and let him drag me over the eastern hemisphere, tip to tush."

Tip to tush, I thought with glee, wishing I could drop everything to write it down. If ever a phrase was worth poaching!

"How long have you been in Whitstable?" I asked, eager to keep her talking.

"Born and raised, then foolishly left to seek my fortunes elsewhere. Happily returned eight years ago. Once Isaac got a bee in his beret about settling down, I insisted we come back here." As I came close to dying with delight over *a bee in his beret*, she studied me over the rim of her glasses. "How do you find England? Traveling alone always offers a richer experience."

I paused. "How did you know—"

"That you're traveling alone? It pushes one to bloom outward. You've got the openness of someone on a solo adventure," she explained. "Most dialect coaches could make a killing telling fortunes. So much can be read in a person's voice. And no, I won't listen to your lover speak to discover his intentions."

"Believe me, there's nothing in his voice I don't already know," I said with enough vinegar in my own voice to add an interesting twist to her profile on me. I lightened up. "Actually, I'm half-English. My dad is originally from this area."

"Really? What brings you back? I suppose some universities are on fall break. Are you a student?"

I laughed outright. "Thank you for that! I'm more than a decade past my college days. That's the nicest thing anyone's said to me in months."

"I certainly hope not." She was serious, and since—having developed a PTSD-related habit of measuring myself against twenty-two-year-old girls—I kind of was, too, I moved on.

"I'm here to sell the family homestead and write something worthwhile." I explained briefly about my upcoming book and my impending doom if I didn't finish it soon.

"I didn't expect to meet an author today."

"It's not that impressive." I confessed to the romances, laid claim to *The Young Edward Rochester*. She surprised me by pulling a copy off the shelf. She had even read it.

"I read everything about Edward Rochester. So many people go straight to Darcy for their ideal romantic hero, but I prefer Rochester. I like my leading men to be capable of wickedness but choose to abstain. Although I have learned that outside of books, a man's wicked streak isn't so easily overcome. Perhaps most men don't have that unyielding Rochester resolve."

At last! Here was a woman I could gossip with over cocktails. I grinned so hard, she stretched out her hand.

"Let's meet. I'm Patricia Whittaker."

I glanced at the cover of my book as I shook her hand. "I should tell you, Mariana Rose is my pen name. In the real world, I'm Marin Beckett. Thanks for the welcome."

Patricia's long skirt swished as I followed her to the counter. Her white hair was swept off her face with a tortoiseshell barrette, but her motions were resolute. I'd have cast her in the role of a hardy pioneer if I was writing her into a book. Everything about her was elegant yet tough.

"Come to lunch tomorrow, if you're free," she said, scrawling down her address.

I glanced at the paper she slid toward me. "Oh, you live in Seasalter, too. I'm on the beach, just around the bend on Faversham Road."

"We're neighbors, then. Which house is yours?"

I suddenly wished I'd kept my mouth shut about my real last name.

"Ah...the skinny blue one," I said, keeping my eyes on her pen as she wrote out a sales slip. To a local book person, the skinny blue one might as well have had *John Robert Beckett Wuz Here* spray-painted across the door.

Patricia's pen paused. I looked up and caught her glancing away from an endcap display of local authors. You don't need me to tell you who was right out front.

The twenty-fifth anniversary edition of *Salt in the Sea* features a close-up photograph of my dad in his thirties. Faded into the background, a woman with a long copper braid has her back to us, staring out at the sea. And in the corner, a little girl with golden curls crouches in the sand.

The rustle of Patricia wrapping my books in tissue recalled my attention. "I ran out of paper bags yesterday. I hope you don't mind plastic." She had the same frank expression on her face. When she asked me to bring dessert to lunch, I knew I could relax. But on my way out the door, she did stop me.

"I knew I heard some long-lost England in your voice. Welcome back."

CHAPTER TEN

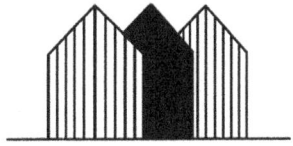

When I got home that evening, an email from my editor was waiting on me. Since working on Saturday isn't Gretchen's style, I crossed my fingers. In between writing about Sam, I'd managed to send her some notes on a pre-*Emma* Mr. Knightley book. Hopefully this meant she couldn't wait until Monday to greenlight my idea.

The news was not good. Velicity was already publishing an *Emma*-themed book in the spring. Apparently Elysienne Fields (real name: Marge Powell) had tried her hand at the literary spin-off for Velicity's new imprint, switching from (what else?) mythology-based romance.

It got worse. Velicity Big Boss Yvonne Lee had announced that each editor must turn in a comprehensive outline of all novels in progress. Next year's line-up was being finalized. If I wanted my book published, Gretchen needed a chapter-by-chapter summary by the next morning. Otherwise it would be bumped from the schedule, along with any chance I had of securing a better contract.

"She wants this tomorrow? And my only idea just got destroyed?"

I looked out the window toward the beach. If I started loading my pockets with rocks in the garden, would I have enough on me to pull a Virginia Woolf by the time I reached the water? Because if I was going to take myself out, I might as well be ironic about it.

I opted instead to pick up the phone. Gretchen answered without saying hello.

"Before you start, let me apologize. I didn't know about the publishing schedule. I had brunch with Kiran Patel this morning. She'd just turned in her report. Took me two weeks, she said. You look so relaxed, she said. When did you turn in yours? I nearly choked to death on my English muffin."

"How could you not know?"

"Deb! Deb misplaced Yvonne's memo. I'd fire her if I didn't need her help with the report. Fifteen authors. Nearly everyone behind schedule. Everyone wants to kill me."

"There's no way I can do the Mr. Knightley book?"

"No! Marge's book is finished. We can't release two competing books. We would look so one-note."

"Yeah." I broke out my head-to-the-desktop routine, poised to bang when necessary.

"What else do you have?"

I didn't say anything. I had nothing to say.

"You always have ideas, Marin. You're one of the writers I never worry about."

"I'm out of ideas. It took me forever to come up with that Knightley thing."

"Well, come up with something else. You are Mariana

Rose, for crap's sake." The clacking of her keyboard stopped. "We could buy some time. If we so much as whisper to Yvonne that your dad is—"

"Absolutely not."

"Marin, you've published twenty-six novels in nine years. No one could claim that your success is based on your father's connections."

I gripped the phone. "I have never thrown my dad's name around the publishing world. I'm not starting now."

"If Yvonne alone knew, who could it hurt?"

As Gretchen rehashed the pros of revealing my literary pedigree, I rehashed a standard lecture: Mariana Beckett, if you have so much as one sip of alcohol in Gretchen Howard's presence again, I will staple your lips shut permanently. One tipsy lapse in judgment and you'll never hear the end of it.

"No," I said again when she paused for breath. And quit bringing it up, I longed to add. I didn't want exceptions. And I certainly didn't want people comparing John Robert Beckett's *Salt in the Sea* to my top seller, *Lust in the Livery*.

Gretchen's irritated sigh drove her resignation across the Atlantic and into my car. "Look, *The Young Edward Rochester* getting optioned put us in a good position. We negotiated a game-changing deal that nets you company support as a mainstream historical fiction author and a lot more cash. But if we don't get something in front of Yvonne now, forget it. Your Rochester book will be a dim memory next year."

So that was it. I was going to lose my leverage and maybe my book deal. If I'd been working last week instead of churning out trash about a gorgeous young Englishman, I might have—

A gorgeous young Englishman.

I had forty-eight pages about a gorgeous young Englishman. It wasn't a literary history of a classic romantic hero, but it was something. It had become more than the initial meeting with Sam; I'd worked in my own David melodrama to give the character of Madison more depth. Plus, there was plenty of heat between Madison and Sean.

But even if I did write one more romance novel, what I had written was hardly a Velicity-level storyline. Velicity romances are the B-movies of publishing, and proud of it. Before *The Young Edward Rochester*, I had thought this was great—the theatrical books are so much more fun to write—but for the Sam-based novel to be accepted, it would have to be shockingly tragic. I'd need more drama than my infidelity crisis could provide, and no plot I'd cooked up since that crisis began was worth an entire book. The only storylines I had been able to carry were rooted in real-life events, my own and those between Sam and me.

"You'll be throwing away an irreplaceable opportunity to take your career to the next level," Gretchen yammered. And I knew she was right.

My conscience was doing its best to be heard, but I made the decision to tune it out. Because the night before, the perfect scenario had been offered up to me. What was more tragic than a little girl clinging to her big brother after their mother's death?

It was a perfect plot, transforming Sean from an object of lust into a leading man worthy of true love. A gorgeous guy with remarkable talent and a world of opportunity open to him. Wounded by losing his mother, crushed by his sister's struggle. Could he help her overcome her destabilizing grief? Could he realize his dreams when she needed him nearby?

It had tension, it had strong characters. It would be easy enough to get inside the head of the protagonist, considering she was me. Plus, I had never tackled a May-December romance.

Okay, more like May-August. Still, it could work.

It was unquestionably wrong to exploit Sam's personal life, but I would be discreet. Sam would never hear of the book, and even if he did, he wouldn't connect it to me. This would be a contemporary story. Mariana Rose wouldn't be the author; this book would be by Beckett Bell.

It was my best shot. It was my only shot.

So I gritted my teeth and took it.

CHAPTER ELEVEN

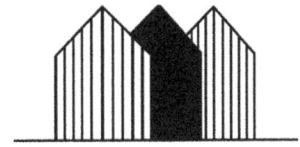

Working through the night to refine my lusty, Sam-inspired novel for Gretchen's report sapped my tolerance for writing romance, so retreating to the archaeological dig in the attic was almost a comfort. For three days, I buried myself in my parents' keepsakes—my mom's meticulous Peace Corps scrapbooks, clippings from my dad's photojournalist days. On a cozy afternoon, I curled up with that stack of love letters from the year they met and educated myself on their rising passion while the rain beat overhead.

But that Tennyson book was haunting me. Why was that book—with its bad-omen-bearing poem—in a box of my childhood keepsakes?

"Give us both some credit, Petite," my dad said when I finally broke down and asked. "Do you think I'd expose my child to that dismal poem? Then consider yourself as a little girl and tell me how long you'd have sat through old Mariana moaning?"

"Then why was that book in my box?"

"You were obsessed with 'The Sea Fairies.' We read it every night. Remember? *'The rainbow lives in the curve of the sand, hither, come hither and see.'*"

"That was Tennyson?"

"You were always a romantic, even back then. You loved the part where the fairies try to kiss the sailors. Don't you remember chasing that little neighbor boy and singing, 'Come hither, and be my lord, for a merry bride—'"

He halted, but the word seemed to hang in the air: *bride*. I could hear the apology building in his breath, but I cut him off to spare us both.

Unfortunately, I seized upon the first idea that popped into my head—the love letters lying in my lap. What flew out of my mouth was far worse than wedding talk.

"I found your letters—" I blurted out before realizing my mistake. It was too late. Although I attempted to cover which letters I'd meant, he badgered me until I finally confessed. "The letters you and Mom wrote each other the year you met."

I cursed myself when his breath snagged in his throat. "Don't give them to Glenister."

"Of course not," I said, wishing desperately that we were rehashing every last detail of my canceled wedding.

"You could send them to me."

"Dad—"

"Send them to me."

Tears already stung my eyes, but this made them fall in earnest. How could I have been so careless? Just reading *Salt in the Sea* could send my dad into a silent depression for weeks. The long-lost account of how he fell in love with my mother—not to mention her account of how she fell for him—could set him back years.

"Daddy, I don't think—"

"It's *Daddy* again, is it?" he said, but his tone was kind—calm, even. "Mariana, I can handle it. Send those letters to me."

"I can't send them," I said with a sniff. Snippets of my parents' infatuated prose crisscrossed my mind. "It will be like she's left all over again. Trust me. I can't send them."

His silence on the line trapped my breath in my chest.

"Maybe you're right," he finally said. "I'm not hankering after another year where I can't get out of bed. My mattress is stiff. It would ruin my back." His wry laugh surprised me so much that I choked on a hiccup. "Hang onto them. When I'm too old to remember who I am, you can read them to me. For laughs."

He seemed determined to continue his comedy routine until I had recovered. His sweetness, combined with my relief that I would not be sending him a stack of lovesick musings from his ex-wife, made me want to send him something, anyhow.

"Something small, it would seem," I said, staring at the dwindling figure in my bank account. My book contract—and thus my advance—were pending based on Gretchen's reaction to my Sean and Madison draft.

For the eightieth time that day, I checked my email. Finally, Gretchen's message was waiting.

Marin! I couldn't put it down! I gave it to Deb and she was hooked, too. We love Sean! It's Simon Quinn from the movie, yes? We love his sister. Of course we love you—Madison!

How much is true and how much is fiction? All I can say is please let Sean/Simon be real! Deb and I are already in love with him. It's on the schedule, the outline was approved. Yvonne even said she loves the younger man angle. I believe 'that hits the hotspot' were her exact words.

Ick. The less I knew about Yvonne's hotspot, the better.

Our one suggestion is that you emphasize the trauma of Sean's little sister. Yvonne feels that making Claire and her psychosis the main conflict in the story will present unique challenges to Madison and Sean. There are so many fantastic plot possibilities—manic aggression, violent delusions—Yvonne thinks this could be our strongest novel of the year. Velicity agreed to the terms we worked out for your new deal. Your contract is in the mail. We'll transfer the money as soon as it's signed. Congrats! And Marin, thank you. We both needed a win like this.

It's going to be okay, I thought, slumping back in relief. But as thrilled as I was that they liked the idea, I hated their focus on the little sister. Since when had her anxiety become a psychosis? I'd never intended Claire to be a knife-wielding maniac.

I contemplated my chances of changing Yvonne's mind, but I knew the answer. In her two years at Velicity, Yvonne had made one thing clear: she's a woman who savors authority.

Well, fine, I reasoned. Turning Claire into a child psychotic will distance my novel from Sam's family. I'll spin the crazy into Claire. She'll be so unhinged, no one could mistake her for anything but fiction.

So my book contract was safe. My thoughts turned to Sam and Ella and their mom, but I swept the guilt into a corner of my conscience. I would find a way to make it different, and where I couldn't make it different, I'd do my best to make it respectful. I owed them that.

CHAPTER TWELVE

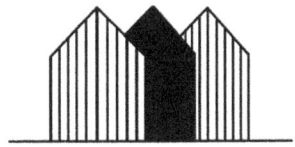

I SPENT THE TWO DAYS THAT FOLLOWED GRETCHEN'S EMAIL stoking the flames between Sean and Madison and fueling Claire's instability. Sixty-five pages in, I had dramatized Madison's attendance at Sean's concert. The only difference between reality and fiction? After Claire cried about the loss of her mother, she stabbed Madison in the thigh with Sean's vintage tuning fork.

With my book finally under control, I was free to work on the other aspect of my Seasalter trip—sorting through the attic. My personal keep pile was growing, but the pile for the Archive was pitifully small. One morning, I pulled my hair into a knot and threw on some worn overalls I'd found in storage. They were perfect for a day of dusty work.

I'd only gone through two boxes when a crate of knickknacks pulled me off-task. Decorating was unavoidable; I dropped everything and began sprucing up my little house. My parents seemed to have had cool, if kitschy, taste back in the day, so there was plenty to work with. A mirror trimmed with oyster shells was perfect above the fireplace. A pelican-shaped letter holder added character to the tiny foyer. After a good polishing, a rack of sparkling glass doorknobs doubled as coat hooks. While I beat the dust out of a colorful hooked rug, I let the shower steam some mid-century curtains stamped with geometric yellow swirls. By late afternoon, the Seasalter house looked like it had grown up with a family.

I was admiring my work when someone rapped on the door. Despite knowing roughly five people in England, Simon Quinn was the last person I expected to see. I ignored my stammering pulse—he really was ridiculously handsome—and ushered him inside.

"This is a nice surprise," I said, leading him into the redecorated living room with a bit of pride. A brand-new look and a visitor to see it.

"I hope you don't mind I stopped by. I was in Canterbury collecting some gear I forgot at Three Wastrels. I would have phoned, but I never got your number." He shoved his hands in his pockets. "By the way, I'm not stalking you. I took your address from the package you so kindly sent to my sisters."

"If anyone is a stalker, it's me. I had to do a little sleuthing to find your dad's address."

When we reached the white sofa, I looked down at myself. I was swimming in the overalls and they were dirtier than dirt itself, as my Grandma Rose used to say. My hair was still piled on top of my head. I reached up. It felt like something was nesting in there.

"I'm not sure why I tend to look my worst when I see you."

"If this is your worst, you needn't worry. What have you been doing?"

I filled him in on my decorating spree. Then I asked for five minutes to change so I wouldn't mess up the couch.

"You feel free to sit, you're nice and clean, as usual." Nice and clean indeed, I thought as I dashed upstairs. He does good things for jeans and a white button-down.

I splashed off in the bathroom and dashed into some jeans of my own, followed by my ancient college sweatshirt.

Nothing flashy for you, I told myself. And no makeup. Okay, fine, *one* swipe of mascara, but that's it. It's your penance for writing fantasy about this poor guy.

Downstairs, Sam was checking out my new display of family photos. He slipped me an envelope colored all over with flowers and hearts. "Ella and Lily commissioned me to deliver this."

I ran my fingers over a smiling sun before pulling out the note inside.

Dear Marin,

We got your presents today in the post. They are very lovely and we love them very much. Lily cannot write as well as I, but she has asked me to send her love and best wishes. Also, would you come to my play at our school's autumn festival? It is at our school. We both hope you will come very much. And thank you for the books.

Love,
Ella Matilda Quinn and Lily Adele Quinn

"You are their new favorite person. Father Christmas can't compete with Marin Beckett."

"Father Christmas," I murmured. Another piece of my uprooted English childhood flashed into focus.

"Brilliant view," he said, studying the sunset rippling on the sea. "Would you like to take a walk?"

The shingle crunched beneath our feet as we headed down the beach. Inspired by the evening light glowing on Sam's face, I envisioned us as characters in a romance-novel beach scene. Sam would be barefoot, his jeans casually cuffed, a sexy way to avoid the surf. My old college sweatshirt was toast, replaced with a flowing white dress. The loose waves of my hair would have been pinned into a twist that, soon enough, I'd symbolically pull free.

Because envisioning real life as a fictional scene is common for me, at first I overlooked the irony of what I had done. Then I remembered: *I was already writing this book.*

And now it's a real book, not some lonely writer's fantasy, I thought, almost writhing with guilt. I looked over at him and wanted to cry for the way I was using him—him, and Ella, and their mom's tragic death. How could I be so awful?

"Do I pass inspection?" he asked, startling me out of my inner monologue.

A tingle spread through my cheeks when I realized how long I'd been staring at him.

"I'm sorry, I got carried away with—" Ugh. Why must every thought in my head escape through my mouth?

"Carried away with what?"

I shook my head. "Nothing."

"Oh, come on. That's not fair."

"No way, it's too embarrassing."

He shrugged. "All right. I was planning to tell you something embarrassing, but I suppose now I won't."

"You were not."

"I swear, it's true."

"What is it?"

"You first," he said with a grin.

Obviously I needed to know what he had to say. I could tell him part of the truth, at least.

"You remember that I also write romance novels?"

"Yes."

"So I'm always scouting for ideas. Sometimes I rework picturesque situations in my head to see how they'd fit in a book."

"And this walk makes the cut?" He shot me the crinkly-eyed smile. "Will it seem like I want you to write about this if I ask you to sit and watch the sunset?"

"Maybe. But it's a good idea," I said, although my own smile faded. I'd already written so much.

"So?" he asked when we were settled on the beach. "Is this romantic enough for a Mariana Rose novel?"

"It's not bad," I admitted.

"What would make it more like your books?"

Well, you could roll onto me and work us into a rhythm to match the pounding waves, I thought about saying. But instead I told him about my white dress and about how sometimes you could pinpoint a character's personality or even a book's entire premise based on the description of something as simple as their hair.

"This would explain why Anne's hair in *The Young Edward Rochester* always fell round her shoulders in 'soft waves.'"

"Or flew out behind her in the wind," I said with a

laugh. "You paid attention to that book, didn't you? That in itself is a little embarrassing. My novels aren't written for close reading."

"I think it holds up," he said, and I was stunned—not by the compliment, but by the words themselves.

How often had I heard David use that phrase in his running monologue on literary merit? *Does a work hold up to critical examination?* It was a question worth asking about his own writing, or that of his colleagues. But never about any book of mine.

"Thank you," I told him. "That's nice to hear."

"You're welcome." He scooped up a handful of pebbles and let them fall through his fingers. "You know, when I got the part in the film, I panicked. I'd hardly done any acting. A few small parts in some friends' film projects at university, but nothing real. I had no idea what I was doing. I was petrified, so I clung to your book during the shoot. It was more than a guide to the character of Edward. It was a security blanket, a talisman—it was honestly almost a friend. And because you wrote the book, well…"

He rested his arms across his knees and looked at me for what we in the romance biz call *a long moment.*

"I suppose, in a way, you've been on my mind for a while, Mariana Rose. Marin Beckett. And if you can believe it, that is not the most embarrassing thing I have to say tonight." His awkward smile vanished. "I came by to apologize for last week. Ella's incident at the pub shook me a bit, but the way I left you outside was quite rude."

"You weren't rude at all. I felt so bad for Ella. Is she doing okay?"

"She's become so anxious since our mum passed that

her mood varies each day. What begins as a moment of sadness sometimes escalates to hysteria. She's often nervous, always quiet. And…" He turned to look at me. "She doesn't connect well to new people."

At first, I'll admit, I thought again of my book. I had used what I'd assumed was an isolated incident of Ella's natural sorrow as inspiration for Sean's sister's emotional trauma. That similarity was problem enough, but I'd followed Yvonne's orders like an obedient worker bee. My character, Claire, was now dangerously unstable—a child psychopath. Which, I would like to make explicitly clear, Miss Ella Quinn is absolutely not.

Then I stopped thinking of that stupid book and listened to what Sam was saying. Ella didn't connect well to new people, but she had connected to me. And I would be leaving soon.

Sam looked out over the darkening waves. "I can't think how to say this."

His nervous glance my way triggered a glaze of ice inside my stomach. Contacting his sisters had been a bad idea.

"I'm sorry, I shouldn't have sent the books. I would never want to hurt the girls."

"Hurt the girls?"

"Yes, since I'm only here for a little while. I didn't mean to force a connection with them."

"I like the connection, that's what I'm trying to say. I'm trying, somewhat inarticulately, to ask you out."

My eyebrows nearly hit my scalp.

"And here was me thinking I was so obvious. You're surprised?"

"Well, yeah. I'm not accustomed to film stars asking me out."

"I'm not a film star. I'm a uni dropout with a garage band."

"A really great garage band."

"Thank you," he said, but seemed to sense my hesitation. "Is the dropout bit a problem, then?"

"No. Not at all." He was staring uneasily at my UW-Milwaukee sweatshirt, which forced me to explain. "Look, I think you're great. It's just, you may not realize this since we've always met in flattering, low-light situations, but I'm thirty-three years old. I have to be years and years too old for you."

"Really, years *and* years?" He was actually laughing. "Age doesn't mean anything."

"No? How old are you, then?"

"I'm not telling if you plan to hold it against me. How old do you think I am? Go on, assess me," he said when I didn't answer. "How old am I?"

All right, fine. I tilted my head to study him. So his dad wanted him to go back to college. You could finish college at any age. I considered the gentle way he had cared for me, how he'd gone out of his way to put me at ease. He might look younger than me, but he didn't look young. The broad shoulders and solid arms, those sculpted Statue-of-David hands…I was going romance novelist on him again. He brought it out in me.

"Well?"

"I can't tell," I confessed. "Twenty-eight?" That would only be five years, I told myself, ignoring the shrew in my head reminding me that my thirty-fourth birthday was coming on quick.

He smiled. "I didn't say I was going to tell you."

"Just because I can't tell doesn't mean I'm not too old. At the risk of sounding like an emo adolescent, you can't imagine how old I feel sometimes."

"Oh? Me too," he said cheerfully.

Of course that was true. If my saga with David had worn me down, losing his mom would certainly have aged him.

He put his hand over mine and stilled my nervous fingers.

"If it's me personally you aren't interested in, that's different."

"It's not you, come on. Who wouldn't find you attractive? I've been fighting myself over it since we met."

"So don't fight anymore." He wore a lighthearted expression that I wanted to match, but he didn't know the most important thing: I was romantically broken. And not sure I even wanted to be whole.

"Marin," he said, as if he'd read my mind, "I haven't forgotten about the update to your author bio. Consider this a no-pressure date."

No pressure, I echoed silently. Space to ease myself back in.

More inspiration for my skeevy new book.

Even now, I hate myself for it, but that's mostly why I said yes.

We made plans to spend a day together as we crunched back up the dark beach to my house. "Saturday morning," he said, when I walked him to the door. "I'll pick you up."

I nodded, focusing on the yellow welcome mat I'd put out that afternoon. The porch light was too bright. I could feel his eyes on my face.

"Do you want to hear one more embarrassing confession?" He laughed when my head snapped up. "I lied when I said I was in Canterbury. I drove over from London just to see you."

CHAPTER THIRTEEN

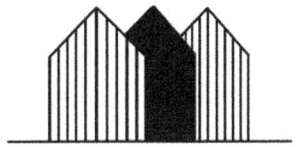

"You look lovely. I'm glad to see you're back in the boots," Sam said when he arrived the morning of our date. "But how do you feel about climbing ladders in that skirt?"

"Ladders?"

"On second thought, leave the ladders to me. You look too nice to change."

I squinted as we stepped into the sunlight. "Where are we going? I can't wait to see how ladders figure into this."

"You'll see. It's a bit of a drive, but I hope you'll think it's worthwhile."

"You're a mysterious man, Sam Quinn." I followed him out the gate, but slammed to a stop before a classic ivory convertible, top down, with two bucket seats and an aura of European cool.

"Are you serious? This is your car?" Of course this is his car, I said to myself. If I were writing this, it's exactly what I'd give him. And since I am writing this, I added guiltily, I'm sure the car will get worked in, too.

"Technically, it was my grandfather's, but he left it to me when he passed away last year. He got it brand new in 1961. It was his prized possession, and now it's mine," he said, opening the door for me.

"It's fantastic." I ran my hand along the chrome in the dashboard.

"Here, I've got something else for you." He leaned across me to the tiny glove compartment and pulled out a delicate white scarf. "My grandmother kept this in the car for long drives. I thought you might want to wear it."

I ran my fingers over the filmy silk without speaking.

"For your hair. The wind?" He waved his fingers around his head uncertainly as I stared at him. I suddenly felt like it wasn't me writing the story anymore. Like this whole thing was an elaborate set-up designed to help me get over a particularly romantic poetry professor.

"Did my sister hire you to do this?" I finally said.

I was mostly joking, but the idea wasn't unreasonable. Nandi was conniving, and as devoted to running my life as she was to cheering me up. She'd also spent her formative years watching old movies with me, so she knew how to set the scene.

Sam gave me a blank look, and then his face fell. "Yes, she did. How will I tell those girls she hired to play my sisters that we're out of work?" He knocked my shoulder playfully. "It's just an old scarf."

Right. And Grace Kelly was just some girl.

I wrapped the scarf around my hair, crossed it at my neck and tied it once in back. I had practiced this scarf-tying trick in the bathroom mirror a million times as a teenager, but this was the first time I'd used it.

Not looking at him over the top of my sunglasses would have been a pop-culture blunder.

"What do you think?" I asked, and he revved the engine.

Sam kept the conversation steady and light as he drove, asking me questions and making me laugh. He was full of stories about his rookie mistakes on the film and being the only brother to five sisters.

"Your parents must love kids. How old was your mother when she had Lily?"

"Forty-two."

"Wow, forty-two." I dug around for my math skills, then casually said, "How old was she when she had you?"

He snorted. "Not a chance, Marin Beckett. Not until you admit that age is irrelevant."

"It's not irrelevant. I like you a lot, but prison doesn't appeal to me, so if you're underage…" I tried to look serious, but I was messing with him. I may have joked to Julie about him being a teenager but, believe me, nothing about Sam is adolescent.

"Of course I'm not underage, woman." He looked over at me and smiled. "I like you a lot, too."

My face began to burn. So much for messing with him.

Eventually, we pulled down a rutted lane, flanked on both sides by a tangled mass of trees. Sam slowed the car to a crawl as we wound our way uphill.

"You're not bringing me out here to kill me, I hope," I said when he took a fork that was more gravel path than actual road. Overgrown brush scraped the sides of the car like fingernails on a chalkboard; the hair on my arms stood up. But after a mile, the brush dwindled, and the twisted path became straight. The trees stretched their boughs overhead, a canopy of leaves shining orange and red. We topped the hill and there was the sea, gleaming and rippling before us. The sun glinted off the water so brightly that spots hung in the air when I looked away.

He pulled up to a rustic two-story stone house, tall and solid, with towering chimneys, high windows, and two pillared porches topped with steeply pitched roofs. Late roses were shedding their petals in the yard, backlit against the sparkling sea.

"Where are we?" I asked in awe.

"My grandparents' house," he said, and I looked at him quickly. Grandparents are not my idea of a no-pressure date.

"Relax, they aren't here. Like I said, my grandfather passed away last year. Shortly before my mum got sick, she moved my grandmother to a care home close to my parents' house. But this is one of the most beautiful places in England. I thought you'd like to see it."

"It's amazing," I said, my eyes following the trim yard rolling into a pasture that rolled up to a cliff overlooking the sea.

"I spent most of my summers here. It is my favorite place to be. On a clear day, you can see the cliffs of Dover," he said, pointing out a white strip across the bay. "And on a very clear day, like today, you can see all the way to France."

"France?" I said, studying the shadow of land along the horizon.

"It's so warm for October." He tossed his jacket in the car and stretched his arms overhead; I glimpsed the waistband of blue boxer shorts and then a taut stomach.

Before I could study it or scold myself for trying, his arms dropped to his sides. The abs disappeared.

"So what's with the ladders?" I said, fishing my mind from the gutter. "Are we repairing your childhood treehouse?"

"Not on this trip." He put both hands on my shoulders and turned me toward a grove of trees. "We are picking apples."

"Really? Oh, fun!" I clapped when he pulled out a paper bag full of food. "And a picnic, too?"

"I bring us a sack lunch and make you pick your own snack and you're impressed with both."

"Doing anything like this in Chicago would be a lot of effort. I'd have to rent a car, fight traffic to the country, haul buckets of apples up to my third-floor condo…"

"But you like living there." This sounded like a statement, but I think it was a question.

"Yes. I like a lot of things about it."

"But?"

"No buts. I like it." I took in the view—blue water, clear skies. France. I do like Chicago. But it was hard to remember with that scenery before me.

"My uncle lives up the road a bit. After lunch, we can take his boat out on the bay, if you like."

I studied the waves, tossing white in the distance. "I'm not a big fan of boats. I get seasick," I added, when he held my eyes.

"We'll keep to solid ground, then," he said, spreading out a blanket at a high point in the yard. He sat on the edge and kicked off his shoes. "Don't you want to take off your boots?" he asked when I was perched beside him. "Enjoy the unseasonable warmth?"

"Oh. No, that's okay," I said, awkwardly tugging the hem of my skirt.

"It's a picnic. You should enjoy the luxury of grass beneath your feet." I looked away. A moment later I heard him say, too quickly, "It's not important."

I glanced up. He had a strange look on his face.

"Wait, what are you thinking? You think I have weird feet!"

"Of course not," he said, but he avoided my eyes.

"Hey, there's nothing wrong with my feet." Whatever he was imagining was worse than the truth, so I gave in. "I don't want you to see my socks. They're old and silly."

His uncomfortable expression melted into mischief. "I'm sorry, Marin. I must see the socks."

"No way."

"How bad can they be?"

"Bad."

He leaned in until his shoulder touched mine, put one finger on the toe of my boot and drew it all the way up. His fingertips brushed my leg as they circled the rim.

"You trust me with your secret socks," he murmured. "You know you do."

With his face so close to mine, I was finding it hard to think. I felt like I had recently written this scene—his warm, clean scent when he leaned against me, his golden-brown eyes gazing into mine. A soft sigh slipped through my lips. How had he turned taking off my boots into a seduction scene?

His fingers moved to the zipper of my boot. He slid it down slowly, leisurely, his eyes never leaving mine.

Despite—or maybe because of—the fluttering in my pulse, I had to laugh. "You really are too much for me."

"Likewise. Hiding your socks." His laughter halted when he spotted the bit of bright blue peeking out of my boot. "Oh my word. Are you joking?"

He yanked off the boot. I buried my face in my hands.

"Papa Smurf. Brainy, Vanity. Smurfette, got to love her." He looked up in obvious delight. "Where did you get these?"

"My dad gave them to me a long time ago." I pressed my palms to my cheeks, knowing they were as red as the stripes on my threadbare socks.

"These are brilliant. Do you always wear cartoon-themed socks? Or is this a special occasion?"

"They're my lucky socks," I said without thinking. "Not that I was hoping to get—"

Oh. My gosh. Stop. Talking. Now.

Yeesh. Nothing but the truth would smooth over this new embarrassment. "I wear them when I need a boost of courage."

I felt his eyes on my face but I refused to look up, instead sliding my feet off his lap to slip off the socks. I chafed them against the warm grass.

"You're right, it feels good." I said, leaning back on the blanket. The wind rustled through the trees above us. It was more relaxing than I'd have thought, lying there with him. "This place is beautiful. It would make a great setting for a romance novel."

"If you were writing this as a scene, how would it go?"

In the book I'm writing now? I'm sure it will go exactly like this, I thought with a pang. But aloud, I only said, "What kind of romance?"

"Er, your choice. I'm not familiar with the varieties."

"I split my time between contemporary and historical. Once I tried the creepy, gothic type, but it didn't work out."

"Why not?"

"I scared myself to death and couldn't finish." His eyes did that crinkling thing again. "In a modern romance, I would probably have them look up at the sky and pick out shapes in the clouds."

This was one hundred percent not true. But I couldn't tell him what I'd really have the characters do in our situation. What our Sean and Madison characters would be doing as soon as I had time to write the scene.

I gave him credit for wrinkling his nose.

"So you'd leave that book on the shelf. Fair enough," I said with a laugh. "In a historical romance, I'd probably have the girl stumble onto the guy while he was out here writing poetry."

I said that before thinking and it made *me* stumble. Of course I wrote about poets; I'd been engaged to one. To hide my sudden awkwardness, I threw out a familiar line that was good for a laugh.

"I like to write about writers. I'm a cliché."

He tendered the laugh; the laugh was accepted. Then he said, "What if it was the scary book?"

"I would keep looking over my shoulder and nothing would get written. The guy and girl would be stranded on this blanket forever."

"That doesn't sound so terrible." He was lying on his back, arm crooked behind his head, eyes closed against the sun. Since he wasn't looking, I studied his face. He had a smattering of freckles on his nose, barely visible against his golden skin. His full mouth met at the corners with the tiniest tilt, a hint of his warm smile. I shocked myself with an impulse to press my finger into the divot on his upper lip.

For a moment, I heard Nandi commanding me to have an adventure, heard Julie urging me to let go and have fun.

I closed my eyes and considered it, but that was all.

AFTER PICKING A HEARTY LOAD OF APPLES AND PICNICKING on the lawn, we cruised back to my house through the late-afternoon glow.

"You're still up for coming to Ella's play on Friday?" he asked as he walked me to my door.

"Sure."

"Then you have a decision to make. You can come for the play only and I'll pick you up at noon. Or you can come for the whole festival and Lily and I will beat you and Ella in the three-legged-race."

"Pretty confident in your racing skills, are you?"

He flicked out two fingers. "Two-time primary school champion."

"Primary school. That was what, four years ago?" Some definite smirk mingled with his smile. "All right, then. Tell Ella to wear her running shoes. Something tells me that you," I poked a finger into his chest, "are all talk and no action."

As soon as I said it, I knew how it looked—like I was daring him to make a move. I dropped my finger and crowded against the door, hoping he couldn't tell I had backed away. When he stepped toward me, my breath caught in my throat, fighting for room with my pounding heart.

He leaned in slowly and I closed my eyes, doing my best not to squeeze them shut. When he was close enough for me to catch his warm scent, I felt his lips press against my forehead.

"No pressure, remember?" He tucked a strand of hair behind my ear and backed down the front steps. "Wear your Smurf socks on Friday. You'll need the luck!"

CHAPTER FOURTEEN

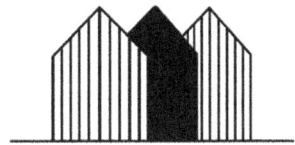

"Attics are such strange, shadowy places. You never know what you'll find—or what might find you," Patricia said the next afternoon. We had hit it off so well during our lunch that hanging out was becoming a regular occurrence. I'd enlisted her help in identifying Archive-worthy mementos.

"What will the Archive want, do you think? The director was so vague."

"That's unsurprising. Without direction, you're more likely to include something peculiar. I'd look for letters, outlines, early drafts. And since *Salt in the Sea* is autobiographical, any object of significance in the book would be interesting. It's a shame your mum flushed your little pet oyster. It would have been ideal."

She wiped a tear from her eye as she chortled before turning back to her box. A moment later, she cleared her throat. "This might be something."

She handed me a black-and-white photograph. Its metal frame was bent, the glass cracked in one corner. In the background, the narrow roof of the Seasalter house rose above the heads of a family—a man and woman, smiling as they squinted into the sun; a scrumptious, chubby baby with his mother's sunglasses clutched in his hands; a little boy perched on the man's shoulders—a boy whose platinum hair beamed as brightly as his smile.

I touched the tip of my finger to the little boy's face. "That's my dad, for sure. And his parents and brother. Wow. I've only seen one other picture of his brother."

Loose and framed photos were jumbled together in the box Patricia passed me. The top one showed my dad and his brother holding shells to their ears, their parents grinning behind them.

"My dad's brother looks around four here. This must have been just before they died." I flipped it over. The names John and Ian were penned across the back in a flowery script.

"I'd tell you how terribly sad it is, but it seems presumptuous since all I know comes from the book. But I'll say this. I don't know how your dad stood it at all."

"He barely did," I said. He barely does, I wanted to add.

I traced a finger over my dad's eight-year-old face—eyes screwed up, his mouth a round O like he was singing. That thatch of blond hair stuck out on his head like a silvery haystack. His skinny little boy legs glowed bronze even in the grey tones of the picture. He had thrown one arm around the bony shoulders of his brother. Less than a month later, the smallest boy would be lost, along with the parents behind them. And my dad would be lost as well, in a different but no less permanent way. I cupped the picture in both hands, like I could protect them if I were gentle enough.

"It's strange to look at these. My whole life, I've associated my dad's childhood in this house with death and despair and crippling anxiety. But this is the other side of the house's history. A happier side. It's just as essential to who my dad is today."

"Did the accident cause your father's panic disorder? Or was it the stimulus that brought it to the surface?" Patricia looked up. "Don't answer, if that's too personal."

"I hardly suspect you of writing an article about us." My dad smiled up at me from the picture in my hand. "Nobody knows whether the disorder stems from the trauma of seeing his family die or whether that was the catalyst for a condition that would have surfaced regardless. But loss is the trigger that's most damaging to him. It always has been."

"How so?"

"He's had four significant episodes, all caused by death or loss. The first, after his family drowned, wasn't treated. His doctors focused on his physical health and left the emotional aspects to his aunt and uncle who raised him in Missouri. He doesn't exaggerate in the book. I only met them once but, even as a kid, I could tell they weren't affectionate people. My dad always says he felt like a visitor who'd overstayed his welcome but had no way to get back home."

"That's the most powerful theme in his book. The displacement of home and all that it means."

"And the most central. The panic attacks began soon after he lost his family, but they were manageable until he had a family of his own. That's when the panic became an obsession. He was petrified that something would happen to my mom or me."

"And it escalated when the three of you came back to this house," she said, because this much was common knowledge, public record in a bestselling book.

"I guess being here, where he lived with his family and where he lost them, brought it all back. Having a wife and baby to worry about didn't help."

She hesitated. "Is it out of line to ask what happened after the book's conclusion?"

For some reason, I felt relieved that she didn't know. So many articles had been written about my family's disintegration that it seemed like common knowledge. I was so used to the routine, I hardly noticed anymore: people would ask if my dad was still a hermit, disparage my mom for abandoning him, laugh about my pet oyster, and that was that.

I lifted out a faded blue cardigan cushioning some of the frames. Although mildewed and dirty like most stuff in the attic, it was exactly like the sweaters my dad still wore at home. I considered donating it to the Archive, then tossed it on the pile I was saving for myself.

"After the search team found our boat, my dad holed up in his office and refused to come out. He was guilt-stricken and convinced we would be better off without him. My mom's parents flew here from South Carolina and the three of them talked him into entering a treatment program in Charleston. My mom and granddad went through every step with him. Afterward, we moved in with my grandparents for good."

"They sound very supportive."

"They were the best. I felt so lucky to live with my

grandparents in the very same house. They helped my dad feel more grounded. For a long time, he was okay."

I told her about growing up in the tall white farmhouse overlooking the Stono River, about planting strawberries with Granddad Cal and making them into shortcake with Grandma Rose. My dad getting well enough to teach, my mom getting a tattoo to celebrate him winning the Fletcher Prize: a tiny JRB over her heart. In one of my less-gracious moments shortly before she'd remarried, I had asked her what Charles thought of that tattoo. Turns out she'd had it removed years before.

That unpleasant memory paved the way for the rest of my story.

"Granddad died when I was eleven. Grandma had passed away the year before. Losing them triggered my dad's obsessive fears that everyone he loved would slip away. The following year, we moved to Chicago to try this intensive therapy program, but nothing helped. Eventually, my mom couldn't take any more. She moved out when I was thirteen and she made me go with her."

I pictured the filigree swirls of her handwriting, all the passion and promises she'd etched into those love letters I had discovered downstairs.

"Maybe it was too much for her to handle alone," I added, forcing myself to give her a fair shake. Patricia was probably measuring my resentment by the way I enunciated my verbs. "After she left, my dad checked himself into a psychiatric hospital. He refused to see anyone for more than a year." I looked up, needing her to understand what came next. "He called me every day. He just didn't want me to see him that way."

She gave me a firm nod.

"He needs to be near the water—it's part of how he manages the obsessive thoughts about his family drowning—so after he left the hospital, he rented a house on Lake Michigan. When my mom remarried eight years later, he donated nearly all of his money, including all future royalties from the book, to psychiatric research. He refused to profit from it again. He couldn't afford the main house anymore, so his landlord rented him the guest cottage near the shore. He moved in and hasn't left the house since."

"He never goes out?"

"Never. Being away from the house makes him panic."

Patricia paused as she processed this. "And your mum?"

I knew what she was thinking. Real estate marketing aside, the love story between John and Isobel Beckett really is one of literature's most beautiful. Even after seeing firsthand the ugly way my parents' marriage ended, when I read *Salt in the Sea*, I get swept up in it, too.

I flipped through a stack of photos before answering. There was one of my dad holding me as a toddler. Two blonde pigtails poked up like antennae on top of my head.

"She doesn't see him anymore. She went back to her social work job and eventually married a guy she met in a support group." I shook my head. "I shouldn't say it like that. Charles isn't *a guy* to me anymore, obviously. I love him, now that I'm not an angry teenager. He's smart and fair and easy to live with. He's Zambian and deeply invested in African social issues, something that's always been important to my mom. I guess that's what she needed."

"That's not a happy story." Patricia reached for the photo in my hands and adjusted her glasses. "It must be interesting, though, having your childhood captured in such a famous book."

"Interesting is one word for it. Of course, the serious commentary focuses on my parents. My contribution seems to be comic relief."

She studied the photo, then looked up to study my face.

"I don't think so. There's a reason the only name he gives you in the book is Bell Petite. You're the clearest symbol of hope that he has. You provide the laughter because, to your father, you're the light that drives away the gloom."

My fingers trembled as she handed back the picture. Our Seasalter house was the backdrop, anchored behind us, slender and straight. My dad smiled into the camera, his arms folded around me. I had one hand on his face, but the other reached out in front of me. At the edge of the photo, I made out a few fine copper strands—the photographer's red hair blowing into the frame. My mother's long shadow fell across the sand.

I'd missed a call from my dad while Patricia and I were raiding the attic. His message was long, his voice pulsing with excitement.

"Petite, I don't know what magic you worked on that Glenister man, but I owe you. The Archive wants to buy the Seasalter house and turn it into a permanent exhibit. Some slice-of-life nonsense. He called it A Walk Through *Salt in the Sea*. I didn't catch the details. Don't really care. If it means the house is off my hands, they can turn it into any fool thing they please."

The message went on, but I could only half-listen. I wanted to be happy for him. But when I tried to imagine the house as a literary tribute, preserving the history within my dad's book, what I saw most clearly was the history I was building in it myself.

Out the windows in the office, the North Sea reflected a ginger-tinted sky. The waves whispered through the quaint diamond panes. Throughout my lonely first month in England, their hush was the only voice I'd heard.

My haven. My hideaway. All night, the words swished through my head. I woke to their beat at three a.m. with an idea that made my breath catch. Within an hour, I had worked up a plan. My renegotiated contract would increase my income by a modest but respectable amount. The money I had saved for my aborted wedding and honeymoon was now fair game. If I combined that with my small personal savings and rented out the house for most of the year, I could just afford the mortgage.

I could keep the house. I could only afford to stay in it a couple weeks each year, but still, it would belong to me.

I slipped downstairs, snagging my laptop on the way to the office. My conscience screeched while I transformed my wholesome date with Sam into a steamy picnic between Madison and Sean. I'd had misgivings about my novel all day. How could I appropriate the family tragedy of this truly decent guy? And not just appropriate it but manipulate it into an absurd soap opera, complete with lavish copulation and a maniacal child? I had almost called Gretchen to say I'd reconsidered, that although my other ideas had been awful, I would keep submitting new ones until I got it right. Or, if it really was too late for that, I'd skip publishing something altogether.

Buying the house meant I no longer had the option of not publishing a book. While I might eventually convince them to consider something new, Yvonne was sure that the book would be Velicity's next bestseller and Gretchen was nearly obsessed with Madison and Sean. If my idea hadn't been a twisted usurpation of Sam's real life, I'd have been ecstatic. Instead, I felt like an opportunistic creep.

But I wrote it anyway. I poured word after word into that book—lies about violence and madness that maligned a real child and distorted her grieving family. And sweet vignettes I couldn't keep from including, snapshots of Sam that held everything about him I had come to admire.

The scene was finished. I crept upstairs. Before falling into bed, I walked to the window and studied the misty dawn breaking over the beach. The waves were whispering to me again.

"My haven," I whispered back with a smile. "My house."

CHAPTER FIFTEEN

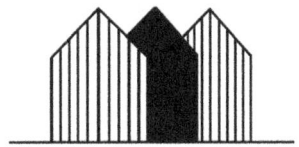

Having discovered a mutual love for classic film, Patricia and I established a ritual: dinner and a movie on Thursday nights. When she heard that our ritual could continue for two weeks every year, she broke out a bottle of champagne. The celebrating made me giddy, but the champagne might've made me paranoid. It was late when I left. Darkness seemed to lengthen the quarter-mile walk between her house and mine.

I plowed up the path from the beach with my keys out and ready. And good grief, why hadn't I left on a light? I slipped into the yard and froze.

A man was sitting on the steps. His face was masked in shadow, but my initial terror evaporated when I recognized the set of his shoulders.

It evaporated into fury.

"What do you think you're doing here?"

"Will you please let me explain before you start yelling?" David said as he rose to meet me.

"No," I snapped, pushing past him. "The sound of your voice makes me sick."

My key ring slipped from my shaking hand. We both leaned down to retrieve it and his fingers brushed mine.

"Get away from me." I jammed the key into the lock so hard, I swear I felt it bend. "Who told you I'm here?"

"I got lucky. Gretchen's assistant let it slip."

"Really, *you* got lucky? What a surprise," I said, and he flinched. "Look, go home. I don't want to do this."

I slipped inside, leaning against the doorframe for support. My heart was pounding so hard, my whole body shook.

David rubbed his palms on his jeans. His nervous gestures, all of them, were as familiar to me as my own.

"I mean it, David. Go home."

"No. I'm not leaving until you talk to me." His tone was so infuriating that I swung the door in his face. He managed to wedge his arm inside. "Marin, I'm sorry. I was so stupid. I got paranoid that you didn't want to get married, that you didn't want to marry me—"

"That was why I said yes when you asked. I said yes because I didn't want to marry you."

"You said yes ten months before you would set a date. The date you agreed to was over a year away. You put off planning until you had no choice and spent two months ignoring me while we scrambled to get it done. What was I supposed to think?"

His words shook me so much that I let the door fall open. This was exactly what I'd been afraid to hear. That despite my best intentions, I had driven him to it.

"You're right," I finally managed to say. "I didn't always want to get married. But when I said yes to you, I said yes.

To you. I made a commitment to you, and I meant it, only to find out that you didn't. For all I know, you were screwing other women the whole time we were together."

His hands had been clenched into fists. I watched them fall limp at his sides.

"You honestly think I'm capable of that? You think I could ask you to spend the rest of your life with me and be with someone else while I said it?"

He looked so stunned that I wanted to believe him.

"I don't know what to think. I don't even know you."

David's voice grew soft. "It's still me, I just made a mistake. I got insecure and then I got stupid. It was just that one day, I swear to you—"

"Don't. Just please, please don't. I don't want to know any of this." I put my hand on my throat like that might keep my voice from shaking.

"Mariana. Please."

I forced my eyes to lock onto his. "Do not ever say my full name again. You and your friend Tennyson turn it into something sad."

"I need you to know how sorry I am. How sorry I'll always be."

"Good. I'll always be sorry, too. When I'm living out the last of my golden years alone because you destroyed my already-fragile belief that love is worthwhile, I'll be sure to remind myself that you felt bad afterward."

He sighed.

"I'm glad to see you haven't lost your taste for melodrama."

There. Right there was a glimpse of the only David I had allowed myself to remember: the condescending, pompous jerk.

"You'll really send me away without hearing me out? I flew four thousand miles on my fall break to see you."

"Oh, excuse me for interfering with your vacation, Doctor Lauer. Have you seen France? It's a short swim across the North Sea. Go ahead, jump in."

He looked like he was trying not to smile. "You're turned around. If I jump in from here, I'll hit the Isle of Sheppey."

"What are you, a geography professor now?"

"So that's it? Six years were worth so little, you won't even speak to me?"

"How much were they worth to you when you took that girl into our home? When you were—"

"Marin, don't."

"No, you don't. Don't invade the one place I've found any peace. Don't act so injured because I won't let you in. And don't trivialize this as me overreacting. This is not me overreacting. This is me saying do not ever show up at my door again."

He stepped back like I'd slapped him. I started to bang the door shut but I hesitated when his hand trembled at his side. I looked at his face, really looked at him for the first time since that horrible day I'd thrown him out. There were lines around his mouth, bags beneath his eyes. His hair hadn't been cut in weeks.

"You look terrible."

"I feel terrible."

Good, I wanted to say, but sorrow settled over me when his shoulders slumped again.

"You look beautiful." When I stayed silent, he continued. "Please let me say this, Marin. You were the best thing about my life. I love everything about you. Please tell me you believe that, that you believe me when I tell you how sorry I will always be for hurting you in this appalling way."

His voice wasn't posh anymore. It was unstudied and kind, like it had been when we met. Before he became Professor David Lauer—Director of the Graduate Studies Program, special lecturer on Victorian literary response to the Industrial Revolution, author of two well-received volumes of new historicist perspectives on the complete works of Alfred, Lord Tennyson. This was the softer, sincere David, the one whose subtle thoughtfulness made him so easy to like. And it was the David he had been almost all the time. I hated to admit it, but this David—oh. This David, I really did miss.

"Just tell me you believe me," he said again. "I don't want anything from you but to know that someday—not now, just someday—you might be able to forgive me."

I looked at him for so long, at the tear that slipped from the corner of his eye, at his hands clenching until his knuckles were white. Even though seeing his face tore open all my thinly scabbed wounds, just him standing there made me feel more at home. He was the only familiar person I had seen in months. And like it or not, he was still the most familiar person in this world to me.

The sky was black but here and there, a few stars poked through, little glimmers in a murky sea. The trite comparisons I could so easily have made (dawn breaking through night, hope breaking through doubt) weren't lost on me when I answered.

"Okay."

Maybe I believed it, maybe not. It didn't matter either way.

David took one step forward, hope flickering across his face. I took one step away.

"No," I whispered, just catching the sob in the back of my throat. I closed the door behind me with a quiet click and shut my eyes against the image of him on the other side. Did he brace himself against it for support? I wondered, as I pressed my own back into it.

When I flipped the deadbolt, I cringed at the finality of it, at how it might sound to his ears. I walked through the dark house without turning on a light. In the bedroom, I stripped off my clothes and dug around for Nandi's sweatpants, stupid-looking ones with *You Wish* printed across the butt that I always mocked. They were completely ridiculous and six inches too short, but she'd insisted I bring them. So I would have a little of her with me when I was most alone.

Cloaked in the comfort of my sister's sweatpants, I listened at the window until I heard him drive away. Before climbing into bed, I pulled in a deep breath and let the salted air scratch away the stifled tears in my throat.

CHAPTER SIXTEEN

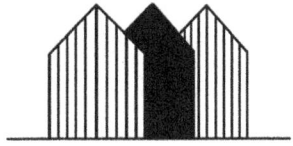

AFTER AN HOUR OF STARING AT THE QUOTE ON MY BEDROOM ceiling, I picked up the phone. For two months, I had been reading a summary of my mom's best qualities every night before dozing off—*you're kind, you're quiet, you're calm, you're bright*—and between the overhead tribute and her devoted letters to my dad and my own memories of the three of us that kept blooming up, I'd started to realize how much I missed her. I dialed her number.

Voicemail.

I tried to imagine myself dumping all this into a message, especially since I hadn't called in weeks. I clicked off at the last second. Julie was introducing her baby boy to his great-grandparents in Israel. Me being upset might upset my dad. Desperate, I called Nandi, who had been my last choice only because she would be murderous with rage.

Voicemail. My message ended in a blubbering mess, so it was no surprise when she called me back the next morning, even though it was two a.m. her time.

"Ugh, I hate him. If I ever run into him on a deserted

street…" She sighed. "The one time I forgot my phone. Poor Mare. If I was there, I'd tuck you in with Redford and Newman and a bowlful of brownie batter. That's it. I'm coming for Christmas."

"Really?!" I squealed, pelting her with questions. We were deep into trip-planning when a knock rang out. My stomach dropped. "What if it's David?"

"If that's David, you shove this phone into his face and let me handle him!" she ordered. I steeled myself for a fight, if needed, and jerked opened the front door.

"Is that look because you're not happy to see me?"

"Sam!" My scowl fell away. "I'm sorry, I thought you were—come in."

This is much better than expected, I thought with a smile. And then I remembered. Holy smokes. I was supposed to be going to the girls' fall festival.

"Who's Sam?" I heard Nandi ask. Sam's eyes flickered toward the phone. I twisted it behind my back.

"Is this a bad time?"

"It's just my sister," I said, taking his coat. When I turned back, I caught him checking out Nandi's stupid sweatpants. Awesome. This time I looked both frumpy and trashy. "I'm sorry I'm running so late. I'll be ready in five minutes."

"No rush. We've got plenty of time," he called as I dashed up the stairs.

I could hear my sister dying of curiosity through the phone.

"Nandi?" I whispered.

She did not whisper back.

"Augh, Marin, spill! Spill! Who is that?"

"I told you about him. He's playing Edward in the movie."

"You're into him! I hear it in your voice. Details! How long has this been going on?"

I decided to save myself some time and trouble. By lying.

"Nothing's going on. I met him for a minute at the wrap party."

Nandi buzzed like I'd given the wrong answer on "Family Feud."

"If you barely met him, how did he know where to find you?"

Grrr, this girl.

"Fine. He invited me to hear his band and then his sisters—"

"You went to hear his band?!"

"Nandi, I'm late. He's waiting for me."

"Oh, he's *waiting* for you," she crooned. "You're into him. Admit it."

"I'm hanging up."

"All right, all right. Go get him, Tiger. Carpe diem or whatever—seize the day, yo!"

I saved time by rolling my eyes at her while I ran for the bathroom, but my battered reflection tripped me up. It would take more than a quick swipe of mascara to repair the damage from my emotional hangover. I'd just rinsed away the makeup smeared beneath my swollen eyes when another knock echoed in the foyer.

Not David, I pleaded as I slipped back downstairs. My racing pulse skidded to a stop when I saw Sam in the open doorway. His broad shoulders blocked my view of the porch, but he turned around with a FedEx box in his hands.

"Oh, good!"

The relief sweeping through me must have shone in my face; Sam looked at me curiously.

"I've been expecting that package for days," I lied. I feigned enthusiasm and ripped into it, then had to paste my smile in place. Looking back at me was my contract for the book that exploited the man beside me.

I snatched it up before Sam could see it and landed in a different scrape. Beneath the contract was an assortment of broken-in Velocity novels, including several of mine. Sam caught sight of a scantily clad couple draped across a book's cover, as well as the extravagant flourish of the author's name: Mariana Rose.

"Look at this!" He lifted it out, only to reveal another book of mine just beneath. He snatched it up, too.

"Sam, trust me, you don't want to read those."

"Are you mad? I've been poring over your Rochester book for months. I can't wait to read more of your work." He dropped onto the sofa with *Aurelia's Mistake*. "This will be the perfect companion whilst you ready yourself."

I ignored his smug grin and turned to Gretchen's note. Why had she sent me a box of used books? *Cleaning my office...inspiration for your next steamy love scene...can't wait to read more about you and Simon. I mean Madison and Sean, ha ha...*

Yeah, ha ha. I shoved the note back into its envelope, then stuffed the envelope and the contract into a drawer.

"I don't suppose you'll agree to read this instead?" I said, offering him another author's book. He glanced at the cover and tossed it aside.

"Donna Pryce? She sounds like a finance analyst. Mariana Rose is the only author I trust to bring the goods, if you know what I mean."

"I don't think *you* know what you mean."

He let my book fall open at a particularly heavy crease in the spine and shot me a cheeky grin, but his eyes widened as they moved down the page. When he looked back at me, he seemed genuinely surprised. And—to be perfectly honest—rather impressed.

"Wow. I had no idea such thoughts were hidden behind your innocent face. I must cool down with some water if I'm to continue with that."

He made a show of filling a glass at the kitchen sink, draining it, and tossing me a smile as he filled it again.

"Did I mention we have plenty of time?" he said, flopping down this time with *Wandering Star*. He flipped to the book's most weathered crease. "I beg you. Take as long as you need."

I counted on the dirty parts to entertain him long enough for me to shower. Ten minutes later, I was rubbing a towel over my hair when I heard voices. I smiled, thinking he'd abandoned my books for TV, but my relief turned to disbelief when I stepped into the hall. Because one voice was Sam's. And the other was definitely David's.

I muttered something not worth repeating as I marched downstairs. I felt Sam watching as I stalked across the room, but I didn't look at him. I pinned David to his seat with my glare.

He looked nothing like the defeated guy from the night before. He was cleaned up and confident, shoulders squared. Maybe he had come by to try making amends again, but the threatening edge to his smile proved that his priorities had shifted when Sam answered my door.

"Darling," he said, coupling a snide tone with a smirk that he directed at Sam.

"Get out," I said, the ragged words snagging in my narrowing throat. When Sam came to stand beside me, David's green eyes glittered. He pulled himself up to full Ph.D. height.

"Your friend was just explaining the complexities of professional salad prep." He adjusted the gold fountain pen tucked into his lapel and flicked a disinterested glance at Sam. "Tell me, the carrots—coins or matchsticks?"

"You know what, David, matchstick that Montblanc up your rear end and get out of my house."

"Four months, Marin. Four thousand miles. You're really not willing to talk to me?"

"There's nothing left to say."

"You haven't given me a chance to say anything!" He gripped my shoulders in both hands.

"Let go of me!" I shoved at his chest until he stepped back. Sam edged in front of me protectively.

"This doesn't concern you," David snapped.

"If you grab her again, I'll prove to you how much it concerns me."

"An admirable display of valor. You can go back to slicing carrots with your dignity intact," David said, stepping toward Sam.

"You can go to hell," Sam replied, and didn't step back. Right on cue, they each clenched a fist.

I closed my eyes to keep them from rolling right out of my face and elbowed some space between them.

"Can you both please put your man-parts away? I'm sure they measure up just fine."

"You don't know from personal experience?" David smirked, and Sam's fist clenched again. I covered it with my hand, lingering a bit for David's benefit.

"Could you give us a minute?"

Sam cut his eyes toward David, but he stepped toward the door.

"Nice to have met you. It was very educational," David called. A dull look of disgust washed over Sam's face.

I'm sorry, I mouthed, and then I yelped, "Hey!" as David snaked his hand around mine. Sam turned on his heel and started toward us.

"I'm fine," I told him, snatching my hand away.

"Fine," Sam said coolly, passing us by. He crossed to the far corner of the room and began to study the books on my shelf.

Yeah, fine, I fumed when he ignored my pointed glance at the door. But sure, stay. Watch me shrivel from the woman you think you know into the bitter shrew that I actually am.

I flipped around to face David. "What part of *stay away from me* do you not comprehend?"

"What is it you're doing over here? Are you trying to get even with me by—"

"By what?" Was he brash enough to insinuate that the guy standing fully clothed in my new house was retribution for the naked co-ed rolling around in our bed?

But this shot was aimed at me.

"By making your smooth white shoulder bare and spreading o'er all your yellow hair." He paused for effect. "Robert Browning."

"Yes, yes, you're a prodigious talent. Few men could call me a slut with an obscure Victorian poem."

"It's hardly obscure. And you didn't answer me."

"I don't owe you an answer. We are done."

He leaned against an end table. Gretchen's box of books fell to the floor. *The Dowager Roused* landed at his feet.

"I thought you were moving away from romance novels. Your Rochester book had so much potential for launching a serious writing career."

I opened my mouth to bite back at that, then shook my head. Not worth it. "David, thank you and goodbye."

"I didn't mean that the way it came out," he said, his tone softening. "You said you could forgive me, Marin. You opened a door when you said that, you know you did."

"I believe what I said was someday, maybe, a long time from now, it might be possible for me not to loathe the sight of you."

"That's not what you said."

"Well, that's what I meant!" I snapped, and that awful ache from the night before flooded his face.

My wet hair was turning my thin robe transparent. I was barely decent and freezing to death. "Look, it's over. Let's forget it."

"How can you forget? Six years, Mariana—"

"Don't call me that."

"Fine. Marin. How can you forget six years?"

"Why don't we talk about what I can't forget? Do I need to break down the images for you, frame by frame? Because I can. I see them all the time. Believe me, I would love to forget."

Longing for the great outdoors now, aren't you? I telegraphed to Sam when he edged into the dining room, probably wishing he could pass through the wall. When I looked back at David, he had slumped onto the sofa. I watched his shoulders shake.

On my list of things to accomplish in life, Console

David had dropped to dead last. For five seconds, I pressed my fingers to my temples (read: I clutched the top of my head with both hands). And then, with a sigh that was more of a growl, I shoved the coffee table back a few feet and perched opposite him. "What?"

"What do you think? I'm a complete idiot. I threw my whole life away. I lost you, I lost my job—"

"You did?" Shock made the words spring from my lips. "Really? You lost your job?"

"Practically. I'm on probation. Disciplinary action for— you know."

"Sleeping with your student." I pushed myself further away. "You can say it. I broke the story, remember?"

I couldn't stop my eyes from lifting to Sam's. He dropped his gaze to the floor. A moment later, he stepped out the back door.

"Brynslee confided in Lois Schenkl, the new head of Women's Lit." Brynslee. That girl's name in his mouth tore a gash through my ear. "Schenkl told the department chair. I've been knocked down to part-time. They may fire me for violating the university's standards of conduct. But it's not that. Coming close to losing my job only reminds me of what I've already lost. You took yourself away like we never existed. Six years, Marin. It was supposed to be sixty."

I failed when I tried not to remember the life we'd planned together. Babies, with my blue eyes and imagination and David's dark hair and quick mind. The house we'd planned to buy someday, an old South Carolina gem overlooking some water, with a little place near the shore for my dad. Two children, maybe three, clinging to a tire swing. My eyes began to burn.

"Please come home and try to work things out. Stop pushing me away. Let me help you."

The house and children melted into that same nightmare scene. Me, exhausted after a rough trip to New York, slipping home unexpectedly to sweet-talk David into flying with me to England for the set visit the next day. Music on in our condo at one a.m. when he was always asleep. His leather attaché on the console. A monogrammed backpack near the front door. And an unmistakable sound down the hall—the creaking springs of our own bed.

"David," I said, biting my cheek, "you can't help me. You're the one who broke me."

He dropped his face into his palms. "I know. Oh, Marin, I'm sorry."

For a few minutes, we both battled back tears. Finally, he looked up.

"What do you want me to do?"

My head ached like something inside was beating its way out. I pressed the heels of my hands against my eyes. It felt like hours before I answered, even to me.

"I want you to go," I whispered, and I heard his throat catch. Before he stood, he pulled my hand into his.

"Mariana. So content to doubt, she forgets to believe." He held my fingers to his lips, his touch so familiar that, despite all that had happened, some part of me instantly felt secure. "I'd hoped to make that better. I'm sorry I made it worse."

My eyes followed him as he walked to the door. For the first time in months, that flame of bitterness I'd been stoking in my chest flickered; instead, I felt the hollow sting of the sweetest parts of our life together passing away. The poems he'd taped to the bathroom mirror to greet me in the morning. How he'd read to me from my own favorite books if I had trouble falling asleep. He would lay with his head in my lap while we watched the snow fall. Six years of firsts that became rituals, inside jokes, and the everyday comfort of mutual routine.

    Gone.

CHAPTER SEVENTEEN

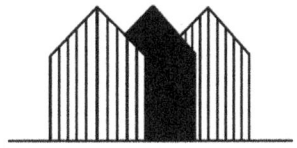

When Julie got back from vacation two weeks later, she was so furious about David's visit that she sacrificed a precious hour of new-mom sleep by calling at midnight her time. I was so glad for the company, I didn't care that she woke me at six.

"The only reason I didn't kill him in July was the C-section. His number's up," she growled. "Garrett, start the car and bring me your bat."

Garrett mumbled in the background, and Julie growled again.

"Dang it. He played the Michael card."

"Well, raising a kid from prison does seem impractical." I shuffled downstairs and flipped on the electric kettle. "It doesn't matter, it's done now. But…"

"But what? You're not thinking of taking him back?"

"No! I'm thinking about something he said. He said I'm so content to doubt love that I don't try to believe in it."

"Yeah? Well, he's so desperate to sound smart that he talks out his tuches, as Bubbe says. We've all got our thing."

"We've all got our thing, as in, you agree, I don't try to believe?"

Julie's response was to not respond.

"Do you think I drove him to it?"

"Of course not. You can't drive someone to cheat. That's a detour jerks go out of their way to take." She paused. "Don't let him throw you, things are looking up. You love England. You're writing again. You're going out with the Prom King."

"I went out with the Prom King. Once. He decided once was enough."

"You haven't heard from him?"

"The day David stepped into my house, the Prom King stepped out." Literally. Sam hadn't just slipped out to give David and me some privacy. He had disappeared without a word.

"Then on to the next. Remember, you're perfecting the art of the casual fling."

"I'll keep it in mind. On that note, I have to get back to exploiting the Prom King's family to save my waning writing career."

I carried my tea to the computer and ignored the way my stomach cramped.

Just push through it, I told myself. I turned to a morbid section on the little sister character and blocked an image of Ella's solemn brown eyes. I'd written three miserable pages when, mercifully, my mom broke in. She had returned my call from the night of David's ambush, and we'd been chatting every few days since. Still, she normally called during the day her time and not the middle of the night.

"I couldn't sleep, so thought I'd see how you're doing. Find anything good in the attic?"

I risked her wrath by mentioning that I'd read those smoldering letters. To my relief, she laughed aloud at my teasing description.

"I'm glad they amused you," she said, and a reassuring ease spread out between us. "But let's keep them out of the Archive collection."

"Are you sure? Those letters were impressive. Maybe you missed your calling as a romance novelist."

"Ha!" she said, and my mood darkened, because I recognized her tone. "I can't imagine I'd contribute much to that field."

I didn't want an argument, but I couldn't quite let the sarcasm slide. "Some of those letters were pretty racy. You'd probably do better than you think."

"I'll stick to case management reports."

"Meaning romance novels are a waste of time?" I had heard this line of reasoning for the past nine years.

"I don't want to fight with you, Marin. If you're happy with your work, that's enough for me," she said, but our chummy camaraderie was gone. After we hung up, I glanced at the chapter in front of me. An eight-year-old child was creeping into her brother's bedroom, a carving knife clutched in her little hands. For once, my mom and I would have been on the same page. Turning a heartbroken, motherless child into a deranged killer was repugnant.

"Enough of that for today," I said through the sour taste in my mouth. I skipped ahead to a scene that was much more fun to write. My guilt gradually faded beneath the escalating heat between Madison and Sean. When the phone rang again two hours later, I'd stoked that glow into eight sizzling pages.

Most of my mind was lingering in a hot bath with Sean and Madison, but it snapped back to the present when a cacophony of giggles erupted from the phone. A bump, a shuffle, and then a small, formal voice: "Hello. May I speak to Marin, please?"

"Lily?"

The formal voice transformed with a joyful shriek.

"Yes, it's me!"

I heard a deep, familiar laugh in the background and had the decency to blush. Not ten seconds earlier, I'd been soaping up a character with an identical laugh—and identical sculpted abs.

For a moment, I splashed back into the tub with those abs. Lily's chatter yanked me out.

"We want you to visit us today and will you come? We're baking fairy cakes and Sam says you can do the sprinkles. But of course it would be lovely if you would let me help." More background chatter. "And Ella, too."

There was another bit of scuffling and then she was back, breathless with excitement.

"Sam said we can make two flavors if I let him talk. Bye." There was a bump and a yelp and then Sam's hello.

"Did you bribe a child to get the phone?"

"I had no choice. She's so quick, she grabbed it after I dialed. Lily, no! We already added the eggs. Put the carton down—" I heard a muffled smack. Sam groaned under his breath.

"You've got a long, wild road ahead of you with that kid."

"A road which leads to the shop for more eggs so my

dad doesn't curse me tomorrow at breakfast," he said with a sigh. "The girls' school is closed today. I just returned from a trip to France, so I offered to stay with them. They've talked of nothing but you all morning."

"Really? I'm surprised, considering I involuntarily stood them up for their school festival."

Even the background noise seemed awkward before he answered.

"Yes, I'm sorry for leaving like that. I thought it best to get out of the way. I meant to call," he mumbled, and then his voice grew firm. "I should have called. I am sorry."

"No worries," I said, patting my own back for sounding so breezy. I almost high-fived myself when I added, "I would like to see *the girls* again."

"Can I bribe you with fairy cakes as I did Lily? Remember, we're making two flavors now."

"I'll come," I told him. "I'll even bring the eggs."

Sam was wiping cake batter from his eyes when he answered the door an hour later. The girls had tried out the hand mixer while his back was turned.

"We prepared two flavors, but only strawberry made it into the oven. We're wearing the chocolate, as you can see."

"The mixer caught my finger," Lily said, holding up her small hand. "Sam promised me ice cream if I wouldn't cry."

"I'm perfecting my bribery skills today," he told me, marching two chattering, chocolate-splattered figures past.

I wandered through the living room while he wrangled them upstairs. In the photos of their mother sprinkled throughout the room, her amber-brown eyes were lit up with laughter. She looked vibrant, and kind, and a bit mischievous, too.

A marriage certificate was framed beside Sam's parents' wedding picture. "Alison Amato Quinn," I whispered, tracing my finger over her signature.

Lace curtains at the windows threw delicate shadows. Sunlight gleamed on the honeyed wood floor. I could feel her there, soothing and right, lingering like a memory or a good dream.

Ella called out, "Stop shoving!" and Lily shrieked, "Too slow!" Six feet clomped downstairs. Even this commotion seemed right. An essential part of the whole she had nurtured.

A few hours later, the fairy cakes we hadn't eaten sparkled in the kitchen. I'd been introduced to the girls' stuffed animal family, enjoyed the pleasure of fingerpaint staining my hands, and helped Barbie twirl Ken around the dance floor. Lily could apparently ride her sugar high until bedtime, but Ella dozed off while I read them a book. Sam's disappearing act didn't come up again until I pulled on my coat.

"So, France. Wow. What were you doing?"

"Touring with my friend Karine's band. She needed someone to fill in on guitar at the last minute." He handed me my scarf as we walked to the door. "Fortunately, SaladBar is staffed by starving artists, so someone is always willing to cover—"

A shrill cry overhead warped into a panicked scream. We cleared the stairs as Lily stumbled into the hall.

"Ella had her dream about mummy again," she said, collapsing against Sam. He picked her up but nearly dropped her when we slammed into the girls' room. Ella had crammed herself into the nook between her bed and the nightstand. She stared without blinking, hands clasped over her ears. Her shrieks sliced like a blade through the room.

I caught the bewildered alarm on Sam's face when he shifted a terrified Lily toward me. He lifted Ella from the floor into his lap, her little form stiff and still tightly curled.

"She needs the flutes. And her flower!"

Lily pointed to a radio in the corner but before I could move, an older version of Sam stormed in and flipped the switch. A soft lullaby fell over the room. Ella's shrieks dwindled and turned to sobs.

"Daddy," she said, holding out her arms.

"It was a dream, darling," he said as she buried her face in his neck. He snapped the switch on a papier-mâché daisy beside her bed. A pink glow hit Sam's disconcerted face. "Now, you see, it was only a dream."

Ella shuddered in her father's arms. He carried her to the window. The afternoon sun struck his face, but shadows fell into the tired lines of his brow.

Sam pulled himself off the bed.

"I didn't realize she still has the dreams," he whispered, placing his fingertips cautiously on Ella's back.

"How could you? You're never here," his dad snapped. "You pop in and just as easily pop out without considering how it affects your sisters."

"Of course I consider them. I live thirty miles away. Why would I come here so often if not for them?"

"Does Amy traipse through France for days at a time? Did Wendy disappear three weeks after your mother died to muck about in some rubbishy film?"

Lily was still clinging to my shoulders. With each tense exchange, she tightened her grip. I carried her into the hall.

"Do you know what I'd like?" I asked, setting her on her feet. "I'd like a fairy cake to take home."

Sam's sharp retort smacked off the walls.

"Could you help me pick out just the right one?" I asked, and she slipped her hand into mine.

She knelt on a stool at the kitchen counter, studying the cupcakes. "It should have loads of icing, of course."

"You are completely devoid of responsibility!" an angry voice shouted above us.

"Should it be orange or pink?" I asked her loudly.

"Pink! No, orange. No, both colors. You need two."

"I do need two." Two cupcakes and two shots of very strong whiskey.

Lily circled her finger above the cupcakes. "She's the one!"

"Are the pink ones girls?" I nearly shouted as Ella's sobs drifted downstairs.

"And orange boys." She pushed another cupcake toward me and licked some frosting off her hand. "Now these are the perfect two for you."

A door slammed overhead.

"Perfect," I croaked before my throat grew too tight to speak.

CHAPTER EIGHTEEN

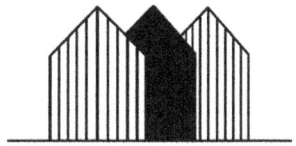

"I don't see the problem. Just explain it to him."

I sighed. Again. "Gretchen, I cannot tell this guy that I wrote about his mother's death and his little sister's broken heart. He's very protective of his family. He'd never speak to me again."

"It didn't bother you when you came up with the idea. Why is it such an issue now?"

"It did bother me, but he was an inspiring stranger. I never expected to know him as well as I do."

"How well do you know him, Marin? Come on, tell me. Is it as hot as in the book?"

"It's not like that between us." Gretchen sniffed, obviously disappointed that the sex scenes were the only entirely fictional part of my book. "Didn't you like any of my new ideas?"

I'd spent the two weeks since witnessing Ella's trauma for myself plotting new stories; surely one of them would work. One had to work, because after seeing their family's struggle up-close, I refused to exploit them in a Velicity-trademark soap opera.

"None of them have the same draw. But the bigger issue is Yvonne. Sean does it for her. She told me she—"

Please! No updates on Yvonne's hotspot.

"Maybe I can tweak it. Make Claire well-adjusted instead of mentally ill. Rewrite Sean as her widowed father instead of her brother."

"The crazy kid is the best part. And I can think of three Velicity novels from this year alone that feature widowed fathers. Besides, Yvonne—*appreciates*—the younger man aspect."

"I can't write this, Gretchen."

"Then send me something I can use. We don't want to risk the deal on this book. It's a pivotal step for your career." And mine, I almost heard her say.

"I know. I'll figure it out."

I hung up and reached for my jacket. The evening was cold, but I needed the beach.

The wind whipping off the sea snatched at my breath. I dropped onto the nearest bench and watched two seagulls fighting while a third looked on. Maybe rivals having it out over a girl? Was there anything in it I could use? Things were grim if I was looking to birds for inspiration.

Writing about the Quinns had been a huge mistake. Sending it to Gretchen had been criminal. Little Ella, with her anxious eyes and solemn face. I was a monster for using her.

There had to be a way to fix this.

But why couldn't I catch hold of a different idea? Had David's betrayal hurt me so much, I couldn't even make up a believable love story? I used to write romance and feel like I was falling in love. Now, I just felt dumb.

But I couldn't walk away. Gretchen was right—a bigger advance, better royalties, the support to shift toward mainstream fiction—this novel would be a game-changer for me. Not to mention that without it, I had no way to buy my Seasalter house. I needed this next book, regardless of how hard it might be to write.

I heard footsteps crunching along the beach and turned to see Sam. We'd made plans to grab dinner after his band rehearsed at Three Wastrels. As he walked toward me, I made him a promise: I would come up with a book that protected us both.

My heart fluttered when he smiled at me. I ignored it by checking my watch. "I didn't realize it was so late. I should have been there to meet you."

"I followed a hunch I would find you here." He offered me a paper coffee cup. "Extra milk."

I pointed at the other cup in his hand. "Extra black?"

He tapped it against mine.

"How's the music biz?" I asked with false cheer.

"I've had my big break. I'm writing advert jingles for a carpet store. Impressive, I know. Did your editor like your latest ideas?"

He knew I was searching for a book concept. He did not know that the concept would replace a book about him.

"She did not." I checked in with the seagulls; only two were left. Maybe the girl-gull had decided she was better off alone.

"What are you going to do?"

I slumped against the bench. "Ever thought of writing a romance? I'll pay you more than the carpet store."

"Yeah, I've sampled your work. I'm not mature enough to write like you. And you can joke about my age all you want, I don't even care."

"That is serious," I said, swooning over the way the wind rumpled his dark hair. When he smiled and his eyes crinkled, my hand inched toward his. Instantly, I pulled it back.

"What would help you write? Did you do anything at home which you could do here?"

I quashed a pang as I remembered working across from David at the dining room table or writing quietly with my dad by his fireplace.

"What?" he asked when I sighed.

"I miss my dad," I said, deleting David from my answer. "He's a writer, too, and we write together sometimes."

"What if we work together? I could come here and write music and you could work on your book. It might help us both concentrate."

"It's too far. How long does it take you to drive here from London?"

"I'm not staying in London right now. I sublet my flat to my friend Karine for a few weeks. She split from her boyfriend and needs to find a new place, and I'm pitching in at my dad's. He's right, I've been away too much since Mum passed. I'm now a part-time underling at his medical office and subservient to the whims of a houseful of girls. I'll be glad for the escape."

"It's still a drive from your dad's place to mine."

"It's not bad. I could come down a couple of nights per week. I'm working on lyrics for an album and four carpet store adverts. Besides, every teenage girl in town is at my house most nights. I could use the peace."

"Every teenage girl in town, huh? They must know you're home."

"They're just visiting Wendy and Jenna."

"Uh-huh," I said, unconvinced.

He sighed impatiently. "This offer expires in one minute, Marin. Make your choice."

I hesitated. The idea of having company—of having Sam for company—was so tempting. But could I think up a new book with the inspiration for my old one sitting beside me?

I watched the wind jumble his curls again. Maybe having him there would be a visual reminder of what was at stake.

"It won't inconvenience you?"

"I told you, it will be helpful to me."

"Okay. But only if you promise to stop if it becomes too much trouble."

"Fine."

"Fine," I said, smiling up at him.

He started to smile back but his eyes narrowed. "Wait. I have a condition as well. You are not allowed, at any time, to make bad study group jokes or refer to me as a schoolboy."

"What will we talk about, in that case?" I said, and then he did flash me a grin. "All right, it's a deal."

"Deal." He grabbed my hand to shake it and looked at me in surprise. "Your fingers are freezing." He pinched the sleeve of my jacket. "This is pitifully thin. Come on, let's warm up by your fireplace. We can order in."

"I'm not cold—" I shut up. Sitting by the fire with Sam did sound cozy.

I jogged alongside him as he hurried down the beach.

He took the four steps up to my door in two long strides and looked back to make sure I was behind him.

I couldn't help but laugh. "I've never seen you look so paternal. It's funny that it's—"

"That it's I, the schoolboy, ensuring you don't get hypothermia?"

"No…that it's with me rather than with the five sisters for whom you're actually somewhat responsible." I shut the door against the frosty night. "Fair warning: I'm not above smashing my finger to get some ice cream out of you."

When I turned toward him, he was leaning against the wall, a thoughtful—almost bewildered—look on his face. His head was tipped to the side, like he was listening to a song I couldn't hear. I looked at him curiously and reached for his coat. He smiled, that one corner of his mouth lifting slightly more than the other.

"In this weather? I'd fix you up with a hot chocolate instead."

CHAPTER NINETEEN

I spent the next few weeks at one end of the sofa, struggling along with a new story and pretending I wasn't far more inspired by the guy kicked back at the other end of the couch. Characters can be stubborn, and mine were not cooperating. I was trying so hard to come up with a new leading man or transform Sean into someone else. The new characters were shadows, not strong enough to take shape, and Sean refused to bend into a cavalier playboy who would reform for love or a troubled ex-soldier searching for peace. I couldn't manipulate him into anyone but who I knew Sam to be.

But I started to get it while he wrote beside me. Sam was more than a model for a romantic hero; he was the real thing. It was his casual kindness, his friendly warmth. How he always found just the right words to put me at ease. His reliable presence had infused so much good into my quiet English life. Somehow, he made the leading men I'd been writing for years as flat as the paper on which they were printed.

Working beside him was also intimidating. He was so diligent. I had seen him concentrate for half an hour, tapping his pen on his bottom lip, until his words spilled out in a rush. His letters were nearly all capitals. Precise but not stiff, just like him.

I tried to imitate his quiet focus, but so much of what I came up with fell flat. All my creativity, all the sweet details and whimsical scenes that had once flowed so easily, had dried up. The only thing I could do well was build upon reality—my own and that of the guy beside me. And I was resolute. I would not do that again.

So we wrote together. Or rather, he wrote and I did my best, all while trying to unravel the confusion in my head. How could I create an original story instead of fantasies based on Sam and me? Why was I obsessed with fantasizing about him? Did I really want to have a fling with a guy who might be the same age as the Homecoming Queen?

Also: did he still want to have a fling with me?

"He hasn't moved a fingernail my way since that showdown with David," I told Patricia. "He took one look at that disaster and decided I exceed the baggage allowance."

Patricia snorted. A few weeks earlier, Sam had attended our movie night and she'd fallen for him, too. Like Nandi and Julie, she was all for me making a move.

"What would I do with a gorgeous lad like him?"

"I've read your novels, darling. You know exactly what to do with him."

"Patricia!"

"Oh, don't look so shocked. He's a grown man." She cackled wickedly. "He's an energetic, robust, fully grown man. Besides, your book might flow better if you practice the romance you're trying to preach."

I had a week alone to consider this, since Sam was back in France accompanying his singer friend, Karine. An hour before he arrived for our next writing night, I went hunting in my closet for just the right look. I had come to a conclusion. If Sam was interested in helping me *move on* for the first time since my breakup, I was ready to go for it.

Everyone kept telling me to have a fling. Maybe something out of character was the best thing I could do. Something like have my way with the gorgeous guy who I'd be alone with all evening.

A bit of red caught my eye—Sam's sweater, the one he had given me the night we met. The V at the neck dipped just low enough to show a subtle but healthy hint of cleavage. And...I bent down in front of the mirror. Yes. If it came to it, I could lean over to offer a glimpse of possible things to come.

I envisioned myself doing this and had to fling open the window to huff some cold air.

Could I really follow through with this? Despite how casually I can write bedroom scenes, actually going there with someone is a serious step for me. And it had been six years since I'd even looked at anyone but David that way.

My head snapped up.

Sure, it had been six years for me. But David had just been dog paddling in the public pool. I gripped the windowsill.

Fair enough. It was time for me to jump in, too.

An hour later, Sam shook a few snowflakes from his wool peacoat and stepped inside. The melted drops that clung to him made his dark hair curl. His hand brushed mine when I took his coat. He was close enough for me to smell his soap, warm and spicy, beneath the December chill on his skin.

"Happy Christmas," he said, offering me a paper bag.

Wine. Yes. We were off to a good start.

"Shall I open this?" When his hands gripped the bottle, I imagined it into a suggestive scene: his long fingers holding it steady, the push and pull and turn of the corkscrew. Was it ridiculous? Of course. Could I spin it to make a reader wish she were twisting in his capable hands? Without question.

I dragged my eyes up his arms and across his broad shoulders, lingering on his neck. Was the skin at the base of his throat as soft as it looked? And his lips were perfect. Sculpted. Masculine. Just full enough. When I finally reached his eyes, I jumped. He was looking right at me.

We carried our wine to the living room and I curled up in my corner of the sofa. He sat at the opposite end, as usual, but instead of relaxing, he reached for his bag.

"Did you make progress while I was away?" he asked, flipping through his notebook.

This was disconcerting. I hadn't seen him for days; for some reason, I'd assumed we would take the night off. Also, while plotting my seduction scene, I hadn't factored in a strategy for distracting him from his work. And he was so much more disciplined than me.

"Marin?"

I snapped out of my scheming. "Huh? I mean, yes?"

"Did you have luck with your book? While I was gone?"

"Oh. Yeah. Some. I sent Gretchen an outline and four chapters on Sunday." I reached for my laptop, which wasn't even on.

"What did she say?"

"I haven't heard back, but it's only been a few days." Although, come to think of it, Gretchen had responded to the draft about Sam and me right away.

"I'm sure she's just busy with the holidays," he said when I frowned. "Do you want to test your ideas on me?"

"At this stage, I know not to ask for feedback. Although I appreciate your willingness to critique my work." I paused. "You'll have to be rough with me, you know."

"Of course," he said, but he was bent over his notebook, already concentrating on something other than me.

After an hour of staring at a blank screen, I was ready to scream. I stood up to refill my wine and reached for his as well.

"I'm all right," he said, so I set my glass down, too. He looked up in surprise. "Don't let that stop you."

"No. I don't want to talk nonsense unless you're buzzed, too."

"Nonsense?" He laughed. "I'd quite like to see that. I suspect you're very interesting when you've had too much to drink."

I had a burst of inspiration. "I guess one more drink won't hurt."

Very slowly, I bent to pick up my glass. From where I was standing, directly facing him, he couldn't possibly avoid the peepshow. I counted to three, then booked it to the kitchen and gulped wine straight from the bottle to drown my nerves.

When I finally pushed myself back into the room, Sam was hard at work, staring at his paper like he was concentrating on those few perfect words just out of reach. It's possible that I huffed when I banged down my drink. I mean, really? Was that the best reaction I could inspire?

"Is anything wrong?" He eyed the wine sloshing in my glass. "Are you having trouble getting started? I noticed you haven't typed anything."

Sure, he would notice that. "I'm just restless."

"Can I help?"

You can help. You can look up once in a while and see me trying to turn you on, I wanted to say. I contemplated just being direct with him and couldn't breathe from the terror. Like it or not, I was stuck with the subtle approach.

"Isn't your sister visiting soon?"

This shift in topic—corrupt to innocent—caught me off guard, but I'm always happy to gush about Nandi.

"I'm so excited. She was eight and I was twenty-two when her dad married my mom, but you'd think it was the opposite. She's bossy and blunt and would fight to the death for me. I'm crazy about her."

"She's your stepsister? You never refer to her like that."

"I don't think of her like that. I was an only child for ages, but I asked for a sister every Christmas." I smiled. "I guess you got all my presents."

I rambled about my family, about my mom and Charles and their trips to Zambia, about how I'm so close to my dad. I mentioned he's a writer and left it at that; I usually do. Lots of people have some basic knowledge of *Salt in the Sea*—a vestige of high school English class—but even people who haven't read it somehow know the embarrassing stuff about me.

I paused for breath. "I don't know why I'm talking so much."

That was a lie. I was talking so much because it was far less scary than making a move on him.

"I like hearing you talk about your family," Sam said. "It's interesting to think that you have an entirely separate life from the one you have here."

"Meaning I actually have a life." I pulled at a loose thread on the cuff of my red sweater. Well, his red sweater.

"Are you bored here? Are you ready to go back?"

Snapshots of home ran through my mind. My condo, so cozy during winter with the snow sifted over the skylights and firelight washing over the creamy walls. Alfred snuggled in beside me, warmer than my flannel pajamas. I did miss home. But what about those shadowy versions of David and me lurking around every corner? What about the smears of betrayal all over the bedroom?

"No." I said this too firmly and tried to play it off. "If I went home now, I'd spend three months wading through dirty snow. I'm staying until spring. Besides, this place will be mine soon. It needs to feel like home, too."

Sam grinned when I finally took a long drink of wine.

"Don't look at me like that," I said, laughing over the rim of my glass. "I've been prattling on for thirty minutes. I can have all the wine I want now. I have nothing left to say."

"That's too bad. I was hoping to experience you unfettered by the drink."

And there it was, the perfect opening. If he wanted me unfettered, I was more than willing. I steeled my nerves. All I had to do was reach out and pull him—

He stuffed his notebook into his bag. I bolted upright.

"Are you leaving?"

"No." He looked startled. "Do you want me to leave?"

I settled back against the cushions. "Of course not."

Put away that work and make yourself comfortable, I imagined myself purring like Mrs. Robinson. I had a vision of myself chain-smoking in a leopard-print slip that I promptly shoved from my brain.

No way, Marin. That guilt-complex cocktail you love so much is off the menu tonight.

I closed my eyes to concentrate. If it meant yanking a stocking up my leg, I was going to see this through.

I peeked at him through my lashes, and—finally!—I caught him checking me out, his gaze fixed a few inches south of my face.

About bloody time. I pretended not to look at him as I arched my back—you know, just had myself a little stretch. It was hard not to smile when his eyes widened.

But then down he bent, right back to his bag. I twisted my mouth, genuinely annoyed, until he pulled out a script. He held it low in his lap, like he didn't want me to notice.

I forgave him for not propositioning me, at least long enough to investigate.

"Do I get to know why you're reading that?"

He hesitated before pushing it toward me. A note was scrawled across the title page.

The execs at Porterhall loved the Rochester footage. Nora Maldonado drooled on her suit during the rain scene. She kept a copy of your audition tape. Study up, my leading man. I expect you to get the green light when we see you in L.A.
~ Jordan

"Sam! How long has this been going on?"

"Jordan mentioned it during the Rochester project. I didn't think she meant it."

"The Jordan I met? I doubt she says anything she doesn't mean." He was frowning. "You don't want to do it?"

"It's more that I don't know how. Why would they choose me when I have so little experience?"

"You must be good at it. Jordan wouldn't have suggested it otherwise."

That something in his face hinting that there was more to Sam and Jordan was back. I decided to take a backroad to the heart of this mystery, throwing out a feeler to test his reaction.

"You may think Jordan is doing this because she wants to sleep with you—" Sam's head snapped up. "—but she wouldn't risk her reputation without knowing you'd be great in the film."

"How do you know that about Jordan?" he demanded.

"Please. You were all she talked about at the wrap party. I won't get into specifics, but you can trust her to handle your PR." Sam rubbed his fingers over his face. "What else is worrying you?"

He hesitated. "It films in Vancouver in May for thirteen weeks."

"Vancouver is a gorgeous city." And maybe he can swing through Chicago on his way, I found myself thinking.

"It's a long time to be away from the girls. My father will never let it drop, and his constant discussion about my life choices makes me long for the silence of my flat."

"Your dad doesn't support your acting?" His expression answered for him. "What about your music?"

"He thinks the entertainment industry is comprised of narcissists and drug addicts."

"Sunshiny. What's he want you to do?"

His entire body slumped into the couch.

"He's a surgeon, like his father. That his only son prefers songwriting to scalpels is a blow he can't forgive. He tends to throw my irresponsible youth in my face as evidence that acting will surely be my next mistake. I've sorted my priorities, but it seems he'll refuse to see that until I pursue work he respects."

"Stick to your plan. There's nothing worse than doing a job you hate." When he didn't answer, I let it drop and turned back to Jordan's note. "Hey, what does Jordan mean, this thing about a rain scene? There was no rain scene in my book."

I glanced up in time to see him shade his eyes behind his hand. His face was flushed.

"Oh, there is a story here," I sang. I scooted closer and gave him his glass. "Take a big drink and tell me all about it."

"You might not like it, you know. I didn't. It goes against the integrity of the story."

"See, you're already talking like a film professional. You'll be fine." I gripped his arm. "Now tell me about the scene that made some woman ruin her suit."

He looked down with a shy smile. He truly was the most adorable man.

"It started as a stupid joke. I was in period costume, wearing a puffed-up white shirt and the tight breeches with tall boots. I looked completely ridiculous."

I laughed for his sake, but I was already picturing it. Oh, Lord. Sam in Mr. Rochester's clothes. It could not get better.

"Well, I'm in the makeup trailer wearing this absurd

outfit, having my hair doused with what smelled like loo spray, when someone mentioned that the white shirt looked like one Colin Firth wore in *Pride and Prejudice*. Suddenly the entire crew starts nattering about some wet shirt scene and how it's the most incredible moment ever captured on film."

"They're right," I said seriously.

"You know the wet shirt scene?"

"Know it? Are you kidding?" I smiled. "Since you're telling me something you consider embarrassing, I'll tell you a secret of mine, if you want."

"A secret of yours? Of course." He tilted his head toward me. He most certainly did not smell like loo freshener anymore. He smelled so good that I leaned in.

"I have a photo of that wet white shirt, appropriately filled with a wet Colin Firth, pinned to the wall in my office at home. A romance novelist needs tools that encourage a certain mood."

"Really? Who else is pinned to your wall?"

"Nope, that's enough about me. Finish your story. The wet white shirt…"

His heavy sigh was more like a groan.

"So while everyone is rabbiting on about the scene, in comes Jordan. She decides on the spot that we need a wet shirt scene."

"I'll bet she did." I let my eyes drift over those abs I'd once glimpsed. "I'm sure the makeup team thought it was a fabulous idea."

"I thought they were going to spray me down where I sat. In the scene, I come upon Hailey—do you remember the girl who plays Anne?—sheltering beneath a tree during a storm. I take off my jacket, gentleman-like, and after hours of hoses and humiliating close-ups, Jordan got her wet shirt scene."

I fought off the urge to lick my lips. "When does this thing air again? I may need another wet shirt inspiration."

"Very funny."

"I'm not joking. I bet girls will tape your photo to walls all over the world."

He threw his head back against the sofa. "I feel so cheap."

"Just think, when you get this new role and Jordan has her way with you—"

"Jordan will not have her way with me."

"Whatever you say."

"You think I can't stand my ground with Jordan?" He cocked an eyebrow at me. "How do you suppose I spent my summer?"

"Ha! I was right. She did put the moves on you."

"And I resisted her. I behaved impeccably throughout the shoot."

I was suddenly ecstatic, but I tried to hide my glee by teasing him.

"Sure, you behaved impeccably working with public television. We're talking about the seductive powers of Hollywood now. Soon, you'll start calling everyone 'baby' and wearing sunglasses indoors. But probably Nora Maldonado will buy you a Porsche. Don't worry, Sam. You'll make an excellent addition to the Hollywood scene." I looked at him slyly. "And I know you'll make an exceptional plaything for Jordan or Nora—"

He snatched a throw pillow and pummeled me. I shrieked and backtracked toward my corner.

"Aren't you clever," he said, laughing as he whomped

me until I collapsed. I pressed my hand to his chest, pretending to keep his playful blows at bay while working up the nerve to pull him toward me. He knelt above me on the sofa with his knees on either side of mine and raised the pillow over his head. His shirt slid up enough for me to glimpse the waistband of his blue boxer shorts and the muscles at his waist.

He gave me a mock glare as he held the pillow above me. "Do you take it back?"

I let my lips curve deviously and slowly shook my head.

And then he launched himself at me, holding the pillow against my face. When he tossed it aside, his own face was inches away, his body pressed along mine. Our laughter faded as we looked at each other. I felt a little dizzy from how close he was, by how warm he felt and how good he smelled. My gaze flickered from his eyes to his mouth. A tiny scar cut across one corner of his lips that I had never been near enough to see.

But I lifted my eyes to his and was surprised by how solemnly he studied me. My palm was pinned against his chest. I could feel his heart beating, beating like I was holding it. And I can't explain it, why I suddenly felt like crying, why his weight against me seemed like an indictment.

I wanted so badly to slide my hands around him. All night, I'd been trying to orchestrate this moment, but when it mattered most, I turned to stone. Our chests, pressed together, rose and fell in sync. I may only have imagined him coming toward me, but my breath caught in my throat.

And then he was gone, back in his corner of the sofa and not looking at me. I sat up, pulsing with disappointment and—ugh, of all things—relief. I kept my face blank like I wasn't affected. Sam's voice was perfectly calm when he spoke.

"The audition may come to nothing. I'm flying to Los Angeles on Sunday and right back on Tuesday. If they were interested, I think they'd have me stay longer."

He began packing up his bag. This time I didn't protest. I walked him to the foyer and watched him pull on his coat. When he opened the door, a few snowflakes swirled in.

Halfway down the steps, he paused.

"I meant to tell you earlier. My jumper looks nice on you."

I looked down at his sweater, then back up at him, but he had already passed through the gate.

CHAPTER TWENTY

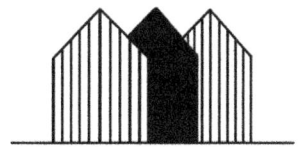

I can't believe you met someone three weeks ago and didn't mention it until now," I told Patricia as we refilled the popcorn bowl during a special holiday movie night. "All your talk about my love life! Meanwhile, your own affair was burning up the phone!"

"We prefer email," Patricia said, queuing up *It's a Wonderful Life*. "It's that Boston accent. I shudder a bit at the nasal short A."

"Does he come here a lot on business? I'll help out at the shop if you want a romantic getaway."

"We'll see. It's strange to consider traveling with a man who isn't Isaac. But that's one of the things Tom and I discuss, the guilt of moving on after a spouse dies. Maybe I was too quick to urge you into something with Sam. Six years of history with your fiancé would be hard to leave behind."

"Losing a milk-livered cheater is hardly the same thing as losing a faithful husband. And as we know, my experiment with Sam was a failure."

Sam had joined us earlier that evening for *White Christmas* and despite our last meeting, things weren't too awkward between us. But he didn't stay for the double feature, and I had filled Patricia in on the drama shortly after he left.

"Trust you to assume that him backing away means he's uninterested," she grunted.

"Should I assume he was just overwhelmed by my charm?"

"I'd at least consider the possibility."

"How many young guys would run away from a girl they like? A girl who is obviously putting it out there?" I wrinkled my nose. "I'm using 'girl' as a euphemism for crone, by the way, which is exactly why he ran away from me."

"If you're a crone, I'm a ruin. You're too polite to say that about me, so mind your metaphors. You're right, a boy interested in only one thing wouldn't back away. But a man interested in how his actions affect you would. And what about how he treats you makes you think he's the first type?" A smug smile took over her face when I didn't answer. "Like you said, he hasn't made a move since he witnessed your argument with David—since he realized how deeply you'd been hurt. What if he's giving you space to decide you're ready?"

I could feel her gloating as I considered this. "You and your mystic, mind-reading voodoo," I grumbled.

"Never mind that, I know you want to believe me." That smug smile bloomed into a wicked grin. "Of course, if you'd rather tell yourself he thinks of you as a piece of tail…"

Our hysterics carried us through the opening credits.

"No one I know shocks me like you do," I said, tossing a kernel of popcorn at her gleeful face. "Look for yourself in a forthcoming Mariana Rose book."

I considered Patricia's words over the next couple of days while preparing for my sister's visit. A Christmas blizzard in Chicago delayed her flight, so the plane that should have arrived at two in the afternoon on the 26th was bumped to four-thirty a.m. on the 27th. When Sam called to congratulate me on my first Boxing Day in decades, he offered me dinner and a place to sleep at his flat to shorten the early morning drive the next day.

"You're staying the night with him?" Nandi yelped when I told her the plan. "I've been praying for this!"

"You know it's not like that. If your flight lands at four-thirty, I'd have to leave my house crazy early to pick you up. I'm just lucky he's living in London again."

"Whatever, you totally want him. Misbehave! Misbehave!"

Her chant echoed in my ears as I drove to his place, but I was in no hurry to throw myself at him after the last fiasco.

"You have the glow of someone kissed by the California sun," I told him when he answered his door.

"I don't know why. I spent most of the trip in one room, auditioning. Or as I like to call it, pretending to know what I'm doing."

I tapped his arm as we settled onto his couch. "But you got the part. That's huge! And you're smiling about it, which is an improvement."

"I'm getting used to the idea. My sisters went mad when I told them. Wendy and Jenna are already listing the celebrities they want to date. They don't seem to hear me when I tell them it's a small film."

"How did your dad take the news?"

"So well that I immediately moved back here. Along with his usual commentary—I'm chasing piecemeal work that will never pay; so few artists succeed, why should I?—he told me I'm shirking responsibility to my sisters and reminded me of my mother's wish that I finish university."

"Ouch." I glanced at his tense face. "What did you say?"

"Nothing I should repeat. But Amy jumped in and reminded Dad that our mum encouraged us to take risks and would've been excited for me. She told me that if I sacrifice the opportunity out of duty to them, I would be shirking responsibility to myself."

"If I ever figure out how to write again, I'm naming a character after Amy."

"Isn't there an Amy in *Wanderlust?* No, wait. Her name was Anna."

"What do you know about *Wanderlust?*"

"Oh, I'm building a whole Mariana Rose library." He pulled a handful of books off a nearby shelf. "I've finished *Mistress Marigold, Never Ever After, Harmony Moon*...I'm half through *The Tempting of the Shrew*."

He laughed without compassion as I squirmed.

"What? I love them. They're the most entertaining romance novels I've ever read."

"They're the only romance novels you've ever read."

"Regardless, I'm sure they rank among the best. Why do you do that, act so embarrassed? What's so embarrassing about your books?"

"It's fictional voyeurism. Plus, when you write steamy novels, some people assume you're promiscuous."

His teasing smile vanished. "Did someone really call you that?"

"Plenty of people insinuate it. David was always getting sly comments from his colleagues. 'That's the kind of academic research one can *get behind*, eh, Professor?'"

Sam narrowed his eyes. "How did David respond?"

"Most of the time he set them straight. Once or twice, he played along."

"Wanker. He should have knocked them flat."

I shrugged. "I'm used to it. There's such a pretentious hierarchy with writing. Some books count, some books don't."

"What do you mean?"

"You know, literary versus commercial versus escapist fiction. I won't debate the validity of the labels. But the stereotype about steamy romance novels is that they're just for getting people off."

"Is that your opinion?"

"Of course not. They're not *Great Expectations*, but they're not trying to be. They're fun." I shrugged. "It's probably worse for me because my dad is a literary writer. I grew up hearing those debates. That's why I use a pen name. Most scholarly types would find it ironic that his offspring possesses such questionable taste."

"They would think that, or you think that?"

Hmm. Another moment where he'd seen into my soul. And I had a feeling my face had given me away.

"Okay, sometimes I do think it. *The Young Edward Rochester* is the only book I've written that didn't get mocked."

"Mocked by whom, critics?"

"Critics don't bother with my books. But my mom thinks they're a waste of space. David implied regularly that I'm not living up to my potential. And his colleagues…well. Which book do you think was the joke at every English department gathering we went to for six years—*A Critical Heritage of Geoffrey Chaucer* or *High Tea and Heartache*?"

"That proves what a great lot of idiots they are. Chaucer is far raunchier than any book of yours I've read. Besides, what those plonkers think is irrelevant. If you like what you write, and you have fun whilst you're writing it, why stop? Why should you try to be someone you're not?"

The minute he spoke, I felt something shift. Like the earth and I had been out of balance, but we'd rotated a click and locked into place.

Do you know those little square puzzles with tiles that slide around to make a picture? For months, I had been sliding around my various ideas, forcing them into pictures that didn't quite fit. But the missing tile—the one that kept the others knocking against each other, the one that sealed the picture tight when it was slipped into place—was the truth in Sam's statement: I had been trying to be someone I'm not. And not just by writing in a style that wasn't truly what I loved, but by doubting that love was worth writing about.

I felt a familiar flash of revelation. I'd caught something that had been hovering just out of reach until I was ready to see it. All the efforts I'd made to create something literary, something less likely to be dismissed as fluff and brushed aside—all those pretenses cracked like cheap veneer. When my jumble of pride and self-doubt fell away, I found the source of the stories I loved to write, stories that celebrated the importance of love.

And Sam was the one who had made that clear.

I eyed the handsome guy in front of me—casual with a subtle, arty edge—as he stacked my books back on his shelf. My mind filled with reminders of how constant he'd been with me. Bandaging my knee the day we met. Writing beside me to help me focus for weeks. Kissing only my forehead after our no-pressure date.

Patricia was right. He had been giving me space.

He used the tip of his finger to straighten *Mistress Marigold* on his shelf. Something warm in my chest began to glow.

"I'll show you to the bedroom," he said, grabbing my overnight bag.

I followed him down the hall, breathless but energized. I was ready. I was finally ready to meet him all the way.

I was ready right up to the moment that he swung open the door to reveal lingerie scattered all over his bedroom: littering the floor, tumbled onto the bed, and mixed into a pile with his blue boxer shorts.

CHAPTER TWENTY-ONE

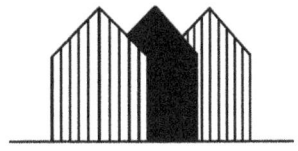

"Then he shoved her lingerie and his own underwear into the same drawer, along with the condoms and birth control pills on the nightstand. In other words, not only is Sam living with Karine, their underwear and contraceptives are cohabitating as well."

Nandi held up a cropped sweater she'd brought from home.

"Nothing that laces around my bare stomach like a ballet slipper, thanks." I had agreed to let her dress me for the informal party she'd badgered me into hosting, but I would not be wearing that. "This whole thing is pointless anyway. I could wear your stupid *You Wish* sweatpants tonight and no one would care."

Nandi grinned. "You like them, don't lie. I saw them in your laundry basket the day I got here." She pinned a sparkly black top to my shoulders. "This will tempt him."

"Did you hear anything I just said?"

"I've heard it all week. I still don't care. Maybe he was doing laundry. Maybe he's just a slob."

"Maybe he's dating a sexy chanteuse."

"You're impossible," she said, but she paused. "When you walked in and saw the lingerie, what did he actually say?"

"He said, 'I told Karine to clean up before she left.' But there's one bed in the whole place. *Half* a strip of condoms was on the nightstand next to it. The underwear—his and hers—was sprinkled generously throughout the room until he stuffed it into the same drawer. What would you think?"

She scrunched her nose as she weighed it out. "Well, fresh starts are the point of New Year's Eve. Tonight is the perfect time to change his mind. You have to try, Mare. That face and those shoulders and his exemplary hindparts? He is delectable."

"Did I mention she's French? She's an edgy, young, French singer-songwriter and she lives in his bed."

"Marin, please shut up. Distract yourself with visions of the beautiful babies you two will make when this works," she said, holding one of her own skirts up to my waist.

"Nandila, get serious. On me, your skirt is a Post-It Note."

She threw it on the bed in disgust. "I hate being short."

"'Diminutive person, explosive personality,'" I said, quoting her dad in a decent imitation of his Zambian accent while she offered me a scrap of deep blue silk. It looked like it might not expose my entire chest if I held it shut all night. "No way."

"Why not?"

"Because it's cut down to the belly button, that's why not."

"It's not as revealing when it's on."

She was right. The top draped so that it showed off a

little but left enough to the imagination. I'd worried it might seem like I was trying to look twenty-two. Instead, I looked like the polished version of myself.

"Again, this is Chinese takeout in my own house. Not necessary," I said, but my protests were waning.

"I'll do your hair in pin-up girl waves. You'll look just like Veronica Lake." Nandi fired her sharpest arrow at my weakest point. Me as classic film star? Check.

"Okay, I'll wear it. With a real skirt of my own." My sister scowled, but when I had on my sleekest pencil skirt, even she looked happy.

"Perfect," she said. "Tonight, be your funny, sexy self. That other girl is French toast."

"Stay until midnight. Just a few more minutes," I said, but Patricia slipped on her coat.

"The year has already dawned over most places I've lived. Let's say I celebrated on Crete time." She draped on a scarf and put her hand on my arm. "Thanks for a lovely evening."

"I'll walk you out," I said, grabbing my sweater from its hook by the door. I made it halfway down the steps before shivering and darting back. Sam was already there, holding out his wool coat for me.

"Saw that coming, did you?" I laughed as I slipped it on.

He tossed me a hat that I struggled up through the sleeves to catch. "Stay warm."

Patricia was waiting on the bottom step. As I reached

her, Sam's phone rang in his coat pocket. My heart sank when I read the screen: Karine.

Through Nandi-acquired intel, I knew Karine was singing at a party in London. She was probably gearing up for a sultry rendition of "Auld Lang Syne." Had she called with a promise to ring Sam's year in right?

For the second time, I climbed the steps. "Sam," I called, coloring my voice with false cheer. I pressed his phone into his palm without looking back.

Patricia took my arm as we walked to her car. I forced some spring into my step.

"So, movie night at my place this week. What do you say to pizza and Humphrey Bogart?"

"It's no good, my girl."

"The pizza or Bogart? Maybe Gregory Peck?"

"I'll always take Peck, but that's not what I mean. You know better than to pretend with me. What just dampened your New Year's spirit? Who was that on the phone?"

I looked away.

"Marin, I don't meddle often, so listen closely. I can't say what's between Sam and this other girl, but that man cares a great deal for you."

"I know he does. He's wonderful to me. But he's just my friend."

"Pffff," was her eloquent response.

"Patricia, he's living with that girl. His condoms are seducing her birth control pills as we speak."

"Shall I remind you of what happens when one assumes?" She rolled her eyes at me. "I've been watching him. If that's how it is between them, then he's trying to convince himself it's what he wants. I won't guess at guff, but I'd say he loves you. He's just not certain you can handle that news."

I carelessly gripped the frosty wrought iron fence. My clammy hands stung when I jerked them away. "You can't love someone you've only known for three months."

"Maybe you can't. Don't presume to know whether he can." Beneath the sleeve of Sam's coat, her hand found mine. "I've been watching you, too. You're terrified to let him know that you care as you do. I know this because you're warm and welcoming with everyone, Sam included. But when anyone hints at something deeper between you—and you can thank your Nandi for hinting nonstop—you lose all your sparkle. You could be listening to a fly buzz in the background for all that your face shows you care."

A hot tear streaked down my cheek. Patricia squeezed my hand. She may be tough, but she's also kind.

"You're braver than you let yourself believe, Marin. What you are is better than fearless. You act in spite of your fear. You wouldn't be in England right now if that weren't true."

I considered this. Throughout my time in Seasalter, I had felt like a coward, like I'd run away from everything wrong in my life. It had never occurred to me that choosing to leave was the bravest path to making things right.

It was an encouraging idea, but it could wait.

"Why do you think he—" My throat was closing; I had to swallow. "Do you really think he loves me? Are you reading his voice?"

My own voice sounded childish and thin. Patricia smiled at me.

"I'm reading his actions. The way he feels about you is evident in everything he does. You don't need special training or mystic skills to perceive it. Just open your eyes and accept what you see."

"He's inside talking to Karine right now. What if I show him how I feel and it doesn't matter?"

"Then you'll know," she said simply. "But I wouldn't worry. What young man who looks like that has no plans for New Year's Eve? Something tells me he did some schedule surgery to be here on such short notice."

Patricia started her car and glanced at the dashboard clock. "Look at that. I stayed to see the old year go out after all. And now…" She lifted her eyebrows significantly. "In with the new."

She drove off, honking the horn once as if to punctuate this thought. I watched her taillights shrink in the darkness as I lingered outside. Laughter drifted up from a house down the beach. In a window, two people embraced, their silhouettes one fluid shape against the amber lights inside.

My lungs shook as I inhaled, but my breath held steady when I pushed it out. The warm air hit the cold night in steamy swirls. I watched them writhe upward and vanish, pretending as I did that they were all my doubts and fears and failures, my suspicion that love always gives way to selfishness. I exhaled until I was empty. Then I pulled in one breath, sharp and clean, and turned to go inside.

Nandi was peering out the window in the foyer. She opened the door for me.

"You missed the big moment. Are you okay?"

I wiped at my wet cheeks. "Do I look that terrible?"

She dabbed at my eyes with a napkin. "Much better. Now you only look cold. Good thing you had someone's big coat to keep you warm," she said with a smirk as I hung up Sam's peacoat.

"Where is he?"

"Phone," she said, gesturing toward the kitchen. She handed me her empty glass. "Here. I need a refill and Sam needs a reminder that you're waiting for your New Year's kiss."

"What am I going to do for entertainment once you leave?"

"I can think of something. I'll make suggestions to both of you if you don't take care of it yourselves." She gave me a friendly shove. "Get going, Marc. I'm parched."

Sam was leaning against the refrigerator. He smiled as I passed him on my way to the sink. "It will be rather late when I get in," he said jovially.

Were they making plans for a New Year's frolic? I tried not to think about it. Instead I rinsed Nandi's glass and focused on what Patricia had said. If he cared for me as much as she thought, maybe this Karine thing was just a hiccup.

"I'll see you then. Happy New Year," he said. And then he murmured, "I love you, too."

Nandi's glass nearly slipped from my hand.

Thank God I had my back to him. What with the wind getting knocked out of me and the new hole in my chest, it was suddenly impossible to breathe.

Keep it together, I thought, grasping desperately for Patricia's words. Face blank. Flies buzzing—

Sam touched my arm. "Here's a special New Year's song for you." He held out his phone.

I glanced up at him. I wasn't quick enough to hide the hurt in my eyes, and I could tell that he saw it when his forehead wrinkled.

"What's wrong—" he began, but I cut him off, jerking

my arm from his grasp. He looked shocked, but I didn't care. I snatched the phone from his hand and turned my back on him as I barked a hello.

"Marin! See how late it is? And I'm not even a little bit tired! And Happy New Year!"

I had been gripping the countertop with white knuckles. I sank against it when Lily's clear voice rang out.

"Happy New Year." My words were weak. I felt rather than saw Sam cross the room. When I peeked at him, his back was to me. He was staring into the garden.

"We learned a new song tonight. Because it's a whole new year, did you know that? I can sing it for you now, listen!"

I was ashamed, that it was "Auld Lang Syne." That song, with the lyrics mixed up and her voice so sweet, and Sam hurt and confused by how angrily I'd turned away…it all blended with Patricia's perceptive advice and Nandi's meddling insistence and my own obsessive need for caution despite the longing I felt. All of it shifted and mingled with Lily's song until I finally, *finally* got over myself.

"That was so pretty, Lily," I said when she'd finished, as another hot tear spilled down my cheek. "I've never heard anyone sing that song so well."

"Thank you. My daddy says I must go to sleep. And he says I should tell you to have a happy New Year and to hang up the phone this instant. And Ella would tell you as well but she's been asleep for ages." The receiver rattled as she tried to hang up. Her giggles only ended when she succeeded.

Sam's phone dangled from my limp hand. I turned toward him. He was standing at the French doors, arms crossed grimly as he stared outside.

I didn't need to summon my courage at all.

I set his phone on the counter with a quiet smack. I crossed the room and, without looking at him, took his hand in my own. I didn't say a word when I pulled him outside. The cold air surrounded us, but I barely felt it. I led him into the darkest corner of the back garden, where only the moon gleamed through the hedges, and I made sure to look at him, really look into his eyes, before I stood on my toes and pulled his face toward mine.

For those first few seconds that I pressed my lips to his, he seemed uncertain, his fingertips hesitant on my back. But when I slid my other hand up his chest to slip my arms around his neck, he relaxed into me. He wrapped one arm around my waist and cradled my head in his other hand, twisting his fingers in my hair in a way that caused my heart to skip.

I kissed him for all the times I had wanted to but couldn't bring myself to try, and for all the times I'd told myself it was something I should never do. I kissed him like I had things to tell him—kissed him slowly for his patience, softly for being so gentle, deeply for how persistently he'd pushed through the walls I'd built. And when it was over, that long first kiss, I kissed him once more, to prove to him I meant it.

I took one step back but Sam didn't let go. He kept his arm tight around me and studied my face.

"I thought you were angry with me," he said at last.

"Maybe you should be angry with me."

He shifted closer to me again. "Why would I ever be angry about a kiss like that?"

"Well, I shouldn't have..." The moon slid from behind a cloud and highlighted the smile playing on his lips. As if pulled by a tide, I leaned in again, then summoned some willpower and held myself back. "I shouldn't have kissed you while you're seeing Karine."

"Karine? I'm not seeing Karine."

Hope flung itself against me, but—hey, I knew what I'd seen.

"You're living with her. Her underwear was all over your bedroom the other day."

"True, and I'm sorry about that. I asked her to clean up for you before she left for her new flat. I told you that."

"You never said she was leaving for her new flat. I would remember, believe me."

"Believe *me*, I remember telling you. I made it a point to let you know she was leaving for the new gaff so you would know she was moving out."

"The new gaff?"

"Yeah, the new gaff. Her new place. She was moving out that day."

"Gaff means apartment? I assumed it was one of the hipster bars you all play. Well, I didn't know!" I yelped when he practically doubled over. "You're not living with Karine? You're not dating her?"

"I am not dating her. In fact, Karine is desperately trying to get you to date me. She told me later she left all those things out intentionally. Her plan was to drive you to me by making you jealous. Because she knew that I'd become rather certain you weren't interested in me."

"You thought that?" I laughed incredulously, but his solemn expression stopped me. "You thought I wasn't interested in you?"

"Marin, you're beautiful and intelligent and accomplished. You've published how many novels? You own your flat in Chicago and you're purchasing a second home here." He shrugged. "I dropped out of university and serve kale to pay the rent."

That's how he saw me? A woman so attractive her fiancé had taken up with someone else? An unknown author of books disparaged as bodice-rippers and then dismissed? And as for how he saw himself…I wanted to tell him how wrong he was, but he went on before I could.

"At times, I doubted you wanted me around at all."

"When have I ever given you that impression?"

"Perhaps the morning of the girls' school festival? Just days after what I thought was a rather nice date, it appeared you'd forgotten me altogether," he said with a rueful smile.

I looked at the ground. Of course I hadn't told Sam why I'd forgotten the festival—that David had ambushed me the night before. I had never considered how my apparent thoughtlessness might have made him feel.

"Or a few weeks later," he went on. "We'd planned to have dinner, but you weren't even home. When I found you on the beach, you seemed disappointed to see me."

"What?" All I remembered was how my heart had fluttered as he'd walked toward me.

And, a voice uncomfortably like Patricia's reminded me, the way you pretended your heart didn't flutter. The way you pretended it didn't mean anything.

The way I'd pretended that none of it meant anything. Not Karine, or Nandi's suggestive comments, or anything else that might end in me getting hurt.

Sam's face was so earnest and open. It wasn't hard to see the hurt in his eyes. I slid my arms around his neck.

"I'm sorry. I never meant for you to think I didn't care.

But you were so reserved with me, I thought you'd changed your mind."

"I've been chasing you like a teenage boy and you thought I'd changed my mind?"

"I thought the horror of a certain egomaniac showing up at my door ran you off. It would have sent me running." Then I snickered at him. "Besides, you might be a teenage boy for all I know."

He hummed impertinently. "You should not have said that. I was quite prepared to reveal my age, but now I'm keeping it to myself to spite you."

"What? That's completely unfair. I've more than proven it doesn't matter anymore." Some instinct told me grumbling would do less good than flirting, so I lowered my lashes à la Scarlett O'Hara and glanced up at him, mentally apologizing to the Indigo Girls and feminists everywhere as I did. "Come on. Tell me."

"I don't think I will," he said, unmoved. "I'll wait until I'm indispensable."

"You're going to drive me crazy with that," I huffed, and he laughed under his breath.

"That's fair. You've been making me crazy for weeks."

He pulled my hand to his mouth and kissed the inside of my wrist. My mouth popped open when his tongue swirled against my skin.

Could he feel my pulse stuttering beneath his lips? When he did the tongue thing again, I gasped out loud.

Holy smokes. I might not be able to handle this new side of Sam.

He tipped my head to the side and trailed his lips across my neck. And it's a good thing I inhaled sharply when he did. For a few seconds, I wasn't sure I would ever breathe again.

When I could speak, I said, "If you hadn't changed your mind, why have you been so hands-off with me this whole time? That's not very teenage-boy of you."

"I wanted you to make the first move." He let my hair fall to cover my neck and pulled back to look at me. "You were going through a lot. I didn't want to pressure you."

"What about that night after you got back from France? I put on an embarrassingly obvious show to get your attention and you hardly noticed."

"Trust me, I noticed you. I was distant for your protection." He moved toward my neck again but I touched my hand to his chest.

"But I was trying to make the first move. What about later, on the couch? Why did you run away from me?"

I didn't realize I was frowning until he smoothed his finger across my forehead.

"Do you know that phrase about the rabbit caught in the headlights?" he asked, and I couldn't help but smile.

"Sort of." Maybe the deer in England are exceptionally brave.

"That doesn't begin to describe the look on your face. I was quite upset with myself. That's why I left so early."

After all my attempts to manipulate him that night, he had worried that he'd pressured me? This realization made me bite my lip.

Maybe he misread my guilt as regret and wanted to redo the moment that had passed. Maybe he was making up for lost time. He put his hands on my hips and pulled me toward him until our faces were inches apart. The air between us tingled. And like that night a few weeks earlier, I let my eyes leave his long enough to study the little scar on his lips.

When I leaned in, I started at that corner, pressing my mouth to the faint line cutting diagonally across his lips. I let myself linger in that one spot, holding his face with both hands. He held still while I placed small, slow kisses from one corner of his mouth to the other. But when I slipped my arms around his neck, he drew me in, running his fingers through my hair in what I would learn was his signature move. I smelled the salt in the cold air, tasted salt on his skin. And, typical for me that night, a salty tear splashed down my face.

He caught it as his mouth moved over my cheek and jerked away. "Are you all right?"

"Yes," I said with a noisy sniff. "I'm just happy."

CHAPTER TWENTY-TWO

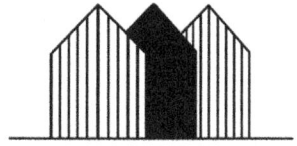

Genevieve Chevalier had been an official Mariana Rose character for a mere six pages before she was rendered unconscious by a runaway carriage. One page later, her violet eyes blinked open beneath crimson drapes suspended from an unfamiliar bed. Her diaphanous chemise swirled around her bare feet as she tripped to the chamber door. Locked.

And then she spied it. Baudelaire's sword, gouged into the floor. A warning against escape.

Genevieve allowed herself ten seconds of silent terror before summoning the Chevalier courage that ran through her veins. She'd just pulled back a heavy wall tapestry to reveal a secret staircase when Sam's voice echoed through the turret.

"Do you know what I think?"

The gloomy castle evaporated into my airy seaside living room. I looked up to see him toss his notebook aside. He slid toward my end of the couch with a certain look on his face.

After Nandi left for Chicago that morning, Sam and I had made a pact to spend our first day alone since New Year's Eve immersed in our work. For once, however, my writing partner was the less diligent member of our study group. And while I was finally inspired to throw myself into writing my new book, an undisciplined Sam was hard to resist.

"I think you are very sexy when absorbed in your work. It's lucky you had that writer's block. Had you been writing like this all along, nothing would've stopped me from making my move."

"What move is that?" I pressed myself long against the couch cushions so he could stretch out beside me.

"This one," he said, pulling me against him. And for a while, the room was void of idle chatter.

"You know the best thing about dating a teenage boy?" I said several minutes later. "I get to make out on the couch like I'm a teenager. I only hope my parents don't catch us."

Sam laughed but pushed himself up.

"I'm joking. My parents won't be home for hours." I reached for him again, but he pulled me upright.

"I promised to let you work. I've done a poor job of it thus far."

I glanced at my laptop. The cursor blinked an urgent message: Hello? Critical deadline?

Sam kicked at his gym bag. "I suppose I could go for a run. Would you lend me your shower when I return?"

Remember those taut abs I had glimpsed awhile back? Yeah, so did I. I ran my hand over his shirt to appreciate them.

"I don't know, Sam. I might not be able to keep a respectable distance."

"What is a respectable distance?" He dropped back onto the sofa, pulling me down with him. "Is this respectable? Because I think this is respectable." And the room grew quiet for a few minutes more.

My laptop beeped as it went to sleep. Sam heaved himself up with a sigh.

"Right. I'm definitely going for a run."

"Yeah. I'm definitely going to get some work done." I woke up my neglected computer, the cursor of which flashed furiously as I smoothed my hair into place.

The abs gleamed when Sam straightened his shirt. I traced one finger across them, one last time.

His hot gaze met mine. We tumbled back into the couch.

My laptop bleeped indignantly.

Consider it research, I told it as the screen went dark.

The muscles at his waist were especially impressive. My lips left his long enough to whisper in his ear. "What are these things called, anyway?"

Sam pulled in an unsteady breath. "Obliques," I heard him gasp.

It started as a hum in my ear, a mosquito's whine that grew more insistent the harder I ignored it. I pretended not to notice when my palms began to sweat. When my heart slammed against my ribs, I was forced to pay attention.

"Don't."

The word was small in the back of my throat, but it swelled until I could barely breathe. I felt sure I had yelled it, but the sound was a bubble bursting.

Sam didn't hear me. He was whispering in my ear, words that were lost in the roar of my thoughts. Moments before, I had pulled him close. In the shift that followed, through the sirens blaring in my head, I heard one distinct message: push him off. When he slid his hand around me to grasp the small of my back, my own hands moved to his shoulders. I shoved him as hard as I could.

He shot up. I rolled away, tugging the sheet along with me. My throat hit the edge of the mattress. The air I sucked in was so dry that I choked.

"Are you all right?"

I couldn't find the breath to speak. First my lungs and then the rest of me lurched off the bed to let in the breeze off the beach.

My bare feet touched down. My legs crumpled beneath me. I watched the knots in the floorboards rush toward my face. Sam stumbled off the bed and caught me before I hit.

"What do you need?"

"Air." The word scraped its way up my throat. I wobbled so much when I tried to stand that he half-lifted me onto the bed before shoving open every window.

The January afternoon poured in, cold and clean and full of light. I took a grateful gulp. The salty wind should've cleared my head. Instead, it began to spin as reality tangled with my memories. Resting my face on my arm, I caught the faint rose fragrance of my own perfume, but beneath it was something cloying and melon, a saccharine scent smeared so deeply into my bed at home that I could still smell it after I'd burned the sheets. A new white sheet that covered me where I lay, whisper-soft and powder-fine, as gentle as the hand stroking over my back. As gentle as a hand that had held mine for years, that had slid down another girl's glowing skin, had run through that girl's shining hair.

I gasped again and my chest seized up.

I'm having a heart attack, I thought, as my lungs strained against my breastbone. A blast of pain sliced down my side. In the back of my mind, I heard myself say, I'm going to die. I'm dying.

I'm dying.

The phrase was too familiar to mistake for my own.

I'm dying. Isobel, I think I'm dying.

How many nights had I woken to those words? Across the hall from my room in the Seasalter house, warm light and ragged whispers had spilled from beneath my parents' door. In South Carolina, my dad's frantic pacing had made the floorboards of my grandparents' farmhouse creak. The strangled cries that echoed through our first year in Chicago, through the last brutal months of my parents' rotting marriage. And later, when I was the only one left to hold his hand: *I'm dying, Mariana, I'm dying.*

It was worse than a heart attack. It was panic. I began to shake.

Static crackled off the flannel backing of the pillow I yanked toward me—the companion piece my grandmother had done to match my favorite, now-tainted quilt. My fingers searched the bumpy surface, read the hand-stitched patterns I knew by heart. French knots, lazy daisies…there. The smooth embroidered strawberries that filled my favorite square, that had once edged the hem of my favorite sundress. At six years old, while my world had pitched and rolled beneath me, I'd clutched that hem in my sweaty hand until the salt had made the strawberries bleed.

A slow breath in. A slow breath out. One at a time. You won't run out.

My parents and I had made up the rhyme together because I'd wanted to help. As a little girl, I would clasp my father's hand and repeat it until he was calm enough to say it with me.

A slow breath in, Marin. A slow breath out. I clasped the words to myself as the bedroom spun around me. A slow breath in. A link to reality. A slow breath out. A chant to outlast the fear.

The throbbing in my chest began to give way to the even sweep of Sam's hand on my back. As my own concern for my sanity faded, I remembered that he probably thought I was nuts. Despite a strong desire to sink through the mattress and disappear, I made myself face him.

"Did I hurt you?" he whispered. He looked so unhappy that I forgot to be embarrassed. I put my hands on his shoulders again. This time, instead of pushing him away, I pushed back the alarms echoing through my head and pulled him close to me.

The room kept whirling around us, but Sam felt solid and still. I held onto him and focused on my dad's words above me—words written for my mom and painted by his hand. If this weren't so terrifying, I'd have found it absurd. Was I really gasping through my own panic in my parents' Seasalter bedroom, beneath the mantra my dad had once used to calm himself through an attack?

You're kind, you're quiet, you're calm, you're bright. The words swirled above us in lavender wisps. I read them until my desperation eased, but the room had been spinning for so long. I pushed Sam away again and scrambled for the waste can beside the bed.

"Can the flu come on this quickly? Do you think you have the flu?"

I shook my head and threw up again.

"Maybe it's something you ate." When I couldn't stop to answer, he said, "I don't like this. I'm calling my dad."

"No," I managed to say.

"He's a doctor, he'll—"

"No!" A medical perspective might've been useful, but I was too afraid to hear what I knew he would say. "I know what it is. Give me ten minutes."

I made up the timeframe to ease his mind, but positive thinking never hurts. When he leaned warily against the headboard, I lay my head on his shoulder to reassure us both. I clutched his arm for longer than necessary, first willing and then allowing myself to be calm. After a long while, he sighed, and I decided it wasn't fair to hide from him.

"Hi," I said, sitting up slowly. I gave him a tiny smile.

"Hi." He didn't smile back. Instead, he bent across me to pick up my shirt.

My pulse felt nearly normal, but my hands were still shaking. He gave me a minute to try before leaning over to button it over my camisole himself.

I watched him frown as he focused. "It's interesting that you start at the bottom and go up. I always start at the top and go down."

He didn't answer. When he tried to fasten the top button, I took hold of his hand.

"I look better with that one open. This one, too," I said, flicking open the second button suggestively.

"Could you not make a joke out of this?" he said tensely. While he generously carried my sick-bag out to the trash, I shuffled to the bathroom to clean myself up."

He perched beside me grimly when I slid back onto the bed. "If I ask how you're feeling, are you going to say *fine*?"

"Would you rather I said fabulous? Or are you looking for something negative?"

"I'm looking for the truth. You don't think it's the flu?" When I shook my head, he said, "Was it a panic attack?"

I stared at him. "Why would you think that?"

"Because I've been with someone when they had one and it looked unnervingly similar."

Hmm. The way he said *I've been with someone* seemed suspiciously gender-neutral. Poor Sam. What if I wasn't the only girl who'd flipped out on him like this?

"Marin! Was it a panic attack?"

"Maybe." Probably. But I wasn't emotionally ready to make that call.

"You've never had one before?"

"No." That much I knew.

"Well, that's great," he snapped, his jaw tightening.

His sarcasm shocked me into retorting, "What's that supposed to mean?"

"It means I'm sorry. It means this is completely my fault. I should have known better." He clutched my fingers. "I did know better."

"How can you think this is your fault?"

He sighed and took both my hands in his. "Marin, forgive me, but I just spent three months watching you recover from what appeared to be a very traumatic breakup. Anyone could have a hard time jumping back into…"

That signature blush colored his cheeks, but I didn't have the heart to comment on it.

"That doesn't mean it's your fault."

"That's exactly what it means."

"No, it's not." I pulled my hands out of his. "That's like saying you made all the decisions. It's like saying I have no choice in this—" He opened his mouth in protest. "—which I know you would never do."

He didn't respond. Yes! Score one for Mariana Beckett.

"Fine." He gave me a begrudging smile. "I suppose we might share the guilt."

"That's better."

I leaned back against the pillows and closed my eyes. As thrilled as I was that he no longer blamed himself, with that distraction gone, I was forced to recognize that I had probably had my first panic attack—my deepest fear made real. Was it a sure sign that someday I would end up alone, unable to function outside whatever sanctuary I could make for myself?

Not without cause, I thought back to the night before I'd left for England, when I'd said goodbye to my dad. Reluctant to leave him, I'd hesitated on his porch and watched through the window as he wrote at his desk. His face was hidden in shadow, but in the golden light of his study, his white hair looked blond again. At that moment, he could have been young and strong and confident, like he had been for most of the time we'd lived in the very house where I lay. Instead of sitting by his window in Wisconsin, he could have been writing in his office downstairs—writing and waiting for the little girl I'd been to climb into his lap.

But he had leaned forward, and the shadows had shifted, settling into the lines on his face. Lines from sorrow, lines from worry, and lines from years of makeshift peace. Lines that told me how well he knew that, even sitting there alone, he was right where he needed to be.

"Can you talk about it with me?" Sam asked, brushing at the tear I hadn't managed to suppress. He slid his palm alongside mine reassuringly. My mind filled with thoughts of us beneath the porch light that night he'd asked me out, how he'd eased my tension with his last-minute confession: *I drove all the way from London, just to see you.* I linked my fingers with his.

"My dad, who I love more than anyone, has a serious anxiety disorder. It's complicated, but panic attacks have always been part of it. He hasn't left his property in a long time because he's afraid of having an attack while he's out."

Sam didn't seem surprised or put off or anything. Maybe he didn't get it.

"Mental illnesses like my dad's run in families. What if I keep having panic attacks, and I get so scared that I end up—"

I didn't want to say it like an insult, that I might end up like my dad. In so many ways, I'd love to be like him. I changed directions.

"It's just, I've worried about this for years and now it's happened. What if it's the first step toward my own mental instability? It feels like the beginning." It was too melodramatic to say what I really thought—that it felt like the beginning of the end.

Sam covered my free hand with his. Until he did, I hadn't noticed that I was compulsively tracing those strawberries embroidered on my pillow.

"You're going to be fine."

"You don't know that. You can't know that."

"Lots of people have one panic attack and never experience another. Most people with a family history of mental illness have no problem at all."

"But the obsessive fear of an attack is usually what triggers one. And I'm terrified of having a panic attack. I've always been terrified."

"That's a good sign, I think. It's always frightened you, yet it's never happened before. Think about it. Your dad's problems started when he was very young. If this was your first panic attack, it's far more likely that you'll be fine."

I looked into my lap, then off to the side. Had I told him when my dad's illness started? Then I looked directly at him and saw alarm in his eyes.

"How long have you known?" I finally asked.

"Since you sent the package to my sisters and I came down to see you. When I looked up directions, your house was listed as a site of historical significance. Home of John Robert Beckett. Setting of *Salt in the Sea*."

That made sense, but seriously? Here in England, where nearly everything is centuries old, the Beckett house is a historical site?

"Perhaps I should have told you before, but I assumed you had reasons for not mentioning it. I didn't want to pressure you." His mouth twisted into a scowl. "That might mean something if I stop saying it every eight minutes."

"It's still nice to hear."

"I want you to know..." He hesitated. "I've read it, Marin. Before I met you."

Of course he had read it, he'd been a psychology major. It was probably required reading. Rightly so, I thought with a sigh.

"Are you angry with me?"

"For what, being discreet? I didn't hide it because I'm ashamed of it, that's like being ashamed of my dad. It's just, so many people know that book. But they don't know us. Sometimes it's nice not to deal with the preconceptions."

"And the misconceptions?"

"Exactly." I bumped his shoulder as he stretched out beside me. "You know, you should really have your own talk show. How do you always know just what to say?"

The sun spread fingers of orange light over the walls. We sat in silence, watching the shadows stretch themselves across the room as the day drained away. When I inched closer to him, Sam wrapped his hand around my waist.

"Now that you know I've read your father's book, I can tell you something I've been thinking of for weeks."

"What's that?" Really, the shape of his mouth is too perfect. Just full enough. And that scar…mmm.

"You hiding your pet oyster in the toilet is one of the funniest things I've ever read."

I groaned and flopped down into my pillow. Humiliating.

"What?"

"You know all those embarrassing stories about me!" I cried.

"You'll be happy to know that the one about the oyster is all I remember."

"Good."

"Aside from your confusion over mud pies and dog mess, that is."

"Hey, that wasn't funny. That was traumatic."

"Oh. And the one where you drew flowers all over your belly and then refused to wear a shirt until they faded away." I closed my eyes. I hate that story more than any other. "Permanent ink as well, wasn't it? Good thing it was summer."

I crossed my arms over my chest.

"Right. There was also the time you——"

My fingers shot out to pinch his side. He laughed softly and leaned his face close to mine.

"I'll buy you a permanent marker if it will produce the same result now. I'll even help you draw."

"Yeah?"

"Yeah."

When he kissed me, I hooked two fingers through the belt loops of his jeans and tugged until there was no space between us. But as my cool fingertips brushed over his stomach, he leapt to his feet.

"I'm sorry," he gasped. "I cannot believe I did that."

He had backed up eight feet from me. That angry look was on his face again.

"You won't come near me now, is that it? Hands-off again?"

He dropped onto the low bench beneath my window without responding. I pushed myself off the bed.

"Don't get up," he said, starting toward me. "You could still be dizzy."

"Sit down."

I was a little surprised at how quickly he obeyed.

I knelt on the bench with him between my knees. When he protested, I put my finger over his lips.

"Thank you. It's wonderful to be with someone so considerate. And although it's the last thing I want, it's probably smart to slow things down. But slowing down is not locking up." I ran my hands over his shoulders. "I think slowing down is like exposure therapy," I said, thinking of my dad's treatments. "We start with the small steps…" One kiss on his left ear. "And move onto bigger steps…" Two on his right. "Working steadily toward—" Three down his neck. "—the ultimate goal."

I hesitated at his mouth, trying to believe what I was about to say.

"I appreciate what you're doing, so much. But I'm not fragile. I'm not going to break." Then I leaned in and kissed him until I proved it to us both.

CHAPTER TWENTY-THREE

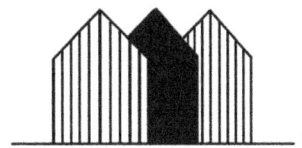

It probably helped that Sam was living in London again. Because of the distance and his job at SaladBar, we only saw each other twice a week, so our agreed-upon course of exposure therapy was easier to maintain.

Not that he would have compromised.

"I'm feeling fine," I would often say, pushing the boundaries against my better judgment.

"I'm so glad," he would always respond, redirecting my energies to whatever else we had planned, from dinner to day trips to dates with Ella and Lily. We cooked each other's favorite foods, hunted for sea glass on the beach, and visited hole-in-the-wall venues in search of new bands. England came alive for me. It began to feel like home.

And in between our rambles, I wrote and wrote. I was steeped in the pages of my new book. In many ways, the lack of action in my real-life relationship helped the story. Pouring all that pent-up longing into my characters was resulting in my steamiest book yet.

One night near the end of January, I was sorting through pictures for a visual outline connecting inspiration images to every scene I had planned. I'd just taped my first clipping to my office wall when Gretchen called.

"Have I got a birthday present for you! I should have waited until Thursday, but it's too amazing. You're getting it early. Are you sitting down?"

"Yep," I said, standing on tiptoe to stick up a photo of Château de Chenonceau. I was used to Gretchen's announcements. It was safe to stand.

"Last week I gave Yvonne the first four chapters of your new manuscript. She's been raving over the romance between Genevieve and Lucien! I was concerned because she was so attached to Madison and Sean, but now that you and Simon are officially together, I think she understands your resistance to finishing it."

"That's great!" I could move forward without restraint.

"It's better than great. Yvonne was in my office this morning to discuss her plans for growing the company. She's realized that our core readership is loyal to Velicity's brand of romance. As she put it, sexy sensationalism sells best. Her new strategy is to hand-select one of our best writers and market her into a brand-name super-author. She's throwing all her support behind you. I told you that Rochester book would lead to big things!"

Actually, Gretchen had been against the Rochester book in the beginning because it lacked the tawdry delights of a regular Velicity romance. But who was I to bring up the past?

"Before we go on, this would require building your brand strictly as a romance novelist. The Velicity kind. Are you willing to do that?"

I glanced at the notes all over the room—plot summaries, character studies, snatches of inspiration scribbled out by hand. Every word that brought Genevieve closer to Lucien reminded me of why I write. My Rochester book hadn't turned out so well because of any complex literary overtones, but because Edward Rochester had inspired it. More than any other literary hero, he is my great romance. And I am a romance author.

I didn't hesitate. "Yes."

"Yvonne is offering you a five-book deal!"

I hit the floor with a bang.

"I told you to sit," Gretchen said with a laugh. "A five-book contract, an annual marketing budget on par with what Velicity used to spend as a whole before the Lee family bought the company, and the avid support of the boss. In other words, Mariana Rose just won the publishing industry's Powerball."

I sat still, not sure where to begin. "What does this mean, exactly?"

"Eventually it will mean television appearances, a multi-city book tour—"

"It means public speaking?"

"It means Lifetime movies with your name in the title. It means multiple translations and foreign rights and your books finding readers all over the world."

That alone was worth the pain of public speaking. My excitement took hold before Gretchen spoke her next words.

"You know what else it means, Marin: money. Lots of money. Get off the floor and go look in the mirror," she told me before hanging up. "Say hello to the next Jackie Collins." My books aren't much like Jackie Collins's, but the fact that I knew that illustrated her point. Jackie Collins is a household name.

For some reason, I needed to follow Gretchen's advice, maybe to prove our conversation had been real. When my own post-shower, pajama-clad reflection stared out of the bathroom mirror, I had to laugh at the contrast between what I saw and how I imagined Jackie Collins. I couldn't remember ever seeing her, but I was envisioning Elizabeth Taylor in that White Diamonds commercial where she tosses her earrings on the table and purrs, "These have always brought me luck." I had a similar fantasy wherein I pulled off my only accessory—the black elastic band around my wet ponytail—and tossed it in front of a dashing gambler. And even in my imagination, the gambler looked at me like I was nuts.

Wine would make me drowsy and I still had work to do, but a celebratory cup of tea was definitely called for. While it steeped, I wandered, admiring my little house. Through the French doors, the back garden was tipped with snow. The windows in my office looked over the beach. My sea glass collection glowed in every sill.

It suddenly occurred to me that with this incredible book deal, I wouldn't need to rent out the house. I could live in it myself. I wanted to be home near my dad for at least half the year, but the rest of the time, I could stay. And if I were going to be around more permanently…well, you know what I was thinking. It would be easier to keep something going with Sam if we weren't four thousand miles apart.

I took a couple minutes to smile until my cheeks hurt, then I gave myself a no-nonsense speech. "No pressure,

Mariana Rose, but if you want this Jackie Collins thing to happen, grab that tea and get to work."

CHAPTER TWENTY-FOUR

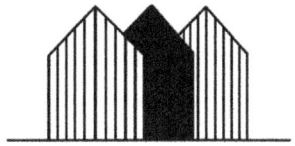

"You should've let me pick you up at the train station. It's too cold to be out," Sam said a few days later when I visited his flat. He slammed the front door on the January wind and held his warm hands to my frozen face.

"That's why I took the bus, so you could stay in. I live in Chicago. We're a cold-hardy people. Besides, you didn't pick me up the first time I came here. Look how well that turned out."

"You may not remember, since you were unconscious, but the first time you came here, I did pick you up," he said, and he swung me into his arms.

I didn't care that it was a cliché. Because even though it was, and even though I'm not one for being carried around, Sam's arms...not a bad place to be.

"I had the strangest conversation with Jordan just now," he said as he settled us onto his lumpy tweed couch. "She wanted to fly me to L.A. next week for a film screening. I told her I couldn't go. I work nearly every day and we have a show that weekend. But she kept at me. Finally, I told her straight out: No, do not ask me again. Do you know what she said?" He looked at me and smirked. "She said, 'I suppose you're too busy discovering whether Mariana Rose's steamy scenes are based on imagination or personal skill.'"

I gave him a weak smile. "I should've warned you. I spoke with Jordan today and it slipped out that I was seeing you this afternoon. She wasn't thrilled, so I tried to downplay it. I didn't want to jeopardize your role in her new film."

"She irritated me so much that I told her she was right, your books are true to life."

"You do not currently possess that information," I said between laughs. "And you did not tell her that."

"I can make an educated guess. And yes, I did."

"Do you still have a job this summer?"

"Of course. She'll probably offer me a pay rise. It's not me Jordan likes, it's the challenge of someone who says no. I only wish she'd take my *no* to heart, as it's the only answer she's going to get." He traced his finger down my filament-fine necklace to the pendant suspended below my throat. "You, on the other hand, will get a very different response."

We stretched out on the sofa and, for the next few minutes, I thought very little about Jordan or anything else I can admit to here.

"True to life," Sam said when he finally looked up. "Your publisher was quite correct to award you that amazing contract. Tell me, that thing you just did to my ear —didn't I read something similar in *Wanderlust?* Exactly how did that scene unfold?" I pulled him toward me for a reenactment, but after a few minutes he leaned back. "How are you feeling?"

Ah, the keystone question of our relationship: How are you feeling? or, If I put my hand here, will you freak out again? His constant vigilance, while thoughtful, could also be incredibly frustrating. But I'd spent my morning sorting through my dad's relics—visual reminders of panic at work—so easing rather than plunging in was less difficult to do.

"I'm fine. I have a surprise for you. Jordan sent me a link to the screener of the Rochester movie. We can watch it together!"

Instead of crinkling into a smile as I'd expected, Sam's eyes filled with fear.

"I can't watch myself. Last year the band filmed a show for my mum, since she'd been too ill to attend most of them. It was torture watching it, even with her. She laughed so hard at me for that..." A distant look crept into his eyes. He blinked it away. "I can't sit through four hours of myself onscreen."

"You have to watch it sometime."

I put on my best smile and whispered something that might make the four hours more palatable. Exposure therapy, remember? It's all about finding the appropriate next level.

Sam's expression was equal parts admiration and awe. "Woman, where do you come up with these ideas? Is this a perk of dating a romance novelist?"

I shrugged cheerfully. "It's a perk of dating this one."

"It's a tempting offer, but I'm not watching that film. If you'd like to leave the show off, however..." He tugged at my sweater with a devious grin.

"You really don't want to watch it?"

"Never."

"You're starring in the movie. Of course you have to watch it!"

"Of course I do not." Behind the devious grin, I saw his jaw set.

In the few weeks we'd been dating, I'd begun to realize that the discipline I'd always admired in him was helped along by a stubborn streak. If I wanted my way on this, I'd have to suck up some pride.

"Look, I wasn't planning to mention it, but today is my birthday. Watching this with you is my one birthday wish."

"It is not your birthday," he said with a laugh. When I didn't laugh in return, he paused. "Today is your birthday? Why didn't you tell me?"

"Why didn't I tell my teenage boyfriend I'm turning thirty-four?" When his confusion shifted to annoyance, I gave him a smooch. "Please? It's a movie based on my very own book. How often does that birthday gift come around?"

He heaved a sigh of acceptance and nudged the remote control my way. But when I reached for it, he grabbed my hand.

"Not so fast, woman. You left an offer on the table. If I'm to survive watching this film, you have to follow through."

Several minutes and, on my part, one shameless performance later, we were settled in with the lights and a couple other things off and the television on.

"That horse was actually called Sam," he said the moment he rode into the film. "Every time the trainer spoke to him, I thought she was speaking to me."

A minute later: "You would not believe how hot that coat was. It must have weighed two stone. It was a really authentic wool, though. The wardrobe mistress tracked it down in…"

And then, "It's rather loud, don't you think? Odd they haven't done something with the sound. Don't you feel that my voice is louder than the rest?"

Then a pause, followed by, "Do I always sound like such a whinger? I sound ridiculous."

And finally, "If I made some chips would you eat them? I wouldn't mind some chips right now. What do you think? Do you fancy some chips?"

I sat up. "Hand me my sweater, will you?"

"Are you cold? Do you want another blanket? Of course, you can have your sweater if you'd rather—wait, was this a bad idea? How are you feeling?"

I clamped my hand over his mouth. "I'm not cold, I need someone strict to monitor the talking in the room. I'm going to pick up Ella."

"I told you, I can't watch myself," he said as I shut off the television.

"Now I believe you." I slid my arms around his neck. "Forget the movie. Seeing you look so delicious in that cravat made me realize something. I have an official portrayer of Edward Rochester at my disposal. You're in a unique position to make a fantasy of mine come true."

Sam's eyes took on a new glimmer. "I have a feeling I'll like the fantasies of Mariana Rose."

"Sorry, it's not that kind of fantasy. But you can't imagine the thrill I would get if you stated, with authority, Edward Rochester's famous line: 'What the deuce is to do now?'"

I waited, but he only grinned. "Go ahead. Here's your chance to make an actual fantasy come true."

I think he almost snorted. "I'm not squandering the opportunity to make your fantasy come true. I'm saving this for a significant moment."

He'd laced enough stubborn satisfaction into his smile for me to see that he wouldn't budge. I sighed and drew a finger down his chest. "Do you have one of those white Rochester shirts? You could reenact that wet shirt scene I've heard so much about."

"Unfortunately for you, I turned in my Rochester clothes." He handed me my sweater with an air of reluctant responsibility. "Do you still want this?"

His eyes lit up when I tossed it to the floor. I ran my hand over the cherished obliques.

"No movie. No cravat. I need something to do."

CHAPTER TWENTY-FIVE

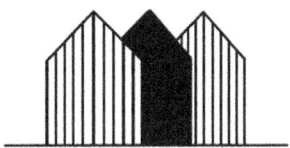

My typical Saturday morning in England usually involved the following: an easy couple of hours spent lolling in my pajamas, sipping hot tea and reading the paper. The third Saturday in February began in the usual way, but I was treating myself especially well, trading my green tea for hot cocoa and piling whipped cream onto a chocolate croissant. I had also set up shop at the dining room table, surrounding myself with index cards, drafts, and enough ideas to carry me through hours of hard writing. I'd designed a day of distraction, balanced equally by edible indulgence and professional sweat.

It was working. By mid-morning, I'd consumed a sleeve of Jaffa Cakes and cranked out six pages. I was foraging through my stash of snacks when I heard a knock.

The smarmy young guy at the door surveyed my tank top with a lecherous grin. I yanked my cardigan shut. The box he held out was stamped with *Alcoholic Beverages. Obtain Appropriate Signatures.*

"I'm Lewis. My route ends at four, if you need a drinking mate."

"Or I could sign," I said, taking his pen.

"Mariana. Fancy name. What do you say to one drink?"

The front gate squeaked. A woman smiled brightly as she picked her way up the walk with a vase of yellow daisies.

"Celebrating today, are you?" Lewis said with a wink.

"I guess I am now," I mumbled as the high from my productive morning drained away.

I set the flowers on the coffee table and read the accompanying card. *Something sunny to brighten your day. Love, Mom and Charles.*

"Well, that's a relief," I told the empty living room. "For a minute, I thought they were from David." Although more than likely he would've sent—

Another bang at the door. Lewis again, leaning against the doorjamb.

"Turns out she had two for you." He handed over a vase of purple orchids.

So much for relief.

"About that drink—" Lewis began, eyes on the tank top again.

"I'll toast you when I crack open the bottle." Since he was leering anyway, I flashed him the *You Wish* across my butt before the door slammed shut.

I carried the vase into the kitchen. The orchids and I regarded each other warily.

"Reinforcements," I said, tearing into the box of booze from Julie and Garrett—one bottle of nice champagne ("to pamper yourself") and another of cheap chardonnay ("to get the job done"). I checked the clock. Eleven a.m.

Well, really, is there ever a time when champagne doesn't help? I asked myself, peeling off the foil as a knock sounded once more.

I jerked open the door, ready to body slam Lewis. Instead I saw Patricia's smiling face.

"Don't shoot. Maybe I should've listened to you and stayed away today. How are you?"

"I was great until I started getting Sorry About Your Wedding presents," I said, gesturing at the bounty I'd amassed. Then I noticed the box in her hands. "I mean, thanks, what a lovely surprise."

"I told your sister I would bring you this, but I know you need to get through today your way. This is the last you'll see of me."

She opened the box to reveal a little two-tiered cake. A tiny bride and groom were stuck into the top.

"Is this a joke?"

"Yes. Pick them up."

I pulled at the figurines. The groom plopped chest-first into the frosting but the bride glided out. Her yellow hair fell in little clay waves down her back. She held her bouquet in one hand, appropriately demure. Her other hand was raised high, and from it dangled the gory severed head of the groom.

"Nandi's final project in 3-D Design. I believe she got an A."

"I would hope so. They even look like us," I said with a shiver.

"It's a joint gift. Nandi's decorations, my recipe." She leaned over for a quick, strong hug. "That was from both of us as well. Now cut me a slice and I'll be on my way. Be forewarned. It's red velvet."

"How could it be anything else?" I said, hacking into the bleeding cake.

I'd just seen Patricia out when my cell phone rang.

"Would it have been this busy if I actually were getting married today?" I asked the little bride on the cake before answering.

"I'm making sure everything's under control," Nandi said. She sounded remarkably alert, considering it was not even six a.m. in Chicago.

"You know, I'm the big sister. You don't have to worry about me," I said, loving her more when she dismissed that with a snort. "I just had some not-wedding cake, by the way."

"Did the jerk fall over when you picked them up?"

"The jerk toppled brilliantly. You should minor in Engineering."

"I'll think it over. Your mom said to ask if you got their flowers."

"They're flourishing on my table right now." I didn't dare mention David's orchids. Nandi would assassinate him.

"Isobel said she'll try calling you again when their flight gets in tonight. I'll spare you her lecture on international phone service."

I felt a moment of guilt for ducking my mom's call the day before. I'd forgotten that, without a family wedding to attend, they'd moved their trip to Zambia up a week.

Enjoy those extra vacation days, folks, courtesy of David Lauer. I popped the cork on the champagne and tipped the bottle in salute.

Nandi cleared her throat. "Okay, new business. How are you spending the day?"

"I'm going to write thirty pages and stuff myself with carbs. Decadent, destructive carbs that make my heart sing and my arteries cry."

"And?"

"And I'll probably wash them down with a few generously spiked drinks. What else do you want?"

"I want your sexy new boyfriend to take you out for some fun."

"My sexy new boyfriend is celebrating his sister's birthday, then he's heading home early to get some sleep. First thing tomorrow, he's off to Hollywood for a week of meetings."

"He's letting you go through this alone?"

I didn't answer. She spat her next words at me.

"You haven't even told him."

"What should I say? 'Hey, Sam, will you blow off Ella's party to watch me cry myself to sleep?'"

"It's a starting point."

"Forget it. He has better things to do than babysit the bride, and I don't need an audience." She started to argue, but I cut her off. "Look, this is how I'm handling it. I'm taking the day to myself so I can feel however I want. If I want to cry, I'll cry, and it won't be awkward for Sam. If I feel like throwing things at the wall, they won't bounce off and hit him. And I won't feel guilty about grieving for the man who broke my heart in front of the man who does nothing but try to mend it."

When she didn't respond, I softened my tone.

"I love you for trying, but no one can do this for me. I have to get through it myself."

"Promise you'll call if you need me. Anytime, okay?

Even tomorrow morning when your head is in the toilet. I'll vicariously hold your hair out of your face."

"I love you. I'll call you."

She paused. "Marc? You really do deserve the best."

I held the phone to my ear until she clicked off. Finally safe from distraction, I spent the next two hours typing up Genevieve's mission to rescue her father from Baudelaire's dungeon, then headed into the kitchen for another chunk of cake.

David's orchids were waiting on me. Thirty stems in a crystal vase, each topped with a waxy amethyst bloom.

Orchids. So finicky they sometimes seem suicidal. For years, I had coddled six plants identical to the flowers before me, flooding them with light every autumn, softening the light each spring. So it felt unnatural—cruel, even—when I pitched the fragile things into the trash.

The card I hadn't bothered to read landed on the floor. Two words stared up at me, both large enough to see from a distance:

Forgive me.

At least it's not Tennyson, I thought sadly. Those words are David Lauer's own.

I picked up the card and let it rest in my palm. The *Forgive Me* seemed to swell the longer I looked. I flung it onto the tangle of flowers and slammed the trash can shut, decapitating an orchid as I did. Its biting fragrance filled the room.

"I have to get out of here."

I hadn't been running in weeks, but I had enough nervous energy to sprint to London and back. I pounded down the beach like I could pound down my sympathetic twinge toward those despondent orchids, toward David's card in the trash. I did my best not to see them. Instead, I pictured everything the day could have held, but wouldn't. The antique lace veil, just like my grandma's, that David had surprised me with. My silk charmeuse wedding dress with our initials embroidered into the hem. Julie's gift to us, those lovely letterpress invitations, that I'd burnt to a crisp. I saw them brown and curl, flake apart, disappear.

And then I saw Sam.

He was walking toward me with his hands shoved into his pockets. Only when I slowed to meet him did I realize how hard I'd been running. I was suddenly concerned that my lungs might explode, but I tried to hide it from Sam, who runs for one hour, minimum, every single day including Christmas and his birthday.

"I didn't expect to see you," I said, attempting a smile. "How was the party?"

"The party ended early," he said quietly. He held out a handful of sea glass, pale pieces of green and blue that gleamed against his palm. "I found you some good ones."

"You always find good ones. Even sea glass is attracted to you," I said as we climbed my back steps. "Did Ella have a nice birthday?"

When he didn't answer, I looked at him closely. A gloomy sorrow filled his eyes. After I unlocked the door, he headed straight to the sofa and slouched into the cushions. He cast a despondent glance at the papers littering the dining room table. "I know I said I wasn't going to stop by. I hope you don't mind. You look busy."

"I can take a break." I sank down beside him on the couch and rubbed his shoulder. "What's going on?"

"Who sent you flowers? Is it a holiday in America?"

"Something like that." I said, ignoring the pain that flickered through me. "How is Ella? How are you?"

He picked despondently at a worn spot on his jeans. "Do you mind if we just sit for a while? I'm trying not to think. And you have such a nice stillness about you."

Now I knew something was wrong. For Sam to say this—Sam, who handles himself and everything that comes his way with a calm and confidence I often envy—something had really upset him.

He stretched out with his head in my lap and tried to smile, but it didn't come off. When I ran my hand down his arm, he caught it and held it against his chest.

"Our mum always had a big family lunch for everyone's birthday," he said after twenty minutes of silence. "We tried to have the same, but we decided it would be best not to mention Mum. Ella has been less anxious recently, but it's never clear when something will upset her. But not talking about Mum only made it more obvious she wasn't there. That she won't be there again."

"Was Ella okay?"

"She's become so serious that, unless she's truly struggling, it's difficult to know how she feels. She didn't seem upset, at first. But as she was opening presents, she noticed our dad had gone missing. She wanted him with her, so while the older girls put out the cake, she and Lily and I went to find him." He swallowed hard. "Ella heard her first."

"Heard who?" I asked in alarm, remembering the Homecoming Queen's bubble-gum-sweet squeals bouncing off my bedroom walls.

"Our mother," he said, throwing his forearm over his

eyes. "She always sang us this birthday song she'd made up when I was small. Given our decision today to act as if Mum never existed, we forgot that, before she died, she'd done birthday videos for each of us. Maybe Dad felt guilty. Or maybe he just missed her. Either way, we walked in on him sitting like a statue in front of the video as Mum sang her birthday song especially for Ella." I felt him cringe against my lap. "It did not go well."

"The video upset her?"

"The video was a shock, so she began to cry, as did Lily. But I made it worse. I yelled at Dad for playing it when we'd all agreed not to involve our mum. My shouting frightened Ella and Lily and brought my other sisters in, who took one look at the video and the sorry scene before them and, of course, began to cry. Then Ella wanted to know why I was 'trying to make everyone forget Mummy.'" He sat up and pulled me into his side. "I was a brute."

"You just wanted to protect her. The shock of seeing the video probably triggered an extreme response for you, too. Some people cry, some people snap."

"It was a betrayal to leave our mother out. What were we saying, that she no longer matters? That we've all forgotten her, so Ella should forget as well? She and Lily are so young, they'll hardly remember as it is."

"They'll remember her. Your mother's touch is all over that house. I could feel it the minute I stepped inside. They'll remember, I know they will."

"How?" he asked, his voice bleak. "What if the rest of us can't work out how to act?"

"You will. You have to let yourself learn what to do and give yourself grace when you make mistakes. That you're this concerned is proof. You'll figure out what's best." I squeezed his hand. "Do I have permission to try and cheer you up?"

"I suppose," he said, mustering a small smile that I could honestly return, since helping him through his bad day had pulled my focus off my own.

"Good. Patricia just brought me the most delicious cake. I'm going to cut you an enormous slice—silence your inner health freak now, Simon Quinn—and then I'm going to teach you to play gin rummy. And I should warn you that I have an impressive record. Roughly six hundred wins to my dad's measly four-fifty."

"You and your dad have played over a thousand games?"

"I told you, he doesn't get out much. Now shuffle these and prepare to get thrashed." I tossed him a pack of cards on my way to cut our cake.

For a gin rummy novice, Sam was surprisingly good. After one lesson and a few practice hands, he won nearly every game. His mood picked up with each success, but after two hours and too many losses, I dumped my cards onto the coffee table and surrendered.

"Remind me not to play you for money," I grumbled, settling back onto the couch, and he pulled my feet into his lap. I closed my eyes with a sigh. "Sometimes you don't even seem real. You're smart, you're talented, you're funny, you're hot. Apparently, you're a card shark. Now you're massaging my feet. Have you always been the perfect man?"

"I'm not perfect. If I were perfect, I would never do *this* just as you've begun to relax." He zipped his fingernail up my foot, laughing when I jerked it away with a squeal.

I paid him back by saying, "Will you treat Jordan to a foot massage next week? Maybe get her to buy you a car?"

"I have a car."

"True, a nice one. Has Jordan seen it? She'll ask you for a ride, if she hasn't already."

He pushed his fingers into my foot with slightly more force. "I'm ignoring your double-entendre this time, but you'd better be on your guard. Your clever wordplay turns me on."

"You don't scare me. I've never met anyone less threatening than you." I rubbed my free foot against his thigh. "A perfect gentleman, right? Completely benign."

"For your information, I have not always been the model of integrity which you see before you." An uncomfortable look crept over his face. "I'm ashamed to think of the women who would tell you, quite rightly, how far from benign my behavior has been."

"What, problems with the slap and tickle?" I laughed, but he did not.

"Not in the traditional sense. But things with the 'slap and tickle' girl did end especially poorly."

"Why especially?"

He hesitated, like he didn't want to admit it, but to me the idea wasn't all that surprising. Sam had always been great to me, but he'd earned his maturity somehow.

"We were rather serious, until I formed the band and spent all my time working on my music career. Eventually, she'd had enough." He smiled grimly. "But never you mind. I've learnt my lesson. Changed my ways. Still, a perfect man would never have to change."

"Are you kidding? A reformed rebel? You've exponentially increased your sex appeal."

"Do you want a list of my many flaws?"

"Yes," I said seriously. "Then I can relax instead of always rolling out my best behavior."

"You? Never. I like you just as well when you're naughty. I'm starting to prefer it."

"See, you did it again. You're charming without trying. You're perfect."

"All right, then." He set down my foot and looked me in the eye.

He was so solemn that my nerves tensed. Did I really want to know the various ways Sam might have hurt a bunch of women? My stomach tightened when he held out his fingers to tick them off.

"To start with, I skive off my chores. I never do the washing up after cooking and I let my laundry pile up for weeks. Secondly, I can be slothful. On occasion, I allow myself to spend an entire day watching football whilst wearing no trousers. Three: I drive a classic automobile which a respectable man would know how to repair. I can barely change the oil filter. Number four, I can't whistle. An appalling shortcoming in an aspiring musician."

I laughed. He couldn't whistle, but he tried all the time.

"And five…" He reached into the waistband of his jeans and pulled out the eight of spades. "Occasionally, I cheat at cards."

"You stole a card? We've been playing with a fifty-one-card deck! No wonder you never saved spades!" I popped him with a pillow, but I had to smile. At least my losses didn't count against me.

"See, not perfect. Slothful, can't whistle—and the cheating, that's pathological."

He looked at me triumphantly, but I shook my head.

"No, no. Even your flaws are interesting. None of those typical 'I snore' answers."

"I've been told that I snore," he added hopefully.

"Sorry, Gorgeous." I shifted myself onto his lap and wound my legs around his waist. "Can I come to your next trouserless football day?"

"That depends. Will you be trouserless as well?"

"What do you think?" I whispered, kissing his ear in the way he particularly liked.

I heard his breath catch in his throat. I'd been teasing him, but that quiet sound made me pause. The steady bass line that underscored each minute we spent together deepened to fill the space between us. I felt it humming in my fingertips as they grazed his face. When he looked into my eyes, I could almost see it, pulsing in the heat of his gaze.

We stared at each other. Our breathing deepened. Then in one smooth, sudden motion he leaned me back onto the couch.

"You look beautiful in this sweater," he said. His mouth followed the scoop of my tank top as his fingers trailed over my cardigan. The soft cashmere sliding over my skin made me shiver in his arms. "You are so beautiful."

I ran my hands over his broad shoulders, flexing beneath his thin cotton shirt. Longing for him fell over me; I pressed myself closer and drew his lips to mine.

After several enjoyable minutes, he ran his finger along my waistband. His eyes never left mine as he brushed the button on my jeans.

And at that moment, in the midst of all that momentum, my cell phone rang.

"It's probably Nandi," I whispered when he looked up.

"She'd kill us both if we stop." He lowered his mouth to mine again but we both jumped when, twenty seconds later, the house phone rang.

I ignored it, my hands flying to his belt. But an immediate buzzkill blared out from that vintage answering machine.

"Mariana? Are you there?"

I dropped that belt buckle like my dad himself had walked into the room. Sam dropped flat on top of me like he was trying to hide. We looked at each other and laughed, choking it back like we were afraid to get caught when my dad spoke again.

"Just checking on you. I know it's a difficult day. Not the day you'd hoped it would be."

The laughter in my throat dwindled and I felt myself shrink into the sofa, as my dad's familiar voice—gruff in tone, gentle in delivery—shoved my reality into the room.

"I keep thinking there's a reason for this disappointment. We never know what good things are ahead. And maybe, when you find someone who really deserves you, if I work hard enough I'll be able to come to your wedding." The word made me flinch. It got worse. "I'd love it if someday I could walk you down the aisle—"

He cut himself off with a grunt and a curse and then paused, the awkward pause of a father trying to fill in the blanks, who knows he's saying the wrong thing but can't sort out what's right.

"I'm sorry, Petite. I'll stop before this gets more grotesque. Call me back if you need me to tell you how remarkable you are and how much I love you." He sighed, a heavy rattling sigh that made me strain toward his voice on the line despite the weight of his words settling on my chest.

The phone fell silent. In the empty seconds that followed, Sam and I were silent as well. He still held me close, he hadn't moved, but cold air seeped between us like he was holding himself away. When he finally pushed up to look at me, I had never felt more exposed.

"I guess it's not a holiday," he mumbled, like for once in his life he didn't know what to say.

I crossed my arms. "Depends on your point of view."

The charge in the air around us had fizzled. While I smoothed my sweater and my messy hair, Sam straightened the cushions on the couch. The perfect gentleman once again.

He traced his fingers over the back of my hand, pressed his lips to my palm and then the inside of my wrist. It still made my breath catch, that trick, and he liked to sneak it in when I didn't expect it. This time it wasn't playful or suggestive. It was familiar, reassuring, but it was more than that. It felt like proof. That it truly was real, this thing between us.

For a while, we lay without talking, my back curled into his chest. I couldn't help seeing all the sad details. That antique veil David had tracked down for me in New York, how I had clutched it to my heart until I got home that night. The sparkly sandals tangled up with David's shoes in the foyer; they didn't belong to me. All those hours wasted in neighborhood diners so I could avoid my tainted home. I pictured my dad after my mom left, shutting himself away for years—years that had stretched on, empty, for decades. And I remembered my first month in England, how I'd had to make myself leave the house. My face burned.

It was dark outside when I walked him to the door. I balled the sleeves of my sweater up in my fists when he slipped on his coat.

"It was a hard day for both of us," I said. "Are you feeling better?"

"Don't worry about me. Will you be all right?"

"Yeah. I'm going to eat some more cake and then talk to my dad. Don't worry, I'll tell him I missed his call because I was doing something morally correct and culturally relevant."

I don't think the smile I forced was convincing. He didn't even try.

"I'll see you in one week."

"Give Jordan a hard time for me."

Before going outside, he stepped toward me, and I thought he was going to kiss me in some quiet, comforting way—quickly on the forehead or softly on my cheek. Instead, he slipped his hand beneath my tank top and slid his palm up the curve of my back. In a novel, I might have written something like *his lips crushed against mine*, except it wasn't the kind of kiss which that usually implies, a kiss that demands something in return. Instead, the strength behind it felt like a message. Like a reminder that he wanted me if I was tempted to forget.

He pulled away and looked into my eyes. And when I tell you this next part, you may not believe me, but I swear it's true. He really is this good.

He put his hands on both sides of my face, his gaze serious and measured and kind.

"If you need someone to tell you how remarkable you are, or how much they love you, you can ring me as well."

CHAPTER TWENTY-SIX

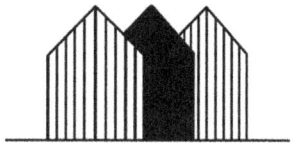

LOVE. SAM HAD SAID LOVE. ON THE DAY I SHOULD HAVE been marrying another man whom I'd sworn to love forever.

Thank you had been an inadequate response, but what else could I have said? Even if I were in love with my much younger boyfriend—which was a *Cosmo* quiz I wasn't ready to take—my would-have-been wedding day was no time to say so.

And love. Really?

I shook my head and began to lay out my notes, chapter by chapter, across the dining room table.

This is not a day for emotional self-assessment, I told myself, ignoring Sam's voice (*love?!*) echoing through my ears. This is a day to be endured and forgotten, I added, closing my eyes against a splintered image of David lifting my veil.

Endured and forgotten through a torrent of work. And maybe a plateful of not-wedding cake.

Okay. Mountain of red velvet on my left. Notes and drafts on my right. Face to the laptop.

"Butt to the chair," I commanded, and got down to business.

Sort of.

Because it's hard to block out your own love life when you're inventing one for somebody else.

Genevieve shivered. The night air was crisp, the water so cold. She tipped her face to survey the stars and her back arched beneath the weight of her skirts...her back arched...arched beneath the beautiful man who had pressed her gently into the couch. The beautiful, thoughtful, too-young man who loves her...who loves her...she is not ready for someone who loves her—

"*Excuse me, Mariana Rose,*" Genevieve snapped. "*This is my book, not yours. You've had me treading water in Baudelaire's moat for hours. Finish this scene so I can dry out.*"

Right, right, back on track. I began tapping the delete key with resolve.

Besides, I told myself, if I do fall in love with Sam, I don't want to be provoked into telling him by my drama with David. If I fall in love with him, I want the words to come naturally. While making dinner, maybe. Me grating parmesan and him whisking up cream for his Italian grandmother's tagliatelle, so good we made it at least once a week. Or while walking the beach some quiet evening, hunting the scattered chips of sea glass that glow along the shore. Sam never fails to find some for me. He'll hold out his hand and they'll gleam against his palm, and my hair will swirl around us as the wind blows off the sea. ("In true romance novel style, I suppose?" he had asked me once on a breezy winter day.) We'll sit in easy silence on our favorite bench, his fingers twined with mine, and I'll look up at him and whisper—

"Augh!" I had deleted half a page.

Pull it together, I barked, sitting up straight. Where was I?

Genevieve shivered as the cold water swirled around her shoulders. She tipped her face to survey the stars and her back arched as the weight of her skirts tugged her down. Her head dipped below the surface, but she clawed at the ledge of the drawbridge and pulled herself up. The ragged planks cut into her palm, but Genevieve dug in with both hands, knowing she was clutching at life itself.

Ugh. The metaphors in this thing are completely obvious, I told myself. She's treading water, she's afraid of change. If she lets herself go, she'll sink and drown. Why don't you come right out and say it? She's fighting love because she's afraid to get hurt.

Had I felt like being clever, I'd have typed out Genevieve's snide response again. As it was, I heard it in my head: *Why don't you come out and say that you're afraid to get hurt so we can get down to business? Because I'm not afraid, I'm madly in love. And since you stuck Lucien in the guillotine and left me as his only hope, I don't have time for this.*

"Next time I'm writing a dishwater character. No more mouthy heroines for me," I said aloud, a weak attempt to distract myself from the issue at hand. And then, as if to confirm that there was no escape, the calendar on my cell phone beeped, reminding me that I'd once had an appointment to keep.

I dropped my head into my hands, and this time David's voice filled my mind.

"Are you sure? Once it's in the Cloud, it's locked in,

Mariana. It's the modern equivalent of signing your name in blood."

"Lock it in, Doctor Lauer. We'll make our deal with the devil together," I'd said, sliding my phone alongside his. I remember kissing his cheek when his face lit up as, after ten months of waiting, we made our wedding date official.

"Face it, now or never," I told myself. The idea of *now* kick-started my pulse, but *never* was a weight that would slow it down for good. When the clock flipped over to ten p.m.—four p.m., Chicago-time; wedding p.m., Marin-time—I stuffed my face with the last chunk of cake, poured myself some of Julie's cheap wine, and bent over my laptop. A playlist glowed out at me.

The Wedding Playlist. All the songs we'd chosen for our big day.

When the Beach Boys began belting out a wish to be older, I spit out my chardonnay. I'd been bumped from my bed by the Homecoming Queen only to take up with the Prom King. The idea of wishing to be older was hilarious. See, I told myself, this isn't so bad.

But it didn't take long. My composure crumpled when Frank Sinatra waltzed in.

"Oh, Frank," I said, trying to laugh. "How could you do it to me?"

He answered by crooning words of devotion.

"Good try," I told him. "I almost buy it. By the way, how many women have you used that line on?" How often had he meant it? Was it worse if it was more than once?

After another foolish love song, I was ready. I slid an envelope from the back of my journal. A chill rocked through me when I ripped the seal.

Item One: Note asking me on our first date, scrawled on a copy of Tennyson's "Mariana":

What if she'd crossed the moated grange and had a drink with me instead of pining for a guy who wasn't nearly as fun? It might have turned into a love poem. If you feel like taking a chance, I'll be waiting for you at the Mystic tonight at nine.

And he had been waiting, with a bottle of red and a ready laugh. And he had waited the day after, and the day after that, until he didn't have to ask which red to order me, and I knew exactly how to draw out his smile.

Item Two: Glassine envelope housing the fragile remains of thirty-two tiny purple orchids. I emptied them into my hand. They had been thirty-two fresh, vivid blooms that had popped up in thirty-two different spots on my thirty-second birthday. The last one had been looped through the prettiest diamond ring.

Item Three: Engagement Photo. The two of us lounging on a blanket at North Avenue Beach. David reading to me from a book of Tennyson. Me with a dreamy, deluded smile on my face.

And Item Four: Wedding Invitation, withheld from the fire to torture myself. Velvety cream paper and rich letterpress details, including Julie's lovely orchid illustration and a rather lovely poem by Doctor Lauer himself.

I made myself see them, the gossamer-fine moments that had made up our life—a life I'd believed was so good. Hadn't it been? David bringing me tea before he left for work. Not breakfast in bed, but almost. On frosty mornings, he'd drape my towel over the radiator so it was toasty warm after my shower. Those purple orchids in every room, thriving in a home filled with love.

Since July, my only clear images of him were those I didn't want—the hectic desire that had melted to shame when I'd walked in and caught him; that horrible anguished sickness when he'd shown up in Seasalter. I picked up the photo and forced myself to see him. Green eyes glinting with intelligence and humor, his warm brown hair with a wash of silver-grey. Across a crowded room, he would smile at me like I was the only person he could see. He had a smile that hinted at all our inside secrets, at something clever and sweet he was waiting to say.

It was a smile every undergrad trembled to see. That was a line from an article in the student newspaper awarding Doctor David Lauer the title of Hottest Professor on Campus. The caption beneath his photo read, "A deep, velvet voice reciting Victorian love poems? Ooh, yes, please." I'd stuck that clipping on the fridge and answered him with a sultry *yes, please* all spring. We had laughed and laughed at the idea of all those kids crushing on their professor.

A smile every undergrad trembled to see. It snapped me back to reality like a slap to the face.

I felt like screaming at his photo. So I did. Then I crumpled it up in my hand.

"Because you are nothing to me anymore. You're sorry that it happened? Great. It was temporary insanity? Sure." Brought on by my lack of commitment? Lack of belief? My hopeless dedication to expecting the worst? Maybe so, who knows?

What I did know was that, at least for the moment, I no longer cared. I wasn't going to sit around like a jilted bride for one more minute listening to Ella Fitzgerald warble "My Romance." Because I knew a thing or two about romance, and more often than not, you wound up trading Ella crooning blissfully for Bessie Smith wailing the blues. And I was done with both.

I flipped the pile of mementos off my lap. Thirty-two brittle orchids flaked onto my vintage rug. I swapped Ella for Ani and ground them into dust.

Half an hour later, I was yowling to Whitesnake with cheerful abandon when someone rapped on the door. Either the police had come to fine me for disturbing the peace or Nandi had hassled Patricia into breaking her promise. I peeked out the window.

It was Sam.

My heart skipped. I didn't know how I felt about his earlier declaration, but one thing was certain: I wanted him there with me. I flipped the lock and leaned on the doorjamb with what I hoped was sexy nonchalance.

"Hello," he said, looking mildly amused.

"You should be on your way to L.A. for a week of meetings and mai tais."

"I'm not really a mai tai kind of guy," he said, stepping inside. "My meetings don't start until Tuesday. Jordan only wanted me to fly in early so she could coach me on what to say."

"Yeah, you're usually at a loss for words." I rolled my eyes, but I was serious when I took his hand. "You didn't need to come back. I'm fine, and Jordan won't be happy."

"Jordan is just relieved she won't contract my tonsillitis. I took ill unexpectedly soon after I left you." He faked a cough and smiled, and his warm eyes did that crinkling thing. He looked so cute that I leaned against him.

"You can share your germs with me." He shivered when I kissed his ear, and suddenly the night took on new life.

"You know, I expected to find you in a very different mood. Vengeful. Heartbroken. Perhaps both. Instead you seem…" I put my hand on his chest and backed him against the wall. He grinned. "Empowered."

I slid my fingers up to trace his lips, then drew them down. "Does this seem empowered?"

Sam didn't answer. In words. But I'd say he agreed.

"Want to meet me upstairs in five minutes?"

"Yes. More than you know. But are you certain that tonight is the right night for you?"

I took a second to ask myself, because maybe he was right. This was not at all how I'd planned my day. Yet as I watched him hold his consideration for me above everything else he might want, all I could remember about the day was how right he'd felt beside me. I leaned into him, looped his fingers with mine. For one moment, the words I wasn't quite prepared to say fluttered against my lips.

But I pressed my lips to his.

"Five minutes," I whispered, and slipped upstairs.

CHAPTER TWENTY-SEVEN

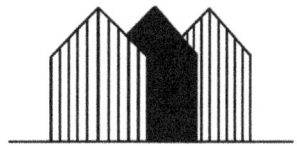

LET ME BE HONEST. I SLIPPED UP THE STAIRS UNTIL I reached the landing. Once out of sight, I vaulted to the top, kicking my dirty clothes under the bed and whipping through the bathroom to clean off the sink. I glanced at myself in the mirror. Face bare but not pasty, that was good. Hair loose and messy but unexpectedly cool. Fine. Good. Now, about my clothes…

The threadbare tank top was not what I'd pictured in this scenario, but it might pass for sexy. However, the tacky You Wish sweatpants I'd changed into earlier were history. I stripped them off and dug around for something else. Jeans are so awkward in the moment and my koala-print pajama pants were absolutely not an option. Anything else seemed like I was trying too hard.

Better too hard than not hard enough, I told myself as I yanked on a jersey skirt.

And then there was the bed. Quilt falling onto the floor, sheets bunched near the end. When I tugged up the flat sheet, the fitted sheet slipped loose. In my frenzy, I tucked it all up military-tight.

"Mariana, take a breath," I ordered and flopped onto the mattress. I felt the hospital corners give way. "Good. And Sam should be up in—" I turned my head to look at the clock. "Twelve minutes?" I'd been zipping around for twelve minutes? Where was he?

I found him reading at my dining room table.

"If you like the steamy scenes in my books, you are going to love what I have planned for you upstairs," I said, draping my arms around him from behind his chair.

I felt him stiffen when I kissed his cheek. His look when he turned toward me wasn't hot or hesitant or even mildly concerned. He was livid.

"Tell me something, Mariana Rose. How long would you have waited before writing up everything that might have happened tonight?"

My hands dropped from his shoulders. I didn't need to see the papers he shoved toward me to know what they were. Earlier that evening, for reference, I had pulled out that Sean and Madison novel. The section I'd flipped to was one of the worst. On the page before him was Claire, Ella's fictional doppelganger, crying into Madison's side over the death of her mother. And then stabbing Madison in the thigh.

All I could do was bite my lip; no words would come to a traitor like me. And all I could think was that this was the end. This was how it would end with Sam. Not for the reasons I'd assumed it would end—I was so much older, we lived an ocean apart. It would end because I had warped his family's most personal loss into a drugstore paperback worth $6.95. It didn't matter that I'd spent the past several weeks writing something completely different, or months before that scrambling for ideas that didn't involve him. That I had written it to begin with was enough.

"You have nothing to say?" he said as I dropped into a chair. "No clever one-liner about art imitating life?"

"It's not what it looks like."

"No?" He snatched up the papers and began to read. "*'It was clear that Claire was traumatized. In the dim light of the pub, shadows aged her delicate face. Her eyes were haunted wells of emptiness. The crying child pressed her nose into Madison's side, as if she could hold on to some fragment of whatever scent had caused her to believe she was with her mother again. And when Sean bent his dark head toward his sister, whispered comforting words only she could hear, Madison found herself wishing she could whisper the same to him.'*"

It was sickening, to hear Sam read it back to me. His tone grew more disgusted.

"*'She ran her hand down the child's silken hair, pressing her close. In Sean's eyes, she saw the hopelessness of a man in despair. Madison reached for him, but before their fingers touched she felt a searing pain as Claire stabbed her—'*"

"You don't know the whole story."

"No, you don't know the whole story. You don't know that for weeks after our mother died, Ella woke up screaming every night. That she slept in Amy's room for months because she was terrified of seeing our own mother dead in her dreams."

I looked into my lap.

"Perhaps these details will make your book more realistic. I haven't seen my father smile in months. He told me the night my mum died that he had no idea how to raise two little girls without her, considering he was fifty-one years old. He's fifty-two now, so your facts are accurate."

"Sam—"

"No, you should know everything. Amy was fired last week for missing a shift when Ella took an anxious spell. She devotes every spare minute to our sisters, although she needn't because Wendy delayed leaving for university to help them adjust. Jenna trained years to achieve Gold Squad-level at the swimming club, but she no longer cares to compete. And surely you'll want to feature Lily. She'll be seven in April. Which would be better for your storyline—if I learn from my mistake with Ella so Lily enjoys her birthday? Or would it be more compelling if I cock it up again?"

He jerked away from the table and turned his back on me. I was afraid to approach him but I got up anyway. Even if I deserved everything he said, I wanted him to have all the facts.

He wouldn't look at me. "All this time, you've been using me for a book."

"No, I haven't." My heart slammed into my throat. "I love you."

I felt my chest split open the minute I said it as the truth in the words came barreling out. Of course I love him, I thought desperately. How could I have pretended I might not?

"Sam. I love you, I do."

He was so controlled when he turned toward me. So deliberate when he curled his lip.

"Thank you." I could almost taste the bitterness staining his words. "I suppose you love Ella as well? Because she loves you, and you've mutilated her. She's a grieving child, not a violent lunatic!"

"I know," I said desperately, trying to touch his arm.

He didn't just shrug me off. He was so repulsed, he backed all the way across the room.

"Okay. For the record, I agree with you. What I've done is despicable. But please let me explain."

"Say what you need to say."

His cold hostility was worse than any volatile rage. I forced myself to meet his eyes.

"I started writing about you the day after we met. It had been months since I'd written one word of any value. I spent the afternoon thinking up terrible ideas and trying not to think about you. Finally, I realized that, for the first time in so long, I was inspired. By you. So I let myself dramatize what happened between us." I rolled my eyes. "I mean, it was a loose interpretation. But there was something about you I liked so much, right away. And I had been empty for so long. I just went with it. It was supposed to be a writing exercise, something romantic and fun that I made up about us. I was hoping that writing anything at all would break through the block I'd had since catching David…"

His expression didn't change but he uncrossed his arms. Then he crossed them right back, killing my hope that his anger had softened. I rushed on.

"It started out innocently—well, as innocently as writing trashy stories about a real person could be. But then my editor called."

I spent the next ten minutes explaining Velicity's production schedule and my contract, about stooping low enough to exploit his family's loss by writing and submitting a partial draft. I spent the ten minutes that followed showing him the unending string of emails insisting to Gretchen that I would not finish the book. Then I followed it up by showing him my new manuscript, which had nothing to do with him beyond the fact that he and Lucien looked remarkably similar.

"The only reason this story isn't rotting in a landfill is that I'm reusing some of the descriptions. In this case, I'm modeling an old tavern on Three Wastrels."

I waited for him to speak, sitting on my hands to keep them still. At last he said, "Why didn't you tell me yourself rather than risk me finding out this way?"

"I hoped you would never find out. It's the worst thing I've ever done. And I did it to you. And Ella…" I pictured the timid trust in her eyes when she leaned against me. The softness of her small hand when she slipped it into mine. "I feel sick over it."

Sam dragged his fingers over a scratch in the table. They stuttered across the surface when he pressed too hard. I summoned all my courage and reached for his hand. He pulled away.

The emptiness in his eyes stung more than the anger I'd expected.

"You'll never look at me the same way again, will you?"

He watched me without speaking. Then he pushed back from the table.

"No. I won't."

All day I had denied myself the comfort of tears, but these words were too much to take. I let my face fall into my hands.

I listened to him pack the few things he kept at my house into his messenger bag. The rasp of the zipper, the shuffle of papers. The clink of the buckles as the flap fell shut. He was going.

Get over it, I told myself. You're not losing a long-term

relationship. This is someone too young, from too far away. Someone with whom, realistically, you had no future at all.

I wanted to cling to these justifications, but the truth pulsing through me was impossible to ignore. I did love Sam. And now that I'd admitted to myself how much, I couldn't just let him leave.

I ripped myself out of the chair and flew into the living room in time to see him slip on his coat.

"Sam, please don't go like this."

He didn't look up as he fastened his buttons, didn't even acknowledge that I was there. Until the clock chime killed our silence.

"It's after midnight. You survived your wedding day." He stepped onto the dark porch and his hard eyes locked with mine. "Congratulations. You're a free woman," he said, and then he shut the door in my face.

CHAPTER TWENTY-EIGHT

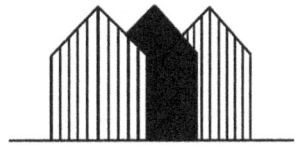

"The person you are trying to reach is unavailable. Please record your—"

I hung up. After three voicemails in thirty minutes, there was no point to a fourth.

Sleep was out of the question. My toenails were trembling, I was so on edge. I thought about writing, but one glance at the dining room table triggered another bout of tears. Finally, I grabbed that half-empty bottle of wine and made for the couch, blessing Julie as I did. The other gifts had been thoughtful, but Julie's cheap wine just kept on giving.

It took a couple of minutes for the fire to get going, but only seconds for my mementos to burn. I pitched them onto the flames without caring. This was no ceremonial cleansing like the burning of the invitations. This was routine, a quick swish of the mop. I tossed in our engagement photo, watched David's hair ignite, dumped a few logs on top. Then I dimmed the lamps, pulled my little house around me, and let it hug me tight.

I tried staring meditatively into the fire. I settled for staring blankly at the wall. I was desperate for distraction when, three hours later, my cell phone rang.

"It's not him, it's not him," I said, grabbing for my skyrocketing hopes. "Do not get excited, it isn't him."

It wasn't him. But it's a good thing I hadn't had the heart to uncork the wine because I knocked the bottle over when I saw who it was.

David Lauer. The bridegroom himself.

"You cannot possibly think I will answer," I said, borrowing a move from Sam that sent him straight to voicemail hell. I didn't bother with the message. He'd been deleted before he began.

And then he actually called again.

"Are you coveting verbal abuse?" I asked his number on the screen. "You must be," I said, when a third call came in. I picked up the phone to switch it off, but this time the call was from Nandi.

"I'm so glad it's you!" I cried, too relieved it was her to consider why she'd be calling me at three a.m.

"Don't hang up," said the very last voice I wanted to hear on my baby sister's phone. Partly because he was Nandi's emergency contact at school; at the time, it had made sense to list him, since he worked on campus. But mostly because if David Lauer were calling me on Nandi's phone, she would have to be—

The air I sucked in got stuck halfway down.

"Tell me," I whispered before my throat sealed off.

"She has a good chance."

"A good chance at what?" I felt the last calm part of my brain unhinge.

"She's going to make it, Marin, you know how tough

she is. She was barely conscious when I got to her, but she recognized me well enough to scowl."

"What happened?" I stumbled upstairs and blindly dumped clothes into a bag. A few pairs of jeans. The crosswalk was unlit. A handful of socks. The driver accelerated into the turn. Pajamas. Underwear. A skull fracture. Three severed fingers. One punctured lung.

"They just took her into surgery. The doctor said reattaching her fingers alone could take a few hours. But Marin," he said, and for the first time he faltered. "There's some internal bleeding that means organ damage. You need to come."

I was already unlocking the car. I leaned against it to keep from doubling over. Organ damage. Nandi's delicate artist's fingers, missing. Not Nandi, please not Nandi, I prayed as I shoved the key into the ignition.

"I can't get in touch with anyone else. Your mom, Charles…no one's picking up."

"They're on their way to Zambia," I said, cursing myself for ignoring my mom the day before. I had no idea when they'd left, when they would land. I didn't even know where they were staying. And my mom was right. Outside the cities, phone reception could be spotty.

"I'll keep calling, you concentrate on getting here safely. Is—anyone —there? To drive you?"

I ignored the catch in his voice when he asked, and the one in mine when I answered.

"No." I hit the A299 and pushed down on the gas.

"Be safe," he said. "I'll see you when you get here." And who'd have ever believed that would be a relief?

I barreled down the empty road and let myself cry, each shuddering wave a new punch to the gut. When I passed the sign for West Malling on the M2, I sucked up my tears and picked up the phone.

"The person you are trying to reach is unavailable. Please—"

"I know he's unavailable!" I shouted, unreasonably enraged by the emotionless recording. By the time the beep sounded, I was sobbing full force again. "Sam, please call me back. It's Nandi."

"It's Nandi—I mean, Nandila Mwenda," I said desperately to the emotionless woman guarding the entrance to the ICU.

"Could you spell that? Both names, please," she said, and we sighed simultaneously.

"N-A-N—"

"Marin."

David was hesitating a few feet behind me, shirt sleeves rolled to the elbow, silver stubble mixed with the brown. We spent an awkward ten seconds trading wary looks before he broke the tension by taking my suitcase.

"The surgeon just came by. She couldn't save her spleen, but they repaired the liver laceration," he said as he led me down the hall. "There's no brain swelling, but she was unconscious when they brought her in, so it's hard to say what may come from the head injury. Critical but stable for now, the doctor said."

He pressed on the door of a dimly lit room. I grabbed for his arm.

"What about—" I swallowed an apple-sized lump in my throat. "What about her fingers?"

He was too slow to respond.

"One," he finally said. "They reattached one."

One. Which meant three. Which meant two, gone.

"Left or right?" I was picturing jars of paintbrushes and pens lining Nandi's desk.

"Right," he sighed, and all those jars crashed to the floor. "But the last two on the right. You know, with rehab...the surgeon seemed positive."

He slid his fingers under mine to pry them off his wrist. Beneath the golden-brown hair on his forearm, five desperate red spots appeared. Five.

"Ready?" He kept my hand in his as we stepped into the room, and if I'd had any thoughts about pulling away, they disappeared when I saw my sister, small and broken in a hospital bed. Tubes crawled out of her nose and veins, snaked up to bags of liquid and whirring machines. Her face was swollen and bruised. She had twisted the wild spirals of her hair into dreadlocks since I'd seen her, but they'd been shaved off on one side. Electrodes studded her scalp. Her right hand was completely bandaged. I ran my finger over her left.

"Hey, sweet girl. You're doing great," I whispered, as near to her ear as I could get around all those wires. "Get better soon, okay? We all need you here bossing us—"

My fingertip hit something rough—the five pretty nails of her fragile left hand. Apple-green polish and the finest swirls of gold glitter cascading down like fireworks. The playful work of an artist with a very steady hand.

I flipped around, unsure if what was hurtling up my throat was a scream or something worse. David stepped up and caught me. I pressed my face into his shoulder to stifle my sobs. He led me to the loveseat against the wall and rubbed my neck while I pulled it together. But when he tried to slip his arm around me, I sat up straight.

"David, thank you. It means so much to me that you stayed with her. But you've been here for hours. Go home and rest."

"I don't want to leave her. I don't want to leave either of you."

I began to withdraw, an instinct, maybe, but I looked up at him and held still. Because something about the way he sat, slumped but tense, knuckles white as he gripped his knees, stripped another layer off that carefully shellacked image I'd been nurturing since July—an image that blotted out everything about him I had loved. But seeing him take care of my little sister reminded me that, for a long time, Nandi had been his little sister, too.

"If you want me to go, I'll go. I know you hate me. I know she hates me. But it feels wrong to leave."

"I don't hate you," I said, and if I'd had any room left for new emotions, I might have felt surprised.

David's face registered all the shock mine must've lacked.

"You don't hate me?"

"No." I sank back against the loveseat.

"Nandi hates me," he said, slumping beside me.

Our eyes met, and I don't know why we both smiled when I said, "Yeah. Nandi hates you."

"Maybe it will motivate her to pull through." David raised his voice and said, "I'm not leaving until you wake up, kid," and the two of us laughed so loudly that a nurse stuck her head into the room.

"I shouldn't have to explain that intensive care patients need a peaceful environment."

David pulled out the posh voice and fired his smile at the nurse. "I apologize, ma'am. We'll restrain ourselves. Although I think the environment is surprisingly peaceful," he said, smiling at me again as we slid into separate corners. "More peaceful than I'd expected."

CHAPTER TWENTY-NINE

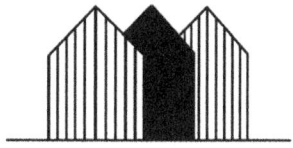

"Ow!" David rubbed his chin. My head had cracked against him when I'd bolted upright. My heart was pounding in time with the beeps exploding from Nandi's bedside.

"She's fine, I'm just changing her fluids," said the nurse adjusting Nandi's IV. "I'm sorry I woke you. You looked so sweet cuddled up together. A very cute couple."

I shook off enough sleep to realize that David and I had drifted together as we'd napped. We were altogether too close beneath a white cotton blanket. I shook that off too and slid away from him.

"I covered you," the nurse went on. "You're wearing your coat, so I assumed you were cold. And you make such a cute couple," she said again, her eyes shooting off cartoon hearts that apparently blinded her to my sour face.

"We're not a couple," I said, but David flashed the dimple side of his smile and said, "Ay, but a light comes from her when she moves and, magnet-like, she drew me in."

"That's beautiful! Did you write that yourself?"

"It's a reference to Tennyson's 'Merlin and—'"

"How is my sister?" I said before the nurse swooned into the dark abyss of Victorian poetry.

She looked startled but managed to blink herself back from the brink. "Her breathing is regular and it's getting stronger. We're watching for symptoms of a bile leak, but right now there's no need for a drain-bag."

Three words I hope never to hear in the same sentence again: Bile. Leak. Drain-Bag. Especially concerning my little sister.

"How long will it take this sedative to wear off?" I asked.

"Hard to say. Her boo-boos are pretty painful and those meds are strong."

Boo-boos? That was worse than the bile bag.

"But she will wake up, right? I mean, she's not in a…"

"Coma?" she chirped. "That crack on the head didn't help, for sure. But she's not in a coma. There's a really good chance she'll wake up."

I waited for her to add something, like *soon* or *by eight*.

"Did you want anything else?" she asked as I stood there expectantly, and I decided I didn't. Hopefully she was just a terrible communicator. If not, I wasn't ready to know what she meant. I passed her the blanket on her way out. "You hang on to that. This hospital is so chilly, you two may need to snuggle again."

"Chilly? I'm being fired in a kiln," I told David, stripping off the coat I'd fallen asleep in.

"That's an interesting look," he said, taking in my threadbare tank top.

"You called me in the middle of the night. I was only

thinking about getting here, I didn't stop to change." He was staring a little too closely at the tank top, so I pulled my cardigan tighter across my chest.

"You've always looked beautiful in that sweater," he said, and his words and expression were so similar to Sam's from the day before that I caught my breath. Was that only yesterday? I wondered, as a different pain sliced through my middle. I tried to block the images of Sam that bloomed into my brain, but my imagination anchored them into place, forcing me to relive how the love in his eyes had shifted to disgust, how his smiling lips had curled into a sneer.

"Marin? Are you all right?" David said when I didn't move. I snapped out of the memory and nodded. "We slept through lunch. Do you want dinner? I could order Thai—"

The phone next to Nandi's bed rang. I nearly knocked him down.

"It might wake her," I heard myself say before running face-first into my senseless words. David slid his right hand over mine while I stood frozen at Nandi's side. He picked up the phone with his left.

"Charles. Did you get a flight?" I kept my eyes on Nandi's motionless face, but when David began updating my stepfather on the bile leak, I walked out the door. And kept walking, until I hit the snow-pocked sidewalk and gulped a breath of frosty night. The chill had set everyone's noses running, so my sniffling didn't attract attention. But when I checked my phone and saw that, after twenty-four hours and at least a half-dozen messages, Sam still hadn't called, I didn't care who heard me.

"The person you are trying to reach is unavailable..."

I waited for the beep and let him have it.

"I just called to say that, for all I care, you can stay unavailable. I realize that mangling your sister's grief for a storyline was wrong and I'm sorry. But your sister isn't going to die from some crap manuscript no one will ever read. Your sister isn't lying unconscious with her liver stitched together and half her hand missing. I would never ignore you in this situation. So kiss Ella and Lily goodbye for me because, regardless of what you think, I do love them. And thanks for being such an unconscionable jerk. You've made it easy to forget that I ever loved you."

I tried to slam the phone into my coat pocket and realized I'd left my coat upstairs. I probably wasn't cold because my blood was boiling. But David seemed to think it was a problem.

"You went outside in this weather with no coat? Do you want to end up with pneumonia in a bed next to Nandi?"

I ducked away from his attempt to cloak me in that blanket. "What did Charles say?"

"They landed in Munich. He sounds shaky." He glanced at Nandi and nearly shouted, "But confident. He's confident about Nandi getting better."

I couldn't help smiling at the anxious way he studied her face. "You think she can hear us?"

"I don't want to worry her if she can." We stood at Nandi's side and I daubed my own lip gloss on her dry lips. "They have a six-hour layover in Munich, can you imagine? They'll be here tomorrow morning."

We watched her quietly for a few minutes before he said, "Where were we supposed to be right now? Bordeaux?"

"Don't."

"Our plane would have been landing. Four nights in

Bordeaux and four months in the Pyrenees. Why did you go along with that plan, anyway? Tracking Tennyson and Hallam's route through the mountains. Four months of back and forth between Narbonne and Perpignan. Not exactly a romantic honeymoon."

"Four months in the south of France is hardly a chore. And you were the one working. I would have been free as a little French bird."

"Yes. 'Mariana in the South.'" He looked so disheartened that I let the reference slide.

"You should've gone anyway. You don't need me to trek after Tennyson."

"At this point, any sabbatical I'm granted will be permanent. Besides, it wouldn't have been the same without you." He didn't look up when he added, "I'm so sorry, Marin."

"David, I don't want to talk about this."

"Neither do I. But given the day, let me say it. I'm sorry. I am so sorry." His words scratched out in a whisper. My own throat grew tight. When he took my hand, I didn't snatch it away. When he pulled me into his arms, I even hugged him back.

"Hell."

We flipped around and there was Nandi, her onyx eyes blinking up at us.

She licked her lips. "Hell."

"Hello to you, too," I said, a bubble of relief swelling from my stomach to my throat. I poured a bucketful of grateful exclamations and happy tears over her, which seemed to leave her unimpressed.

Nandi cleared her throat. "Not hello. Hell."

She swung her gaze from me to David, David to me.

Then she turned her eyes on David and tried to burn a hole right through him.

"I died, didn't I?" she finally said, her voice rough from disuse but fueled by fury. "I died and I'm in hell. That's the only way you could be touching my sister."

"No, honey, we were just—" I paused. What had we been doing? Not making up, exactly. Maybe making peace.

"Why were you hugging him? Have you completely lost your mind?"

"At least we know your memory is intact," David said, and Nandi glared at him until he took a step back.

"Look who's up!" sang the romantic nurse as she bounced into the room. "Rise and shine, you sleepy little sweetie!"

Nandi threw a scowl at her, then jerked her head toward David. "Could you please have him removed from this room? By force?"

"Somebody woke up a grumpypants!" The nurse smiled at David. "Patients are often emotional coming out of an experience like this, but don't you worry. In a few days, her smile will be sunshine-bright."

Nandi shook her head. "This has to be hell."

A happy, hiccupping sob slipped out of me. She turned toward me with her proprietary blend of exasperation and disgust.

"Marc, I am begging you. Quit sniveling and act normal." She frowned at David and the nurse. "You're my only link to reality."

I did my best to suck up my tears. "I just didn't expect you to be so much like yourself."

"Who did you expect? Someone who doesn't mind you cavorting with this jerk? Did you think I had a lobotomy?"

She picked anxiously at the electrodes on her head. "I didn't, right? Have a lobotomy?"

"No," I said, smiling to hide my sorrow over what she truly had lost. "Charles and Mom will be here in the morning."

"Some guy named Phil has called five times, he's been so worried," David said, and Nandi tolerated him long enough to accept that choice bit of news.

"How long have I been in here?" she said, seeming to remember that there were worse things than catching David with his hands on me.

"Since last night. You—"

"Miss Mwenda, welcome back."

The doctor in the doorway was tiny, maybe five feet tall, with razor-sharp hair and a matching bedside manner. She almost glanced at David and me.

"You can wait in the hall while I examine her."

"We'll be right outside," I told Nandi, kissing her cheek and her forehead, too. She rolled her eyes.

"While you're out there, get a grip."

I doubt she was suggesting I grip David's shoulders, but that's exactly what I did when we fell together in relief.

"She's going to be okay," I whispered.

"She's going to be great."

The breath I'd been holding for nearly a day eased its way out. When I inhaled again, my nose didn't burn from the pungent hospital with its base note of despair. The air I took in was a twist of spring, laced like a gift through a bitter-cold day. And it had a familiar sandalwood finish that used to make my knees go weak.

I hadn't paid enough attention. I'd let us slip into a favorite spot—my cheek pressed into his shoulder, his chin resting on my head. His soft t-shirt was smooth and warm against his solid chest.

It's only the stressful day, I told myself when I leaned into him.

It's just my sleepless night, I said when I closed my eyes.

"I did provoke her into waking," David murmured against my hair. "Finally. Something I managed to get right."

"You got a lot of stuff right this time." He squeezed my fingers, which reminded me that I had things to figure out. "How do I tell her about her hand?"

"Maybe I should tell her. If she feels like lashing out, she'll enjoy yelling at me."

"No, I'll do it. I just hate to think about how she'll feel."

"We could tell her together. When she's angry, she can beat me up, and when she needs to cry, you'll calm her down."

"We'll play it by ear," I said as the doctor left the room, but one look at Nandi told me she already knew. She was worse than hysterical. She was mute. And she was cradling her bandaged hand.

I nudged the IV stand aside. The stunned way she leaned into me said more than shouts or tears. But after an hour of near silence, she looked up at David.

"I hear they saved my middle finger. You'll be my inspiration in rehab."

David actually smiled.

"With that for motivation, you'll be perfect again by next week," he told her, and for one moment, Nandi's twitching lips betrayed her. Because once upon a time, she'd been as loyal to David as she still was to me.

She tolerated him until visiting hours ended, when

David dared to tap her on the knee. "All right, kid, I'll give you a break from my presence." He glanced around the room before his gaze lit on me. "Well. Take care."

"You, too," I said, knowing I should say something meaningful, but too lame to figure out what.

"Wait," Nandi said. She looked at me. "I need to spend the night alone."

"What? No. I'm not leaving you here."

"Marc." She gripped my arm and I noticed how hard she was breathing. "You know how you said you needed Sam to stay away?" She cast a smirk toward David. "You remember Sam, Marin's movie-star man-friend?"

David's eyes hit the floor.

Nandi turned back to me. "It's just, I get it now. I get why you needed to do the wedding day alone," she said, and David's eyes sprung back up to my face.

"Nandi, you're hurt," I told her. "I can't leave you—"

"I get it," she said, each word dropping rigidly into place. She leaned against me again and I fought off the instinct to clutch her to my side. "No one can do it for me, remember? I have to face it myself."

It was just like this girl to use my own words against me. I felt her shoulders relax when I nodded. "If you need me, I can be here in ten minutes."

"From your place? No less than fifteen. But okay." She didn't bother looking at David when she said, "Did you drive here, Doctor Dipstick?"

"Our car's downstairs," said David, who didn't look away from me.

"No, *your* car is downstairs. She doesn't have a car anymore," she growled, then she pinched her lips together.

"Doctor Ross said you stayed here the whole time. So, thanks or whatever."

From the casual way she picked at her cast, I could tell she meant it. She proved it by granting him the privilege of driving eight city miles out of his way to take me home.

"But don't even think about trying anything with her." We were almost out the door when she called, "Oh, yeah. Um, Alfred's probably pissed. I forgot to feed him before I left last night."

Poor baby. I hadn't considered my sweet cat once since I'd gotten to Nandi. I pictured Alfred's portly face.

Oh help, I told myself on our way to the car. Meal-free for a whole day. I'm going to hear about this.

"You're going to hear about that," David said. "Alfred was probably offended by your absence to begin with. Without food, he'll threaten to sue. Sorry. I should have thought of him."

"I should have thought of him. He's *my* cat," I said, although technically we'd adopted him together.

The streetlights flashed across David's profile when he pulled into traffic. I saw his jaw tense.

After twenty-four hours of unsettling surprises, I should have learned to expect them, but I was shocked when I found myself sympathizing with David as I weighed the impact of all that he'd lost. The only family he'd had in the city. The job and respect he'd worked years to secure. Our condo; although I had bought it before we met, together we'd turned it into a home. Even the lumpy grey cat who, until a few months earlier, had never been anyone but our cat. Our cat, our car, our circle of friends. When you pulled the sinews of our lives apart, not much remained on either side that hadn't grown into the other. No wonder the snap had been so messy.

Messy. More like a bloodbath, I thought as we pulled up to my building. The syrupy, spoiling cantaloupe scent that had haunted our apartment before I'd left for England suddenly flooded my nose.

David had slumped behind the wheel. Maybe he could smell the cantaloupe, too.

"Do you want help with your suitcase?"

"No," I said, so sharply he flinched. I cracked open the door to let some February into the stuffy car. "Listen, thank you again for taking care of Nandi. I really appreciate how you came through for her."

"Charles asked me to stop by the hospital before class tomorrow morning. I could pick you up on my way."

"It's not on your way."

His hands gripped the steering wheel. "I could pick you up anyway."

"I don't think spending more time together is a good idea," I told him. And to prove my point, my heart turned a flip when he unclipped his seatbelt and leaned toward me.

"Don't you miss us, Marin? Don't you miss me? Because I miss you. As awful as the past few hours have been, I'm so glad I got to spend them with you."

Regret anchored his expression, but hope ghosted in his eyes. When he picked up my hand, I felt another wave of unsettling warmth. It had begun to wash over me every time he got close.

"Marin," he whispered, but I turned away. It was easier to think without looking at him.

Nandi's habit of leaving on lights hadn't changed. Three floors above us, a warm glow filtered through the sheers at the living room window. A year before we would have gone up together. For months, I hadn't wanted to go up at all.

"David, I don't think—"

A little pointy-eared figure leapt into the window seat and began scratching its paws against the glass.

I swore at myself and jumped out of the car, fumbling for the keys in my purse. Loitering downstairs while my cat was starving. I should call the ASPCA on myself.

"Sorry, buddy," I said when I got to Alfred. He yowled pathetically with each twist of the can opener and glowered until I dumped the food into his bowl. But when his little jaws were clamped around his first ferocious bite, he allowed me to scratch behind his ears.

"Goodness, I missed you," I told him, and he flipped his feather-duster tail in my face.

"He's angry, so clearly he missed you, too," David said from behind me as he dropped my suitcase. The knee he'd twisted at his last faculty 5K cracked when he crouched beside us. He offered his hand to Alfred and got a tail-slap in return. "It's nice to know you still care, pal."

His grinning eyes held mine, long enough for me to know I had to move. But when I sprung upright so did he, so that we were still face-to-face, eye-to-eye, in the middle of the home we had shared for years.

The sink was piled with dirty dishes—stacks of vibrant Fiestaware, an early wedding gift from David's parents. Nandi's trail of assorted Converse stretched from the living room into the open kitchen we'd remodeled, an early wedding gift to ourselves. Textbooks lay scattered over the new walnut floors. *The Catcher in the Rye* was splayed open on the velvet sofa that had been our first joint purchase four years before. All around me were reminders of what I'd once valued most: the man I had loved, the life we had built, the sister I'd almost lost. And how the man I'd loved had been there when my sister was so alone.

My eyes swept across the room, but when they fell on David, they locked with his. He took one step toward me and, when I didn't step back, he took me into his arms. His hands slid into spots so familiar they were practically a custom fit—the small of my back, the nape of my neck. He leaned in until we were pressed together, leaned me back until I had to hold on. That sandalwood scent wrapped around me until I forgot that I should let go.

My heart pounded beneath his fingers as they skimmed over my shirt. His lips brushed mine and I gasped in surprise. Electricity pulsed through me from the taste of him. I pulled him closer and the sparks burst into flame. And then his hands were roaming wildly and mine raked through his messy hair. He backed me across the room until I was pressed against the wall.

"Oh, I've missed you," he whispered between shaking breaths.

I opened my eyes to answer and froze. Somewhere between that gentle first kiss and the feverish last, the edges of my worlds had blurred together. I looked into his eyes and was stunned that they were green instead of golden brown.

I jerked away so hard my skull smacked against the wall.

"Hey," he said softly and cupped the back of my head. But when his fingers slid into my hair, I jerked away again, and this time I pushed him off. His hands dropped, limp at his sides.

"I'm sorry, I can't do this," I said like some horrible cliché. Like a shallow archetype, the woman who says yes but means no. Or maybe says no and means yes? Whichever. The only difference between that stale character and me was that she flirts with disaster, whereas I had almost dragged it into bed. "Sorry," I said again. "I can't."

"Because of him?" His voice was a jumble of sorrow and regret and something a lot like annoyance. It was the something that fueled an annoyance of my own, one that burned right through the truth in his words.

"Because of her," I snapped. I ignored the ache sinking into his face by shaking my head to clear it.

Try cracking it on the wall again. Maybe you'll pound some sense into it, I told myself. I forced my mind to color in the details of his betrayal that had lately begun to fade. And when the venom I conjured didn't burn hot enough, I grabbed my suitcase by its handle and marched down the hall, determined to shove myself headfirst into the scene of the crime.

"Marin, wait," he said, but my trembling hand gripped the doorknob. I threw a defiant look over my shoulder, then threw open the door to welcome the sting that would come from the sight of our bed.

But our bed was gone. In its place was the hand-carved teak headboard I'd fallen in love with on our last weekend getaway. It had been an impractical love. The heavy headboard had a price tag to match; I'd reluctantly left it behind. Now it was standing in my own room, against walls that had been green when I left but were now a pale, buttery cream. My tired IKEA floor mat had been replaced with a plush wool rug. The new duvet was bright white, fresh and clean and airy. And folded at the end, still in the dry cleaner's plastic overwrap, was my grandmother's quilt, made new.

I crept across the room. With the quilt clutched to my chest, I ran one finger around the grooves of a gleaming teak lily.

David was hesitating outside the room. He didn't come near, even when I said, "How did you do this?"

"I asked Nandi to do it. Obviously, she restricted my involvement to handing over my credit card and tracking down the bed." He looked straight at the floor and shuffled another step back. "The, uh, mattress is new, too."

The mattress was so tall that, when I perched on it, my toes lifted off the floor. The tufted top pillowed around me. Alfred barreled into the room and made himself comfortable on what had been David's side of the bed.

David stepped back again and bumped into my office door.

"You were right. I shouldn't be here." He started toward the kitchen without looking up. Within seconds, the front door closed.

It took me a minute to push my stunned body off the bed. He was on the first-floor landing before I got the words out.

"Tomorrow morning, if you don't mind, a ride to the hospital would be great."

CHAPTER THIRTY

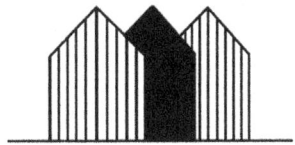

"You got anything for me in there?" David asked the next morning. He tapped the box of doughnuts I'd bought to celebrate Nandi's big move from the ICU to a regular floor.

"Possibly." I pulled out his favorite apple fritter and watched his eyes light up.

"You are, quite simply, a beautiful human being." He shoved half the doughnut in his mouth at once. "A jewel," he added around a wad of masticated dough.

"You are, quite simply, grossing me out right now," I said with a laugh as we rounded the corner toward Nandi's new room.

My mother must have heard us coming. She was charging toward us, face blazing as brightly as the curls falling out of her braid.

"Marin, why on earth would you leave Nandi alone last night?"

"It's nice to see you, too, Mom. Doughnut?" I offered her the gross one—jelly-filled.

"David spent hours waiting with her so she wouldn't be alone. Charles and I are rushing like mad from the other side of the world. But the minute she wakes up, you decide it's time to go."

"It's what she said she needed. She can decide for herself, she's nineteen years old."

"Yes, she's nineteen. She has no business staying alone after such an ordeal."

"Try telling her that. She—"

"She cried all night. She made herself sick."

I stopped so suddenly that David smacked into me, then I shoved the doughnuts into his hands and stormed down the hall. But when I burst into Nandi's room she was propped up in bed, convincing Charles that she should tattoo the shaved side of her head.

"Just a little one, Dad. As a reminder that I've been given a second chance," she added solemnly.

Charles gave her the shrewd smile he reserved for Nandi, but when he hugged me, his hands were trembling. Over his shoulder, I gave her a thumbs-up.

"Well done, kid," I heard David say from the doorway, and Nandi's eyes narrowed. David sighed. "I'll wait outside."

"No, we must thank you for your care of Nandila," Charles said, clasping David's hand. "We would have preferred no one else in our absence."

"Ha!" Nandi sneered.

"Cut it out," I said.

She was horrified into speechlessness. Unfortunately, my mother was not.

"From now on, we'll call you before we call Marin. You seem to have more staying power."

My faithful protector paused in her disapproval of me to rush to my defense.

"Isobel, I made Marin leave."

"Why didn't you call me?" I scolded her. "I'd have come right back."

She rolled her eyes. "Why is everyone making this into a thing? So I cried a little. Big deal."

"You don't puke on yourself from crying *a little*." My mom was looking at Nandi, but she pointed her words at me.

Nandi tried her best to surge upright. "Haven't you people heard of alone time? I wanted five minutes by myself to get used to the idea that I'm a gimp."

The sound disappeared from the room as the rest of us quit breathing. A few awkward moments passed before David turned to me.

"I thought the gimp's affliction was confined to the leg," he deadpanned. I saw my sister try not to smile. But my mom was in no mood to joke.

"There's nothing funny about this. You shouldn't have left her alone, Marin."

"Isobel, I told you, I asked her to leave."

"Then she should have had the backbone to tell you no."

I was torn between guilt over leaving Nandi to cry herself sick and aggravation with my mother for not letting it go. But when my mom turned toward me and said, "You're her sister. You should have stuck it out," something inside me snapped.

"The way you stuck it out with my dad?"

I heard lungs all over the room distend when everyone sucked in their breath again.

"That was different," my mom whispered.

"You're right, it was different. Nandi wanted to be alone. Dad begged you to stay."

There was almost an audible whoosh as my mother's indignation deflated. She pulled her arms around herself until Charles took her hand.

"That is all now, from both of you. Let us simply be thankful that Nandila will soon be well."

I crossed to Nandi's side. "How are you doing?"

"Are we still talking about this?"

"I want to make sure you're okay before I go. It's crowded in here. And I have a sudden urge to visit my dad," I said without looking at my mom. "I'll stay with you tonight. We'll design head tattoos."

"Do you want to take the car?" David asked. "You can drop me off at work and I'll swing by here later and pick it up."

"Thanks," I said, ignoring the alarm flashing in Nandi's eyes.

"Marin..." My mom's voice was small when she called across the room.

"You all need some time together. I'll see you later," I told her, too tired to fight but not ready to make peace.

I called my dad on the way out of town. The chocolate chip cookies he always makes me were hot when I arrived two hours later.

"The groceries aren't delivered until Wednesday. I'm running low on milk."

I pulled a jug from my tote bag. "Cookies without milk would be criminal."

"My Bell Petite. Let no man say we didn't raise you right."

I rested my face against his shoulder when he pulled me in for a long hug. The wiry fibers of his wool cardigan tickled my nose, but the cedar-chest scent calmed my nerves.

"How's...is it Nandi?" he asked, although he knew quite well it was. My mother's second family is a sensitive issue.

"Better. They moved her to a regular floor."

"Give my best to whatever nurse has to keep that pistol in a hospital bed," he said while I poured the milk. "You've had a rough couple of days. How are you feeling?"

How are you feeling? The words echoed back to me in Sam's voice—it was gentle on the first go-round, mocking on the rest.

"I'm okay," I began, and then I stopped myself. I didn't need to make excuses with my dad. "No, I'm not. My sister almost died on my canceled wedding day and my ex-fiancé keeps making me forget he's a pig. This teenage jerkhole I've been dating just dumped me—"

"You've been dating a jerkhole?" he said, another perfect example of why I love him. Faced with two curious options, he always focuses on the right one. Daughter dating a teenager? Bizarre. Daughter dating a jerkhole? Unacceptable. "Who is he? What does he do? Assuming he's not in high school."

"His name is Sam. He's an actor...slash waiter," I added, enjoying the sardonic way my dad grimaced. "How do I keep finding these guys who seem perfectly normal and then—boom—they turn out to be capable of something nasty? David, no problem at all plopping into bed with a student. Sam, so childish he won't return an emergency phone call."

"It's because there is no normal. And we're all capable of anything."

Thus sayeth the sage, I grouched, slouching against the tabletop. "It doesn't matter, I'm done with dating. It brings out the craz—" I halted before my mouth ran away with itself.

"It what?"

"I had a panic attack," I told him.

"Oh, I see, dating brings out the crazy in you," he said, and fortunately he laughed.

"Sorry. But yes, I had a panic attack, and I understand now why you'd do anything to avoid one. It was awful."

I was afraid to look at him, sure I would read in his eyes the certainty that, indeed, I was teetering on the edge of mental instability.

"When was this?"

"A few weeks ago."

"Were you out?"

"No, I was at home." And thank God for it, I added silently. No wonder so many people with panic disorders stop leaving the house. The idea of that happening in a public place—the dizziness, the puking, the being sure you're going to die—was petrifying.

"What were you doing when it happened?"

"I was…" A filmstrip of risqué images flickered through my mind. "I was exercising," I said, trying to sound casual.

His mouth pulled to the side as his eyes narrowed.

"With the jerkhole, I assume." I felt my face heat up. "Pretend for a minute this isn't the most awkward discussion we've ever had. Were you thinking about Jerkhole the First while *exercising*?"

Of course the answer was yes. It had been years since I'd been that close to anyone but David. Sure, the novelty of someone else had been exciting. But there was the vulnerability of it, too—the sucking-in-your-stomach part of any new romance. Not to mention that, for each stroke of a hand in reality, I saw the mirror image slipping over that girl in my bed.

"You know enough about panic attacks to work up some of the symptoms once you began worrying about them, but my guess is you had an anxiety attack," he said. "The terms get used interchangeably, but they're not the same thing. A panic attack happens for no reason. An anxiety attack is provoked by stress. And you're an expert at ignoring stress until it blows up in your face."

I didn't need to respond to the part about me. We both knew that was true. But could he be right about the anxiety thing?

"I've done some research, obviously," he said when I asked him about it. Since one wall of the books lining his study was devoted to the subject, I decided to take him at his word.

"Before you broke up with David, did you have—" My father squirmed, and then growled, because squirming is not something he does well. "Did you have problems in this area?" When I shook my head, he said, "Did you have another attack the next time you, er..."

"We didn't—I mean, I haven't been—I thought it was better to stop."

"I'm sure the jerkhole was thrilled about that."

Another filmstrip rattled off, a sequence of kind eyes smiling into mine, of lips that never hesitated to pull back and hands that worked hard not to get carried away. *How are you feeling?* There was warmth in the voice when I heard it again.

"He understood."

My dad heaved an irritated sigh, like he couldn't believe he was forced to discuss this with his daughter. "You shouldn't keep yourself from…exercising. *If* you feel ready—" He grunted in exasperation. "All I'm saying is if you treat it like a problem, it's more likely to become one."

So much for my stint as a psychologist.

"Do you think that covers it or do we need to keep discussing this?" The dread in his eyes as he asked was equal to the horror in my voice when I yelped, "No! No. Thanks. I think that's answered my question."

"Good," he declared, and the kitchen buzzed with the relief rising off us both. After a few minutes of recovery, he said, "If you'd rather not deal with the house—or with the jerkhole—you don't need to go back to Seasalter. That Glenister man called last week with another offer."

"I hope you told him no. I love Seasalter. I love that house. I'm not giving it up because of some infantile Englishman. And listen, Dad, I know you don't want to hear this, but I'm paying full price for the house."

"No, you're not. You shouldn't even have to buy it, you should be inheriting the place, but I need—"

"Exactly, you need the money, and now I can pay you what it's worth. What you'd get from someone else if you weren't selling it to me." I cut off his protest. "Last week I asked your attorney to amend the selling price. Also, she locked in our closing date, along with your closing date on this place with your landlord. Why didn't you tell me Ulrich was pressuring you?"

"Ulrich is a pillock. Not worth mentioning," he said,

reminding me that, despite his almost-vanished accent and a mostly Midwestern upbringing, he was English at heart. "Now call and get that price back down where we agreed."

We spent the next few hours splicing arguments over the selling price into updates on life in general. I'd bitten into one last cookie when he said, "Before you go, tell me what happened with your mother this morning."

"What do you mean?"

"She called me," he said, and I blinked.

"Excuse me?"

"We talk now, from time to time." The cookie turned to glue in my mouth. "She comes over for dinner sometimes," he added, and I tried to swallow and choked.

He whacked me on the back.

"You neglected to mention this why?" I asked when I could talk again.

"Your mother worried about how you'd react." He looked me over. "How are you reacting?"

At first I couldn't answer. If he'd said Elvis had been to dinner, I might have believed him. My mother coming for dinner was impossible.

"Mariana?"

"Yeesh, give me a minute. I need to piece my identity back together." My answer, I realized, was dependent upon his. "How do you feel about it?"

"We've come to an understanding."

"What understanding?" I said, but he waved the question away.

"Just don't give her a hard time."

"But—"

"I know you're angry with her, but you've always done

your best not to let it poison things between you. Don't give into it now."

He was giving me more credit than I deserved. Sure, I'd managed to maintain a neutral relationship with my mother. The explosive battles we'd had during my teenage years had mostly ceased. But the peace had come at the expense of any bond we'd once shared. Our days of weeping over *Casablanca* together were done. They'd given way to a series of conversations that grew more strained and less frequent every year. Maybe I hadn't cultivated the friction between us, but I hadn't done much to relieve it.

My dad never bothers with a poker face. He tossed his trump card into my lap by saying, "If you won't do it for her, do it for me."

But I wasn't letting it go until I knew a few things. If there was any chance that my mother's reappearance could shake the balance he'd knocked together, I would bar his front door myself.

"Does it hurt you, being around her?" I asked, and he answered me frankly, like he always has.

"Yes." I opened my mouth to argue and he said, "But not as much as being without her. It will never be the same between us, I know, but I'm willing to redefine our relationship if it means we can forge some kind of peace."

I hid my scowl behind a long drink of milk.

"Say it out loud, Mariana. Your face is saying it for you anyway."

Say it out loud, really? Fine. No problem. Happy to oblige.

"What will you do if she disappears again? How can you ever trust that she won't? And how can you be so civil to her when she's been ignoring you for years?"

"Because I love her," he said, and my heart hit the roof of my mouth. "There's no point in hiding it. Anyone who wants to can pick up *Salt in the Sea* and know exactly how I feel about her. That makes me seem pathetic to people who know she left, but if I cared what people think, I would never have written that book. I didn't write it for them. I wrote it to tell the people I love most how much they mean to me. I wrote it as a love letter, to her and to you."

"Dad—"

"I've loved her for forty years and she's always known it. Why would I pretend that I don't?"

"Because she shattered your heart. Because she left you alone when you needed her most."

Because you almost didn't recover, I thought desperately. Because I can't stand to lose you if it happens again.

My doubts unfolded in the silence between us.

"You worry too much, Petite. I'm not fooling myself. Your mother isn't coming back to me. But I've spent twenty years living with her memory. I'd like to include the reality of her in the years I have left, however sparse that reality might be."

He smudged away the tears I couldn't manage to hide. "If you love someone enough you can forgive anything." His fingers trembled when they reached for mine. "Forgiveness is illogical most of the time. But then, so is love."

CHAPTER THIRTY-ONE

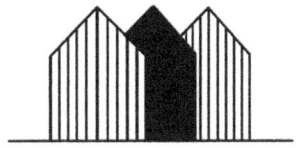

The silence outside Nandi's hospital room was eerie enough that I picked up my pace. I pushed through the half-open door, almost expecting her bed to be empty. But she was there, and so was David, and they were staring each other down.

"What's going on? Where is everyone?"

Nandi crossed her arms as best she could around her bandaged hand.

"The *family* needed some sleep. They left this interloper here to babysit me, although I'd much rather be alone." She turned to David. "I see what you're doing. You're trying to worm your way in. She's not giving you another chance!"

David looked at me with weary eyes. "Nandi has been reminding me that I don't deserve you."

"Nope. And as long as I have even one stump of one finger, I will throw you out," she snapped, and the real issue behind her attitude became clear.

"Calm down. This isn't good for you." I put my hand on her shoulder. She shrugged it off.

"You're just as bad, hugging him and being all nice and borrowing his car. What would Sam say?" I glanced at David. Nandi's straining voice hardened. "Don't worry, I gave Professor Perv the scoop on your hot new romance."

"Nandi…" I said, but I couldn't follow it up. I wasn't ready to tell her I'd set a new personal record for Relationships I've Ruined.

"I let him know you're so in love, you only leave your sex cave every three days."

I'd never told Nandi that Sam and I hadn't made it all the way into that cave; I'm sure she'd convinced David that we were spelunking night and day. Which, when I considered it, was an assumption I didn't mind him making. Still, Nandi was getting out of hand.

"Relax. Do I need to call the nurse upstairs for some grumpypants medicine?"

My sister was not amused. Nor was she thrilled when David and I laughed together. She was so irritated she didn't even call him by an insulting nickname.

"Look, David, thanks very much for helping them scrape me off the street. Thanks for staying with me while they stuck me back together and thanks for waiting around until everyone else got here. But guess what? They're here. And you shouldn't be. So just go."

"As you wish. You obviously won't be happy until I do." David started toward the door.

"Have a nice life," she called as he passed by her bed.

"That's enough." I turned toward Nandi. "I get that you're having a hard time today, but taking it out on David isn't fair."

"He shouldn't be here. He's not in this family anymore."

"He's been very good to you, Nandi. He waited up all night while you were in surgery, and not because you were alone. Because he cares about you."

"It's all right, Marin. I'm not helping by being here. I'll call you later."

Nandi jerked up so hard that she cried out in pain. "See, I told you, he's trying to win you back!"

I smoothed her hair from her hot face.

"Honey, David knows we're not getting back together." I turned to where he was hesitating in the doorway. "You know."

A succession of emotions flickered over his face but, by the time he crossed the room to us, his mouth was pressed in acceptance.

"I know."

"It's not that it hasn't felt good, being with you. It reminded me of why we were together for so long. I'm grateful for that. I needed that," I said, not caring when my voice began to shake. "It felt almost the same, didn't it?" David nodded. "But it's not the same. And we're not the same. And no matter what space we try to push ourselves into, we're not going to fit. I can stop being so angry, but I know myself. Well enough to know I can't get beyond what happened."

"I know you well enough to know that, too. Mariana," he whispered.

I stopped trying to hold my burning eyes open and let the tears fall wherever they wanted. David was swallowing like his throat had sealed shut.

"I can admit this now. It wasn't only your fault," I said. "You were right, I wasn't there with you, not really, those last few months. We were hurtling toward the wedding and, as much as I loved you, I was so scared that afterward everything would change. I should have talked about it with you. Instead, I kept it so close that I caused the change myself. So for that, David, I'm sorry."

I gave Nandi credit for keeping her mouth shut that whole time, but her restraint was wearing thin. She groaned under her breath when David pulled me in for a hug. When he pressed his lips to my forehead, she pretended to puke.

"Don't rile yourself up, kid, it's a friendly kiss. We're in a period of transition," he said, squeezing me once before turning me loose.

"Relax," I told her. "Try to remember how much you guys liked each other. You know, the good old days."

Nandi sighed fantastically. "Maybe I hit my head harder than they thought. I don't remember that at all."

"Did they put diva-syrup in your IV today? I know you hit your head, but you didn't come out of a three-month coma. This isn't 'The Young and the Restless.'"

"And if you must be melodramatic, pick a respectable model. Aim for Lydia Bennett or even Scarlett O'Hara, at the very least."

Nandi screwed up her face at him, and this time I agreed.

"You know, if you and I are going to be friends, you have got to stop doing that."

"Doing what?"

"Glorifying classic literature in ways that put down all the rest. In case you forgot, the books I write are shelved with everything else. Okay, no one's ever going to equate *Luciana and her Lovers* with *Tess of the D'Urbervilles*. It's still an entertaining book."

"It's a lot sexier, too," said a familiar voice from the

doorway. A familiar British voice that sent a jolt straight through me.

"Thank God!" Nandi yelped. "Not a moment too soon. Professor Perv has been moving in."

Sam didn't even glance at David. He also didn't take another step.

"What do you want?" I finally said, congratulating myself on sounding like I couldn't care less.

"I tried calling—"

"Yeah, I blocked your number. You made it so clear I wasn't worth your time that I started to feel the same way."

Somewhere beneath the blood pounding through my ears, I heard Nandi groan. "Really? Ugh. This is 'The Young and the Restless.'"

But then Sam said, "I couldn't get a direct flight to L.A. when I rescheduled on Saturday. I had a five-hour layover in Chicago, so I thought we could talk," and everything else washed away in the wave of disgust that hit me.

"Did you really? Well, how nice for me that you would stoop so low."

He opened his mouth to speak and then seemed to think better of it, turning toward Nandi instead.

"Nandi, sorry, how are you…feeling?" He said the last word so lamely that Nandi blinked. When he looked back at me, his ears had turned pink. "I'd like it if we could talk. I'd hoped we could talk."

"I'd hoped we could talk, too—*the eight times I called you* when I thought my sister was dying."

"Maybe you should go," David spoke up. He didn't need to use the professor voice; his everyday voice was serious enough. "These two don't need some new stupidity upsetting them."

Sam spared David a glance.

"Why are you here?" His tone—not jealous, not offended, just indifferent—was like flicking a match at the anger he'd fueled within me.

"You know what he's doing here? He's being an adult. He's putting aside our differences to help. It's what grown-ups do in an emergency."

"He's also trying to creep his way into Marin's new bed," Nandi said.

David had apparently reached his limit. His shoes squeaked against the tile when he jerked around. "Did you not hear what I said to her five minutes ago?"

"I don't trust anything you say to her."

David huffed. Nandi huffed. I huffed at them both.

Sam shuffled his feet. "I've decided to stay in Los Angeles for a while. I'd appreciate the chance to speak to you before I go."

I'd been basking in the heat of my anger, so it was especially annoying to me that, when he said this, my entire body went cold.

"How long are you staying?" the weak side of me blurted. My prison-warden side cursed her, then pricked up her ears.

He shrugged. "Jordan thinks if I move to L.A., my career prospects will improve."

The silence that stretched out between us was too much for Nandi, whose recent knock to the head seemed to have done away with the dab of patience she'd been born with.

"Wow, you two are stupid. It's a layover, Mare, he doesn't have all day. Go!" Her eyes halted, mid-roll, when they touched on David. "You should already be gone."

David sighed like he couldn't wait.

"Do you need anything?" he asked me, glancing at Sam.

"No, she doesn't," Nandi said. "She's had everything from you she can stand, so—"

"You! Calm down or I'm calling a nurse." I shook my head at David. "Escape while you can."

David buttoned on his coat. He jerked his head toward Sam. "Sure I can't escort him out?"

"I'll take care of it," I told him, dropping the car keys into his palm. "Thanks for the loan. And thank you again for everything you've done."

"Is that a 'you're dismissed' thank you or a 'let's get together soon' thank you?" he said on our way to the elevator.

"It's an 'I'll call you' thank you."

"Maybe even an 'I'll call you for dinner tomorrow night' thank you?" He grinned when I gave him a look. "Last-ditch effort. Don't tell the boss." He nodded toward Nandi's room.

"Trust me, I won't."

He slipped an arm around me.

"See you later. I love you." We both froze. David half-smiled, half-sighed. "Habit. I'll work on it."

I glanced over his shoulder to see Sam waiting with his back pressed to the wall. He never even looked our way.

When the elevator doors closed, I trudged toward him. "There's a waiting room over here." We both trudged down the hall.

Over the frozen expanse of Lake Michigan, the last smudge of daylight was giving in to night. Only one lamp burned in the corner, so although we faced off near the window, it was difficult to see.

"Well?" I asked after an endless silent minute.

"I spent hours on the plane trying to think what I should say to you."

"I can see you came up with volumes," I said after another minute ticked by. When he still didn't speak, I glanced at my watch. "Okay, then, thanks for the chat. I need to get back to Nandi."

"I read the whole manuscript."

My indignation faltered at this reminder of my own transgressions. "What?"

"I took it. When I left that night. I didn't believe you and wanted to read the book myself. Which I did, and it infuriated me. I read it every time you called, to ensure I would stay angry."

"Good strategy."

"No. Because the more I read it, the less I could deny you were telling the truth. Usually when I read your books, no matter what they're about, it's clear you had fun whilst writing them. And those scenes based on us together were…well. I could tell they were yours."

That's right you could, I wanted to say. As love scenes go, those were some of my finest.

"The sections based on Ella weren't anything like your other books. They were depressing. With no humor at all to balance them out. I've read enough of your work to know you didn't want to write those scenes."

Since I'd been saying this all along, I didn't feel obliged to answer.

"I had a list of things to tell you tonight but, after seeing Nandi, smashed up as she is, all I can say is I'm sorry. I have been such a prick."

"*Prick* is putting it nicely," I said, but I sighed when he flinched. "Look, forget it. We both sinned. We're even."

I turned my back on him and headed toward the door, but he caught me by the wrist. When I whirled around, he flicked out his index finger.

"One: I've got a hot temper and a short fuse. Two: I'm impressively skilled at cutting others with my words. Three: I'm irrationally overprotective of the people I love. Four: I'm stubborn beyond reason and I sometimes enjoy it. And five," he said, tapping his thumb, "the more I care about someone, the nastier I react when I've been hurt."

Those same five fingers found their way to mine.

"I have plenty of flaws, obviously. But I'm never too proud to admit I've been wrong."

I'd nearly chewed through my lip trying to be tough and still my nose began to drip. This was so frustrating that my eyes gave in, too.

"I'm sorry." He whispered it while brushing away my tears and again when he swept my hair from my face. He whispered it as his lips moved over my cheek, once more when they paused near my mouth. But he didn't let his mouth touch mine.

I wasn't altogether ready to get over it. But his arms were solid when he wrapped them around me, his fingers were gentle tracing over my back. He pulled us together, put his mouth to my ear, and this time he whispered something different—the three words that, if I'm honest, I'd most wanted him to say.

I felt the release in his shoulders when I slipped my arms around him, felt him relax when I brought my lips to his. My own relief was so strong that, at first, I felt limp. But it wasn't long before our reunion took an enthusiastic turn.

"Whoops!" A visitor stepped in and stepped right back out. Our hands snapped back to respectable places. Sam snuck a look at his watch.

"I hate this, but I have to get to the airport. Jordan will fire me if I push—" I started in on his ear again. "Push back my—flight—again."

"I'm sorry I can't ride—along with—you." His fingers toyed with the hem of my blouse. "Nandi's having—a hard —day."

These words seemed to penetrate our brains. I took his hands in both of mine.

"She is having a hard day. I can't leave her alone."

His steady eyes held mine. He looked so solemn that my heart plummeted.

"I forgot. You're moving to L.A." I had a fleeting vision of Sam frolicking with Jordan in the California sand. And one of me stumbling down Seasalter's shingle beach, alone.

"I said Jordan wants me to move to L.A. I'm only staying for a while. No more than a month. Jordan has lined up some auditions—hey, one is for a Chicago detective series." I immediately pictured snippets of life with Sam in my home city, until he added, "Only set in Chicago, of course. It films in L.A. But I could visit, if I get the part."

"That's great!" I tried my best to look overjoyed for him, but I must have grinned too widely.

"You'll hurt your face doing that. What's wrong?"

I wasn't about to be the girlfriend who guilt-trips a guy into staying. I decided to pretend to be the girlfriend who's suspicious of other women.

"Are you staying with Jordan while you're there?"

Sam's eyes took on a little shine. "You are so cute when you're jealous."

"Well, Jordan's not subtle when she wants something. What if she slides into your bed some night?"

"I'll slide out and make for the nearest hotel."

The playful tone in his voice disappeared.

"I promise you, Marin, you never have to worry about me and Jordan. You never have to worry about me with anyone at all. And really," he said, his eyes crinkling, "after weeks of painfully slow exposure therapy, surely I've proven my self-control."

I winced. "Yeah, about that. Turns out I was wrong. Apparently, it's best to get right back in the saddle."

Sam suddenly grew very still. And stayed that way, for a pretty long time.

"We had fun anyway. Think of all the board games we would never have played. So many movies we would never have seen."

I think he kind of blinked.

"The good news is I've been given a clean bill of health." I walked my fingers over his belt. "Therapy complete."

"A clean bill of health? You saw a doctor?"

"No, my dad explained it to me."

"You spoke about this with your dad?!"

"He knows a lot about panic. I wanted to see what he thought."

"Your dad knows we were—that I was—with his daughter?"

"Sam, I'm a thirty-four year-old romance novelist. He knows I've been up to some stuff."

"And now he knows you've been up to it with me." He

was shaking his head. "That's done it, then. Your father will never like me."

"Don't be silly." Although after that whole *jerkhole* conversation…well, I could smooth it over.

"I know about fathers and daughters."

"Been chased with a shotgun before, have you?"

"Shotgun?" His voice cracked. He scowled when I laughed. "I have five sisters. I'm never warm to the guys who come round. My father is worse than I am."

I linked my arms around his neck.

"You're a very good big brother. I'm sorry I invoked your wrath with my writing." I turned serious when I added, "It won't happen again."

"I'm sorry I behaved like a childish plonker. From now on I'll talk things out with you, rather than shut you out."

"Good. I don't want some stupid misunderstanding turning this into a bad melodrama. No more secrets," I said. But then: "Oh."

Sam leaned away. "What 'oh'?"

I bit my lip for so long that he narrowed his eyes.

"Remember on Saturday when you said—in that really mean voice—'Congratulations, you're a free woman'? Try to keep that in mind when you hear that I made out with David."

Guilt: gone. Incredulity: present. Anger: seemed to be on the rise.

"You what?"

"Yeah. Last night. For, like, a minute."

"A minute?"

"Definitely no more than two." When it looked like his self-professed short fuse was about to ignite, I said, "Hey, buddy, it was a rough day, he'd been great to Nandi, you were *unavailable*, and I was too tired to think straight. And as you said before slamming the door in my face, I was a free woman."

His lips buzzed when he blew out a sigh. "When you put it that way, I suppose there's not much I can say."

"Nope." I stood on my toes and performed one of my best moves on his throat until he shivered against me. "I much prefer making out with you."

I proved it to him for a few minutes before he forced himself to pull back.

"I am going to miss that flight if I don't leave this instant." He stood opposite me with a tortured look on his face. "Then again, a month is quite a long time," he said, reaching for me. "I don't even know if I want to be an actor."

I summoned all my restraint and stepped away.

"But you need to find out. A month will fly by, you'll see. And maybe we can, you know, get creative with a video chat." I smiled at the intrigued way he lifted his eyebrows before leaning in for one last quick goodbye.

Twelve minutes later, his cab screeched away from the curb. I watched him go, cringing as the car took a corner at life-threatening speed. When I turned to go inside, my phone rang in my pocket.

"I just remembered. While reading your manuscript, I realized you lied to me." He laughed under his breath. "Picking out shapes in the clouds, indeed. We should visit the countryside often, now I know your true idea of a romantic picnic."

CHAPTER THIRTY-TWO

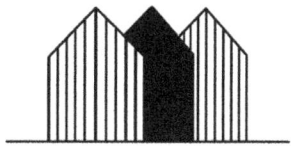

A MONTH, IT TURNS OUT, DOES NOT ALWAYS FLY BY. AND since my creative video chat idea had proved too awkward to be useful, I was beginning to feel too tightly wound. Which explains why, when I got back to Seasalter during our third week apart, I made a habit of pausing the Rochester film to stare at Sam in that thin wet shirt. When Patricia came over one sunny Friday at the end of week four, I didn't notice poor objectified Sam gazing out at us. Even more embarrassing? She'd walked in on this before.

"You do realize that for us to watch television we'll have to turn off the film?" She laughed and settled onto the couch. "Did you discover why Sam wants us to watch?"

"No. He's being so mysterious," I said, passing her a mug of tea. "Yesterday he sent me a train ticket with instructions to pack a weekend bag and meet him today outside St. Pancras. And he told me to watch this morning, but he wouldn't say why."

"Oh, to be young and in love," she said with a tolerant

roll of her eyes. "It's a good thing he went to L.A. You might never have finished that novel otherwise."

The delay in my own romantic endeavors did have one upside—I'd transferred my energy to Genevieve and Lucien and delivered my book a week early. It was sitting in Yvonne Lee's inbox, waiting for my champion's stamp of approval.

"You're right. Plus, the trip was good for Sam. He had six auditions and signed with an agent. I won't deny that Jordan knows how to make things happen."

"What about you? Are you going home now that your book is finished?"

I watched the steam swirl off my tea. "I'm going home in May. I think I'll rent this place weekly to summer tourists and come back again this fall. Skip the Chicago winter."

"I assume this summer you'll sneak off to Vancouver for a sexy set visit or two." She gave me a dry smile. "You don't fool me."

The generic music of a morning talk show grabbed our attention. The host smiled a glaring, red-lipped smile straight into the camera. I was so distracted by those glowing lips that I almost missed her words.

"Fresh off the plane from America, we have Simon Quinn and Hailey McNamara, stars of the new serial *The Young Edward Rochester*, premiering Sunday. Good morning."

"Good morning," said my very own Sam, live on national television.

Patricia clutched my arm and we both squealed. This is one more thing I love about her. She's tough as rawhide, but she's not too gruff for a squeal now and then.

Sam sat casually nearest the host. Beside him, I

recognized Hailey from the wrap party, her red hair shining beneath the studio lights.

"Sam seems relaxed. Must be looking away from the monitor, eh?" Patricia chuckled, as Sam chatted with the host. His thin grey sweater showed off his broad shoulders and the hard plane of his stomach. I pictured the obliques and bit my lip to hide a guilty smile.

Patricia shook her head at me.

"Like a cat nibbling a canary," she said, and then snorted. "That Gloria Martin wants a bite of him, too."

Gloria Martin giggled through those blood-red lips. She uncrossed her legs and leaned toward Sam.

"I must say you don't look as though you were on an overnight from Los Angeles."

Sam didn't blink. "Hailey always looks lovely. But I'm a boring travel companion, so that may have helped. I started in talking and she got a full night's sleep."

"Don't believe a word from him," Hailey said, flicking Sam on the shoulder. "He kept me up laughing half the night."

Red Lips looked into the camera.

"You heard it here first. His sense of humor is as dazzling as the rest of him."

"He has it rough, that boy," Patricia said with an acerbic laugh.

After a while, a chair was placed beside Hailey's and out came Jordan. She and Red Lips volleyed questions at Sam until I felt bad for Hailey. At one point, Jordan leaned all the way across her to touch Sam on the knee.

The host allowed Hailey to introduce a clip of the wet-shirt scene—hand-selected by Jordan, no doubt. Red Lips cleared her throat on-air when it was over. She was leaning so far toward Sam that she almost slid out of her chair. Jordan looked proprietary and Hailey was teasing him and Sam had that faint flush in his cheeks, so rare and so cute.

It was official: Simon Quinn was national news.

Near the show's end, Gloria Martin held up a copy of *The Young Edward Rochester*.

"Simon, any truth to the rumor you're dating the book's author, Mariana Rose?"

It was obvious the question caught him off guard. Both eyebrows shot up.

"Hardly anyone knows who I am. I doubt there are rumors going round about me." His eyes flickered directly into the camera; for half a second, he was looking at me. Then he smiled his best crooked smile elusively at Red Lips. "You would need to contact Ms. Rose's people for comment."

Patricia and I keeled over laughing. I'd get my people right on that.

"I'll bet you ten quid that rumor originated an hour ago with a whisper in what's her name's ear from Jordan 'Any Press is Good Press' Palomo."

"Jordan seems to know how to generate interest. I suspect she'll use whatever she can to promote the film. And I have a feeling that interest in Simon Quinn will soon be high."

I turned back to the television in time to see the credits roll. Sam was looking at the floor with his hands in his pockets, but Hailey must've said something funny, because he glanced up with a grin. Jordan took one step forward. Red Lips put her hand on his arm. I shook my head with a smile. Because I had a feeling of my own—one that told me Patricia was right.

"Are we lost?" I asked Sam a few hours later as we drove through the countryside. I gave him a playful nudge. "Do you need me to call my people for directions?"

"Do I look lost?" He reached across the gearshift for my hand, but he wasn't being romantic. He pushed it toward my face. "Another sign ahead, woman. Cover your eyes."

I adore surprises, so I followed instructions. But when I got the all-clear, I said, "Do I look lost? Because I am. Do you ever plan to tell me where we are?"

He grinned. "Don't you like the thrill of putting yourself in my capable hands?"

I thought about cracking an innuendo-laden joke, but it seemed too easy. And anyway, from the look of the cottage we'd arrived at, we were apparently in a Beatrix Potter story. Before I could get too excited about holing up in the cottage with Sam for three long days, he said, "We're not staying here, I'm just collecting our keys. I'll be right back. No snooping."

The place we rolled up to a few minutes later was the exact opposite of the charming cottage. This was a centuries-old stone house, beautiful and dramatic but imposing, like it had elbowed its way into the surrounding hills. Sam's car looked so out of place in the driveway that I wanted to laugh, but I didn't; I had a spooky feeling it might offend the house.

"Is this a bed and breakfast?" I asked, but that seemed unlikely. A diluted light in a single window didn't feel quite hospitable enough.

"No. I believe we're the only ones here this weekend."

He was smiling at my confusion. I gave him a suspicious look.

"Is this a 'spend the night in a haunted house' kind of thing? Where you get a thousand bucks if you survive until dawn? Because I've seen the movies. The house always wins."

"A thousand, really? That pale, rather peculiar bloke who gave me the keys only offered me five hundred."

"Sam…"

He leaned beside me against the car.

"It's a large place, isn't it? Three stories high. It's not vast but still, it's considerable." Out of the corner of my eye, I saw him glance at me before saying, "If I had to guess I would say this was a gentleman's house at one time. It's not large enough to be a nobleman's seat."

I barely heard him. I was distracted by the fading sun slipping behind the clouds, by how the house seemed to pull the shadows around itself like a cloak. I edged closer to Sam without looking away from the empty windows. It was the kind of place I didn't want to turn my back on.

"I like that wall running round the top of the house. What are those called? Battlements?" He slid his eyes my way. "Very picturesque."

"I didn't know you're such an architecture fan. Seriously, is this where we're staying?"

"Yes." He pulled me to him with a little smile. "You really don't know where we are?"

"Should I?"

The little smile grew large. "I thought your extensive research would offer you some clues. Not to mention I've been almost directly quoting a very famous description of this place which I'm certain you know by heart."

I looked around again, then followed his eyes to the house's stone tower.

"I don't think there's anyone in the tower," he whispered. "But one never knows for certain."

I whipped my head around to look at him, then looked again at the house. My mouth fell open when I realized what he'd been saying. I couldn't really quote the description by heart, but I could come close.

"It was three stories high…the proportions weren't vast but they were considerable…" I paused to try to get it right. "A gentleman's manor house but not a nobleman's seat… and the battlements around the top gave it a picturesque look."

He beamed. "That's what I expected from the author of *The Young Edward Rochester*."

"This is where you brought me? North Lees Hall?"

"Charlotte Brontë's inspiration for Thornfield. As close as one can get to Edward Rochester's house outside of fiction."

I studied the house again. When I knew what to look for, I saw that he was right—I had seen it before. Instead of intimidating me, it began to beckon, its history and significance as seductive as its isolation had suddenly become. In the deepening dusk, the light shimmered out of that one window like a flame. And that irony wasn't lost on this Brontë fan.

Sam slipped his arms around me. "After all these months in England, I thought it was time you saw this house up close."

Oh, it was time, all right. I slid my hands up his chest and whispered the only word I could find.

"Perfect."

In the beginning, our kiss was rather sweet. But it had been weeks since we'd been alone and sweet quickly turned scandalous; we stumbled toward the house. I brushed my lips across his throat while he unlocked the door. When it swung open behind us with a quiet creak, we gazed at each other levelly. But before I pulled him inside, he caught me around the waist.

"Marin," he said in a low voice. He lifted one eyebrow and gave me a suggestive smile. "'What the deuce is to do now?'"

A few breathless, giddy seconds passed before I recovered my speech. "Wow. I mean, truly, slam dunk. How long have you been planning that?"

"Oh, a while," he said nonchalantly, closing the door behind us.

CHAPTER THIRTY-THREE

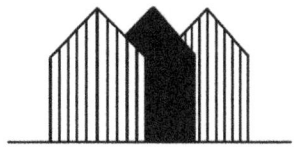

"Did you know North Lees Hall is a heritage preservation site? It's managed by a nonprofit," Sam said, flipping through a brochure the day after we'd returned. "I'm going to send a donation. Each year. For the rest of my life."

"Me, too," I sighed, throwing my arms over my head as I stretched out on the couch with my feet in his lap. "Along with a note: A good time was had by all. Repeatedly."

Sam shook his head with a smile. "Couldn't help yourself, could you?"

"It's my bread and butter. I have to keep my skills sharp."

He traced his fingers over my hip. "Your skills won't have a chance to grow dull," he said, and I pulled him alongside me.

We were reveling in a sweet break from responsibility. Gretchen told me Yvonne Lee had "licked up" my new book, which, disturbing visual aside, was excellent news. We were starting revisions the next week. Sam had received the advance half of his salary for the film he would begin in May. Since, as he said, it paid roughly the same as his job at SaladBar, he'd stepped away from serving kale to focus on his sisters before leaving for Vancouver.

We were reveling blissfully five minutes later when we heard a knock. Sam's dad was dropping off Ella and Lily on his way to a medical conference.

Sam put some space between us and went for the door. He didn't get far.

"I need a few minutes to think some boring thoughts," he said, shooting me a cheeky grin on his way upstairs.

When I answered the door moments later, Lily launched herself at me.

"Marin! We brought our climbing penguins game and will you play with us? And we're excited to stay with you for a whole night and part of tomorrow as well." She pranced around as she chattered. Ella leaned against me with her shy smile.

Doctor Quinn looked tired. In the few months I'd known him, his hair had grown more grey than brown. He had the same mouth as Sam but it was flat, like he'd pressed it into a line for too long. Sometimes he seemed absent, sometimes cold, but I don't think either was true. In the wedding photo hanging in his house, Sam's mom is smiling straight into the camera, but Doctor Quinn is smiling at her. That loss would wear anyone down.

"I'm sure they're in good hands," he said, almost to himself, as the girls ran into the kitchen. It was disconcerting, his habit of nearly speaking to me, but not quite.

"Won't you come in for a moment? Perhaps you'd like coffee or a nice cup of tea?" Also disconcerting? My

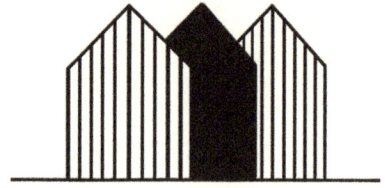

LET'S CONNECT!

Amazon Author Page - Sarah Madelin
Website - SarahMadelin.com
Meet-Cute Facebook Readers' Group
Facebook - @sarahmadelinbooks
Instagram - @sarahmadelinbooks
TikTok - @sarahmadelinbooks
Pinterest - @sarahmadelinbooks

ALSO BY SARAH MADELIN

NOVELETTES
Love on Hold - The Prequel to Love on Paper

NOVELS
Love on Film - The Sequel to Love on Paper

WITH GRATITUDE

more. My brother perfectly illustrates what it means to walk through life being cool and kind.

My twin kiddos delayed my book's publication by years for the best possible reason. They make me laugh and give my life meaning every day.

Finally, my husband Mike listened to me revise sentences ten different ways and read my many drafts at least ten different times, even though romantic women's fiction is not really his thing. That's true love, and I'm grateful to have him.

WITH GRATITUDE

Maureen Feakins welcomed me warmly into her home. Sue and Terry allowed me to experience a real Seasalter beach house. Kara Louise at The Whiting Post outfitted me in quirky English style. Amber Abrams distracted me with Amarula, laughs, and bad theater. Ray and Janet Adams went out of their way to help me explore the charming village of Fairlight and inspired me with their view of Dover's white cliffs and France's shadowy shore. Derek Barlow and his sweet mother, Rose, were wonderful impromptu travel companions who became cherished friends.

Indigo Girls, Gregory Alan Isakov, Bootstraps, and Rosie Thomas inspired me with music that kept me writing. Chris Rae and *The Septic's Companion* offered this American girl loads of fascinating British slang. L.M. Montgomery and Carl Sandburg taught me who I am as a person. Marisa de los Santos and Jennifer Crusie taught me who I am as a writer. A smiling catalog model who represented Marin in my mind popped up for years to encourage me with her sunny smile. A fetching French athlete who had the same face and birthday as Sam brought my leading man to life.

Danyelle Ferguson, Allison Gygi, and Judy Mendelson offered me incredible feedback and unfailing support in the best writing group an author could have. Kelsie Stelting listened to my fears and dared me to go for it anyway. Sally Henson gave me the blueprint to finally get this thing out in the world.

My dad recognized that I was a writer before anyone else and always encouraged me to work at it. My mom was the first to love Marin's story; she never stopped asking for

With Gratitude

Remember when Julia Roberts won the Oscar for *Erin Brockovich* and told the conductor to axe the exit music because she'd been waiting forever to give that speech? Well, I've been waiting 11 years to thank the people who helped me get here, so please excuse my long-windedness.

My earliest readers and supporters, Allison Perkins and Allyson Wolcott, helped me plod my way through the very first draft of this book. I can't imagine how bored they were by our endless conversations about fictional characters, but their input was invaluable.

Babies Allison, Julie, and Jenna gave me sweet smiles and sticky hugs that made me feel better when brooding over some tricky plot points.

Beta readers Faith Boldt, Penny Cromwell, Olivia Haberman, Alex Harrison, Teri McKean, Kelly O'Connor McNees, Sandy Schultz, and Jamie Lou Thome offered me great insights on how to polish and pare down my crazy-long first draft.

The wonderful Lee Whiley read my revised draft with a Kent Coast local's eyes and ears to prevent Sam from sounding too much like Hyacinth Bucket.

The lovely folks I met during my research trip to Seasalter made my month in England unforgettable.

I reached up to my shoulder and hooked his fingers with mine.

"I thought you said I was going to regret it?"

Thank you for reading this sample of *Love on Film*, Available in April 2022!

"You got someone better in mind?" Sue called from behind the counter.

Sam slapped some cash into the vinyl folder containing our bill.

"Sue is a pearl amongst so many grains of sand. She has my full support." He turned toward the kitchen with his hand over his heart. "You're a gem, Sue."

She waved a dismissive hand at him from the pass-through, but I saw her smile when he turned away.

We were walking home when he stopped and pulled me around to face him. The sun was in his eyes; he squinted down at me.

"Do this for me. Just think it over while we're apart. If you decide at the end of the summer that you really don't want to get married, I won't mention it again." He slipped his arms around my waist and looked at me with serious eyes. "Truly. I would never want you to do something you may regret."

He was too earnest for me to dismiss the idea. I nodded.

"Good." He slung his arm over my shoulder as we walked.

"You're the one who needs a lesson in regret. I can't believe you told a teenage loudmouth you proposed to me. Two days, tops, and it will show up on Perez Hilton. And he wants you for himself, so you know he'll be glad I turned you down."

He smiled. "Actually, Marin, you're getting the lesson in regret. You are going to regret your little speech about the kitchen. Because when we get home, I'm going to demonstrate my skills in the kitchen. And possibly in the shower as well."

that then I'm happy to let you. I'd just prefer that you do it because you want to and not because we have a legal agreement that says you have to."

"I've never heard of anyone being bound by law to physically carry their spouse," he said, leaning over to kiss me once. He pulled back and flashed his bedroom eyes at me. "Come on. Marry me." His seductive look turned to frustration when I smiled and shook my head. "Sue, talk sense to this woman."

Sue didn't look up as she stacked our plates.

"Someday he'll stop asking." She snatched the chopstick Sam was fidgeting with out of his hand and tossed it into an empty bowl. "And you're not getting any younger."

Ah, the betrayal! I looked up at her. "Really, Sue? Et tu?

"The truth hurts. Chasing a toddler with forty-year-old knees hurts more."

"My knees won't be forty for four years, thank you very much. And since when am I chasing a toddler?" I called before she disappeared into the kitchen.

"Oh, now you don't want to have children, either?" Sam asked in a suspicious tone.

This was getting ridiculous. "Of course I do. I'll have a baby with you right now, let's go." I was halfway out of my chair when he pulled me back.

"I said have a baby, not make a baby."

"I know the difference. I'm equally interested in both." I tossed back the remainder of my lukewarm tea. "Look, can we go? If we keep talking about this, Sue will badger us into having eight or nine kids. And then she'll expect to be godmother."

wants me wearing a suit to an office every day. Preferably the office opposite his."

"Then it's a good thing that what he wants matters less than what you want. Although no one who's seen you in a suit would blame him," I said. "I am surprised about the magazine. How did it happen this time?"

"How does it always happen? My agent pushes until she gets her way."

"Renee makes good money promoting your pretty face. But she can make even more promoting the rest of you."

He rumpled his hair. "I don't want to talk about Renee. We'll be apart all summer. Before we go, I want to know why you won't marry me so I'm not in a strop the whole time I'm working."

"Oh, not a strop!"

"I'm serious," he said, clumsily flipping the chopstick again. "Tell me why."

"It's just not for me. We've already talked about this."

And believe me, we had—at length. Evidently, I had declined with too much gusto when he'd asked me in jest a few weeks before. What had been a flirtatious joke had become a sore spot with him.

"Is it because you think I'll eventually want to leave?"

"No."

His eyes clouded over. "Because you think you'll want to leave?"

"No. I've already told you. If you're willing to haul around my frail eighty-year-old butt when you're a spry young thing of seventy-one—"

"Seventy-two."

"Fine," I said, willing to compromise at eight years instead of the true eight and a half. "If you're willing to do

LOVE ON FILM - CHAPTER TWO

From Sam's pained expression, I could tell he agreed with her. Sue flicked him with her dish towel and marched into the kitchen.

"I'm sorry about your skirt," he said as I dabbed at the stain.

"It's fine, the sauce blends in with the poppies." I looked up at him and smiled. "You're going to regret telling them you asked me to marry you. That little redhead is the kind who talks."

"Good," he said, awkwardly flipping a chopstick through his fingers. "Maybe if enough people talk me up, you'll see my finer points and reconsider."

I put my hand over his. The chopstick wedged uncomfortably between my pinkie and ring finger.

"I love your finer points. I love all your points. I just don't want to get married. Anyway, are people your age allowed to marry without their parents' consent? Because I doubt your dad would approve of you marrying me. An older woman. The author of lascivious romance novels. I'm a corrupting influence on his only son."

"That joke wasn't funny when you made it last month. And for your information, when my dad was my age, he had been married for two years. My dad was my age when I was born. Also, as you know quite well, he thinks you are a stabilizing influence. He was thrilled when I moved in with you. His happiness would be complete if I would quit acting and settle into what he considers a real profession."

I bristled at that. "Send him a copy of your bank statement. He'll change his mind."

"He would pull out a magazine like the one I just signed and I would, quite rightly, lose all credibility in his eyes. He of blocky printed capitals and sharp cursive points. Mine was all loops and swirls. I paused to study them. They looked nice together.

"Thank you," Lucy began when I passed the book to her, but a new voice thundered behind us.

"What are you girls doing? Are you bothering my customers?" The girls parted, Red Sea-style, as Sue charged in. She glanced at the shirtless photo of Sam with a disapproving grunt. "In this restaurant, customers are entitled to privacy. Regardless of how they toss it aside when they leave," she added with a pointed look at Sam before turning to glare at Darcy. "The best moo shu pork you've ever tasted. No wonder you've been stuffing your face with it all week. Get going. Don't let me catch you bothering these people again."

Darcy smiled at me in a way that wasn't altogether friendly. "Cute skirt. You've got chicken in your lap." I looked down to see one of Sam's chopstick casualties bleeding sauce onto my new orange poppy skirt.

"Out!" Sue bellowed.

Lucy's face had gone from pink to white.

"I'm really sorry." Her fingers were shaking. She dropped the book into my lap. "Oh, I'm sorry!"

Yeesh, I thought as I handed it to her. This kid needs a Joan Jett mix tape to build up her confidence. "It's okay. It was nice of you to say hi."

Her deer in the headlights look faded a bit. Before she left, she whispered to me, "It's the most romantic story I've ever read." Then she glanced at Sam once more and fled.

Sue shook her head at the girls before lecturing Sam. "If you pose half-naked for all of America, it's your own fault when America won't leave you be."

The loudmouth redhead giggled again and pulled a new *Entertainment Weekly* from her bag. A familiar man smoldered out at us from the pages, sans shirt. His jeans were slung low on his hips, highlighting some very pretty oblique muscles.

Well, well. How had the magazine talked him into that?

Sam looked like he was in physical pain when he saw it. He glanced at me and half-scowled, half-smiled when I gave him a thumbs-up.

Darcy shoved the magazine at him. "Would you sign it, 'Dear Darcy, I'm fantastic in the kitchen'?"

"No," Sam said, scrawling his name on the photo. He jerked around to face the other girl. Cheeks flushed, her big doe eyes filled with horror, she nudged a book toward him.

"Could you please sign that for me? If you don't mind?"

It was a copy of my memoir. A battered, dog-eared copy, I noticed, feeling rather flattered.

"Of course. What's your name?"

"Lucy?" she cheeped, like she was no longer sure.

Sam dashed off the inscription, saying, "You know, Lucy, *she* wrote the book." I heard the flutter of Lucy's gasp when he said her name.

"That's okay," I said with a laugh. "It'll be worth more if he signs it."

Sam rolled his eyes without looking at me and slid the book toward Lucy. She squeaked when his hand bumped hers.

"No. I mean, yes. I know. I was hoping that you might…if you would…" She stared at me in desperation.

"Sure." I tried to give her a soothing smile. A second later she stopped rocking on her heels. Progress.

I signed my name beneath Sam's, his signature a blend

started to say, but she seemed to get dizzy when Sam flashed her his brightest smile, full-strength.

"Not at all. I'm just asking her to marry me. She turns me down twice a week." I'm not sure if they have the phrase *how do you like them apples?* in England, but the smug smile he gave me said something very similar.

I gaped at Sam. Both girls gaped at me.

"Are you crazy?" the one called Darcy yelped. "How can you turn him down? He's so perfect!"

Sam looked away from my triumphant face. This round was going to Mariana Beckett.

I propped my chin on my hand and stared at him longingly.

"He is, isn't he? Those eyelashes. That rugged, rumpled look he has when he doesn't shave. Mmm. And have you ever seen a sexier mouth on a man? I mean, look at it."

The girls complied. Readily. I watched him bite the inside of his cheek, which only made his mouth more delicious.

"Let's be honest. There's not a better backside in Hollywood." Sam's neck turned red. Even the fawn was beginning to blush. But Darcy was taking it in stride. I leaned toward her conspiratorially and lowered my voice. "And you would not believe how great he is in the—"

"Marin!" Sam's eyes held a delightful mix of shock and mortification.

"In the kitchen," I said innocently before shooting Darcy a suggestive smirk. "He's *fantastic* in the kitchen."

Sam jerked toward the girls.

"Right. Can I do anything—er, what can I—" He glanced at the redhead and let a frustrated sigh slip through his lips. "Was there something you wanted?"

girl galloped forward, a mane of red hair swishing around her. She pushed her way to the table, bumping the fawn aside as she inserted herself at the corner between Sam and me.

"We've been coming every day since we saw the picture in the *RedEye* of you guys eating here. About time you showed up. If I have one more egg roll, I will puke."

"Darcy!" the fawn hissed.

"We were in the *RedEye*?" Sam asked me.

"Last week. Back cover," I said. "Nandi told me."

"Oh, right," he said vaguely. He turned to the girls. "Can I do anything for you?"

The redhead giggled hysterically. I could see her answers to that question gyrating inside her head.

Sam looked at me wearily. Until the previous autumn he had lived on the fringe of the movie business, doing bit parts in big films for minimal pay and big roles in indie films for almost no pay at all. But in late October, as my memoir hit the shelves, Sam hit the big time with an overproduced, under-cerebral movie called *Splintering Dark*, billed as sci-fi film noir for the Comic-Con set. Apparently the idea was to woo starry-eyed romantics with glamorous costumes and a smoldering hero while working in enough explosions, time warps, and side-boob to satisfy hormonal techno-geeks. And the idea had been a good one; the sequel had wrapped in March.

Sam wasn't in love with the over-the-top movie or his sudden popularity with teenage girls, and he was still overwhelmed by the concept of devoted fans. When I wrinkled my nose into a You're-So-Cute-When-You-Entertain-The-Public grin, he grimaced at me again.

"I'm sorry, I hope we're not interrupting," the fawn

chopsticks long enough to roll them at me. The broccoli between them bounced to the floor.

"Because you're so perfect." I shrugged cheerfully, but when he scowled, I said, "How about perfect for me? Can you accept that?"

He caught my hand and twisted my fingers with his. "I might be able to stomach it."

A gruff moan sounded over our heads.

"I don't know how much more of you two *I* can stomach," Sue grumbled. She scraped Sam's lunch mishaps into her dishrag. "Would you marry him already? Then honeymoon in China so he can practice with chopsticks. It will save me an hour of cleanup every week."

Neither of us said anything as she stalked away. But a light gleamed in Sam's eyes when he looked into mine.

"What do you say, Marin?" He traced a circle around my ring finger. "Will you make Sue the happiest woman in the world and marry me?"

"Sam," I said, touching my hand to his face. Then I patted his cheek. "No. But thanks for asking."

He leaned back in his chair and crossed his arms. One corner of his mouth pulled to the side in a stubborn smirk.

"Are you going to eat that peapod?"

He narrowed his eyes at me. I snagged it off his plate.

Sam leaned forward. "Marin, you are the most—"

"Hi," squeaked a voice to my right. A teenage girl approached us tentatively, twirling a wisp of blonde hair around her finger. She gazed at Sam with sweet, uncertain eyes that belonged on a baby deer. "I'm sorry. I mean, excuse me."

"Holy Sichuan, I can't believe it's really you!" Another

LOVE ON FILM - CHAPTER TWO

Our tabletop was a battleground strewn with chicken and bamboo.

"There's no shame in using a fork," I told Sam as he concentrated on the Kung Pao teetering between his chopsticks. He shot me a victorious look when he managed to bring the bite to his mouth.

"Why are you laughing? I'm getting it," he said around his mouthful. He looked up at our server. "Sue, tell her. I'm getting it."

"You've been getting it for a year and a half," Sue said as she filled his water glass. "You're the reason we put paper over the tablecloths."

Sam grimaced at her, then pointed a chopstick at me. "Poke fun while you can, woman. You'll be choking on that laughter soon."

"I hope not," I said, snatching a piece of fallen chicken. "I love watching you flounder at something. It's so rare."

"Because I'm so perfect." Sam took his eyes off his

LOVE ON FILM - CHAPTER ONE

"Come on, let me see." I traced a finger over his fist until he unfolded his fingers.

Sea glass. Frosted bits of clear and Coke-bottle green and my favorite aqua blue. The kind he had brought me when we'd first started dating. It used to line the windowsills in my Seasalter house.

"What are you doing with this?" I asked, and his little smile deepened. He slipped it into his pocket with a shrug, then slipped his hand into mine.

"Saving it for someday."

suppose it's a good thing I won't need to count the floorboards again. At least not in that bedroom." He wrapped both arms around my waist. "I'm sorry I left you. It couldn't have been easy, listening to a stranger instruct you in your own family history. It irritated me, so it must drive you mad."

I shrugged. "*Salt in the Sea* was required reading in my AP English class. Writing a book report on my dad's mental health cured me of being sensitive."

"How are you feeling after that, honestly?" he asked.

The whole truth. That's what we'd promised, and a deal's a deal. I folded my hands on his chest.

"Honestly? Very tired, rather hungry, somewhat sad, slightly disgusted. But so happy to be with you." I leaned my head against him.

He pulled me close and I felt his whole chest tighten when he swallowed. A minute later he said, "I will make this up to you, Marin. Someday, I promise, I will make this right."

"It's already right. The best thing you can do for me is stop beating yourself up. Walking away—from the book deal and the house—was my decision, and I would do it again if I had to." I pushed back to look at him. "Now smile at me or I'll buy you a keychain from the gift shop in my garage."

I kissed his clenched jaw until it relaxed and then slid my hand down to his. It was curled into a fist he seemed reluctant to open.

"What have you got?"

"Nothing," he said, but he ducked his head. For the first time all day, a real smile played at the corners of his mouth.

"Sure," I said, scribbling my name on the title page. Mrs. Collins's mouth gaped so widely, I thought her bridge might fall out. I gave her a no-hard-feelings smile. "My stepdad is from Zambia, by the way."

Patricia was waiting for me in the foyer. I ran my hand over the pelican's brass bill before passing through the front door. When the gate slammed shut behind me, I refused to look back. The sweet guy waiting for me felt bad enough without watching me languish in regret.

"I've never seen Sam so uptight," Patricia said as we walked toward where he was staring grimly out at the water. I could see his fists clenching inside his coat pockets.

"Guilt is his go-to reaction when anyone mentions the Seasalter house. Instead of acknowledging that it's my fault for writing about him, he blames himself. He won't let go of the belief that I gave up my book contract and lost the house because he got so angry when he first found out I'd written about him." I watched him drag the toe of his black Chuck Taylors through the shingle and felt some guilt myself. "I shouldn't have brought him here, no matter how curious I was about how the exhibit turned out."

Sam's bleak expression didn't lift when he saw us. Patricia gave me a knowing look and continued up the beach to her house, leaving us with a promise to meet for breakfast before we left for Chicago the next day.

I hooked my fingers around Sam's arm and pulled him toward me.

"How's it going, gloomy?" I asked, pushing my bottom lip out at him. "You missed the best part. My parents' bedroom has wall-to-wall green shag carpet. With matching green walls. It's like standing inside an avocado."

I watched him muster a half-hearted smile for me. "I

(and accepting that nothing remained of my own love nest but the quote painted above the bed), Patricia and I headed downstairs. I spent a solitary moment in the little sun porch office where first my dad and then I had written some significant words. He had banged out literary greatness on his green Olivetti typewriter. Thirty years later, I had banged my head on the desk before deciding to write smut about Sam—a decision that, when I refused my editor's demand that I publish the story, had ultimately cost me the house.

I ran my finger over the chipped white paint on the desk we had shared, three decades apart, and listened to Mrs. Collins relate the details of my parents' split: eight years after the publication of *Salt in the Sea*, after years of dealing with John Robert Beckett's paranoid delusions (*lucid panic attacks*, I corrected), Isobel Beckett took their daughter Mariana (*Marin for short*) and left him to deal with his illness alone. When Isobel remarried a man from Zimbabwe (*at least it starts with a Z…*), Mr. Beckett cut off contact from all but a few individuals. For almost twenty years, he didn't write a word (*he didn't* publish *a word; he wrote plenty*) until his daughter's broken heart reunited the couple.

"They came together for the sake of their only child," Mrs. Collins said dramatically. When I laughed aloud, she glared at me. "Fortunately, the couple has rebuilt their friendship after so many years apart. Mr. Beckett published an acclaimed book of essays last year. It's available in our gift shop."

"I just bought one." The mother of the girl who had recognized Sam turned toward me. She held out a copy of *Love on Paper*. "I bought your book, too. Would you sign it for me?"

LOVE ON FILM - CHAPTER ONE

"Mum, that was Simon Quinn," I heard her say, her voice a cross between a hiss and a shriek. Her mom's eyes shot up to mine.

"It's always the teenagers," I whispered to Patricia. "He could be wearing a Halloween mask and they'd sniff him out."

"He does have a rather distinctive presence," she said with a smirk.

"I know you're talking about his butt, Patricia." I laughed, and then snapped my mouth shut. Mrs. Collins's expression said she was ten seconds away from making me write a hundred lines of *I will not disrespect important works of literature.*

My stomach cramped a bit during our tour of my childhood bedroom. Clearly Richard Glenister, the director of the Archive, had raided my own memoir for inspiration. The room was filled with details I'd described in *Love on Paper:* the star-patterned wallpaper, my clubhouse in the crawl space, the lace handkerchief swaddling one of Whitstable's famous oysters. It was the little yellow rocking chair my granddad had made for me that stung the most. I'd forgotten it in the attic when we'd sold the Archive the house and hadn't remembered until it was too late.

It was the strawberry-embroidered dress laid out on the bed that forced me out of the room. It was unnervingly similar to the one I had worn on what, at that point, I still considered the worst night of my life. Me, locked into the hull of a tiny sailboat, my dad lashed to the deck by a rope and his own panic. Just looking at that dress, I felt the boat pitch beneath me. It was the only provocation I needed to get out.

After glimpsing the love nest of John and Isobel Beckett

withering look. She had been explaining something—the house tour based on my dad's book or the family saga in general—that I hadn't heard. I had been too busy staring with regret at my mom's crewelwork tapestry, which I had forgotten to pack after selling the house. Mrs. Collins must have misinterpreted my regret as mockery. She looked at me when she said, "Although it's not commonly known, Isobel Beckett—or Isobel Beckett-Mwenda, as she's called today—is a talented visual artist. While the décor of the time might not agree with our modern aesthetics, one must applaud her for weaving elements of her family's story into even a simple needlework project."

This particular needlework project involved two deer lapping at a spring while an owl looked on. I'm still not sure what elements of the family story were supposed to be represented. Also, my mom has a solid sense of style, but the reason she isn't known as a visual artist is because she's not one. As she said herself when she heard the comment, three fill-in-the-grid tapestries don't make her Grandma Moses.

My purposes for going on the tour weren't clear, even to me, but I wasn't there to prove that the London Literary Archive had missed the mark when they'd converted the family homestead to a tourist attraction. And I certainly wasn't going to set Mrs. Collins's slightly inaccurate story straight. I gave her a chipper smile and sealed my lips tight.

We were stuck on the landing waiting for our look into the bedrooms when Sam touched my arm.

"If you're doing all right, I'm going to wait on the beach." He pulled his hat over his eyes as he slouched downstairs. Even so, when he passed a girl on the bottom step, she drew in a sharp breath.

frightening, I'd ask for my change. A suggested donation of eight quid each..."

"Stingy," I told him. "This is a museum now. It's educational."

The three of us rounded the corner into the living room and, despite my best intentions, I couldn't help but gasp. The airy white walls of my pretty beach cottage had been covered with dark wood paneling. Vines trailed from macramé plant hangers grouped in the corner. The built-in bookshelves were dominated by a green vinyl recliner with a split in the seat. My deep linen sofa had been replaced by a shabby plaid couch with a bit of stuffing poking through one cushion.

My brow wrinkled. For one thing, while money hadn't been abundant for my parents in our Seasalter years, I'm pretty sure they would have patched up the furniture. Let no one say that my mother isn't handy with a needle and thread. During her time in the Peace Corps, she had outfitted more kids than Fräulein Maria and she had done it without a stockpile of brocade drapes.

For another thing, our mid-century curtains with the big yellow swirls completely clashed with that Christmas-plaid couch.

Patricia looked at me warily and I didn't want to know what Sam's face was doing. Both of them had worried that I would break down the minute I saw the remodel. And it was tempting. But since flinging myself onto that ugly couch was out of the question, I took a deep breath and pulled myself together.

"My mom would regret her decision not to provide guidance on the décor if she saw this," I whispered.

Mrs. Collins stopped mid-sentence to give me a

shut up. All we're good for is disturbing the peace." The gate creaked again like it agreed.

As the line advanced, I heard someone laughingly utter the words "pet oyster." Someone else mimicked the sound of a toilet flushing. I glimpsed the decades-old imprint of my parents' handprints arched above my own as we climbed the cement steps. Sam's fingers tightened around mine.

"What do you think? Did my pretty sea glass kitchen survive the period remodel?" I asked, knowing that the little house I loved—the little beach cottage that had almost been mine for keeps—would look very different now that it had been restored to look as it had in my dad's famous memoir.

Patricia looked doubtful. Sam refused to look up.

"No? Any bets on what hideous color the kitchen appliances are? I'm going with olive green. No, wait— deviled-egg yellow."

Patricia grinned, Sam frowned, I laughed. The tour guide, a stern-faced woman who had introduced herself only as Mrs. Collins, pursed her lips at me. I filed away a mental snapshot of her; she'd be a perfect model for an uptight headmistress character.

"Hey, check it out," I whispered to Sam as we filed into the foyer. "They're using my pelican letter holder as the donation jar!"

He gave me a look that resembled the headmistress's and pulled out his wallet.

"I'll get it," I told him, but he scowled.

"I'm not letting you pay to walk through your own house," he said, stuffing thirty pounds down the pelican's throat. He gestured toward Mrs. Collins. "If she wasn't so

LOVE ON FILM - CHAPTER ONE

From outside, the Seasalter house looked much the same—tiny and straight, holding itself brave against sea winds and the strangers milling in the front yard. But it seemed tired, almost grey instead of the pale blue I remembered. An anemic crust crawled over the brick foundation, like the salt had stung it harshly in the two years I'd been gone. When we passed through the gate it creaked at me—a crotchety rebuke.

Sam clasped my hand like we were in line at a wake rather than queuing for the noon tour of the London Literary Archive's newest attraction, "A Walk through *Salt in the Sea*." I felt him tense when anyone entered the yard.

"Is it always this busy?" I asked Patricia as a family of four lined up behind us.

"This is tame. You should have seen the crowds last summer. And they don't just keep to your house. They're up and down the beach."

"The locals probably wish the Beckett family would

Sequel to the Novel
LOVE ON PAPER

love *on* film

SARAH MADELIN

Read On For An Exclusive Preview!

Thank You!

I am so excited to share *Love on Paper* with you. I hope you loved reading it as much as I enjoyed writing it. If you did, would you consider leaving a review? Even a line or two can make a huge difference in an author's career. Thank you!

Want to keep up with my author news? Please join my **mailing list** at *https://sarahmadelin.com/subscribe*. I'll send the inside scoop on life, new releases, and works in progress. Sometimes, I'll even include a special update from Marin herself!

If you want exclusive content in an inclusive group, please join **Meet-Cute, my Facebook reader group**, at https://www.facebook.com/groups/meetcutereadersgroup. We'll share encouraging words with each other, you can ask me questions and vote on ideas for upcoming books, and you'll even get the chance to review advance copies—including the sequel to this book, *Love on Film*.

Be sure to check out **the first two chapters of the sequel, included right here at the end of this book**.

Thank you for reading, everyone. It means the world to me!

xo,
Sarah Madelin

naughty photo or two? I wondered despairingly. I was about to go against my better judgment and suggest it when he said, "Marin, how much detail are you planning to share in this memoir? Because you're very skilled at certain types of writing and I'm not sure I want—it's just, people we know will surely read it—"

Now I was visualizing his signature blush.

"Sam. Believe me. I would never jeopardize your freedom of expression. Ever. I promise to close the door on any scene before it gets too intense."

And since I keep my promises, I'm afraid that's as far as we can go at this time.

"You don't need my permission to write your own story."

"I know that. But now it's your story, too."

A splash. A tap. The muffled pat of a towel. A declaration, three words long. Well, four, including my name.

"I love you, too. Now will you tell me what you think?"

"If I'm certain of anything, it's that you will do whatever it takes to respect my family. At this point, you could write Ella's biography with my blessing." He laughed quietly. "You should give the Archive a heads up. You may have stumbled upon your bestseller."

"I'm more interested in how jealous Gretchen and Yvonne will be when another publisher gets the real-life Simon Quinn in a book. They were crazy about Sean, and he was a pale imitation of the real you."

"You're very sweet to say so." His razor scraped by again.

"I thought you'd finished shaving."

"I missed a spot. Why? Is it bothering you?"

"In a sense. I can't keep from visualizing you. Inappropriately."

The splashing was conspicuously louder when he said, "Why stop? I've been visualizing you throughout this call. I assume you're wearing black stilettos?"

"Brown wool socks."

"Even better," he growled.

I decided to get in the spirit of things while we had time. "What are you wearing?"

"I stepped out of the shower two minutes before you called. So...not much."

Why, oh, why are we not a couple who might text a

how you and I got here, I would need to tell them a little about your family."

I heard a grunt followed by a series of little scratches, like he was going over his upper lip, and hoped the grunt meant he couldn't speak but he was listening and not that he hated it so much he was speechless. I rushed on.

"I would do the same thing with my family, in much greater detail. And the David thing will have to go in, since we wouldn't be together if he hadn't…hmm." I grew thoughtful. "I've never looked at it that way. We wouldn't be together if David hadn't—"

He saved me from saying it aloud.

"Let's just agree that sometimes good can come from evil. We don't have to send him a thank you card for stabbing you in the back." A vigorous splash rattled in the background.

"So what do you think?"

"I think he's a pillock who threw away the loveliest girl in the world."

I smiled. "What else do you think?"

He hummed hesitantly. "Are you sure you want to open yourself up in that way?"

"Gretchen and Yvonne are opening up most of it for me. And I'll admit, I like the idea of turning their manipulation against them. They strung me along for months with half the truth about my big book deal, and now they're exploiting my dad to boost sales. At least if I tell the story, I can keep it honest. Besides…" I had to laugh. "I've spent my whole life as a book character. I'm a Beckett. We're good on paper."

One long scratch of the razor sailed by. After a minute of silence, I said, "Do you hate it?"

finally drop the Beckett from her hyphenated last name." I heard water sloshing. "What are you doing?"

A rough scrape sounded before he answered. "Shaving. I have to be ready for the makeup team the moment I arrive on set."

I had a vision of him shirtless before a steamy bathroom mirror, which I mentally wiped down. Might as well picture him from the front and the back.

"So what's your plan for coming out, as you say? Are you going to have your *people* release a public statement?"

Sam laughed, but I was too nervous to join in.

"I do have a plan. A good one. But if you're uncomfortable with it, be honest." I took a deep breath. "I'm thinking of writing a memoir. About the past year."

"Oh?"

"Including everything that happened with Velicity."

"Really?"

I waited for a reaction I could interpret. There wasn't one.

"A lot of what happened with Velicity involves you. Some of it involves your family."

He sounded guilty when he said, "I'm all too aware of that, Marin."

"I know you're aware of it. I need to know you're okay with it. Before you say anything, let me clarify what I'm thinking. Unlike the Madison and Sean story, which focused on your family, I would focus on my family, my experience in England, and what happened with my publishing deal. It's annoying that Velicity mentions our relationship in every promo for the Rochester book, but they've crossed a line by bringing my dad into this. That said, to explain my fallout with Velicity and show people

III. A Memoir.

BEFORE PITCHING MY BIG IDEA TO LYLE, I HAD TO HASH IT out with Sam. He had a four a.m. call time, but when he picked up the phone at two-thirty in Vancouver, the crazy fool had just come in from running.

"Where do you even go in the middle of the night? Aren't you afraid of tripping over something in the dark?"

"They have the most incredible things here, Marin. They call them treadmills. Bloody brilliant, these Canadians."

"Oh, right. Well, keep it up. You're twenty-six now. It's downhill from there."

"I don't plan to let myself go until I'm your age. After that, what's the point?" he said with a snort. "You sound exceedingly cheerful for this time of night. Are you writing?"

"Kind of." My hands were sweating. I wiped them on his blue boxers, which I'd appropriated to wear while we were apart. "I've made a decision. I'm coming out of the closet."

A few seconds of loaded silence drifted over from Vancouver.

"About my dad, I mean. And I should say I've been outed. It's all over the industry that Bell Petite grew up to have a way with a dirty turn of phrase." I gave him the lowdown on my conference with Marge.

"These Velicity people are so vindictive. Will this upset your dad?"

"No, he'll love it. He likes my books—although we both pretend the sexy parts don't exist. My mom, however, may *the Sea.* You and your little pet oyster. The first time I read that book, I was pregnant with Ariadne. Your cute antics had me aching for a baby girl. All these years and none of us had a clue!"

For a minute, all I could do was stare. I'm not sure I breathed until she touched my arm in concern.

"What gave me away?" I tried to smile for Marge's sake, but inside I was about to ignite. Gretchen. She was the only one who knew.

"I read it online last night. I know I saw it on Love Notes…"

Love Notes? The most popular blog for romance fans?

Marge shook her head. "But I read it first in yesterday's *Consumer Romance Report*. In an article about the second edition of your Rochester book being released with the TV movie."

Despite its decidedly unromantic title, *Consumer Romance Report* is the foremost industry publication in the genre. If my family history had made the magazine, it was well on its way to being common knowledge. It meant one thing.

Gretchen and Yvonne had devised a new plan to increase sales: capitalizing on the hallowed name of John Robert Beckett.

Any residual respect I'd had for Velicity dissolved. In its place was an idea, a tiny sprout of a plan that would bloom into the very book you hold in your hands.

"It's amazing," Marge was saying. "This whole time Mariana Rose was John Robert Beckett's Bell Petite."

I smiled at Marge as my sly satisfaction began to build.

"Actually," I said, offering her my hand, "his Bell Petite has been Marin Beckett all along."

"Mariana Rose, aren't you the sweetest thing to come down here on a day like this!" She pulled me into what we both would have been professionally obligated to describe as her ample bosom. "Who knew Chicago in July could feel so much like Alabama? It's hotter than Hades out there, but you look so nice and cool. You skinny little things always do. I've looked like a pig on a spit since we got here."

"No, you look great. I love what you've done with your hair."

"Image consultant," she said, patting her auburn-coiffed head. "Ned thinks most of this Velocity super-author business is hooey, but even he admits to liking me as a redhead."

She cast a fond look at Ned, his hands folded across his own ample bosom. He looked like he'd pay good money for a La-Z-Boy and a cold beer.

"And so you've given up romance," she surprised me by saying. "I wish you luck, but I hate to see you go. I know your readers will, too. Your stories are so much fun."

"I left Velocity but I'm not giving up romance. I'm going indie. I'm setting up my own small press and I just signed with agent Lyle Michaud to handle foreign translations and media deals."

"Lyle Michaud! Well, you skipped to the front of the line!" After effusive congratulations, Marge said, "I'm glad to hear you're sticking with it. I should've known, but you know how rumors fly when someone splits from Velocity. I thought maybe you'd decided to try another genre. Something more like your dad's book, even."

My astonishment must have splashed itself across my face, because Marge laughed.

"To think you're that same sweet little girl from *Salt in*

opportunity to right an old wrong. If the Archive puts all the details in place, there's certain to be an oyster living the good life in the upstairs toilet. One that won't ever be flushed."

His fingers met mine.

"That's a life saved, Marin. All because of you."

II. An Idea.

JULIE, MICHAEL, AND I WERE OUTSIDE THE HAROLD Washington Library when it happened. One minute, we were strolling our way to story time. The next, an enormous photo of Marge Powell grinned out the window at us: Elysienne Fields, bestselling author of the new *Courting the Fates* series, was in Chicago for a book signing.

I studied the poster. "What do you think? Could I have worked the purple sequins if it was still my book tour?"

Julie shook her dark head doubtfully. "Marin, you can wear anything. But that sequined top would wear you."

I checked my watch. "Can you two enjoy *Stellaluna* without me? I want to say hello."

I leafed through Marge's new book—hardcover!—while the crowd dwindled. A grass-green John Deere cap glinted in the corner; Marge's husband Ned was dozing on a folding chair.

Marge herself was holding court in high style. I was used to seeing her at the few conferences I attend each year in embellished sweatshirts that she makes for fun. But no glitter paint or leaf appliqués had touched her plum pantsuit. When she waved at me from across the room, the stones in her chunky bracelet sparkled.

shoulder. "The conversation with your mother sounded tense."

"Conversations with my mother tend to be tense. Regardless, I wish I'd called her last week. She said she would've bought the house if she had known what was going on."

"You'll write a bestseller and buy it back yourself someday."

That was an idea. "Someday."

"The Archive will probably cock it up and flog it in a hurry."

"I—" Wait, what? I leaned back to look at him. "'Cock it up' I understand. But 'flog it' can't mean what I'm thinking."

"Mess it up. Then sell it."

"Those are actual sayings?"

"They are. But I didn't put them together to be perverse. You did that all by yourself."

His eyes crinkled. I considered swooning. Instead I smiled back.

"Do me a favor and repeat that phrase verbatim when you meet my mother next month."

We carried our dinner to the coffee table that doubled as his dining room. Maybe he thought my appetite wasn't hearty enough, because after a while, he said, "I doubt the heritage site will catch on. You should get started on the bestseller."

"Yeah. It's no North Lees Hall. How many people could care about that house?"

Neither of us said anything. *Over Twenty Million Copies Sold* speaks for itself.

"You know," Sam said slowly, "this could be an

telling it, so it didn't take long. To her credit, she seemed genuinely sorry about the loss of my contract.

"I wish you had told me before letting the house go. I'd have tried to find a way to buy it myself."

"Why?" I couldn't help asking, and a minute later I think she sniffled.

"You and your father didn't live there alone. It means something to me, too." I'm positive she blew her nose, but she didn't give me a chance to say anything. She cleared her throat and her voice became brusque again. "I thought you were coming home last week. Nandi told me you're living with your—do you call him your boyfriend? I thought that term might offend both of you, considering."

"Considering what? That I'm forty-five years older than him?" I scowled into the phone. Sam looked up from the stove and scowled at me. "I'm not living with him, I'm staying with him. We're both going to Chicago next month."

"And he'll be staying with you?"

"No, I got him a hotel room. I can only stand so much of him," I said, blowing him a kiss. "Mom, as you just pointed out, I'm old enough to make my own decisions."

Besides, I thought about telling her, I'll gamble what money I've got left that, within an hour, he'll charm you into asking him to marry me. Or maybe asking him to marry you.

A few minutes later, I leaned against Sam's kitchen counter while he poured white wine into his standard cream sauce. He'd decided to experiment with his grandmother's tagliatelle recipe.

He stirred with one hand while the other kneaded my

demonstration of my fresh and original moves. I was about to oblige when my phone rang again.

"You are one popular woman today," he said, pushing himself up to make dinner.

I swore when I saw the caller. "It's my mother. I forgot to call her about the house."

"Tell her you've been busy taking advantage of me. Send the conversation in another direction entirely."

"Very funny."

"Marin!" my mother snapped. "You might have mentioned that you and your father have agreed to turn the Seasalter house into an amusement park. What is this about it becoming some kind of roadside attraction?"

"Mom, it's the London Literary Archive. I doubt they're installing a Tilt-A-Whirl."

"Someone just called asking about my china pattern from back then. As if I bothered with china. I was fresh out of the Peace Corps. I'm not sure we had dishes at all."

"Tell them that. They'll probably do an exhibit of us eating our oatmeal from turtle shells you picked up in Cameroon." Some insolent part of me smiled at the choked intake of her breath.

"Why would your father want our privacy invaded like this? What happened to selling the property to some nice young family?" She sounded so WASP-ish, I was surprised she didn't immediately correct herself. "As if the book wasn't exhibition enough. Why doesn't he sign up for a reality television show as well?"

"I think he's in talks with one of the networks," I said in my own special brand of pain-in-the-rear. Then I gave her the short version of the real story. I had gotten good at still bringing what's-his-name, the *actor*, when you come home next month?"

I slipped out of Sam's bedroom and lowered my voice. "You know his name, Dad. And he's important to me, so be nice to him."

"I'll do what I can," he said with a grunt. "Tell him to bring a smock. He can take over porch-painting duty from the other jerkhole."

Word had traveled through the university grapevine coordinated by my nosy sister that the jerkhole in question was seeing an economics professor who favored shorter-than-average skirts. Nandi said she had hair like summer in the Amazon, but she appeared to be in her thirties. Not that we're judging.

I had twenty minutes to run my hands through the tousled hair of the not-yet-in-his-thirties guy at my side before Patricia called to say she'd saved an article for us about the successful adaptation of books into films. It mentioned *The Young Edward Rochester*—book and movie—and prominently featured a photo of Sam. A photo from which scene, you ask? Here's a clue: when I mentioned it, his face turned pink.

I had almost convinced him to stand under his shower in a white button-down so I could compare the period look to a modern one when Nandi called with news from her feminist literature course. Guess whose book was cited during a lecture on the romance novel? Turns out someone in the English department (say hello to Doctor Lois Schenkl!) thinks *In Your Dreams* by Beckett Bell inverts traditional gender roles in a fresh and original way.

Sam had yet to read *In Your Dreams* and requested a

Epilogue. Addendum. Afterword. Notes.
They're Just Less *Sound of Music*-y Ways of Saying
Every Ending is a Beginning.

I. An Ending.

MY DAD'S ATTORNEY CALLED THREE DAYS LATER TO SAY THE Literary Archive had closed on my Seasalter house. My dad himself called a day after that to tell me that he was the proud owner of his very own slip of lakefront Wisconsin.

"Not too bad for an old man like me to finally have a place of my own. Maybe I can write about it. A Virginia Woolf knock-off for the OCD crowd. Might be a big hit in the psych ward."

"You're not an old man. And I'm not discussing the psych ward comment," I told him, causing Sam to pause in his laundry-folding and glance at me. "I'm happy for you. What are you going to rip out, now that you're legally allowed?"

I said this jokingly because we'd been hacking into that house for years, paving walks and painting rooms. But he was full of plans.

"I want an office off the back, someplace I can work and see the water. I feel inspired. And the paint could use a touch-up. I should hire someone for that, too," he said, surprising me. I'd always taken care of that stuff. "Are you any other way, with you in Chicago and me God knows where all the time." I nodded. "I'm serious, Marin. If we're doing this, I'm doing it all the way. It would be nice if you'd let me."

I gave myself a moment to sit still and feel it all: joy, gratitude, relief, release. I put my hands on his face. Then I slid them down to the buttons on his shirt.

"All the way, really? You want me to let you do it all the way?" One. Two. Three buttons undone. "You set that up, I know you did." Four.

A mischievous grin crept over his face. "I don't know what you're talking about." Five.

Six. I reached around him and flipped off the lamp. "Please, I'm a professional. Well, I used to be. I can spot a come-on like that with my eyes closed."

"In that case…" He tipped me back, his lips at my ear. "To borrow a bit of your innuendo, close your eyes and come on."

your point."

"Good. Because I've read enough of your books to know how these misunderstandings unfold. So if you have a secret lovechild hidden away or you're a Romanian princess in disguise, I'd prefer to know now. Unlike you, I'm not a fan of surprises."

And so we've come to it. Did I tell him the truth, that I'd lost my book deal? Or did I keep this one secret so he would never find out why?

It was a little bit of both.

I told the truth about losing my contract. I told a lie about why. Despite my best effort, the lie was so bad that Sam took one look at my face and called me out. When I tried to lie again, he got angry. So finally, I told the truth. The whole truth. You know him well enough at this point to visualize what followed: shock, then guilt, then a lot of guilt, then negotiation. And finally, the reluctant acceptance that it was too late to change things anyway.

"This is entirely my fault. If I hadn't been such a prick...I know how you feel about Ella. Anything you'd consent to publish would be respectful of her and my family. I would never have let you give up something so important." He took my hand. "I'll make it up to you, Marin. I'll find a way to make it up to you someday."

"No, it was my choice. And it was the right choice. Even if I'd rewritten it to be completely different, Yvonne would have had us performing like trained dogs in bookstores across America." I shook my head. "There are other publishers. I'll figure it out."

He slipped his fingers into my hair. That steadfast light in his eyes never wavered when he looked at me.

"We'll figure it out together. I don't think this will work

Because I struggle to see how you've concluded that this is just a casual fling."

I sniffed loudly. "Will you believe me if I say it's not you, it's me?"

"Yes," he said, so definitely that I laughed. "That's better. I much prefer hearing you laugh to watching you cry. Although tears are preferable to you pretending you're fine. That's horrible."

This made me pause. "Why didn't you tell me earlier that you knew about the house?"

"I only learned of it fifteen minutes before I arrived. I was processing it. And you seemed determined to believe the worst about me. You deserved to suffer," he said with a smirk.

I pursed my lips and nodded. "That's true."

"I'm joking," Sam said, rolling his eyes to the ceiling. "Marin. You are the most exasperating woman I have ever met."

All I could do was nod again. "Yeah. Me, too."

"All right. Let's clear this up. Do you remember when I found your book draft about my family?"

Mingled with the fear that maybe Patricia hadn't covered for me as well as I'd thought was a streak of incredulity. "Do you think I'm likely to forget?"

"But do you remember what you told me? You said I would never again need to worry about finding myself in a poorly plotted melodrama because you weren't honest with me."

Now this was actually insulting.

"What do you mean, poorly plotted? Do you know how much work went into keeping this from you?" Another unimpressed look floated my way. I sighed. "Okay, I see everything I told him was true. The only lie was the omission.

"My dad needs me at home. It's not fair to leave him alone so much. He wouldn't sell this house to me for what it's worth. It's his only real asset. If I had gone ahead with my plan to buy it, I would have deprived him of money he needs."

When I glanced up, his blank look had been replaced by a kind one I knew well.

"Your father is lucky to have you," he said quietly, and I smiled, mostly out of relief that he'd believed me.

But, I told myself, Sam is so genuine it wouldn't occur to him—

"Now why don't you tell me what else is going on. Because if that were all, there's no reason for you to have kept it from me."

Maybe it was the dumbfounded despair in my eyes, or the idiotic way my mouth fell open. Regardless, he sat there with an expectant look until I broke down and told him that I didn't want him to be stretched in so many different directions, between me and his family and the career opportunities opening up for him. As I talked, Patricia's admonishments looped through my head and flew out my mouth as well. Eventually, I found myself curled into his side, the last of my mascara staining his shirt.

Despite the supportive way he ran his hand over my back, when I finally stopped talking, the look he gave me was somewhat unimpressed.

"I'm confused. In what way have I demonstrated to you that I plan to pop into and out of your life on my whim? Is the tone of my voice wrong when I say that I love you?

We looked at each other without speaking. I twisted the bag's twine handles around my fingers until they throbbed.

"Patricia said to tell you she always keeps her word, unless the words aren't worth keeping." I enjoyed a vision of my hands around Patricia's neck. "She also said she hopes you'll still speak to her."

"Oh, I've got plenty to say."

I sat down, hard, next to him. His face was still expressionless. Where was the upbeat guy I'd left downstairs? Then I realized that, whatever he knew, he'd known about it all night.

Until that moment, I hadn't understood how good an actor he is.

"So. Where to begin?"

"What did she tell you?" I asked after a minute.

"I'll be honest, Marin, that sounds like you're trying to determine how much I know so you can calculate how much you can continue to hide." His blunt words and blank tone made him hard to read, so I was surprised when he drew my face toward his. He kept his hand on my cheek after he pulled away. And he said, gently, "Why did you sell your house? That's what Patricia said I should ask you first."

Relief is not a strong enough word for what flooded through me. I have to admit that, instead of wanting to wrestle Patricia to the ground, I felt grateful that she'd protected what was most important. She had given me this one clear signal, a heads-up so I would know to think fast.

Sam's gaze was too steady. If I looked into his eyes, I would never pull it off. I clutched my little quilted pillow and focused on the embroidered squares. When I spoke,

Get it over with, I snapped. Get it out and get back to Sam so you don't lose more time.

A few minutes later, I trudged to the bathroom. There was no way to hide my blotchy face, so while I mopped up my smeared mascara, I thought up an excuse.

I had a fight with Nandi, I imagined myself telling him. Or my mom, that was even better. We had an argument, but I'm fine. No, I'd rather not talk about it. Stupid family stuff.

Stupid, stupid, stupid stuff.

I pulled open the door. Sam was leaning against the opposite wall.

"I had a fight with Nandi!" I gasped. "I mean my mom. I had a fight with my mom. About Nandi."

"Did you? I'm sorry to hear that." He walked into my room and sat on the bed. "Do you want to talk about it?"

Good thing I rehearsed this, I thought sarcastically as I followed him. "I'd rather not."

I flipped on the bedside lamp. When I turned around, he was holding out my cell phone.

"This was in the kitchen." His tone was matter-of-fact, his face blank.

My face, on the other hand: open book. An epic tragedy, probably.

"Sam," I started, but I couldn't go on. I couldn't even say I'd been on the landline. The only receiver was downstairs. Then I noticed the bag beside him. And the familiar logo splashed across the front. He handed it to me.

"I stopped at Patricia's bookshop to buy you some entertainment for tomorrow's flight. I came away with an entertaining story myself."

in his arms, pushing my face into his shoulder so he couldn't see it.

"Your sisters are so lucky. If I had a big brother, I'd want him to be just like you."

"Really? I've no interest at all in having you for a sister. None whatsoever." He slid his hand a little lower than what could honestly be considered my back.

"You're not eating," he said a few minutes later as we picnicked by the fireplace. "Not fond of Amy's kebab recipe?"

I tried to smile. "I could listen to you say 'kebab' every day for the rest of my life. In your accent, it's extremely cute."

The long look he gave me was also cute, but in a let's-go-back-to-my-place kind of way.

Maybe he will come to my place. For a few days, now and then, for a while. It's not over yet, I reminded myself. But I could feel the telltale nose-drip starting, which meant I had three seconds to leave the room before the tears showed up.

"Was that my phone?" I called as I fled, timing a much-needed sniff with the clomp of my feet on the stairs.

In the bedroom, I pushed open every window and curled up in the dark. I held my eyes open wide, like I could dry them out, and dragged in a few deep breaths. The air smelled like salt, and something else, too. Salt and earth. New leaves and wet streets.

Spring. This must be how spring smells in Seasalter, I thought, pulling my sleeves over my hands. I tried to forget that I wouldn't be around to experience it, but the sob in my throat pushed its way out. I let my face fall into my pillow in defeat.

CHAPTER THIRTY-FIVE

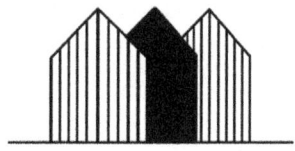

"I've brought you loads of good things," Sam said when he arrived at my house a few hours later. He handed me a sparkly pink bag. "First and foremost, to prove you're forgiven for missing her party, Lily insisted you have your share of plastic treasures. Very important items, all. Secondly, I insisted you have the largest piece of birthday cake." He held a huge forkful to my lips, then pulled some plastic containers from a bag. "Party leftovers for dinner: marmite on toast, tomato bouncers, chicken kebabs. As I said to the children at the party, no poking others with your skewer. Especially since I'm the only other person here. Finally, look what I found on the beach near my grandparents' house yesterday. All for you."

I froze when he spread out a handful of sea glass. The largest piece was the prettiest—a dime-sized drop of aqua. A frosted splash of sea.

Behind me, Sam slipped his hands around my waist. When he lifted my hair to press his lips to my neck, I turned fact that I'm a meddling old goat keep you from stopping in tomorrow to tell me goodbye."

I reached up long enough to cover her hand with my own.

"Now you are being ridiculous," I said before pulling away.

I stared into my lap, thinking maybe Patricia really is psychic. I'd been tiptoeing around that question for weeks, comparing how I felt about David—and how I felt about myself when I was with David—to how I felt about Sam. The conclusion I kept coming to left me with a strange combination of sorrow and relief.

"What does this have to do with my house?" I asked finally.

"Maybe nothing. But do you remember telling me that David compared you to Tennyson's Mariana? Because you like to expect the worst?"

I saw where she was going and had no desire to hear it. She didn't give me a choice.

"You're willing to give up an awful lot for someone you are selling so short." She waited a minute. "You're selling yourself short, too."

"I'm not doing anything."

"Exactly. You're not doing anything, you're not saying anything. You're keeping it all to yourself so that you hold all the cards. Tell yourself whatever you want. You're doing it so Sam won't lose time with his family? You're sparing him the hassle of being tied down? Gobshite. You're doing it now to avoid him doing it later. Because that's the kind of faith you have in him and in yourself."

Her words were harsh, but even I could tell her voice held nothing for me but kindness.

"You expect it to end. So you're setting the end in motion, my friend."

My nose dripped just before the tears broke free. Patricia slipped me a tissue.

"Tough love, Marin. It's my specialty." She opened the door but leaned over to touch my shoulder. "Don't let the sell the book you just finished. Then you can buy it and rent it out like you planned in the beginning."

"Selling my book could take months. I asked my dad's landlord for more time when my contract fell through. He's done waiting on us. The house in Wisconsin is tiny and old, but it's lakefront property. He could sell it to a developer tomorrow. And he's considering it."

"There are other houses on Lake Michigan. Your dad would adjust."

"No."

Patricia sighed as I rolled to a stop near her bookshop. The rain thudding on the roof of the car filled the gap in our conversation. I looked over at her with a rueful smile.

"You told me once that you don't meddle. For the record, Patricia, that statement is false." I could feel her deliberating as she looked at me. "If I tell you to say it, will you bite my head off again?"

She smiled. "I will miss you, you know. Seasalter will lose some flavor when you go." She picked up her purse but didn't open the door. "Try not to hate me when you hear this."

I bit my lip and nodded.

"I've been thinking about this for the past month, since you let me know what you're planning to do. I know this is presumptuous and I have no right to ask. But now that you've had some distance from your breakup with David, did losing him break your heart? Or was it his betrayal that hurt you most?" She let the words settle before she continued. "I don't expect an answer. It's just a hunch I've had, that maybe David wasn't the great love of your life. Six years is a long time to be with someone and still hesitate to set a wedding date."

"I don't have a grand scheme, Patricia. All I'm doing is going home a little sooner than planned. Sam's visiting next month on his way to Vancouver. I'll tell him about selling the house then. He'll think it's because I've realized I shouldn't leave my dad. Which is true, by the way."

Her eyes nearly rolled into the back of her head. "Protecting your dad is your pet excuse."

I was too tired for that fight, so I ignored her comment. "If Sam finds out not publishing that book cost me all of my income and one perfect house, he'll feel terrible. And then he'll try to convince me that publishing it won't matter and, hey, why not make a mockery of his family tragedy? Who wouldn't love to be exploited in a histrionic book? And then it will always be this horrible thing between us. So don't bring it up."

"God forbid I bring it up. I was sworn to secrecy before you breathed Word One to me, wasn't I?"

"Had I known you would be this difficult, I'd have kept quiet. I should've sent you a callous email."

I felt shaky, like I'd had too much coffee. I hate arguing. Especially with someone I respect.

"I know," Patricia said. "I hate fighting with you, too."

"Would you stop doing that?" I exploded. We fell silent. Finally, I looked at her. "I'm sorry. This thing is wearing me down. I'm not happy about it. I just don't know what else to do."

She put her hand on my arm. "Start being honest with the people you're protecting. Tell Sam you've sold the house. Let him respond instead of deciding for him that a long-distance romance will cramp his style. Rather than tell your dad you've changed your mind about buying the house, tell him the truth. Maybe he'll hold onto it until you losing the contract itself. If you had any conviction that the two of you would stay together after you go home, you'd tell him that much of the truth."

I didn't respond. Sam was reluctant to leave his sisters to film in Vancouver, and he'd won a new role shooting in Amsterdam all fall. He'd be away from home often enough. He didn't need one more international obligation.

She scowled at my silence.

"What's your plan, to *email* him when you get home and say you're not coming back?"

"Don't be ridiculous," I said in a flat voice.

"Don't you be ridiculous. Have you ever allowed yourself to believe that you can build a life with Sam? A real life, Marin, one where people do more than tuck themselves away in a beach house. No. You think he's too young and too handsome, and because of that he'll eventually tire of you."

"You sound exactly like Nandi when you tell me all about myself."

"When she hears about this, she'll rip into you, too. And you know why."

Because neither of you can resist the urge to run my life? I thought.

"No. Because we love you, you self-destructive ninny."

My simmering irritation began to boil. "You know, the mind-reading thing is getting old."

It was like I'd never spoken.

"Once you've had some time apart, you'll let Sam know—in a callous, casual way that's the exact opposite of how you really feel—that you've sold your house here, like it meant nothing to you. And then you plan to watch him drift away."

"You think I'm being an idiot. I see it in your face. And—ha! I hear it in your voice, too."

Patricia twisted in her seat to face me. "Do you know what I think? I think you assume too bloody much."

"Well, sorry," I said, flicking the wipers up a notch. "Unlike you, I can't read minds. I can only go on what I think is best."

She sniffed. "You excel at deciding what's best for everyone else. But your logic is flawed. And your motivation, although you refuse to see it, is selfish."

I felt an all-over flash of anger.

"Are you serious?" Because let's be honest—I'd given up a million-dollar book deal to protect one man I loved and, as a result, lost a house I loved to protect the sanity of another.

"Out of respect for Isaac I won't say 'as a heart attack.' But yes, I'm absolutely serious." Her face softened. "I know you think keeping Sam in the dark about giving up your book deal is best. Maybe you're right. But I see only one reason you aren't telling him you've sold the house. You've decided for him that he's better off without you."

I flipped on the defroster; all the hot air from the passenger had fogged up the windows.

"I have a very good reason for keeping it from him. He's listened to me gush about loving my house for months. If I tell him I've suddenly decided not to buy it, he'll know something's wrong. He's not stupid."

"He's also not an arse, but you expect him to throw you over once you're gone."

"I don't expect anything."

Patricia snorted. "You may be able to hide the reason you lost your contract, but we both know you can't hide

"Would you be so kind as to leave us her—oh, excellent. This will be helpful indeed."

Indeed, I thought, scribbling my mom's number on his card.

"Please wait a few days before calling. I'm going home tomorrow and I'd like to explain the sale of the property personally." So she doesn't flip out when she hears that her very own wax replica might be erected for posterity in the Seasalter house.

"And just to confirm, the original quote is still painted on the ceiling in your parents' bedroom?" The man's small eyes danced in their sockets.

My bedroom, I wanted to say. "It is."

Richard Glenister beamed at me. He tried to beam at Patricia but his radiance faded—she looked angry enough to club us both with her purse.

He attempted a sober look before offering his hand. "Thank you, Ms. Beckett. It's an honor for us to acquire the property. I assure you, it will be a heritage site many will treasure."

When I stretched out my own hand, I did my best to ignore my shaking fingers and the sensation of Patricia's wrath burning a hole through my back.

"Thank you, Mr. Glenister."

"Say it," I told Patricia as I drove through Whitstable's wet streets near the end of our silent ride. "I know you're thinking it."

"What is it you think you know now?" she snapped.

CHAPTER THIRTY-FOUR

When Patricia and I dropped off my dad's papers at the Literary Archive a few weeks later, Richard Glenister was brimming with enthusiasm for the impending heritage site, A Walk Through *Salt in the Sea*. He quizzed me for twenty minutes on my childhood memories of the Seasalter house.

"For instance, do you recall whether the bath fixtures are the same? Or if the doorknobs are original, that sort of thing? We want to restore the house to its former condition to give visitors a true understanding of the book's setting and its significance to your family."

I tried not to picture my pretty beach house being ripped apart to make room for fake wood paneling and stained linoleum. I also suppressed my desire to box this totally innocent man on the ear for even implying that he could understand the house's significance. I only said, "I don't remember much. You might speak to my mother. I'm sure she could tell you more."

pictured my dad sitting alone on his porch in Wind Point. Lily's clear, contagious giggles bubbled through the glass, followed by Ella's quiet laugh.

It was this or nothing, Gretchen had said, but she was wrong. It was nothing either way.

"Marin? Are you there?"

My head felt heavy and painfully hot, like something inside was trying to beat its way out. I pressed my face against my hand and took a second to steel my shaking nerves.

"Tell Yvonne I went with nothing," I said, and hung up the phone.

your hand. She won't just back out of the five-book deal. She's prepared to drop you altogether."

The last thread holding up my stomach snapped.

"We've worked together for nine years, Gretchen. How could you not tell me this?"

"I was hoping there'd be nothing to tell. I've busted my butt for weeks to convince Yvonne there are other ways to capitalize on the film. But she's determined. It's this or nothing."

From the dining room, I heard a deep laugh followed by a shy one and looked up to see Sam and Ella stacking all their penguins together. The overhead light made her blonde hair shine. I turned away and stared out at the water, at the waves bobbing against the overcast sky.

They're a permanent part of literature, those waves. And so am I, and so are the two of us together, forever linked in the climax of my father's book. Our turbulent boat trip was the incident that forced my parents to leave Seasalter. It was confirmation that all their plans would take a backseat to the illness that had clawed its way into the front. And it was common knowledge, this beginning of my family's collapse.

Salt in the Sea. A book so celebrated, it's never gone out of print. It ripped the covers off my family, opened us up for gossip and critique. But it's also an indelible portrait of who we once were. A scrapbook that holds the part of my family I didn't get to keep.

I looked around my little office, at the clean white walls and the windows framing the fretting sea. In the garden, rose bushes nodded in the not-quite-spring breeze. I pictured myself standing beneath the porch light with Sam that first night he'd come to my Seasalter house. Then I would've won the contract anyway. The Sean and Madison book just accelerated things."

"What things?"

"Yvonne wants to release your Sean and Madison book to coincide with our second printing of *The Young Edward Rochester* and the film's American TV premiere. She wants you and Simon to promote both books, along with the film, as the romance behind the romance novel. She thinks it will catapult sales and show the industry that Velicity is a major player, all in one stroke."

"That is brilliant," I admitted.

"Yvonne has ideas for making the stuff with his family less personal. She knows you'll never agree to the part about the crazy kid. Maybe we could make it a mystery. Turn the mom's death into a tragic murder instead of just cancer," she actually said.

"*Just* cancer? Are you kidding me?"

"You know what I mean. The point is, we'll use the truth as inspiration, because it's the linchpin of the conflict. You know, 'How can Sean and Madison stay together when his family needs him in England?' But we'll pump up the drama so much that it's obvious the family stuff is fake. During promos, we'll play up the cute stuff that's real, like when you fainted and he caught you, and then you discovered that you were both connected to *The Young Edward Rochester*. Yvonne is right, it's a really cool way for Velicity to capitalize on the miniseries."

"Gretchen," I said firmly, "I'm done inventing fantasies about this man. And Velicity has no right to his reality. It's nonnegotiable."

"I know how you feel," Gretchen said slowly. "But your future with Velicity depends on this. Yvonne's going to force

"No!" Ironically, she sounded offended. "Do you think I want you to sue us?"

"I'm starting to, yeah."

Sam's phone rang; another marriage proposal, no doubt. Lily pressed her nose to the office door and grinned at me.

"What ending is Deb talking about?" I asked, doing my best to wave at Lily.

"I had a junior editor write a placeholder based on what little you've mentioned about your real relationship. Yvonne thought if we mocked up an ending that proves we can tell the story respectfully, you might agree to finish it yourself."

Sam appeared at the door, pulling Lily back. He pressed his palm against the glass, a small hello. My stomach began to churn.

"Nothing about that story is respectable. Yvonne has to know by now that I won't publish it."

"Yvonne loves the Sean and Madison storyline; moreover, she loves that it mirrors your real-life romance."

"Some of it mirrors our relationship. The rest of it makes a soap opera of his mother's death and turns his sister into a psychopath. I won't do it."

"Soap sells, Marin, as well as true love, and that book has both. Yvonne knows that better than anyone."

I paused.

"Why is this book so important to Yvonne?" She didn't answer. "This has been her plan the whole time. My big contract was a cover to get this book." It seemed ludicrous, but I felt sure I was right.

Gretchen was quiet. "If it makes you feel better, you

ears began tingling. Do you ever get that, moments before everything hits the fan? Like intuition is warning you to duck.

"Maybe Gretchen thought it was good enough where you stopped to—"

"How did it end?"

Deb clearly suspected that I'd lost my mind. "Sean and Madison went to the premiere of the movie he starred in, the one that you wrote. I mean that Madison wrote. And everyone was taking their picture and saying it was a real-life fairytale. Like it really is."

The phone almost slipped from my sweaty hand. "I didn't write that."

"I…oh. I don't know…"

"Do you have this year's publishing schedule? What's listed for me?"

"*Genevieve at Midnight* is slated for December. And an untitled book, for release in August."

Of course. Bring Sam to Newport, so Yvonne can badger us both into publishing that horrible story. Like hell I would.

Deb must've sensed I was about to blow. She transferred me back to Gretchen.

"Marin!" Gretchen's voice was snippy. "I was on with Vanessa Laurent. Do you know how rarely she returns my calls?"

"Why? Did you attempt to publish her manuscript without permission, too?" I heard a weak clattering, like she'd dropped her pen or maybe her evil-genius monocle had fallen out. "Deb just informed me that she loved the fairytale ending to my unfinished Sean and Madison novel. Did you really plan to publish it behind my back?"

beveled glass sliced him into a mirage of shifting shapes.

"Why? Is she in love with him as well?"

"Are you in love with him?" Gretchen asked, zest flooding her voice again.

"I meant as well as everyone who watched the English premiere of the miniseries last weekend. His phone's been jumping out of his pocket with marriage proposals." I watched him hug Lily as she climbed into his lap and thought, Yes, God help me, I'm in love with him. He makes it impossible to be anything else.

"Oh." Gretchen sounded disappointed in me again. "Anyway, Yvonne's very interested in meeting him. He did portray a Velicity character, you know."

I didn't comment on the absurdity of Velicity claiming Edward Rochester—young, old, or dead and gone—as its own. Somewhere in Yorkshire, Charlotte Brontë was whirling in her grave.

"I'll check with him. He's doing a new film this summer, so he'll be busy."

Gretchen was silent. Finally, she said, "Well, hopefully we can arrange the trip to accommodate him," before passing me off to Deb.

"Where did I put the dates Yvonne's assistant sent?" I heard Deb rustling through papers and pictured her desk, the one chaotic spot in Gretchen's streamlined office. "I just finished the book about you and your new boyfriend. It's so romantic! Gretchen showed me his picture and oh! is he cute. Does he have a brother? I don't care if he's young."

"What book did you finish?"

"Your Sean and Madison book. I loved it, how you met without realizing—"

"I didn't finish that book. I'm not going to finish it." My

"Why?" Ella grumbled the next afternoon. Her pile of penguins had collapsed first, followed shortly by mine. Lily was more interested in creating families for her penguins than stacking them on her plastic iceberg; she'd arranged them wing-to-wing like they were holding hands. But Sam's mound of penguins grew tall until the last one perched triumphantly on top. "Why does Sam always win?"

"Because he cheats," I told her.

"At cards, woman, not penguins. Some things are sacred." He turned to Lily. "Now?" The two of them made explosion noises when they toppled his penguins, the carnage spilling over the dining room table. Ella giggled with her hand over her mouth.

At this typically inconvenient moment, my editor called. I ruffled Ella's hair before stepping into the adjoining office. "Win this one for both of us."

Gretchen was full of news. The marketing department was creating a press kit devoted to me and my books. They wanted new photos of me from myriad ridiculous angles—glamorous, romantic, down-to-earth. There was talk of hiring an assistant to handle my work exclusively. The assistant's main task: coordinating public appearances to establish Mariana Rose as Velicity's flagship author. Gretchen mentioned hiring a PR coach. By the time she was finished, I could no longer distinguish between elation and intimidation.

"Yvonne is inviting you for a weekend at the Lee family's summer home in Newport. You can coordinate with Deb on the arrangements." Gretchen paused. Her next words lacked their usual bite. Instead, she sounded cautious. "She'd like Simon Quinn to accompany you."

I glanced at Sam through the office's French doors. The

jobless? Because I assure you, I don't." He called to the girls. "Have fun tonight."

Lily dashed to her father's side for a hug. Ella allowed him a hug as well, but she watched him leave without a word. She slipped her small hand into mine as I closed the door and looked up at me with eyes that understood more than they should.

A cheer from behind us told me Lily had spotted Sam. She ran halfway up the stairs to meet him. "Where have you been?" she demanded as he lifted her up.

He looked at me when he answered. "I was counting floorboards in Marin's bedroom. Do you know how many rows there are?" He tapped the tip of Lily's nose. "Forty-six."

Ella squinted shrewdly. "Marin said you were changing a light bulb."

"Did she? Hmm. Then I did that as well. It's ready anytime Marin wants to turn it on again. Is Dad bringing in your things?"

The three of us, even Lily, just looked at him. Finally, I stammered, "He said to tell you hello."

Sam stood still. When his eyes met mine, one corner of his mouth was pulled to the side. He raised his eyebrows, shook his head once, and turned to his sisters.

"Well, you're here. And Marin is here. I honestly can't think of a better reason to go out for pizza. Can you?" He looked at Ella when he asked this, because the little girl in his arms was already celebrating. Then he held out his hand to us both.

nervous habit of turning into a stodgy English matron whenever I spoke to him: *Please* come inside, Doctor Quinn, *do*. It would be *most* lovely if you would take tea with us.

He didn't answer. The distracted look in his eyes made me add, "Sam's on his way. He's changing a light bulb for me." It was a decent excuse.

Doctor Quinn took a step toward the door. "Please tell him I said hello."

Really? Sure, things between Sam and his father were tense, but he hadn't seen him in over a month. Would he really leave without speaking to him? Was he oblivious or would he intentionally hurt him like that?

"I know Sam would like to see you," I said carefully. "He'll be right down."

"I'm catching the ferry to Calais. I'm sure he'll understand."

"I'm sure he will." I stared so hard that he finally looked at me, but the lines of his face didn't soften. "He understands that you disapprove of nearly everything about him. How can you be so unsupportive of all that he's accomplishing?"

"Accomplishing? He earns a pittance waiting tables and these trifling entertainment jobs pay even less. He's twenty-five years old. What is he accomplishing aside from refusing to grow up?"

"He's twenty-five?" I heard myself say. I paused for two seconds to process this. I hadn't even wondered about his age in weeks; I'm proud to say, I no longer cared. "Okay, fine, he's twenty-five. He's smart and responsible and insanely talented, and people in the position to know about talent believe in him. You should, too."

"Do you plan on supporting him when he's forty and

Made in the USA
Monee, IL
19 April 2022